THE FEET OF A SNAKE

'Racy and readable'

Guardian

'Tremendously exciting . . . one of the most disturbing thrillers I have read in years'

Annabel

'A novel which for excitement and enlightenment makes the annual Ludlum thriller seem like a soporific . . . handled with a plausibility that will find you reviewing the events of the last decade with alarm and dismay'

Bestsellers

'A valuable insight into the minds of the Iranian middle class'

William H. Sullivan,
Former US Ambassador to Iran

About the Author

Barry Chubin is an Iranian who went to school in England, where he captained Wellington School at cricket and later represented Somerset at schoolboy level. After university in America and various appointments in Iran involving energy and oil, in 1972 he was speech-writer to the Shah of Iran on OPEC and oil matters.

He was also responsible for liaison between the National Iranian Oil Company and the US embassy in Teheran during the mid 1970s. In 1978 he was special envoy representing the Prime Minister of Iran shortly before the Ayatollah Khomeini came to power.

Chubin's access to the Shah, to OPEC ministers, the multi-national oil companies and to American officials gave him a unique insight into the workings of international oil dealings and the drama of the Iranian Revolution.

Fluent in English and French as well as his mother tongue, Persian, Chubin has now made his home in the South of France, where he is at work on his next novel.

The Feet of a Snake

Barry Chubin

CORONET BOOKS
Hodder and Stoughton

First published in Great Britain
in 1984 by Hodder and Stoughton Ltd

Coronet edition 1985

British Library C.I.P.

Chubin, Barry
The feet of a snake.
I. Title
823[F] PR9105.9.C55

ISBN 0-340-37664-3

Printed and bound in Great Britain for Hodder and Stoughton Paperbacks, a division of Hodder and Stoughton Ltd., Mill Road, Dunton Green, Sevenoaks, Kent (Editorial Office: 47 Bedford Square, London, WC1 3DP) by Richard Clay (The Chaucer Press) Ltd., Bungay, Suffolk

I have never seen
the eye of a needle,
the feet of a snake, or
the charity of a mullah.

Islamic Proverb

While most if not all the material in this book about oil in Iran is representative of the wheeling and dealing that took place in that country, THE FEET OF A SNAKE is above all a work of fiction. In particular, the character of the salesman at Harrods in London is my own creation. In no way is it intended to cast doubts on that fine store's impeccable reputation or reflect on the high calibre of its employees.

Barry Chubin
London December 1983

This book is dedicated to all those who for ever lost a part of themselves in the name of a violent God: the Iranians, who lost their country, their loved ones and their self-respect; the American hostages and their families, who were so brutally and shamelessly used; the media-men who once again allowed their Nielsen ratings to cloud their better judgment.

1979

Washington. Friday, October 19: 10.00 a.m.

It was the dull look on the dead girl's face that had really shaken the old man. Those fixed, dilated eyes, locked on to the ceiling . . .

He stretched and turned listlessly on to his back in the crisp white linen sheets of the king-sized bed. Then lay still for a moment, his eyes closed. Gradually he raised his right arm and caressed his mop of white hair, then the fleshy wrinkles around his eyes. He massaged harder, digging into the crevices as though a burning pain lay buried deep in the tunnels of his mind.

Only then did he open his eyes to face a new day. He looked up at the large square ceiling of his bedroom, but the beautiful colours and textures of the previous night's opium dream had vanished. Instead his young daughter's frozen face faded in, superimposed as a hideous fresco on the white ceiling.

It's only the opium, Ali Mahmoudi consoled himself, remembering the depression that sometimes followed the drug's euphoria. But it was of little comfort; there was nothing to look forward to, and so much to regret.

"*Heyvanha*, animals," he cursed out loud, in rage as much as grief.

He could not recall how he had crossed the city back to his Watergate apartment the previous night. Nor could he recall the drugstore from which he had so desperately called Gina in Aspen. Sickeningly only the sorrow and the guilt and the craving for escape came back to him. He remembered the urgency with which he had removed the opium cake from the laundry cupboard and hastily unwrapped its covering aluminium foil. He remembered too how he had unsteadily carried it all – the small brass tongs, the elongated pin, the *vafoor* pipe, the small coal briquets, the opium itself – on a silver tray to the library, and how he had trembled with impatience at the maddening slowness of the briquets in the fireplace.

Alone, sprawled among deep Persian cushions on the floor in front of the blazing fire, he had at last lifted the old embossed tongs and picked up a small glowing coal, brought it to the pipe bowl and sat back awaiting the bitter-sweet aroma of fantasy.

And Gina? he thought, massaging the tense surface of his scalp again; his first daughter, the eldest, the last. Had she moved quickly, taking the precautions he had taught her?

He hoped so. Dear God he hoped so.

The shrill chirp of the trimline telephone jerked the old man out of his misery. He turned towards the bedside table and feebly stretched out his hand.

The familiar voice of the operator sounded in his ear.

"Morning, sir. It's ten o'clock. Your breakfast is on its way."

Mahmoudi murmured his thanks and replaced the receiver, turning once again on to his back. Instantly his thoughts reverted to his younger daughter. Why had they killed her? An innocent child who knew little and cared less. What could possibly come of it?

The soft two-tone chime of the doorbell sounded and the old man dragged his aching body from the bed.

"One moment, Guttierez," he called, struggling into a bathrobe as he made his way towards the steel-plated security door. Slowly he fumbled with the locks and chains, then at last turned the knob.

The door came into him fast, knocking him sprawling against the chest of drawers in the hallway and sending a priceless antique *Ju* ware vase crashing to the floor. Two men in white stepped in swiftly and Mahmoudi knew instantly his time had come.

One of the white-uniformed men half raised a pistol and a hiss of air erupted in a sharp jab that stabbed his right thigh. He grabbed at the limb and looked down. A small dart had pierced his flesh through the dark-blue towelling. After a moment he collapsed.

The two men worked with mechanical proficiency.

"Get the cart," said the more heavily built of the two as he knelt beside Mahmoudi. As his companion left the room he quickly lifted the old man's left eyelid. Satisfied with the fully dilated pupil, he ripped the dart from Mahmoudi's leg and waited for his return, and for the all-clear.

Soon the two men were lifting the body on to the collapsible stretcher-cart, then wordlessly, with the efficiency of experience, they set about their individual assignments. The heavy man peeled off Mahmoudi's soiled pyjamas and half-heartedly dried his groin and thighs with them before disappearing into the bathroom. He tossed the soiled ball of cloth towards the tub and washed the skin-coloured, paper-thin surgical gloves covering his hands. By the time he returned to the living-room Mahmoudi's body had been wrapped in a grey wool blanket and strapped down.

The smaller man unfolded a lightweight cotton pillowcase and wrapped it round Mahmoudi's face, leaving just sufficient space for him to breathe; but nowhere near enough for identification. He then collected a fresh set of clothes from the bedroom and stuffed them in a large brown paper bag that was folded on to one of the end rungs of the cart. Together they then wheeled the stretcher into the hall.

Seven minutes after the two men had knocked on Mahmoudi's door an unmarked ambulance inconspicuously drove away from the loading dock of the Watergate complex. Twenty minutes later it entered a huge, empty, well lit basement garage, across the Arlington

Bridge in Crystal City, less than a mile from the Pentagon.

"You awake?" the heavier man asked roughly as he tapped Mahmoudi's cheeks and lifted his eyelids.

"What is going on?" slurred the drugged man, still dazed and disoriented.

"You're okay. Just lie still."

Mahmoudi narrowed his eyes to improve the focus. He felt a parched burning sensation in his throat. The feeling contrasted sharply with the ice-water running through his limbs.

"I'm gonna tell you exactly what's happening so you're not surprised by anything."

The man spoke sternly.

"We're both gonna pitch in and help. I'm gonna undo the straps and you're gonna get dressed. If there's any resistance we'll put you back to sleep. Only this time it'll be something far blunter than a needle." He released the arm straps and the second man silently offered Mahmoudi a glass of water.

Mahmoudi took it gratefully and moistened his mouth; the burning in his throat eased and his mind stirred to life. Perhaps he could negotiate with them. Make them an offer. Anything. Any amount. He shook his head muzzily.

Gina! The name reverberated in his mind, sending a shudder of adrenalin through his body. Had she listened? Was she safe? In London? He took another sip of water and summoned up all the energy he could muster.

"I will stay here quietly and I will not misbehave or give you any trouble," he whispered. "I will also pay you whatever you wish – say, fifty thousand dollars each – delivered right here within the hour, if you release me."

It was a pathetic attempt and he knew it. Not even the words came out right. But he had to try; the alternatives were worse, and somehow he had to break free to make that call to Gina.

"This ain't Iran. Your money's no good here," said the

man as he dumped the clothes from the paper bag in a pile at the end of the stretcher.

"Untie me," commanded Mahmoudi in frustration. His feet flailed at the cuffs on his ankles as he struggled to sit up. The pile of clothes fell to the floor. "You animals, you . . ."

The man stepped forward and placed a massive paw on Mahmoudi's chest, pushing him back.

"Don't get excited, Your Excellency. The Colonel wants to see you."

Washington. Friday, October 19: noon.

Trouble-shooter, thought Mahmoudi disgustedly, as the two men sandwiched him through the doors of the elevator that had brought them from the basement and across a huge green-grey marble lobby that extended two, maybe three, floors in height. Eyes posted at different vantage-points followed them. Not for one moment did the armed guards on the catwalk above or those in the lobby itself break their silent vigil. They followed the three men through the visual identification procedures at the control desk and into the elevator.

That was the official term – trouble-shooter – thought Mahmoudi sardonically. First, second and third secretaries, political officers, consuls, petroleum attachés, private businessmen, even occasionally ambassadors, were espionage operatives. But that was in their "official days". When they reached retirement age or a scandal barred their hidden identities, they became trouble-shooters, consultants, advisers.

The private high-speed security elevator came to an abrupt stop on the twenty-sixth floor, but the doors did not open. The smaller of the two men pressed a series of numbers that changed daily on the wall panel inside the elevator before the doors separated to reveal a large fluorescent-lit reception area that was again characterised by silence and antiseptic coldness. Four uniformed security guards stood at the ready, scattered in various corners of the room, as the doors slid open.

"All this for a trouble-shooter?" murmured Mahmoudi glancing distastefully at the two men.

They ignored him. Silently, and with only the faintest of nods around the room, they guided him past their watchful colleagues and well-kept row of plastic shrubbery to a desk positioned before a large double door. An elegantly dressed middle-aged secretary glanced up from the screen of her word processor. From above her half-moon spectacles her eyes beckoned them to enter.

Once inside, the two men left Mahmoudi, and the door shut behind him with an authoritative snap that sounded suspiciously like an electronic lock. From the empty lobby and the speed of his reception Mahmoudi knew he had been expected. But now, inside Colonel Grover Cleveland Bell's office, he was not so sure. The hunched figure at the huge polished desk seemed totally preoccupied with the mound of papers before him.

As Mahmoudi stood waiting, he felt sick with fear. He knew from experience that it was part of Bell's natural make-up to unnerve, but the knowledge was of little comfort.

The figure behind the desk glared at the papers in front of him, heedless of his presence. Mahmoudi recognised the man's cold, calculating tactics. Still he was transfixed by Bell's constant leer, worn as Bell himself had once pompously told him, as "a testament to my will, a badge of dedication to my country".

The muscles and nerves that had been torn to shreds by North Korean shrapnel had been rebuilt with great care and exquisite delicacy by America's finest surgeons. But even they were unable to reconstruct the most sensitive of organs. The otherwise distinguished features were locked into a slight contortion, resulting from non-existent nerves and paralysed muscles that froze the flesh from the right lip up to the cheekbone and earlobe. There remained, too, a razor-thin scar that no amount of surgical wizardry had been able to erase.

Trophy or not, thought Mahmoudi, looking away with distaste, it was a sinister image. But one which its owner used effectively – often, and to maximum advantage. To calm himself, Mahmoudi turned to take in his surroundings.

"Ali!" said Colonel Grover Cleveland Bell at that precise moment. His eyes registered Mahmoudi's head snapping towards him. "It's so good to see you again."

He put down his pen and slowly, deliberately, removed his glasses before walking across the room. He almost had to bend to take Mahmoudi's right hand, for he towered above the short, plump, former Cabinet Minister to the Shah.

"You haven't been here before, have you?" he asked, forcing himself to smile effusively and noting Mahmoudi's haggard condition. It belied the fact that only a year ago this was one of the most powerful men in Iran; the man to see if you wanted to peddle anything – armaments, computers, construction projects, refinery equipment, trucks, toys, tankers – anything. With a small commission to this Jack-of-all-trades – *bedeh bestoon*, as it was called – you could sell anything, and at any price you chose, if the fee was right.

"How do you like my paintings?" Bell asked, pointing to a wall.

Behind the couch at one end of the huge room hung a small grouping of Leonardo da Vinci cartoons, including the original hang glider and the bicycle that predated its "invention" by four hundred years. Beside these classics were more modern designs – two Leroy Nieman paintings of the younger Mohammed Ali in full swing, and a clashing multi-coloured design by Nicola Simbari depicting two beautiful nude showgirls in a torrid embrace. They added both colour and contrast to the collection.

Mahmoudi looked away. "I am sure you did not drag me here to talk about your office or to show me your paintings," he ventured, trying to sound haughty.

Bell placed a patronising arm around his slumped shoulders and steered him towards his desk, noting again as he did so how much Mahmoudi had aged.

"I enjoy paintings myself," he said, walking behind his shining oak desk and sitting in the matching ladder-backed chair. "Leonardo got to the truth through his passion for detail, which is why I admire him. It's a philosophy I have lived by, and recommend highly."

Bell's face became slightly softer as deep lines etched themselves either side of a wide, thin-lipped mouth. His cold, light blue eyes, however, remained emotionless and the face slightly flat on the right side.

"But I'm boring you, and we have things to discuss."

He picked up the tortoiseshell glasses and placed them on the tip of his aquiline nose. A neat stack of computer print-outs sat beneath his folded arms.

Mahmoudi knew the pleasantries were over. He shifted uncomfortably on his seat. Fear, opium withdrawal and the death of his daughter were the major parts of his shattered world. The continuing revolution in Iran was a minor aggravation by comparison. His little hands tugged at his collar and then smoothed his hair.

"I'm sorry about the death of your daughter," said Bell in a tone that reflected little sympathy. "But the fault lies squarely on your own shoulders. I guess it's convenient, even natural, to lay the blame on others, but for the record, we had nothing to do with it, despite what you may think. She was running with a sick, decadent crowd; drug addicts, promiscuity, that sort of thing, and someone killed her."

"Then how did you find out about the existence of the tapes?"

"Pardon the cliché, but we have ways. And they're a little more sophisticated than killing teenage junkies."

The bastard knows he doesn't even have to lie convincingly, thought Mahmoudi. But he stayed silent; antagonism was counter-productive at this point and his priority now was to keep Gina alive. On the phone last night she had listened to him for once in her life. Not because of her sister's death – for Gina the shock of that was a surface reaction that would soon pass – but because she had sensed the danger. Usually she never took anything seriously, except her jewels, her clothes and her playthings. But the question was, had the mood lasted? Had she moved quickly? Would she be at the call-box at the appointed time? Don't be conspicuous, my darling, he had warned her. Use another name. Call yourself Maria Montez – the actress on whom he had doted from a distance in his youth. It was the only name that had come to mind.

Bell's sudden turn towards him jolted Mahmoudi back to the present. He watched the tall man behind the desk remove the half-moon glasses from his nose and point them at him.

"There seems to be an epidemic of irrationality among you Iranians. The Shah's acting like a spoiled brat; why the hell doesn't he just listen to Washington and abdicate? And you, Ali, why do you refuse to answer my calls? Why can't we meet like civilised human beings instead of my dragging you in here like a common criminal? You'll have to stay with us now until this absurd business is cleared up once and for all," he said, like a schoolmaster feigning disappointment at a wayward charge. He added as an afterthought: "I can't imagine what prompted you to make those tapes in the first place. You knew how sensitive that information was."

Mahmoudi felt his heart miss a beat and his stomach churn uncontrollably. As he looked away from the menacing glare he prayed that Gina had listened and moved quickly.

He shook his head from side to side, loosening his tight shirt-collar with his right index finger.

"You ask yourself why I have to make tapes like those

after twenty-five years of friendship with your country? They were protection. After so many years, I know all too well what you people are capable of doing in the name of democracy and freedom. No one is ever safe with you. When their usefulness runs out, they become expendable. And there are no exceptions for friendship, are there? Not even His Majesty was immune."

Mahmoudi sighed wearily and looked at the looming figure.

"I am tired, Colonel. Sick to death. One of my daughters is dead. I am marked for death, and we both know it. Do what you will."

Bell stood slowly and looked down at Mahmoudi. He now understood. What he saw, more than what he heard, told him that the man before him was a pathetic shell of his former self and had no cards left to play. Bell banked the observation and correlated it to the computer summary of Mahmoudi's personality that sat on his desk only a few feet away. There would be no need for any of the machine's findings. There would be no need to revert to the inquisitor's basic code of conduct: to go for the balls. No need to break down the man's cunning and wily brilliance by intimidating him. The computer profile was now obsolete. Mahmoudi had collapsed. He would need no threat of physical violence to make him cooperate. In fact, if he had known the extent of the man's disintegration, he wouldn't have gone to such dramatics to drag him in. He would have used more conventional means.

No, he thought again. There was still information to extract from Mahmoudi, but now the inquisitor walked a delicate tightrope. He had to be careful not to drive the man over the edge. He had to offer him solace and hope.

"Nobody," he said with vehement sincerity, "is going to kill anyone, Ali. You're tired and the pressure is getting to you. Leila's death was a hell of an unfortunate incident and you have my deepest sympathy. Besides, I think we can solve this thing without too much of a mess. We've formulated procedures to recover the tapes from your house, presuming, of course, they're still there."

Yes, thought Bell, as he paced a few steps. He'd share some information with Mahmoudi and boost his confidence. There was nothing to lose and everything to gain. After all, he would be no threat; he would be in custody for the rest of his limited life.

He turned and paced back. Bait him with a little information.

"We've selected an individual for the job. For various reasons we had to rule out sending in our own people. In the circumstances, it was considered too risky to involve this country directly. For certain other reasons the President has ruled out the Israelis, and our other allies are willing to help but only in a superficial way. None of them is prepared to undertake the actual mission, which is typical of the bastards. Always sitting on the fence."

Bell lit a short thin Davidoff Ambassadrice cigar. As he did so he noted Mahmoudi's eyes had stopped darting. The old schemer was nibbling.

"We need a complete plan of your house in Teheran and the combination of your floor safe. Do you have them?"

Mahmoudi stared at Bell silently as his once-agile brain strained to regain its power. He tried to weigh the options, to assess his interests. The information Bell wanted was not crucial; he knew too much already. He knew where the tapes were; all he wanted was the safe number. If he did not comply willingly, Bell could easily bypass him. He could blow the safe open if need be. On the other hand, if he cooperated perhaps it would buy him time. Perhaps he could break free long enough to contact Gina. And there was still the other matter. Yes, maybe there was a chance.

"I will help you," he said finally as he fumbled in his coat pocket. Abruptly he remembered the coat had been pulled from the closet by his kidnappers. "May I please have something to write with. Your animals forgot to pack my pen."

Bell slid a pen and a pad of paper across the desk. Wearily, Mahmoudi wrote.

"That is the combination number of the safe," he said, handing the pad back. "If I am not mistaken I have a plan of the house at my apartment in Cannes."

"My pen, please," said Bell, beckoning.

Mahmoudi pushed it across the table as Bell stubbed out his barely-used cigar.

"How will you do it?" asked Mahmoudi, not the least bit interested in the answer. What he needed was more time to think and plan. But the answer was more than he had bargained for.

"Michael Adel," replied Bell casually, pleased but not surprised by the shock on the old man's face. "He'll get them out for us." He paused, before adding dispassionately, "Gina and he were lovers, weren't they?"

Mahmoudi looked sharply at Bell, then more slowly down at the dark brown parquet of the floor.

"He is the father of my grand-daughter, Natalie," he answered softly, obviously embarrassed to have his daughter's long affair with Adel dragged up in this setting. "But, of course, you would know that sort of thing. That is your forte, is it not?"

"Of course," answered Bell. "I know Adel quite well myself. We met when he was at the National Iranian Oil Company and saw quite a lot of each other while I was on assignment in Iran. There are several reasons why we chose him, but we needn't go into that. Let's just say that a combination of the ancient *qanat* irrigation system of your country and the fact that his father's house is only one away from yours was the clincher."

Mahmoudi's embarrassment and surprise turned slowly to disbelief.

He had always liked Michael Adel. In fact, he would have been pleased to have him as a son-in-law, not least because he had been the only stable influence in Gina's whole life. He had to admit, though, in this moment of doubt, that it had never been clear whether this bright young whizz-kid was more American than Iranian or vice-versa. He had known Adel's father since they had been boys attending the old Alborz College together in Teheran. After a long stint in the United States old Adel had returned to Iran with an American wife and two little American sons. Michael, the elder boy, had grown into a bright and dynamic young petroleum engineer. He was wholesome and refreshingly American, yet fully at home in the intricacies of Iranian society. After a few years in the oil company, he had set himself up in the oil services industry, and by a combination of hard work, charm and good business sense he had amassed great wealth.

The fixer in Mahmoudi, the operator whose survival and success had always depended on up-to-date information, was instinctively curious. Had Bell somehow coerced Adel into a role in this venture? Or had he misread Michael Adel? Had he been one of Bell's stooges all along?

"I find it difficult to believe that a boy like Adel would willingly lend himself to this sort of thing. He is a very decent man."

"You surprise me, Ali," said Bell, glancing at the computer print-outs lying on the table beneath his elbows. "Nice he may be, but beneath that playboy exterior lies a ruthless character. Ask your daughter."

This time Mahmoudi did not rise to the bait. "Even if you are right, he had every opportunity to enrich himself at the oil company and he always refused to take the short-cut to wealth. Why should he subject himself to danger and help you steal now?"

Bell lowered his eyes to the papers on his desk as his hand dropped beneath its surface to the bell-button hidden there. "There are, Ali, several sides to Michael Adel. And most of them you know nothing about. But don't worry about it. He'll help."

The door of the office opened and the two kidnappers entered.

"You haven't been formally introduced, have you?" asked Bell as he looked over Mahmoudi's left shoulder. "His Excellency Ali Mahmoudi. Jim Gleeson," he said, pointing to the smaller, quieter of the two men. "And Bill Davis."

Ali Mahmoudi glanced swiftly at the two men – a gesture that held in it a world of contempt.

"These gentlemen will accompany you for the next few days," said Bell, looking at his watch. "We'll meet in Cannes in three days' time. In addition to your house plans, we have other business there." Bell stood and approached Mahmoudi as the twisted grin returned to his face. "But before you go, Your Excellency" – the last two words were clipped – "tell me just how you obtained those tapes. You've piqued my professional curiosity."

Mahmoudi stared up. For one brief moment he felt an urge to defy Bell. But he controlled the impulse; it would only be a short-lived satisfaction. Play along, he thought. Loosen the reins by appearing helpful. It's the only hope.

"It's so simple, you probably wouldn't believe me."

"The best plans always are, Ali."

"Christmas, nineteen-seventy-four, I gave Jacey one of those Eraser-Mate pens. Very good for doodling, scribbling and so forth. I had it encased in gold at Cartier's in Paris. Luckily he liked it and always carried it with him.

"I had something else done to it too," added Mahmoudi pausing. "The pen has a very large eraser on the top and there is – how do you say it? – a microphone that works off any noise . . ."

"A SAM," interrupted Bell glancing at the two men behind Mahmoudi.

"A what?"

"Sound-activated microphone."

"Ah, Colonel, what a professional you are. That is what the man called it too."

Mahmoudi's teasing irritated Bell. "And how did you record?" he snapped.

"That was more or less luck. I was kept on standby – as you say it – waiting outside the meetings in case I was needed. I was in the room next door when Jacey was giving his presentation, a few feet away with only a wall separating us. The microphone taped straight on to a little IBM tape-recorder in my pocket. I had to change the small miniature tapes often through the long meetings, but I was alone in the room and so it was not a problem. Later I transferred all the material on the small tapes to regular cassettes and destroyed the miniature ones. I was so happy I obtained them and so lucky that the meetings were so . . . so . . . crucial. I thought afterwards that they would provide me with protection if ever I needed it."

The old man lowered his head and gave a hollow laugh. "Protection," he repeated bitterly.

Bell nodded at the two men, who moved towards Mahmoudi.

"Help Mr Mahmoudi back to his apartment and see that he has everything he needs."

The old man offered no resistance. He slid off the chair slowly and stood. "Be careful, Colonel. There are exceptions to every rule," he said as he turned towards the door. "Michael Adel may prove to be your exception."

He walked a few feet, then stopped abruptly and looked back.

"Oh, Colonel. There is something else you might like to consider. It does compare well with the tapes you seek."

Bell rose from behind his desk, hooked the granny glasses on to the end of his nose, and walked slowly towards Mahmoudi.

"In many ways the papers are remarkably similar in value to the tapes, Colonel. They are my recollections; diaries of various activities in Iran."

Bell's instincts sensed danger. Experience dictated caution.

"Various activities?"

"The stealing."

"What stealing, Ali?"

It was Mahmoudi's turn to smile.

"Oil-stealing, Colonel."

Cannes. Friday, October 19: 6.30 p.m.

At precisely that moment – six time zones away – the Côte d'Azur was hardly the glamorous place the French tourist industry so proudly advertises. The Mistral wind had burst out of Africa like a freight train. It boomed and tumbled through the darkness, building great roller-coaster waves that piled up on the beaches in crashing confusion and hurled themselves against the flotillas of deserted private yachts in their off-season moorings.

In Cannes, rain lashed the sparkling promenades and bowed the palm trees. The town's main boulevard, La Croisette, which in summer played host to the world's jet-set, was deserted, and only one man braved its more exposed southern flank.

The lonely runner exhaled every fourth step as he wove past the Majestic Hotel, down past the expensive boutiques: Hermès, Gucci, Lanvin . . . past the Blue Bar and the Palais des Festivals, where the antics of the Cannes Film Festival signal the tentative start of *la saison*.

This gets harder every day, he thought, as he broke his run in front of the elegant Carlton Hotel. He crossed the deserted street and the small pink-paved parking lot that sets the hotel back from the boulevard, and mounted the six steps to the hotel's awning. There he bent forward to catch his breath.

"*Vous êtes fou*, Monsieur Adel. Running in this weather," huffed the doorman, reaching to offer the bended athlete a towel.

"Pull in the stomach, Jean. You're beginning to look like an egg," panted Michael Adel.

The doorman straightened his moustache and then cradled his stomach. "*Ça, c'est présence.*"

"It's fat, Jean," quipped Adel as part of their daily banter.

"No, Mr Adel," responded the doorman without hesitation. "We French are not mad like you Americans. Whenever we feel the urge to exercise, we merely lie down until it passes."

Adel smiled, conceding the game.

"Did Madame and Mademoiselle Natalie return with you?" enquired the doorman.

"No. They should be here by the weekend." Adel towelled his mop of curly black hair and wiped his blue plastic jacket and running shoes. "You'll probably see them before I do. Natalie is sure to want a club sandwich on the way home." He exchanged the towel for his car keys and the newspaper which the doorman picked up for him every day, saving him the trouble of entering the lobby.

"Stay here, Jean. No use both of us catching pneumonia," he said as he moved away.

"Oh, Mr Adel," the doorman called after him. "Did you see your friends?"

A look of casual surprise crossed the athlete's rugged, handsome face as he turned back. "What friends, Jean?"

"A couple of American gentlemen." The portly doorman shrugged. "They said they'd drive along the Croisette to find you running."

"Didn't see a soul. Did they leave their names?"

"No, sir."

"Well, they shouldn't have a problem finding me. My telephone number is listed." Adel nodded kindly at the doorman before turning into the pouring rain. A few steps down the narrow hotel driveway he slid quickly into the front seat of a sleek white Aston Martin Lagonda and waited for the new V8 engine to warm up. Two Americans? he thought. He wasn't expecting anyone.

Dismissing the question, he slipped the car into gear.

The doorman smiled and shook his head in admiration. There goes a fine gentleman, he thought, wondering if Monsieur Adel had looked after himself during the revolution in Iran; had money in America or Switzerland or somewhere. Monsieur Adel had been working in Iran, he remembered hearing; had a lot of investments there apparently. It would be a shame not to see him again. Like so many others who had dropped out of sight over the years after some distant political convulsion or other. He watched as the car turned right on the *Croisette* and disappeared. It would be a shame if that happened to Monsieur . . .

Abruptly, his thoughts were jarred by the sound of a motor kicking to life to his left, in the small parking lot fronting the hotel. A dark blue Peugeot 504 pulled into the traffic behind the Lagonda. Inside were the same two Americans who had asked after Michael Adel.

Washington. Friday, October 19: 1.34 p.m.

Colonel Grover Cleveland Bell watched the short, dishevelled-looking man turn and amble away towards the huge photochromic windows. "What oil-stealing, Ali?"

"Of course, my papers are not documented with signatures or contracts. Such things never are," said Ali Mahmoudi in his precise English. "They are simply the recollections of an old man who seeks to spend the rest of his short life in peace and quiet."

Brusquely, Bell waved dismissal to his two subordinates; but even as they departed Mahmoudi did not turn. He spoke instead, slowly, softly into the window, the hot vapour from his breath clinging to the cold glass.

"I have written it all down in great detail, Colonel. Before the revolution. In the form of diaries, recollections – how do you say? *aide-mémoires*. It is all in a safe-deposit box somewhere in Europe. It was prudent of me, no?"

"I'm not sure I follow you, Ali."

"It is not difficult, Colonel. I have made detailed notes of the whole set-up by which the Western oil companies used us and how their senior executives enriched themselves. Oh yes, and in the process made some of us very rich, too. But that is all in the past now."

He paused and turned to smile at Bell's puzzled expression. "My notes detail exactly which officers in the old Anglo-Iranian Oil Company pushed their pet Iranian executives after the 1953 nationalisation to the pinnacles of power in the National Iranian Oil Company and the Iranian government. After all, we – and I was one of them – were all part of the early cadre trained by the British . . ."

"What has all this got to do with us, Ali?"

"It is quite simple. Through these corrupt friends, or *doostan* as we were called, your oil companies and their executives enriched themselves shamelessly. Oh, what a lovely story it would make one day. The Watergate scandal would pale in comparison. Not very good for political stability in the West, wouldn't you say, Colonel?"

"And how was this stealing purportedly conducted?" probed Bell.

"Many ways. Having established their network of *doostan*, the foreign oil companies would use us as they wished. For example, after we nationalised the oil industry, the companies came to us to negotiate discounts on future oil sales, ostensibly to amortise the investments they had made over the years to develop the oil facilities in Iran. We would engage in tough negotiations and finally concede, say, twenty cents a barrel to the offshore trading company that represented all the oil companies. Of course, that was perhaps eight cents too much and by prior agreement – reached in secret sessions in Geneva – we all shared that eight cents through a complex web of offshore bearer share concerns. By we, Colonel, I naturally mean certain individuals in your oil companies as well as a few of us Iranians. And eight cents a barrel for, say, three or four million barrels per day is not an inconsequential amount, is it? Especially over a period of some years.

"Don't look so bored, Colonel," said Mahmoudi as he turned back. "It's all documented. Names, dates, amounts, bank accounts. But, above all, names. And it goes back a long time, not just to the more recent boom."

Thrusting his hands into his trouser pockets he took a few steps before stopping again.

"And once OPEC was established we all, the Western oil company executives and the *doostan*, had a very profitable time bypassing the OPEC equal mix provisions between light and heavy crude. The oil companies would pay us huge bribes – millions of dollars per year – to give them a favourable mix of light oil over heavy. We Iranians would supply the light, breaking OPEC rules. We'd bank the bribes in Switzerland. Clean. End of story, Colonel?

"But no-ooh. Ooh-noo. Because who would come pecking at those accounts in the middle of the night? People like . . ."

The significance of the half-dozen names mentioned by Mahmoudi was not lost on Bell. He was naming the chairmen and presidents of America's and Europe's largest oil companies as well as senior banking and government officials on both sides of the Atlantic.

"That's right. These gentlemen and a handful of us Iranians were partners in perhaps the biggest swindle in history."

Mahmoudi moved towards a leather armchair.

"Oh, I nearly forgot the SCTs," he said as he slumped into it.

"The what?"

"Shuffling credit terms," smiled Mahmoudi. "You see, I was a professional too." He burst out laughing at his own joke.

"What were shuffling credit terms?" asked an irritated Bell.

"OPEC regulations allowed its members to offer a maximum of sixty days' credit and that's what all the contracts between Iran and the oil companies stipulated on paper. But who drew up and policed these contracts on the Iranian side? We did. And do you know what else we – the *doostan* – insisted upon? That the money be paid to Iranian government deposit accounts in Switzerland. The oil companies always paid promptly within sixty days into these accounts. The only snag was that they were not Iranian government accounts. The real government accounts, maintained in Chase Manhattan branches in New York and London, were actually only credited after 120 days. So sixty days' interest on oil shipments was always unaccounted for. Calculate what that was, Colonel, when oil prices had climbed to ten or twelve dollars a barrel. About one, sometimes one and a half million barrels a day were being treated in this way. That's ten to fifteen million dollars per day earning two months' interest. What's that add up to, Colonel? What is that per day? And what happened to it? Why don't you ask" – and out came the names again – "for the exact figures and where some of that money went. Oh, it was all so cosy, our little partnership."

Mahmoudi suddenly paused looking reflective. "I wonder if they're still doing it with the other oil-producing countries. Is it also happening in Saudi Arabia, Nigeria, Venezuela?" His pensive frown gradually gave way to a broad grin that erupted into a mocking cackle.

Bell stared at him and waited for the laughter to subside. It was unlikely, he thought, that Mahmoudi had made more than one copy of the documents he was referring to. But that wasn't good enough. He had to get a precise handle on them. He had to be certain.

"You've recorded all this?" he prompted, after Mahmoudi had eventually taken hold of himself.

"And more, Grover – may I call you that? I have also outlined the activities of the myopic meters. Have you heard of them?"

Bell shook his head.

"That was perhaps the jewel. It was so brazen. You see, we in Iran were equipped to export eight and a half million barrels of oil per day, but even at the highest point only six million barrels were ever officially transferred to tankers. That left two and a half million barrels a day of extra capacity that we never used – not officially. It was for *emergency purposes* – only the 'emergency' was unofficially always there. All we did was bypass the meters with auxiliary pipelines that simply had no meters, and, *voilà*, the oil was never registered."

"Pipelines and pumping stations with no meters, Ali? How's that possible?"

"I said auxiliary pipelines. Lines designed for use in temporary emergencies when tracking output was not important. When the main pipes were inoperative after an earthquake, or during a fire and so on."

"How much flowed this way?"

Mahmoudi was pleased with Bell's interest.

"It is difficult to put a figure on it. Sometimes it was more, sometimes less. But it was always there. Somewhere between five hundred thousand and one million barrels a day. Even at the twelve dollar a barrel price current just before the revolution, that is somewhere between six and twelve million dollars a day being siphoned off. Twelve million a day, Colonel!" he exclaimed.

"Where did all this money go?"

"I have written down only what I know: some of it came back to us *doostan*. Much of it went to our friends in America and Europe who were doing the buying on behalf of their companies. Where the rest went I don't know. Your imagination is as good as mine. But what I do know is written in detail. Names, Grover. Names, names."

Bell frowned. "And you're saying no one ever questioned the oil company figures?"

"Of course not!" snapped Mahmoudi, irritated by the absurdity of the question.

"SAVAK – the secret police – were always there, lurking somewhere in the background. His Majesty had conveniently created a *bête noire* which provided us with wonderfully effective cover. No one dared question what went on because the enormity of these myopic meters meant it had to have been . . . ah . . . approved."

Mahmoudi shook his head and chuckled. "The funny thing, Colonel, was that it was so impressively efficient. We did not need more than two people at most. Two people in just the right positions in the oil company. And towards the end, Colonel, in the last few years before the revolution, it was inefficient to have to go through two men, so both positions were filled by one man, making the operation even more streamlined. I ask you, is that not impressive?" concluded the old man with another round of belly laughter.

Bell squinted and his fingers drummed his bottom lip as he let the silence hang.

Then he pushed himself out of the deep armchair and walked quickly to the desk. "That's a hell of a tale you have there, Ali. Could do quite a lot of shaking up in the world. And that is the last thing we need."

"Bigger even than Watergate, isn't it, Colonel?" said Mahmoudi, driving home the nail. "It is the biggest swindle in history. And what poetic irony that its stars are the most upstanding and upright pillars of the American and European business establishment. Up to now it was always us 'dirty little Arabs' who were the thieves. It would be fascinating to see how your public would react if they learned that what we stole was a pittance compared with the so-called pillars of your society, would it not?"

"You don't want to leave documents like that lying around. It could be counter-productive."

"Rest assured, dear Grover. If I have no worries, you

have no worries. For my own protection I have made only one set, which the depository has been instructed to release only on my death. And then only if it is . . . ah . . . how do you put it? . . . unnatural."

Bell sifted through a pile of papers on his desk, selected one and studied it for a moment before placing it back in its allotted slot.

Then he stood and paced towards Mahmoudi. "You seem to forget, Ali, that we are on the same side. We have no quarrel with you. There's no animosity between us."

He put his hand on Mahmoudi's shoulder and produced his natural leer of a smile. "Look, Ali, you've been under unbelievable pressure lately. It's all gone wrong for you and it's a shame. But don't let it get to you; don't take it out on your friends. I assure you, you will never need to use that file – not against us. We are colleagues. We'll always look after you. Even if it means we have to put up with these occasional tantrums of yours." He laughed, his features again attempting to convey kindness and sympathy.

Mahmoudi smiled back. "Perhaps you are right, Colonel."

"You need a holiday, Ali. A long vacation, away from telephones, newspapers and television. Maybe after Cannes you should just take off – destination unknown sort of thing," said Bell. He moved back around the desk and pressed the button again.

"I'm running a little late, Ali. I do hope we can meet again before Cannes, though. Perhaps you can come over for dinner."

The two men entered the room and Mahmoudi turned to see them. His stomach turned as he looked back at Bell. He had to call Gina in London. He had to tell her what to do.

"I won't need these . . . these . . . two . . ."

"Just for protection, Ali," Bell said as he guided Mahmoudi towards the door. "They won't get in your way. We have information that suggests the Khomeini people have hit-squads heading this way. I'd feel more at ease if you had someone looking after you."

He looked from Mahmoudi to the two men. "I don't want you getting in His Excellency's way. Stay in the background," he instructed.

"Well, Ali. We'll be in touch," he said, shaking hands with the old man.

Mahmoudi smiled contentedly. He had the leeway to distance himself from these two ghouls for long enough to call Gina from an untapped call-box. All that remained was: how?

"Goodbye, Colonel," he said as he turned to leave. "And thank you."

Bell held the door open until the three men had walked through the reception area. Then he walked swiftly to his desk and picked up the telephone. He pressed a button and waited.

"Miss Pringle," he said when a voice answered. "Mahmoudi's file. The papers from his safe-deposit box at the bank in Geneva. Have them brought up. I want to see those diaries of his again."

Cannes. Friday, October 19: evening.

Michael Adel drove carefully through the light evening traffic, heading the powerful car northwards, up the narrow winding lanes to the hills of Super Cannes behind and overlooking the city. He did not look forward to the empty house; without Sam and Natalie it was too big, too quiet, too cold. He did not enjoy it without them.

He thought of his daughter. She was still a serious child, observing everything, taking it all in. But she was happier now; the memories of her mother's home were fading, and she had gradually warmed to the love and security Samira had so carefully and generously provided.

He drove on, oblivious of everything but his own thoughts. It was amazing that from that simple chance meeting with Samira had begun a love-affair that was to affect not only his life but Natalie's.

It had been – what? – almost three years ago now. Sitting over croissants and coffee at an outdoor table of the Café Flore, a little Left Bank bistro on the Boulevard Saint-Germain, Adel had had a late night and little sleep. He had glanced at the headlines of *Le Monde* but nothing gripped his attention and the paper remained half-folded beside his plate. The bitter, strong coffee warmed his stomach as the caffeine started to affect his sluggish brain. He looked up to see a girl seated two tables away dropping her eyes as they met his. It was commonplace to find women sitting alone in Parisian cafés, but somehow this one seemed vulnerable. She was a small, slender girl, almost delicate. *Recherchée*, the French called it, with fine small bones, not at first glance unlike thousands of French women who possess that indefinable air of delicacy and innate chic. Yet it was her eyes that were startling. They were large and brown and limpid – so openly trusting that his immediate impulse was to warn her against strange men, like himself. He looked at her unobserved and with growing interest. Her long jet black hair was tied loosely by a ribbon at the nape of her neck. Her face was dark and striking, with enviably high cheekbones that gave her features a starkly sensuous cast. Her long slender legs were encased in skin-tight Levis which she had tucked into knee-length burgundy boots. A puffy silk chemise fluttered against her taut nipples with the light morning breeze.

Yes, she was different from Parisian girls, Adel mused, not because she lacked their intuitive style – she had that in abundance – but because she lacked their awareness, that knowledge of their own sexuality and how to use it. Yes, he thought again. She was vulnerable; she lacked the protective carapace that helped survival in a harsh world.

"*Vous êtes américaine?*"

She looked at him with just a hint of a smile and nodded. "Yes. How did you know?" Her voice was youthful but husky, and her accentless French was guarded.

"It's been years since I saw a lavaliere," he replied nostalgically.

She touched the necklace with the Greek symbols.

"The man must be very dear to you."

"He is." She brought the necklace to her lips and left it there. "But how do you know about lavalieres?"

He switched to English. "I'm American, too."

She smiled and her face was warm and sensuous and disarming.

"Well, maybe we should start at the beginning," he said. "What's your name?"

"Samira," she replied and her large brown eyes looked openly into his.

"Samira what?"

"Ferragamo. My father was Italian, my mother French. They both emigrated to the States. What's your name?"

"Adel. Michael Adel. And that's half-American, half-Iranian."

Her eyes held a trace of surprise as she looked at him, her chin resting on the palm of her hand, her elbow leaning on the table. "You look far more American than Iranian."

He smiled. "In the present circumstances, that's a compliment, I suppose."

"It is. You'll laugh, but in Paris I've come to love what everybody mocks Americans for – the simpleness and childlike honesty you find among them. There's no guile in America."

They ordered more coffee and talked for a long while. Then they strolled along Boulevard Saint-Germain, to St Clotilde, the ancient church hidden among the trees. Then northward again along the Esplanade des Invalides, on to the sculptured Pont Alexandre III.

Along the way she spoke of her frustration as a

student at the Sorbonne and how she loathed the French men she knew, students and teachers, who "treated all females as playthings". She found France, her mother's country, disappointing and pretentious, even though she blended in so well. And she missed the earnestness of her four undergraduate years at Brown University and the simple honesty of the American way of life.

Adel leaned on the bridge rail beside her, charmed by her open innocence, and they watched the river. A *bâteau mouche* moved into view and she waved and smiled at the crowded deck.

"So what are you going to do with yourself?" he asked, not knowing why her artless chatter was so enticing.

"I don't know," she said, her eyes on the river. "I've got to come up with something that stimulates me."

"What does the man in your life say?" He pointed at her necklace.

"Nothing. It belonged to my father. He's dead now."

He looked at her, amazed by the interest she provoked in him. She was enthralled by things he had not even observed – at least not for a long, long time. And her concerns seemed so trivial, so innocent and young. But it was her enthusiasm and zest for them that was catching. In normal circumstances, boredom should by now have set in and the search for excuses started. But somehow he was captivated by her spirit and charm. It was like a journey back through time, back to the carefree days of a college campus.

Besides, he thought, they had been together for several hours now and she hadn't once mentioned Louis Feraud or Givenchy or Dior, which in itself was a blessing. She hadn't even brought up Régine's.

Suddenly she smiled mischievously. "Come on, I'd like a crêpe," she said as she took his arm.

"Let's make that a full lunch," he asserted.

For a second she hesitated. Just as suddenly, the doubt vanished. "Okay," she conceded.

After that, they had met every day and Paris took on a

new meaning. Somehow she managed to organise their days according to her own tastes, ignoring his suggestions of more luxurious surroundings.

"Yaach," she would say in response to every name he mentioned.

And, strangely, he found it attractive; refreshing, even. Gone were the fashionable stamping grounds of the rich and the jet set. The expensive and over-rated restaurants, discothèques and night clubs. Gone, too, were lissom high-priced call-girls. Instead, he saw the city by day and with Samira it took on a new light. They did the traditional tourist things and he loved it. They walked along the Seine, went to the Tuileries and the Louvre, watched and made bets on the men playing *boules* in the Luxembourg Gardens.

And they often went to her small but tastefully furnished apartment in an old building on the Avenue de Bosquet on the Left Bank. But she never visited his hotel or made the smallest concession to his regular lifestyle.

She tried cooking, but was not very good at it, so he took over, with omelettes, entrecôtes, croque monsieurs, and feeble attempts at hamburgers. In fact it was his cooking that had put their relationship in clear perspective.

"God, the French," he complained bitterly one evening, as he sucked the fresh burn blister on his index finger. "Can't grind beef. Purée it, even if you plead with the butcher. Whatever you do, it tastes like wet mortar. Why the hell do we go through this cooking ritual every day anyway?" he asked, not altogether in jest. "We can eat well occasionally."

"I have to be a little different from the others, don't I?" she had answered petulantly. "Besides, I like eating what we cook."

"What *we*? What *we* eat together, *I* cook. You can't cook to save your life," his voice had been harsher than he had intended.

"I know you can pay for the best. You've made that

boorishly obvious." She had been wounded and her voice was angry. "You prefer that life, don't you? Dinner at Lasserre and then Régine's, and then a fuck at the good old George V. You really don't want a normal relationship, do you? One with ordinary human moods and feelings. One that grows with time. No, you always want to buy a short cut. You need six waiters hovering around, bowing, scraping and calling you 'sir' before you can have a good time."

Her eyes brimmed with tears and her cheeks were flushed with anger as she spoke.

"I hate that part of you. This is all an act, isn't it? Nothing means anything to you; especially women. You just buy them with your 'worthless' money. I'm just a challenge. Someone you can't have that easily. Go on, then. Call Madame Claude. Get one of her whores. I'm not what you're used to."

Adel smiled reminiscently as he downshifted the Lagonda's automatic gears to negotiate the steep gradient of the final stretch of the hill. From that one small kitchen incident, his whole life had changed.

He shifted the gear back to drive as the road straightened out and remembered how he had stood absolutely still, frozen by her outburst. She had been wrong, yet there was truth in what she had said. Not since those blissful but infuriating times with Gina had he really cared about a woman; not since those carefree, glamorous illicit days with Jane Bennett had he felt such sheer excitement. Dear loyal, romantic, secretive, screwed-up Jane, he thought. So anxious to love, yet so terrified of her husband and scandal.

Yes, Samira was different. It was such a different kind of love with Samira, the very antithesis of those physical, feckless relationships. It was honest and innocent and clean. She was a different kind of girl, too; fragile and unaffected and pure. She brought out in him qualities he had long since forgotten; qualities he had buried in his efforts to impress. With her he was human again, the image had vanished. Her innocence and openness had made his posing absurd. She loved him, that was obvious. But she loved him honestly for what he was. She knew nothing of his past. All she cared about was the present.

Suddenly, in that one frozen moment, he had loved again. For the first time since his schooldays, he had felt the strong urge to explain.

"Sam . . ." he said hesitantly, afraid by habit to bare what he had kept hidden for so long. But the words were uncontrollable. "You're right."

Softly, deliberately, he had sought to relieve the tension within himself. He had told her about his past, about Gina and Natalie and his chosen shell of endurance. He had told her about the glass bubble society he lived in and the insecurity and alienation he felt in Iran and how, to survive, he had slowly adopted the characteristics of a chameleon. He had told her about his business, the strains it placed on him and the relief he felt when spending time on site at the oil fields in the desert, away from the corruption in Teheran.

But the pressure of the pent-up forces had been unsatisfied. It had demanded more: a full, total commitment.

"I love you, Sam. As much as I'm capable of loving, I love you."

She had looked at him, her eyes filled with sympathy and excitement. But she had held her gaze, contemplating her answer.

"I love you, too, Michael," she had replied at length. "But don't be that way with me. Don't be hard. You don't need it with me; you don't need to act. I love Michael Adel, not the money or the restaurants or the cars. They won't get me through the night. Only you will."

Adel turned the car off the Chemin des Collines, high above Cannes, into the driveway of his home. She was the best thing that had ever happened to him, he thought as the burly gate-keeper stepped out to open the wrought-iron gates. Adel guided the car through the entrance and followed a left-curving driveway lined with pine trees. The house followed the ubiquitous Mediterranean form – white stucco, Moorish arches shading walkways under red tile roofing. But it was large, even by the Riviera's opulent standards.

At the far end of the building, mist rose from the heated swimming pool which extended into the house, beneath a glass wall. To the front of the house lay a vast expanse of lawn which was bordered by exquisite varieties of flowers.

To the left of the pool, a barbecue pit squatted in the semi-darkness beneath the summer shade of the surrounding palms. It was Sam's enclave, a source of delicious charcoal aromas on summer evenings.

Behind the house, in a clear semi-circle, stood a forest, mainly pines. Hidden behind the thick foliage was a paddock with a tack-room where his wife and daughter kept their horses and a small gymnasium where he worked out daily.

But the *pièce de résistance* of the mansion lay directly in front of it. It was the breathtaking view of the Mediterranean, from Golfe Juan and Juan-les-Pins to the left, to Porte la Galère to the right. He would never tire of this view, thought Adel as he walked to the front door.

"Storm's getting worse, John," said Adel as he entered the lobby.

John Usher was English and had been in Adel's employ for several years now. Tall, balding, bespectacled, he was Adel's personal butler, but he was also a confidant and friend.

"You have a visitor, sir." Usher reached to take Adel's windbreaker. "A Mr Donald Anderson, an American gentleman . . ."

Adel turned sharply, his eyes narrowing.

"He did say you were old friends, sir," said a surprised Usher, handing him Anderson's calling card.

"That's true enough, John," Adel answered distantly as he studied the card.

In addition to Anderson's name, the card carried an

embossed golden seal of a spread-eagle and the legend: The United States of America, Department of State, Near East Section.

London. Friday, October 19: 7.00 p.m.

The stunning girl with long jet-black hair felt foolish and out of place. Never in her entire life had she considered looking inconspicuous a difficult – or desirable – task to accomplish. Never, that was, until now. Moreover, hers was – as she was the first to admit – only a half-hearted effort. Her expensive Fiorucci jeans, and her exquisite Parisian mink jacket made it impossible for her to blend into the mundane commuter traffic heading home for the weekend. Her suntan and immaculate coiffure only served to widen the gap between her and the throng battling its way through Knightsbridge underground station.

She glanced distastefully at her gold Piaget watch before aimlessly picking out two more fashion magazines from the rack and dumping them on the growing pile beside the cash register of the news-stand. Thankfully, she thought as she paid for her purchases, it was nearly seven o'clock.

She dropped the change carelessly into her bag, snapped the H-buckle closed and threaded her way against the heavy flow of human traffic towards the decrepit telephone booths at the far side of the station.

What was she doing? she wondered dejectedly. All this panic, all this talk of danger. Fake names, dead lines, flights across the world and not being able to call one's friends. But this was the final straw. It was crazy. Secret long-distance calls. Had the old man's mind been affected by Leila's death? Or was it the opium . . .

The last few yards were relatively easy to cross, the crowds decreasing as she walked further from the escalators. On the right side of the three booths stood a group of scraggy, chanting Hare Krishnas but she pouted and ignored them, hurrying instead towards the welcome sound of ringing that had suddenly erupted from the centre telephone booth.

"Hallo . . . hallo."

"Yes, Father," replied the pretty girl, instantly recognising his impatient voice.

"I cannot talk for very long. We are going through the *ghosl* ceremony with your sister's body."

Gina Mahmoudi's heart sank as she visualised her sister's corpse being elaborately washed and wrapped in the sheet-like *kafan* according to Islamic tradition.

"I have managed to be alone for just a moment. So listen carefully, my darling."

"Why on earth didn't you use a coffin, Father?"

"I begged them to give me a few last moments with Leila and this was the best way. Now, you must do as I tell you."

"But, really, Father, you should have . . ."

"Listen," snapped Ali Mahmoudi in a frenzied whisper. "I have only a moment. They will be back soon to accompany me to her grave. The opportunity will be lost. And both our lives depend on you listening."

Cannes. Friday, October 19: 9.00 p.m.

"That was delicious, Michael," said Don Anderson as he stood from the dining table. "Do you eat like this every night?"

Adel nodded at Usher. "Only when John here is hungry."

Usher smiled but said nothing as the two men went

through the low, arched hallway separating the dining and sitting areas.

"How about a drink, Don?" offered Adel.

"Sure, why not?"

Adel pointed to a comfortable corner of the lavish living-room. "Make yourself at home. I'll be right back."

All evening it had been tense, he thought as he walked to the rustic wooden bar in one of the two alcoves that stood along the left wall of the room. Despite absurdly polite conversation, gossip about old friends and genial recollections of the past, which had only prompted Anderson to recount the events that led to his divorce, the atmosphere had not reflected their once deep friendship. On the contrary, it had been decidedly strained.

Perhaps Anderson's divorce had been one of those which left a bitter aftertaste, thought Adel. His own involvement with Gina had not ended in divorce but it had been a gut-wrenching experience, nevertheless. He remembered the depths of his own depression then and gave his friend the benefit of the doubt.

Adel strolled back and handed Anderson a brandy glass with Bas Armagnac in it. "How long will you be with us, Don?" he asked, placing the bottle on the glass table in front of his guest. "I hope it's not one of those all-American hit-and-run jobs."

"Afraid so. Two or three days at the most," replied Anderson. "But tell me, Michael, what do you make of the situation in Iran?"

Adel sat at one end of the couch, surprised by the abrupt change of topic. Was Anderson at last leading up to the purpose of his visit?

"I'm sure I feel the same way as you," he replied guardedly. "We both worked too long in that environment to believe the crap we're being fed. There's something missing that makes the whole thing . . . ah . . . unbelievable. There's more to the Iranian story than we're being told."

Anderson shifted uneasily in the deep armchair.

"You don't believe it was a straightforward, domestically motivated revolt, then?"

Adel studied his old friend yet again: he had gained a good deal of weight in the last two years but the chubbiness had only served to enhance his clean-cut boyish appearance. The blond hair was still cut short and combed tidily; the blue eyes retained their honesty, though the dark circles beneath them were new. They suggested hardship or strain; or both.

"I don't know what to think, Don," he responded. "It's not intellectual or fashionable to believe in the conspiracy theory these days but there are too many unanswered questions, too many coincidences for my taste. Somehow it jars."

Adel told his friend about his doubts: his incredulity at the apparent ineptness of the CIA; the fumblings of the dreaded SAVAK, the CIA-created and operated Iranian secret police; the seeming fickleness of Iran's much-vaunted army; and the apparent treachery of its two senior commanders, whose switching of sides had guaranteed Khomeini's success. The case of one of the generals seemed particularly odd – he had been the *de facto* controller of SAVAK, the Shah's right-hand man and childhood friend. Now he was setting up a new Islamic secret police for Khomeini.

Anderson remained silent as Adel related the incongruities. Now he was talking of the nervousness of America's Arab allies in the Gulf and Middle East, how they were drawing lessons from American indifference to the fate of its friends in Iran.

Anderson grimaced and let out a long hiss of air.

"Yeah, the Iranian revolution has had a devastating effect. Unfortunately, a lot of people feel the way you do," he conceded worriedly. "The Saudis and Sadat in Egypt are very discouraged. They believe we let the Shah down, too."

Adel sat forward in his chair. "They have every reason to be worried. It's going to get a lot worse out there. The whole Middle East is a powder-keg and they've unleashed a lunatic, a nut who preaches a violent God in an ignorant, backward part of the world. He's a time bomb, ticking away."

"You're exaggerating, Michael. Khomeini's bad. The Shah's gone – and I won't argue with you about the how or why of that . . ."

"Why not, Don?" snapped Adel.

Anderson did not reply. He reached for the bottle of cognac. It was late, he was tired and the worst part was still to come. The whole conversation had started off badly, he thought dejectedly. What he had hoped to avoid seemed impossible now. He stood and stretched his tired, aching body and strolled away from the sitting area, past the hanging fireplace in the middle of the large room to the open verandah doors.

It had stopped raining and the night was clear and crisp. Below him lay Cannes and the glittering night lights of the Croisette, yet up here it was serene, secluded. Soon, he thought, it would be something quite different.

The thought jolted Anderson. He felt sorry for Adel. Here was a charming, carefree guy who worked hard and played harder. In the murky world of Iranian big business he had acquired his riches honestly and with his personal integrity intact. His uncomplicated, almost childlike rules of right and wrong appealed to Anderson's puritan streak. Besides, he thought, the wealth Adel had acquired had never changed him. He enjoyed spending rather than flaunting his money and he always attributed his wealth to luck, saying that making money in a corrupt society was neither something to be proud of nor much of an achievement. "It's not making money that's difficult," he had once said in a rare philosophic mood. "Making money with distinction is the hard part."

Anderson felt uncomfortable and ill at ease as he entered the room and looked at his friend. He doubted that Adel would believe his position. He wouldn't believe that he had no choice; that he was just a messenger.

"What do you know about the military equipment we have in Iran, Michael?" he asked bluntly as he sat again, the timbre of his voice wavering.

Adel set the magazine he was flicking through aside, and shrugged. "Not much except that some of the more sensitive stuff must have been removed." He was not about to query Anderson's change of subject; the man was obviously here for a purpose and he'd get to it in his own time.

"Exactly. All of it. All the sophisticated material at least has either been 'liberated' or destroyed. The most important items we had there were the F-14 Tomcat fighters. They're among the most sophisticated equipment we've got. They're the backbone of our tactical military capability. The Shah bought eighty of these fighters armed with another of our most sophisticated and sensitive items – the Phoenix missile. Towards the height of the unrest in Iran, these missiles, along with other sensitive equipment, were 'liberated' by shipment to bases in Turkey and Israel. With them went all the software and technical manuals that were in Iran for training and maintenance purposes."

Where could all this be leading us, wondered Adel.

"All, that is, but a commentary on the Phoenix missile system," Anderson clarified softly. "To be more specific, the tape of a verbal presentation of the manuals. Which is, needless to say, as valuable as the manuals themselves. The tapes contain everything there is, the essential information regarding the missile, onboard computers, over-the-horizon radar, digital to analog processors, the brains of the thing."

Adel let out a low whistle.

"You've guessed it, Mike. If these tapes fell into the hands of the Soviets, US security is screwed. Even more so if this data is added to the information gathered last year from the break-in at one of the sub-contractor's offices in California. That compromised the engineering skills, so they already have the manufacturing knowhow. If they get the information contained in the manuals it'll give them the entire thing, lock, stock and barrel. The manuals would give them step by step instructions to follow. And these tapes give them just about that."

Adel shook his head and smiled an irritated smile as he stood. He combed his hair with his right hand and paced calmly towards the wall.

"That's about par for the course, isn't it?" he said, pressing a wall-button. "Kind of completes the picture of incompetence the US managed to paint in its involvement with Iran."

"It was a mad scramble in those last few days, Mike. There was equipment scattered throughout the country – some to be destroyed, some to be evacuated. Despite the chaos, despite the logistical excesses, everything we knew about was successfully liberated. This set we knew nothing about. Not, that is, until a few days ago."

Adel stuck his hands in his trouser pockets and sauntered back. "Who made these tapes?"

"I don't know," replied Anderson, shaking his head. "It's a major security leak. The immediate problem is . . ."

The sound of knocking interrupted him.

"Come in," said Adel.

"Yes, sir." It was Usher.

"Coffee, please, John."

Anderson waited for the door to close before continuing.

"The immediate problem comes from the level of Soviet infiltration within the Khomeini movement. It seems that somewhere along the line, the Soviets recognised the strength of the revolutionary movement and were prepared for it. They've acted quickly and efficiently.

"The leftist infiltration of the Islamics is so widespread, we haven't yet been able to get a handle on it. The country is in total chaos; no law, no order, no administration; everything from the armed forces to private factories, from government ministries to political trials, from banks to the media is run by small Islamic revolutionary committees, or as the Iranians call them, *komitehs*. These organisations fall under the general umbrella of Ayatollah Khomeini's Islamic Revolutionary Council."

The words tumbled from Anderson's mouth in a staccato, robot-like fashion.

"It is here that the communists have moved quickly and effectively. They've infiltrated the key *komitehs* and have a stranglehold on the entire government apparatus. It's an intelligence nightmare. Sometimes they've done it in religious guise; sometimes through the students and militants and so on. But they've done it well; they've gone in deep."

Anderson reached nervously for his glass and gulped a mouthful of brandy.

"If the revolution were just in the hands of a bunch of Khomeini fanatic rag-heads, we'd be less worried. They'd never find the tapes and, if they did, they couldn't figure out their importance. But we're dealing with infiltration of the revolution by highly trained radical left-wing elements. And that means Soviet access to those tapes."

Anderson stopped suddenly and his frown deepened. His face was flushed and his brow sweating.

Three thousand miles was a long way to come and cry over spilt milk, thought Adel as he reached for his cigarettes on the side table. What was Anderson leading up to? Why was he telling him all this?

"Michael, they want you to get those tapes out."

Adel snapped his head towards Anderson. The statement was so unexpected that he sat stunned, unable to respond.

"You'll have good support."

Anderson's meek assurance stirred Adel's brain. Had Anderson drunk too much? Was this whole visit the symptom of some kind of breakdown? Good God, could he be serious?

"Your name has received the highest-level approval, Michael. A lot's riding on you."

Still, Adel could find nothing to say. He sat staring at his old friend incredulously.

"Meetings and briefings and orientation sessions have been set up for you over the next few days."

"Don, tell me I'm hallucinating," said Adel finally.

He lit the cigarette in his hand when Anderson did not respond.

"Why me? Why some civilian jerk with no experience? We must have operatives trained to do this sort of thing. If we don't, the Israelis certainly do. Or the British. The Germans even."

Anderson rubbed his sweaty hands on his trouser legs. He spoke in short jerky bursts. "That's not possible; we can't use our own people; there's some sort of problem with it. I don't know what it is."

"Why the hell not?" snapped Adel. "Is this another brainwave of the Carter administration: holding back the specialist to give the amateurs a chance?"

Anderson shook his head. "Look, Michael. I don't know all there is to know about this thing. I only know what I've been told." He gestured helplessly with his hands.

"Only thing I can think of is that the President doesn't want anything to tarnish the Camp David Agreement. He's pleased as a kitten with it; it's still too fresh and vulnerable."

"Marvellous."

Anderson looked at him and shrugged. "That's a personal opinion. It's not official or anything," he said. "Maybe it's because the Soviets are looking for a reason to cause additional unrest in Iran and destabilise the region even further. But I don't know. I wasn't told. I can only guess . . ."

There was a knock on the living-room door.

"Come in," said Adel, surreptitiously holding up his hand in a signal of silence. It was an unnecessary gesture and he was angry with himself for having made it. Usher entered carrying a silver tray holding coffee and cups. He placed it in front of Adel.

"Shall I pour, sir?"

"Thanks, John, we'll do it ourselves."

The door closed before Anderson continued. "In any event, that takes care of the US and Israel. As for the West Germans, well, they rely too heavily on Iranian oil to get involved. In fact, they're anxious to establish good relations with the new government as quickly as they can. Same with the Brits. They have seventy thousand jobs dependent on car sales to Iran. From what I've been told, all these countries are willing to help but none of them would actually carry out the operation for us."

Adel poured the coffee. "Milk and sugar?" he asked gruffly, annoyed by the unsteadiness of his hand.

"Both."

"Well, they're willing to do more than I am. I won't lift a finger. I'm not going in as some half-assed spy to get my neck chopped off. You'll have to find someone else."

"The assignment," said Anderson slowly and deliberately, avoiding Adel's eyes, "is of grave importance to us."

"Jesus Christ, Don!" snapped Adel. "Are you people nuts? I couldn't do it even if I wanted to, which I don't. I don't know a damn thing about this sort of thing."

Anderson said nothing. He sat staring at his cup.

"Do you people really believe you can sit around some mahogany table in the State Department and decide that a perfect stranger should go into the middle of a revolution and steal documents or tape-recordings or whatever from under the eyes of a bunch of raving maniacs?" Adel's voice was rising.

"I mean, where do you people get these ideas from? You fuck up the entire country and then expect a rank amateur perfect stranger to risk his life to save your asses. Who the hell comes up with these ideas?"

Anderson finished his coffee in one gulp, then poured himself another cup. This time he did not add cream or sugar.

"It's not the State Department," he said quietly.

"The CIA then," snapped Adel, stubbing out his cigarette. "What the hell's the difference?"

Anderson shook his head. "This is unofficial."

Adel felt a slow sinking sensation; and the flow, the fast flow, of adrenalin.

"Who is it, then?" he asked with unmasked trepidation.

"I don't know, Michael. And I'm not authorised to discuss it."

Adel grimaced as the anxiety turned to anger. He lit another cigarette and shook his head. "You're nuts, you know that? Crazy. You walk off the street and ask me to risk my life but you aren't authorised to tell me who I'm doing it for." He shook his head again. "You can't be serious, Don. And if you are, forget it."

Anderson looked away and sighed. It was a long, deep, troubled sigh.

"You have to do it, Michael," he said, his voice soft and low. "They have leverage."

"What the hell is leverage?"

"Your daughter," whispered Anderson, his voice tinged with embarrassment. "They'll use Natalie."

The words shook Adel as slow-motion images of his little daughter flashed before his eyes; instantly his mind was paralysed, his body cold and heavy.

"What . . . what does that mean?" he stuttered. "What do you mean – 'they'll use Natalie'? What has she got to do with this?" The words came out soft and full of doubt. It was the tone of a man who did not want to hear the answer.

"I don't really know, Michael. And again I'm not authorised to go into it," replied Anderson as he turned away from his friend's incredulous and tormented stare. "The Colonel is going to take that up with you. Monday. Right here in Cannes."

Cannes. Saturday, October 20: 2.30 a.m.

It was almost two hours since Don Anderson had left and Michael Adel was still on the telephone, this time to the operator in the Bahamas.

"Please note the number for future use, sir." The lilting tones of the young West Indian woman caressed the transatlantic line. "The phone number of the Lyford Cay Club is 742710. Now what was the name of your party, again, sir?"

"Case," barked Adel impatiently. "John Alexander Case."

He lit a cigarette and tossed the match into the ashtray already brimming with butt ends. After the total failure of the last two calls, he had a strong feeling that he would be using it a lot more before the night was out. He leaned forward and emptied the ashtray in the wastepaper basket beside the desk.

The call to the Bahamas was the third since Anderson had left, but none had produced the answers he sought. Case, he thought fearfully, was the last and the best of his reliable sources. He stubbed out the cigarette and reached for the letter-opener that lay beside the phone.

He had to find out, he thought, nervously twirling the miniature sword in the fingers of one hand. He had to know where Bell stood. Whom he represented. Was he still with the CIA? Or did he represent some private arms manufacturer worried about secrets carelessly left lying around? Was it a squeeze play to entrap him? Some crazy scheme of senile, demented ex-spooks? For what? Why?

None of it made sense.

He glanced at the picture of a smiling Natalie on his

writing table. And what the hell were State Department officials doing running errands for retired spies anyway? Was it a bluff? Or did Colonel Grover Cleveland Bell still count for something?

In his government career Bell had been powerful. Just how powerful was not generally known. He was one of the handful of men whose names constantly cropped up on the sidelines, looming shadows on the outer perimeters of Washington's power structure: Edward Bennett Williams, John J. McCloy, Larry O'Brien. But the linkage with Bell's name was not business or law or even government work in the true sense. It was to the CIA – and to the "dirty tricks" covert operations directorate at that. Vietnam, Watergate, Iran. Publicly he had emerged unscathed – as indeed he always did – from his association with the collapse of the US position in Iran. He had just drifted quietly away, this time into apparent retirement and consultancy work. But the silence surrounding Bell was eerie. It had always puzzled Adel. No one else had escaped so quietly. President Carter, Secretary of State Cyrus Vance, National Security Adviser Zbigniew Brzezinsky, Ambassador William Sullivan, General Robert Huyser, even the lowly head of the Iran desk at the State Department, Henry Precht, had all been hauled over the coals. The media had had a field day, and yet there had been no mention of Bell.

Why? And why were people so reluctant to talk about him now? A retired intelligence consultant?

It didn't make sense.

As soon as Anderson had left, Adel had singled out three people who could help him piece together the answers he needed. His call to Jake Holzstein at the *Washington Post* – an old classmate from Stanford, with whom he had kept in constant touch – had begun with the usual banter. Holzstein's gossip on the Washington scene was prolific, indiscreet and punctuated by high-pitched giggles. But when Adel had casually slipped in Bell's name, Holzstein's tone changed perceptibly. It stiffened and the titters disappeared.

"He's around," said Holzstein brusquely.

"I heard he was doing consultancy work."

"Isn't everyone in Washington?"

"Who for, Jake?"

There was a silence before he answered. "Why Bell, Michael?"

"No reason in particular. He's the only old Iran hand I haven't heard about since the revolution."

"In the middle of the night in the South of France, you're wondering about old Iran hands?"

"Why not?"

"Is everything all right?"

Every statement was a question, noted Adel. "Sure. Did you say he was retired?"

"I don't recall saying anything, Michael."

After they had hung up, Adel had stopped only for the briefest of moments to contemplate Holzstein's sudden and uncharacteristic resistance to gossip. The bizarre sense of mounting suspicion drove him on. Immediately he placed a call to Putney Chatsworth, who he knew had only just retired two months ago to his native Charleston, North Carolina. Chatsworth was a first-class backgammon player, whom Adel had come to know well in Paris, while Chatsworth was living there. Many an afternoon had been spent locked in combat together in the games room of the Travellers Club on the Champs Elysées. Chatsworth was unofficially designated as the political counsellor at the US Embassy, but it was an open secret that he was the CIA station chief in Paris.

"Why, Michael, I didn't know the old Colonel played backgammon," bellowed the southern voice, when Adel had asked after Bell. "I'm just an ole country boy these days, spendin' my time on the boards, if you see what I mean." He had laughed. "What's eatin' you anyway, boy?"

"A friend of mine's been offered some work with Bell,"

he said, opting for a different approach, "and he was wondering . . ."

"And how's your cute little wife?"

The call had drawn another blank. All it had achieved was to increase the tension and arouse the weird feeling that an inexplicable wall of silence surrounded Bell, even among men he had always considered friendly and talkative. The connection he was now waiting for was his ace. It was also his last reliable card.

He had first met John Alexander Case in Iran after his appointment as chairman of Enerco. Case had come to pay his respects to the Shah and subsequently, as head of the world's largest energy company, his audiences were frequent. Often the work he had in the country filtered down to Adel at the National Iranian Oil Company. The discreet deference paid to this prince of commerce, by governments American and foreign, was always reflected in the mannerisms of the people Adel saw him with – the nervous sheepishness of the Shah, the tense hand-wringing of former CIA chief and one-time ambassador to Iran, Richard Helms, the obsequiousness of Ambassador William Sullivan. Even the indestructible Bell had always assumed a subservient manner in Case's presence.

Adel and Case had developed a rapport at their very first meeting. Soon the relationship deepened and Adel had become aware of Case's genuine liking. It grew gradually from one of an avuncular magnate with a bright young nephew to a more personal one, and the transition occurred at the very place Adel was now calling. "You're the only one in the entire Iranian oil company it doesn't cost me to see," he had once said, only half-jokingly. "And a pretty packet at that."

Case, concluded Adel, was a knowledgeable man, among the inner sanctum of the American élite and a good friend. He knew he could rely on him.

The telephone line clicked.

"Lyford Cay Club. May I help you?"

"Mr Case, please. John Alexander Case." He was tired of saying the name.

"Mr Case is in the card room, sir. I'm afraid he's not to be disturbed for another two hours," replied the club operator without hesitation. "He requests all callers to call back then, sir."

"Look, this is an emergency," snapped Adel. "Tell him it's Michael Adel on the line from France and tell him it's urgent."

"Ah . . . one minute, please."

The phone clicked again.

Adel rubbed his moist, aching forehead with the fingers of his left hand and leaned back. He could just picture the astonishment he had caused by his impertinence: the confused operator anxiously turning to the manager and he nervously to Mrs Case in their private villa, each unwilling to take responsibility for breaking one of their trustee's instructions. And he was just as certain Mrs Case would overrule her husband.

In fact, he had a good relationship with all the family. His friendship with Shirley, their nineteen-year-old daughter, had started right on the very white couch the invalid Mrs Case would probably be sitting on when the manager called.

As he waited, he recalled vividly the genteel luxury of the club, a world apart from the poverty and squalor of Nassau and the garishness of Paradise Island. He recalled the Uncle Toms – gliding around the pool serving English dowagers, German landowners and "old money" from Boston, New York and Philadelphia – and the flashes of resentment and anger he detected behind the mask of servility on those glistening black faces.

He remembered too how, while he was a house-guest of the Cases, their daughter had insisted on taking him to Paradise Island one evening when her parents had been invited to some formal affair in which she had no interest. Strolling back along the narrow rolling path to the bungalow in the early hours of the morning, she had suddenly dangled a small plastic bag of marijuana in front of her.

"Can you roll?" she had asked, smiling at him coyly.

"What makes you think I smoke?"

"This lump of hash was in your toilet case," she had shot back.

He remembered how he had stopped in his tracks.

Before the night was out, however, they had smoked several joints. In between they had gone for a midnight dip and then, wrapped in bathrobes embroidered with the Enerco arms, they had sat on the deep couch overlooking the gently sloping white sand of the shore and the calm, almost still, moonlit sea.

It was then that she had kissed him. Gently at first, stiffly as is the uncertain way of one with no experience. And then harder . . .

The telephone clicked again and the worried voice of John Alexander Case came on the line.

"What is it, Michael?" asked Case. "What's wrong?"

"Ah . . . nothing that urgent, Mr Case. I just need your guidance on something rather quickly."

"Thank goodness for that," responded Case with a sigh of relief. "You had me worried there for a moment, Michael."

"Thank you for your concern, sir. I hope I didn't disturb your bridge game."

"Poker actually, Michael. In fact, your timing's superb. You just saved me from sitting patsy with two anaemic pairs, so I'm doubly pleased to hear from you. Now what is it you need to know?"

Adel was uncertain as to the approach he should take. "How are Mrs Case and Shirley? Are they enjoying the sun with you?"

"Yes, Michael, they're both here and they're fine." His tone was laconic.

Adel chose the straight, direct approach. "I need to know about Colonel Bell, sir. Is he still with the government?"

"Who?"

"Bell. Colonel Grover Cleveland Bell, sir. You remember, he used to be in Iran."

There was a moment's silence before Case answered. "You know, that's a good question. I don't really know, Michael. There've been so many changes in Washington lately that it looks like the Minnesota Vikings' offensive line."

"I know, sir," said Adel, with mounting anguish. He leaned forward on the desk and rubbed his temples. "But it's very important to me. I need to know if he's still with the government or if he's retired. Would it be possible for you to perhaps enquire on my behalf? You travel in the same circles."

Case hesitated again before speaking. "He's a fine man, Michael. That much I can tell you without checking. He's also the sort of man who will always be an insider. But as for checking, well, we're all going to be down here for the next two weeks and it's not the sort of thing to be discussed on the phone. What is it you need to know exactly?"

"Is he sanctioned, sir?"

"Grover Cleveland Bell," retorted Case with a raw edge to his voice, "doesn't fart in his sleep without covering his ass, Michael. I wouldn't get in a pissing match with him, if I were you."

The rest was a blur. Adel had heard enough. The wall of silence was complete.

1975

Paris. April.

The Air France flight 194 Teheran–Paris banked to the right. Below, the futuristic Roissy-Charles de Gaulle airport stood shining in the sunlight of a clear, early spring morning.

As Michael Adel set aside the *Herald Tribune* article on the emergence of Senator Muskie as the most likely challenger to Gerald Ford in next year's Presidential elections, the Boeing 707's engines whined high and the plane burst forward towards its final descent. Almost simultaneously, Michael Adel felt a strange excitement at the thought of what lay ahead. What he had to do was unfortunate. But it was also unavoidable and overdue. He reflected on his motives for the thousandth time but again dismissed the pangs of guilt; revenge was not the deciding factor. Gina had nearly ruined him and simply for her own pleasure, but that was unimportant now. What was essential was Natalie and her well-being.

He hadn't been in Paris for over a year; not since he had left his job at the oil company in Iran to go into private business there. As he had expected, the 1973 oil price hikes had burst upon Iran like a giant Christmas cracker – every sector of the economy was in a state of dynamic boom. Fortunately the area he had chosen was the most expansive of them all and consequently he was feverishly overworked; the engineering and construction work had been pouring into his company and the oil-field sites were scattered all over inaccessible areas of Iran. He had spent most of the last year commuting between his office in Teheran and the sites, working harder than he would have liked.

But now the company had taken shape and would run itself. He was freer and richer than he had a right to be. In the past eighteen months, he had made over five million dollars and that was in the first year of operations, when capital outlay was at its peak. He knew the whole Iranian economy was out of control; there was just too much money for some, too fast an expansion, and the pie was being shared by too small a portion of the population. It would blow up sooner or later. But for now, the future was promising. He was one of the privileged few. And his money was cared for with tender Swiss hospitality.

The Peugeot 504 taxi pulled up in the narrow access lane running parallel to Avenue George V. Adel stepped out in front of the Hotel George V and paid the taxi.

"*Bonjour, Monsieur Adel.* It's nice to see you again," said the dark blue uniformed doorman.

Adel had forgotten his name, but gave him a warm smile.

"*Merci,*" he said as he lifted the slim black leather briefcase and the larger aluminium case.

The doorman reached for the luggage.

"That's okay. I'll take them myself," Adel said firmly as he headed for the glass doors. He was unwilling to risk the contents at this late stage.

As an old client, he was exempted from the formalities of registration at the reception desk on the left of the luxurious lobby. Monsieur Palli – and a crisp one-hundred-franc note – made sure that within minutes he was in the familiar brown and beige of Suite 633.

"Monsieur Palli, are the other two suites in order?" he asked the formally attired receptionist.

"Of course, Monsieur," Palli responded with a ready, wide smile. "Will there be anything else, Monsieur?"

he said backing towards the door, eager to peek at the denomination of the crisp note in his hand.

"Thank you, no," said Adel, closing the door behind him.

Very little had changed in these rooms during the past decade. The suite was small by comparison to others offered by the hotel, but Adel preferred it because of its relative isolation and quiet. The front door opened into a small but well-designed sitting-room. To the left was a larger sized bedroom with a huge double bed in the middle. On each side of the bed were mirrors which accentuated the spacious cupboards behind and provided an elegant *belle époque* environment. At the end of the bed stood an antique buffet-type chest of drawers. A television, a bar, and a small sitting area in front of the bay window overlooking the hotel's deserted back courtyard completed the room.

Adel noticed the packages he had asked Usher to deliver placed tidily on the bed; he was uncharacteristically excited. Quickly he made two phone calls, eager to move on to the work that lay ahead. The first call was to Catherine, Madame Claude's secretary, to confirm the evening's arrangements; the second to the sixth-floor maid to pick up his suits and shirts for ironing.

The camera assembly was not difficult. Over the past year he had worked hard to acquire an expert's understanding of photography. The equipment he had was the simplest and most efficient available and in addition to one main system, he had two back-up systems to ensure a fail-safe operation.

The primary system worked off two infra-red lights camouflaged as decorative lamps. One he placed on the chest of drawers in front of the bed and the other on the left side of the room; they would trigger the necessary light for the still photography. He hid the two tripod-mounted Nikon F2 photomic cameras in the cupboards on either side of the bed and positioned them at an angle covering the mattress.

The two cameras were loaded with infra-red film in

five hundred frame magazines with lens apertures set at f-5.6 and speed at 1/125. Both were motorised and attached to individual electronic timers which Adel set to give an exposure every ten seconds; both were blimped to ensure silence. The camera furthest from the bed – about fourteen feet from the camera film plane – held an 85mm, f-18 Nikon lens. The second, about six feet from the centre of the bed, was equipped with a 28mm Nikon f-2.8.

The second system was a Sony video camera customised for him by a specialist firm in Amsterdam for fifteen thousand dollars; it was adapted to handle extremely high-speed film. He placed the video camera on a tripod and set the unit inside the left-hand cupboard. That provided a medium view of the pillows. He adjusted the tripod, focused precisely and locked the tripod firmly.

The three hidden cameras covered the bed, one from the right, two from the left. He also clipped the microphone to the top of the video camera and adjusted the sound level to the predetermined number "5".

For the best part of the next hour he carefully wired the cameras and microphone to a small central control panel and placed the switch in the closet beside his shoes and the video recorder.

He ran the wires along the border of the cupboards and underneath the edge of the carpet past the radiator, then along the carpet edge into the cupboard, where the central control lay.

With wiring completed, he rolled down the outside window shutters, drew the curtains and doused the lights. In the darkness, he carefully pulled the highly sensitive film cassette from a lead container and placed it in the recorder. He then plugged the central control unit, video cassette recorder and video camera into electrical outlets.

Next to the central toggle switch were three light-emitting diodes – LEDs. One for each system. He snapped the central switch, and the LED glowed green.

Satisfied, he turned off the system and covered the video recorder with a heavy black felt cloth.

He turned on the lights and glanced at his watch; it was 4.30 p.m. In four hours, Gina Mahmoudi would knock on the door. Carefully he pushed all the cupboard doors shut, except the three that held the cameras. These he left open a few inches to allow the necessary clearance for the lenses and attached to the three metal hinges of each cupboard door specially made, long, heavy, prism-shaped magnets that jammed the doors. He adjusted the magnets until he had exactly the required openings, knowing that once the magnets were attached it would be impossible to open or close the doors by sheer strength; the wooden doors would splinter or crack before the magnetic fields were broken. The only way to neutralise them was to slide the powerful magnets rather than pull at them.

Adel slid the magnets off and on once or twice and tested the system several times before he was completely satisfied.

The six-hour flight, the two hours of engineering and the nervous excitement had tired him. He picked up the telephone.

"Operator, I'd like a wake-up call at seven-thirty this evening," he said, lighting a cigarette.

"*Oui, Monsieur Adel. Dix-neuf heures trente*," she repeated.

"Oh, and one at seven-forty-five, to be certain," he added.

He lay back and took one last drag at his cigarette. By this time tomorrow his daughter Natalie would be out of that insane asylum her mother called home. He would have her, and all this dirt would be over. It was unfortunate that it had to be this way, he reflected; he would have preferred a more civilised approach but Gina had made that impossible. She had spurned his offers of an amicable solution, and since they had never been married there were no courts to resort to. Anyway, he thought – taking a malicious pleasure in knowing that it was a humiliation Gina would never forget – it would all be over soon. And he would have Natalie.

He relaxed and within minutes was fast asleep.

London. Same day: 8.30 a.m.

Gina Mahmoudi rolled over in her king-sized bed and glanced at her bedside clock. It was eight-thirty in the morning. An ungodly hour, she thought, as she tried to remember when she had last seen this time of day. Strangely, though, she felt vibrant and alert. She turned towards the night table and pressed two buttons simultaneously. The first smoothly parted the silk curtains. The second operated the window shutters with equal deftness.

It was a typical murky, rainy London day and it marred the handsome back courtyard view of her town house in Montpelier Square. Although she rarely made use of the small private park, she loved the scene it provided on those balmy summer days. And it gave her a perfect conversation piece, an ice-breaker, at the start of her regular soirées.

She moved swiftly out of bed and covered her naked body with a white satin floor-length dressing gown. She suddenly thought of her daughter, Natalie. She was growing up and, despite the nurse, becoming much too demanding. She would have to go off to boarding-school soon, but where? Cheltenham? Heathfield? Roedean? They were too close to London; she would be home too often – almost every weekend – and then there were the long holidays. All the prestigious schools in England seemed to be on holiday twelve months in the year, she thought. No, Switzerland was a better idea. She'd have her lawyer look into the possibilities there.

Gina was well aware, and often a little sad, that she was not suited to motherhood. When Natalie had been younger, it had been much easier; she had given Gina enormous pleasure. She had been a novelty, another part of herself, but as she grew older she was becoming an individual who needed so much loving and attention and time. It was a full-time occupation and Gina resented it. Not that Natalie was materially deprived; she had the best that money could buy.

Gina loved her house. She hated sleeping in strange beds and although Natalie lived on a different floor of the house and was forbidden to enter her sleeping quarters, so that she could bring her men home, it was still a nuisance. Yes, Switzerland was one choice; it had excellent educational facilities and Natalie could acquire polish, learn languages and cosmopolitan ways there. Switzerland, she thought, would be best for everybody.

She picked up the phone and pressed the button marked "I".

"Gerda, I'm up and about," she said, cueing her housekeeper to deliver the usual pot of black coffee. Suddenly she was hungry.

"And two soft-boiled eggs and some toast," she added.

"That's better, madam. You should have breakfast every day. Coffee is not good for you," Gerda said with a heavy Austrian accent.

Gina walked into the bathroom and slipped off her gown. The shower was tingling and the thought of a whole week with Adel excited her. She caressed her body with the soap and thought of the last time she had been with him. It had been in Paris, a long time ago now. He had picked up that girl at the François I Discothèque and they had seduced her together. He had let her make love to the girl over and over and he had watched, smoking hashish and popping amyl-nitrate for them at just the opportune moment to keep their highs going. She shuddered as she recalled how, when she was going down on the girl for the third time, he had picked the exact right moment to join the fray. How he suddenly stood up and entered her from behind.

It had hurt, but she loved it. It was quintessential pleasure.

Yes, she thought, she would enjoy the coming week with him and perhaps, this time, she could even hold on to him.

Gina stepped out of the shower glowing and grabbed a pink towelling bathrobe. As far as she was capable of loving anyone unselfishly she loved Adel. Perhaps it was because they had first met a lifetime ago in Iran when they were both children and they had grown up together. He had been an outstanding athlete, she pretty and spoilt. And she had been so proud to be his girlfriend. He had been so kind and gentle, patient with her tantrums yet shyly dominant as teenage sexual awareness developed and bound them close together. He had always had a weakness for lame ducks; frequently during the holidays he brought home the lonely, over-sensitive boys for whom boarding-school, with its inherent sadism, was sheer torture. She liked those qualities about him, his gentleness and understanding.

He had never changed, she thought. He was and always had been a survivor. But he was also a simple man whose success came through hard work and intelligence rather than ruthlessness or corruption. And he knew her so well. He understood her every action and forgave her everything until she goaded him beyond endurance. She wanted to see him suffer, to abandon his unquestioning acceptance – and he did. But at what cost? No one had ever replaced him, though God knows there had been enough candidates.

Then Gerda came in and disturbed her reverie.

"Here we are, madam," she said, placing the green and white Wedgwood breakfast set on the table in front of the window. "And the mail," she added.

Gina said nothing. She was deep in thought and could not be bothered with another of Gerda's long conversations.

Oh, she had got him back – when she had told him she was pregnant. Until two months after Natalie's birth, to be precise. Under his care her pregnancy had been a healthy one – only a little alcohol, no cigarettes. But it had not been the same. Sometimes she found him staring at her, a hard, bitter look in his eyes. It frightened her; it was a quality she had never seen in him before and she knew it was her fault. The only thing that really worked – perhaps even better than before – was their sexual relationship. The gentleness and affection had dissipated, replaced by a violent, animal-like quality. And for her it was even more enjoyable. Somehow, though, the frequency decreased. They saw each other less and less; and, more often than not, it was for Natalie's sake.

The telephone rang. Anyway, she mused, so long as she held on to Natalie, his precious little Natalie, she would have part of him.

"Hello, 584 2521." She never quite knew why she pretended privacy when half the town had her number.

"Hi," said the deep mellow tone.

"Hello, Enrico darling," she said with feigned lilting delight. "How was the Caribbean?"

For the third time that morning the voice said, "Boring without you, darling."

Count Enrico de Sapio was one of the current popular jet-set gigolos and one of her regular escorts. He was generously endowed but not sexually prolific. He served his purpose more as an agreeable companion on whose elegant arm she could appear at parties, discothèques, dinners; and he was not in the least possessive – indeed, he had acted as her pimp on a number of occasions when she had wanted a particularly delectable but rather inaccessible young man. For Gina, he was decoration for twenty-eight days a month and a stallion for two. It was an arrangement that suited them both.

"I'm dying to see you," he said.

"I'm dying to see you too, darling, but I'm off to New York today," she lied.

"What a pity, and I've been saving myself for you."

Gina thought for a minute. Perhaps she could fit him

in before her flight to Paris. But the thought of Adel pre-empted the notion.

"Darling, you're adorable. I would simply love to see you, but my flight leaves at one and I have a million things to do. Save yourself for me a bit longer, I'll be back next week," she said, injecting a note of sorrow into her voice.

"Oh, what a shame . . ." They chatted aimlessly for a few more minutes, then their conversation ran out of steam. "So I'll see you when you get back, my love," he said, eager to put down the receiver. He was wise enough to know that in his line of work, his career was short; time was mean.

" 'Bye, darling. Call me next week."

She put the phone down and realised that it could never work with Adel. She could never be faithful to just one man and she really had no wish to be; there was too much variety in this world to be tied down. On the other hand, she thought, there was no one quite like him.

"I'll always keep a part of him," she said aloud as she bit into the thick toast and marmalade and thought of his precious little Natalie.

Paris. Same day.

At eight-thirty in the evening Gina Mahmoudi closed the door of her suite behind her. As Michael Adel's note had instructed, she made her way down from the seventh floor, glancing out of habit to check her make-up in one or two of the gently lit mirrors along the way. But it was a routine action; her mind was preoccupied by his unusual behaviour; she could not understand why he had not met her at the airport, nor why they had separate suites. Maybe he had business to attend to. Even so, it was unlike him to invite people the first night they were together after so long. She shrugged off the questions as she descended the hotel's ornately sculptured wrought-iron back staircase and made her way to Adel's suite.

At the sound of the chimes, Adel closed the top button of his white shirt and tightened his striped black and white tie. He picked up a tumbler of Glenlivet from the coffee table and walked towards the door. He felt remarkably good; the anxiety had subsided, giving way to controlled excitement and determination.

"Hello, Gina," he said warmly, his heart missing a beat. He had forgotten how attractive she was.

The seductive dimpled smile on her face formed a pout as she rose on her toes. "Hello, darling," she purred.

Adel bent down and kissed her cheek. It was the same Azzaro perfume on the same body and it produced a flood of bitter-sweet memories. He felt, too, the slight tremble in her hand. He placed a guiding arm against the small of her back and gently brushed her in.

"How are you?" he asked. "You look fabulous."

"Thank you."

"First a drink," he said, pointing at her as he headed towards the bar. "White wine still?"

She moved towards the Picasso lithograph on the beige cloth-covered wall. "That would be lovely."

A bottle of Corton-Charlemagne 1969 lay in an ice bucket, already opened. Alongside it, in the large silver-plated bucket, were two others, unopened. It was a rich, spicy, lingering white Burgundy, which was ageing magnificently. Not unlike Gina, he thought, as he poured it into a crystal wine glass and handed it to her.

"It's been a long time. How've you been?" he asked.

"Oh, fine. Travelling a lot and keeping busy in general. I was in Beverly Hills in the spring and all I did was think of you, darling. I kept remembering how you love it and how nice it would have been if you were there. We never did go there together, did we?" she asked, as she arranged her lissom body on the settee opposite him.

He shook his head. "No. We never did. I guess I like it

because I grew up in the neighbourhood," he said, in casual reference to his college days at Stanford which was in the neighbourhood as far as she was concerned; a thousand miles was nothing to Gina.

"How's Natalie?" he asked.

"Oh, she's fine. Growing and talking non-stop. She's such a happy child and so independent; everywhere we go she's the centre of attraction. She's so pretty I envy her."

Adel felt a surge of anger, but he controlled it, careful not to let it show in his tone. "You know, it's been two years since I saw her."

"Oh, darling, we must arrange something. Perhaps you should come and have tea with her one day."

Two years now, thought Adel, feeling his determination mounting. For two years this was the sort of answer he'd been getting. Every civilised effort he'd made to establish some sort of normal relationship with his daughter – to stop her lonely descent to insecurity – had foundered in a sea of flippancy and lies. But soon, he thought, soon it would end.

He was pleased to see Gina's glass already empty. He picked it up casually and half-filled it. Gina was a hard drinker but she was no fool; he must not be seen to be plying her.

"Lack of beauty has never been your problem," he said, holding out her drink. "You just take it too seriously."

She smiled and reached for her glass.

Yes, she was still a stunning woman, he thought as he sat back again and studied her. Her elegantly cut jet-black hair fell to just below her shoulders and her lips formed a permanent pout below sleepy bedroom eyes. If it wasn't for the thin lines around her eyes, due less to her thirty-three years than to her fast lifestyle, she could have been the innocent girl he had known so many years ago. Beneath the floating white chiffon dress her slender, long-limbed figure showed no sign of ageing. It retained its youthful hardness: her breasts pressed firm, inviting and round against the almost transparent, material.

"Might as well get over the free samples and start into the real portions," she said, walking to the makeshift bar and exchanging the already empty wine glass for a tall crystal tumbler. "Who are your guests tonight?" she asked casually, as she filled the larger glass.

"Oh, I thought you'd enjoy a little bit of variety," replied Adel suggestively.

She looked up at him and blushed as she discarded her shoes and curled up on the sofa, tucking her feet beneath her. At least one of her concerns was unfounded, she noted with relief.

"And what would you do if I said no?"

"Faint."

She laughed and came over to him. Silently she knelt in front of him and kissed his lips – a long, tender kiss.

"You know I love you when you're being a bastard, don't you?"

She closed her eyes and moved her hands softly down his body, enjoying the feel of his chest beneath the thin cotton shirt. They moved down, past the silk of his trouser-tops and then they stopped. With a facility that comes only from experience, she undid his zipper and then slowly, almost tantalisingly, felt for him. Like a mischievous child with a lollipop, she dipped her head and took him in, yet now her hooded eyes looked up at him – teasing, tempting.

Pleasure overwhelmed him as blood suffused his body. Gently at first and then harder he pressed her head down, forcing himself deeper. She complied willingly; deeper and deeper, with every bow of her head, his heart beating faster, his body heat rising . . .

Suddenly she stood, her face blushing red, moisture dampening her forehead. She lifted the skirt of her dress and, unencumbered by underwear, she turned to sit on him, so that he could enter her from behind, the way she had always liked it.

The doorbell, with its soft two-stroke chime, interrupted.

She cursed obscenely, dropping her skirt only half in mock anger. "I suppose we can't tell them to come back later?"

Adel smiled and stood up.

"Why?" he teased. "We can take up where we left off just as soon as the ice melts. Only you'll have more to play with," he said, turning his eyes suggestively.

Adel opened the door to reveal two extraordinarily beautiful young girls – a testament to the good taste of Madame Claude's organisation. One was a brunette with shortish *flou* hair, cut just above the shoulders. Her large brown eyes were almonds in shape and colour and they were accentuated by high cheekbones that hollowed out her cheeks, giving her a sleek animal quality. Tall and slim with full inviting lips, she was no more than twenty-three years old but she had about her an air of supreme confidence.

"*Bonsoir*," she said. "My name is Claudine and this is Barbara." She pointed to her blonde friend.

Barbara looked even younger and, to judge solely from her appearance, less experienced, but she was no less attractive. She had long fluffy blonde hair that fell well below her shoulders. The skin that covered her delicate doll-like features was smooth and unseasonably tanned, setting off the blueness of her eyes and the blondeness of her hair.

Both girls were elegantly and expensively dressed – the mark of the professional. They wore mink coats which, when removed, revealed diaphanous evening dresses beneath. Nothing resembling underwear broke the smooth lines of their slinky yet tasteful garments.

Almost immediately, Gina had drinks in their hands. Just as quickly she had turned her attention and charm to the more inexperienced and vulnerable Barbara.

Adel leaned back in his chair and surveyed the scene; there was little else for him to do. The girls were relaxed and enjoying themselves and Gina was in her element.

Like a lioness stalking her prey, she had little use for her mate.

The plan was going well – almost too well, thought Adel as he felt a sudden pang of anxiety. Would it work? Were the machines operating properly? The cupboards . . . He felt an urge for reassurance.

"Excuse me a minute," he said as he walked towards the bedroom. "I have to make a call." He locked the door behind him without waiting for a response.

Carefully he rechecked the camera angles, the wiring, the magnets and the rest of the sensitive equipment. It was all in order, functioning perfectly. But still he felt a gnawing feeling of doubt.

He sat on the bed, pulled out the bedside drawer, and took out the engraved Victorian silver cigarette case he had placed there in the afternoon. It was full of ready-made joints of the highest quality hashish – acquired, rolled and delivered by Usher. Alongside it lay a green and white Limoges china pillbox.

The hashish would relax him. As for the girls, he thought, inspecting the cigarettes, it would break whatever ice was left and ease any inhibitions that might exist – though that was doubtful from what he had seen. He smiled, knowing that as far as ice-breaking was concerned, Gina by now had made their thousand-dollar fees seem like mere icing on the cake.

He lit the thinnest, mildest joint and took in a deep breath. The bitter-sweet smell spread immediately throughout the room, the smoke billowing around the bedside lampshade. He inhaled deeply and held his breath.

For the umpteenth time he considered what he was about to do, and again came to the same conclusion: he simply had no choice. Gina marched to a different band. And its instruments did not include love or caring or compromise. Even for their own daughter. He crushed the joint and headed for the door. He . . . no normal parent could stand aside and watch the destruction of his offspring.

He stepped from the bedroom to find the three girls talking and laughing happily. From the quality of the hotel's service he knew it had to be minutes after ten-thirty, for in their midst stood two trolleys covered with a magnificent selection of *canapés* and several bottles of Dom Perignon 1955 Champagne in ice cold buckets. Next to the ice buckets stood a large crystal bowl containing a mound of Iranian caviar surrounded by chopped onions, finely chopped hard egg yolks and whites, and parsley.

Gina had convinced the girls that they would be more comfortable in bathrobes and both had complied. She was in full flight.

"Caviar is good for you," she said, scooping spoonfuls on to small side plates and adding the various spices, butter and toast. "The Iranians say it's an aphrodisiac and the Russians claim it gives you stamina. Either way it can't do us any harm."

The girls responded eagerly and Adel marvelled at Gina's authority.

"Here, this will help your appetites," he said, opening the cigarette case. "Leave the food for later."

The girls did not need much persuading; they were delighted by a new diversion. Between the hashish, the wine, the food, the conversation, one sensual pleasure quickly followed another in an orgy of self-indulgence. It was nearly midnight before the foreplay subsided.

Adel opened the small china box and extracted a miniature golden spoon from it; he poured several spoonfuls of white powder on the dark brown marble table-top and formed eight lines of cocaine with a matchbook.

Claudine lit up at the sight of the coke. "Ahh . . . *J'adore ça. Il ne nous manquait que cela*," she said eagerly as she moved over and inhaled two lines, one in each nostril, through a short straw.

"*Ça, c'est chouette*," said Barbara, delightedly waiting her turn. "It's been ages since I've had any. Where did you get it?"

Gina stood and picked up the china box from the table, a little annoyed that Adel had stolen her thunder by producing the ultimate in fashionable aphrodisiacs. As she did so, and before Barbara had a chance to inhale her lines, she brushed the white powder from the table with a flamboyant gesture that totally disregarded its value.

Barbara was shocked and, from the look on her face, very disappointed. She stared at Gina questioningly.

"Come on," Gina commanded. "I'll show you how to use it properly." Her voice was soft and husky as she smiled and took Barbara's uncertain hand.

Adel immediately recognised the carrot and stick approach so often used by Gina. It was crucial, Adel thought, that the film record Gina's dominant role in the seduction scene. He didn't want some clever, high-priced lawyer claiming she had been drugged and coerced.

"Show us all," said Adel, as Gina pulled Claudine from her chair and tugged her gently towards the bedroom.

Gina looked provocatively over her shoulder. "Join us."

He followed the three girls into the bedroom and immediately turned off the bedside lamp, pitching the room into darkness and camouflaging the cracks in the cupboard doors.

"Darling," complained Gina. "Give us a bit of light. We need to see what we're doing."

Adel opened the bedroom door wider to allow more light from the sitting-room to filter through. He turned to see the faint outline of her white dress fall to the floor.

The two girls were already lying on the bed. Barbara had disrobed and lay naked on her right, her head propped up by a pillow. But for a minute triangle of glowing white skin and blonde hair between her legs, her body was a light coffee colour, tanned by the Caribbean sun. Her eyes were dilated and yearning as she watched Gina step out of her dress. The hashish was taking hold, thought Adel, observing her fingers gently circling the centre of the small mound of white.

Claudine sat on the huge double bed, her back resting on the headboard, her arms hugging her own legs, her lips suggestively sucking the smooth shining flesh of her knee. Her robe was open at the front and her breasts, pressed as they were against her thighs, were large and firm.

Gina caressed his face as she brushed past. "Join us!" she whispered, the alcohol and hashish slightly slurring her words.

"You're stoned," he said, smiling.

She pointed to the two girls with her eyes. "So are they, my darling," she whispered, turning towards the bed.

Adel felt in his pocket for the miniature remote-control mechanism; he pressed the button that activated the equipment and immediately the invisible infra-red lighting flooded the darkness. He looked at the cupboard doors to check they were as he had left them – opened sufficiently to allow the cameras to record. When he saw no problem, he lit another joint and sat in the armchair at the end of the bed. They don't need me, he mused. Which was just as well. It was preferable that he keep out of the cameras' range.

Gina moved between the two girls and opened the tiny china box. Without the aid of the spoon she tapped a generous portion of the rich white powder on to the patch of hair between her legs.

"Now try it," she tempted Barbara in a deep, husky tone. "It's really much nicer this way."

And Barbara did. She went down on Gina and sniffed. Deep, life-enhancing inhalations that slowly became a mad, desperate hunt. Like a terrier, she pawed and licked and dug for the buried aphrodisiac with her tongue. The more she found the more she sought, her sensual impulses fusing in uncontrollable animal desire.

Gina lay back in ecstasy, her hands guiding Barbara's head. But her eyes were devouring Claudine; they closed and opened in burning desire, travelling with naked lust over Claudine's buxom form. Physically, though, Gina ignored her. Instead she suddenly pulled Barbara's head away from her body in a violent yet passionate movement.

It was a momentary action as she spread another generous dose of cocaine between her legs. For the next fifteen minutes the two women clawed at each other; tongues flicking, lips devouring, fingers moving from one nerve centre to another, a tangle of knotted arms and legs. As the burning passion grew, Gina turned towards Claudine. It was time to produce yet more.

And she did. She collected a generous portion of the white powder on her index finger and gently penetrated Claudine. She knew the itching, tingling feeling it would create. She knew because she was experiencing it herself.

Almost immediately, Claudine was burning inside and out. Soon she would yearn for something to alleviate the itch. To relax the aroused, burning nerves. And Gina provided the balm.

Eventually ecstasy took hold. Gina lay on her side while the two girls devoted themselves to satisfying her. And she came. How many times was difficult to tell, but she came. And came. Finally, exhausted, the three girls slumped back in sweat and fatigue, knotted together in a tangle of arms and legs, sheets and pillows.

And Michael Adel had what he had come for.

He sat up and forced himself to concentrate. It had been a wildly sensuous scene and he had been aroused to fever pitch but he had resisted the temptation. After ten minutes of silence he stood slowly and opened the cupboard door as discreetly as he could and took out the leather briefcase before turning off the central switch. Then he silently collected the two Nikon cameras and placed them in the briefcase. With the video cassette he was more careful. Guarding against light, he withdrew the oversized cassette and immediately placed it in its lead container before putting that, too, in the briefcase.

"What are you doing, darling?" came Gina's exhausted, hoarse voice.

"I'll see you in the morning," he said softly. "There're two envelopes in the drawer beside you. Give one to each of the girls when you've finished with them."

Gina slowly pushed herself up on to her elbows. "But, darling, I thought . . ."

He bent over the limp, sweat-soaked body of Barbara and kissed Gina's damp cheek. "I'll see you in the morning," he said gently but firmly.

John Usher was consuming his third "Nino Special" in the newly decorated bar of the hotel, when Adel entered the virtually deserted room. Only three Arabs apparently felt at home at this late hour and they sat in one corner talking loudly. Somewhere in the background, Frank Sinatra fought a losing battle for attention.

Usher stood up from his stool as Adel took the two steps up from the sunken sitting area to the bar. Adel handed him the briefcase and nodded at the head barman.

"How are you, Nino?"

"Fine, Mr Adel. Are you staying with us a few days this time?"

"I'm afraid not. I'm off in the morning."

He turned to Usher. "You won't get any sleep tonight, so take it easy with those, John," he said, pointing to the half-finished cocktail. "Everything okay?"

"Yes, sir."

"When can I have them?"

"They're waiting for them right now. They'll work on them through the night."

Adel nodded and was silent for a moment. "Okay. Bring them up to my room at nine in the morning then," he said, "but be careful."

He turned to leave, then turned back. "Thank you, John."

Paris. April.

As a rule Michael Adel was a late riser, but an unusual exhilaration that morning forced his body clock to operate ahead of time. Neither the operator nor Usher had disturbed him and he knew it had to be early as he threw off the bed covers and got up. He looked around the room and noted that Usher had set up the video cassette recorder and attached it to the television. He checked the wardrobe for a fresh change of clothes and then spent the next two hours bathing, dressing and eating breakfast. He was practically finished with the morning's papers when John Usher knocked on the door.

"Good morning, sir."

Adel glanced at the briefcase in the tired, unkempt man's hand. "How do they look, John?"

"I think you'll be satisfied, sir."

Adel nodded gently and took the briefcase. "Good." He moved towards the centre of the room. "I'll be leaving for Cannes almost immediately, John. Why don't you stay over tonight and get some rest?"

"Thank you, sir."

"And don't forget to take care of everything in both suites and Miss Mahmoudi's quarters too."

"I will, sir," said Usher, before leaving.

The results of the photography were as good, if not better, than Adel had expected. The film and accompanying stills gave a blow-by-blow account of the previous night's action. It covered every lurid detail from three different angles, providing an incontestable document of a drug-induced orgy. Even more important, so far as Adel was concerned: nowhere in either the stills or the movie was he implicated.

As a work of art, Adel thought, the lighting was a

little on the dark side, but as an instrument of blackmail it was flawless. Gina's father could never absorb a scandal of the magnitude these pictures would cause.
And she needed her father's money.

Paris. April.

Gina Mahmoudi was awake and eating a hearty continental breakfast when Michael Adel entered.
"Good morning, darling," she said, as she returned from the door to a croissant dripping with honey.
Adel smiled nervously but said nothing. He placed the portable video recorder he carried beside her breakfast tray and connected it to the television and a nearby wall plug. As he set up the apparatus, he noted out of the corner of his eye the look of surprise and confusion on Gina's face.
"What *are* you doing?" she exclaimed.
"You'll see in just a minute."
He loaded the cassette into the machine and turned towards her, eager to conclude the whole sordid affair when he noticed a second cup on the breakfast tray.
"Is someone here?" he asked apprehensively, glancing towards the bedroom door.
"Yes, darling," replied Gina with a mischievous grin. "Barbara was so tired I let her stay. She's still asleep."
Adel walked to the bedroom door and closed it gently. Barbara's presence was probably a blessing in disguise, he thought. Gina was less likely to cause a scene with her next door. He returned to sit opposite Gina and reached to pour himself a cup of coffee.
"Gina, I'm going to take Natalie from you."
The carefree look of mischief on Gina's face evaporated.
"You're no mother for her and you know it. Your

money provides her with food and shelter, but that's about all she gets from you.

"When I agreed to let you keep her, it was because I believed you would provide her with a better life. You convinced me that a mother's love is more important to a child than a father's and I was willing to go along with that.

"But, I should have known better." His voice was bitter now and a shade louder. "In your case I should have known better."

"That's not true, I –"

"Let me finish," he snapped. "The child is suffering and miserable. She never sees you except at parties when you bring her in to show her off like a prize pekinese. If it weren't for her nurse, you wouldn't know if she was dead or alive. There are men crawling in and out of that house like it was an army enlistment centre. And you go on your merry way as if she doesn't exist. No love, no caring, no warmth, no responsibility. Hell, that's no home for her – it's a bloody brothel," he said angrily, the words erupting uncontrollably. "It's only a matter of time before it catches up with her, Gina. She needs a simple, orderly, secure upbringing."

She stared at him in disbelief, slowly curling up on the sofa as if suddenly overcome by a deep winter chill.

"Go fuck yourself," she spat at last. "You self-righteous, pompous little trader. What gives you the right to lecture me about how I treat my daughter? MY DAUGHTER . . ." she shrieked.

As her invective gathered pace, Adel walked over to the bedroom door and locked it. He wanted no interruptions. He then turned slowly, walked over to the small screen and pushed the start button.

Gina froze. She uttered no sound as the small black and white picture flickered to life.

"I hope you get the general idea," said Adel calmly. "But if you miss anything, I can ask the concierge to send up a larger screen." He paused to watch the writhing of the three women. "Not exactly a picture of motherhood, Gina."

The effect was devastating. It took hold immediately and he knew he need say no more.

Her voice, when it finally came, was trembling and barely audible, her face a sickly white. "You can have your fucking daughter, you bastard," she whispered, a haggard expression on her face. Her arms were wrapped around herself to ward against the cold front of fallen blood pressure.

Adel turned immediately to leave. There was nothing to stay for. Only the smell of victory lingered. And it was unbearably foul.

1979

Cannes. Monday, October 22: 9.45 a.m.

The white stone pile of the Carlton Hotel blazed in the late October sunlight. The week-long cold spell had abated and suddenly the town basked in the warmth of an Indian summer. Elderly couples swarmed along the ocean boulevard admiring the blend of natural and man-made beauty. Some strolled along the beach front, taking advantage of nature's kindness; others sipped coffee in sidewalk cafés, bistros and boîtes. Still others browsed in the luxurious boutiques for something they didn't already have; in Cannes, need is not the prerequisite.

Adel inched his car through the pedestrians, unusually impatient with the unhurried movement of the elderly winter residents. His mind raced furiously with nervous anticipation. Not only had his calls to three well-informed friends drawn a blank, but four days of incessant probing had proved equally fruitless. At the first mention of the name Bell, people who otherwise were afraid of nothing shied away; powerful, previously reliable friends in positions to know. Government people, doyens of private enterprise, the media, intelligence operatives and even people on the other side of the law – all refused to talk about Colonel Grover Cleveland Bell.

At last Adel reached the hotel's semi-circular driveway and pulled up between the white pillars of its awning.

"Now that we have nice weather you're not running,"

joked the doorman as he opened the car door and handed him a newspaper.

"Thanks, Jean." Adel rolled the paper and strode away quickly, leaving the plump figure looking after him, surprised at his uncharacteristic abruptness.

In the east wing of the hotel, two floors above the huge patio bar area, a lace curtain ballooned outward towards the pillared balustrade of a balcony. Colonel Grover Cleveland Bell's head appeared briefly, looking down.

The lobby was quiet in this off-season period, and Adel walked briskly through the almost deserted space, ignoring the recognition of the idle hall-porters. He entered the elevator and snapped the newspaper open. Every day the headlines screamed of the chaos in Iran. An old proverb came to mind: "*They have sown the wind and they shall reap the whirlwind.*"

What was worse, he thought, he was getting caught up in it. And he was about to meet the man who had manipulated him into this no-win position.

He remembered Bell from Teheran as an affable acquaintance, whose sophisticated manner belied his reputation as a tough and ruthless operator. After his arrival in Iran following Watergate, his role as the CIA supremo for Central and South-West Asia had become an open secret. Propping up the Daoud Khan régime in Afghanistan; neutralising Mostafa Barzani's Kurdish revolt in Iraq; formulating the Algiers accord between Iraq and Iran; monitoring Soviet missile-launchers from the highly secret US radar facility outside the North-East Iranian village of Behshahr; arranging the assassination of the Baluchi chieftain Amir Akbar Khan whose graduation from opium smuggling to regional politics had proved inconvenient; financing the British aid programme to the Sultan of Oman. Bell was even credited for manipulating US congressional approval of AWACS sales to Iran, using his notorious "file card" system on legislators to ensure a positive vote.

Adel knew Bell as a ruthless man whose commitment to furthering his "understanding" of US foreign policy interests knew no limits. Any state should be glad to have a Bell who could do its dirty work with such thoroughness. And one or two others did.

As he raised his hand to the doorbell, Adel was aware for the first time in his life that he was genuinely frightened. He hadn't a card to play with. And Colonel Grover Cleveland Bell was not a man to be bluffed.

The door opened to reveal a tall, gangling man whose face had marked time since Adel had last seen him. At sixty, the Colonel, as he liked to be called, despite his far higher seniority, still looked younger than his age. His thinning hair was still brushed straight back, only it was perhaps whiter now.

"It's so nice to see you again, Michael." The half-smile on the left side of his face contrasted sharply with the tautness of his right cheek. "Come in, come in."

Years of schooling at Switzerland's exclusive Le Rosey School, Harvard, and in the intelligence community had given the Colonel more than a fair share of social ease and *savoir faire*. The veneer, however, could not quite mask the eyes. And time had not been kind there: it had ploughed deep furrows that accentuated the coldness and cunning that lay behind the open, disfigured gaze.

"Please sit there – best chair in the house," the Colonel said affably, pointing to a padded, high-backed Louis XIV armchair.

Adel looked at the corner Bell had chosen and his mind raced. He thought: There's always a reason with people like Bell. Every move, every phrase is calculated. The chair, he observed, was one of four in a circle around a marble table. It looked comfortable enough, but it faced the wall, leaving the large room behind him out of sight.

He refused Bell's invitation and chose instead the chair opposite, facing the room.

The Colonel did not acknowledge the rebuff. He sat

beside Adel, rubbing his palms together in polite welcome. The most comfortable chair in the house remained vacant, Adel noted, as a breeze carrying the aroma of fresh sea air entered the room and blew the light lace curtains of the bay window towards him. Faint sounds of traffic filtered in from the beach-front below, all but drowning out the sound of a distant campanile announcing the hour of ten o'clock.

"It's always a pleasure to see old friends," said Bell. "My years at the Military Mission in Iran are among the most memorable of my life. The friendships I developed there are a continuing source of pleasure to me." He paused and the two men studied each other. "Would you care for a drink?"

Adel shook his head. "No, thank you," he replied as he openly surveyed the room. One of the connecting doors of the suite was slightly ajar.

Bell looked at Adel, his smile unaffected, but behind the joviality his mind was working overtime; it scanned its memory of the psycho-graphic summary on Michael Adel which Operations Directorate had provided.

Fundamentally subject's make-up is reactive rather than active; a counter-puncher with lightning quick, shrewd, agile mind that relies on IQ of 153 and total confidence in both perceived self-image and physical prowess. Self-effacement is innate and should not be translated as self-doubt. Avoid open confrontation physical or psychological. Keep all contacts hostility-free or heavily weighted against subject.

"Very well," he said, smiling. "First let me say this." He relied on his habitual stabbing of the air with his right index finger to induce confidence and sincerity. "I wanted our first meeting to be private, man to man, if you will. I didn't think it was necessary to drag in a bunch of bodies to sit around and discuss the details at this stage."

He looked Adel squarely in the eye, only half-expecting an answer.

"You must realise, Michael, that the circumstances

in which we find ourselves are highly unusual and our options clearly limited. The danger to the United States is severe. In fact, this thing is potentially catastrophic for the entire Free World."

Adel did not reply.

"Don Anderson tells me you're roughly familiar with what we have in mind."

"Yes," replied Adel. "About as familiar as you are with my reaction."

Hostility considered counter-productive to desired goals. This stimulus will meet with rejection. Barring subject's known weaknesses for wife and daughter, based on daughter's life history, only alternate mode of approach to stimulate willing cooperation and confidence is breakdown of subject's innate barriers of mistrust. Considered unfeasible within specified time-frame.

"Anderson also informs me you're a little disappointed by the events in Iran."

"Bitter," said Adel, staring coldly.

"I beg your pardon?" Bell cocked his left eyebrow and readied himself for the first thrust.

"Bitter. Bitter is a more accurate description of my feelings."

"Michael, that's a very natural response. The revolution in Iran was an unfortunate thing and it came at a particularly bad time for you. I know your construction business was doing extremely well. Why, your tax write-offs must have been close to three point two million dollars."

Adel was startled. That was the exact figure agreed with his company's auditors in New York only twelve days ago.

"Not to mention your family's real estate holdings in Teheran and on the Caspian coast. But we all lost, Michael. Perhaps needlessly. The Shah was a good friend of mine, but unfortunately he was a bad listener. He wouldn't listen to me; in the last few years he wouldn't listen to anyone. He chose to ignore all the extraordinary problems that are by-products of unduly rapid modernisation programmes. He simply went too fast and . . ." Bell lifted his hands in conclusion.

Adel nodded. "That's one way of looking at it."

Despite prescribed impactive mode of first contact, ie Anderson, second contact should appeal to subject's romantic make-up and simplistic viewing of the world and self-imposed adherence to strict but simple ethical standards.

"Michael," he said in the same patronising tone, "the fact that we need to call on you is the result of a build-up of unusual circumstances. Rare circumstances. We analysed the options closely before we found it necessary to select you. God only knows, we would have preferred to use a professional operative and not trouble you. But unfortunately that's not possible."

He paused and studied Adel before continuing. "I appreciate the personal dilemma we are putting you in, but we have no choice. I assure you, we'll be indebted to you. I hope you never need to call on that debt but it's a good promissory note to have."

Adel brushed some imaginary dust from the trousers of his safari suit; it was a nervous action. "Tell me, Colonel. How many of these promissory notes did the Shah have?"

"Yes," responded Bell promptly and without passion. "In retrospect perhaps we should have helped him a little more. But, as I said, it all got out of hand. Oh, I imagine there are plenty of conspiracy theories around, especially among your Iranian friends," he added. "Only problem is, if there aren't any conspiracies, they invent some. The CIA subverted the Shah's government. Or the oil companies did it, or the State Department, or President Carter."

"You're right," said Adel disciplining himself to mirror Bell's calm. "All sorts of silly rumours abound and it's not just among the Iranians. Even Alexander Haig and George Bush have jumped on the band wagon." He allowed his voice a sarcastic note. "They've both suggested that General Huyser's role in Iran should be studied more closely. But I'm sure that's just campaign talk, aren't you?"

Bell casually uncrossed and re-crossed his legs. "Well, they're wrong. 'Dutch' Huyser had nothing to do with any of this. The fact is, the Carter administration blew it. The clowns couldn't handle it, that's all. In retrospect, it's very clear that despite a build-up of crisis signals from very early on, when the actual revolution erupted in October of 1978, Washington was simply unprepared. The indications were there, but they just blew it."

Adel rubbed the corner of his right eye. "You are an opponent of the conspiracy theory and an advocate of Murphy's Law, then."

Bell cocked his head to the right. "How's that?"

"Well, you seem to be an expert on it," responded Adel. "'If anything can go wrong, it will.' And that's what you want the world to believe, isn't it? Approximately forty thousand Americans lived in Iran, Colonel. Scattered throughout the country, working in the most sensitive areas. We had at our disposal the so-called dreaded SAVAK secret police, the CIA, the Defence Intelligence Agency, the Army, Navy, Air Force of both Iran and America. We had the friendly government intelligence agencies, MI6, Mossad, SDECE and so on. And still you say Washington wasn't aware! It wasn't prepared!" He shook his head. "Well, the only thing you have going for you, Colonel, is that no one gives a shit. That's all. But that doesn't mean anyone believes it either."

Despite US citizenship, upbringing and education, subject by nature possesses complicated thought process that is suspicious and mistrusting. This should not be stimulated.

Bell returned Adel's cold glare and decided to test Operations Directorate's advice. His tone shifted dramatically.

"For whatever it's worth, that's what happened. I

don't expect you to be convinced, or even swayed, by the logic of reality. After all, you are part Iranian."

"Whether you like it or not, Colonel, I'm an American and that's exactly why I find it so unpalatable. Lying and stealing, extortion, kidnapping and murder are not part of the *American* ethic. Didn't Vietnam and Watergate teach you anything?"

Bell settled in his chair as he extended his legs in front of him and reflected on the impressive accuracy of Operations Directorate's report. The guy's acting true to form. He's a college kid who never grew up. Everything is black and white and conveniently simple; he's a romantic, and therefore predictable.

"I'm surprised at you, Michael. Who said anything about kidnapping or murder or blackmail? That's not what we do. We're not gangsters, Michael."

"What the hell do you call 'leverage', then?"

Bell shook his head and smirked. "From what I hear about Gina, you're far better versed in that sort of thing than we are."

Adel was shaken. Did Bell know about the Gina and Natalie episode at the George V four years ago? Of course he knew. Dirt was his profession.

"Let's have a drink, Michael. I have most everything right here, but the room service is excellent if you'd prefer something more exotic."

"Scotch is fine," conceded Adel, his throat dry, his nerves edgy.

Bell walked to the marble-topped Empire console that stood against a wall beneath a Gobelin tapestry. The console had been adapted to hold a small refrigerator and a well-stocked bar of miniature bottles. He poured a bottle into each glass, adding water and ice to Adel's, and handed it over before sitting back in his chair.

"To success," he offered, raising the crystal tumbler.

Adel glared at him. "I have no interest in the success or failure of your operation, Colonel."

"Michael, you know how critical this is for our country. As I shall explain, you are uniquely equipped to help us. You must look at this in . . ."

"Look, Colonel, I'm not your man," snapped Adel. "You need a professional, someone who's trained – willing. I'm not, and if there's no blackmail, no leverage, no pressures on me or my family, then I'd just like to get up and leave."

"I see," Bell intoned calmly. He crossed his long legs. "But, Michael, it's a question of degree, isn't it?"

Adel tensed and waited. He lifted his glass and took a sip of whisky.

Only known effective stimulus available within required time-span is threat to daughter or wife, Bell recalled.

He said, "We're not in a clear black and white situation. It's all a matter of degree."

Beneath his silk shirt Adel could feel the moisture building. "I'm not with you."

Bell looked at him and thought: It is time to jolt him again, to throw him off balance.

"It means, Adel," he said sharply, "that it's a question of ownership. I understand Natalie's mother is undergoing severe psychological strain as a result of your actions. And it would stand to reason that any court of law would find your deeds reprehensible, even criminal, perhaps."

So that was what the bastard had in mind. Using Natalie to tighten the screws again. The thought of Natalie being returned to Gina repelled him. Which is exactly what it was designed to do, he thought.

"Help yourself to another drink, Michael," Bell offered. He sat, his hands pressed together in front of his mouth.

Silently Adel did so, his mind desperately searching for a way out.

"Let's settle this thing amicably, Michael. We're wasting valuable time. None of this has anything to do with the Phoenix," said Bell, once Adel was seated.

"This may come as a surprise to you, but I couldn't

give a damn about your missiles. Besides, you should have thought about the possibility of compromise when you cashed the healthy payment cheques from the Shah. It's too late now; the missiles don't belong to us. The Iranians bought and paid for them. But that's something else that doesn't quite add up. Documents as sensitive as the Phoenix manuals were certainly never available to Iranians. Not the military. Not the highest government officials. Not even the Shah. How the hell could tapes of a presentation of the manuals fall into the wrong hands?"

Bell smiled sheepishly and leaned forward. His left hand massaged the stiff, unmoving side of his face. He thought: He's weakening. Back off a step or two. Leave him alone a minute. Let it take hold.

"You grossly underestimate the abilities of His Excellency Ali Mahmoudi."

"What does Mahmoudi have to do with this? He got what he wanted from the Shah by providing women for him," snapped Adel. " 'Pimping', it's called. And what a coincidence: he also happened to be the representative of just about every major American arms supplier in Iran."

Bell rose and walked to the bar. "Mahmoudi made the tapes," he said, pouring himself another straight whisky. "Somehow he got close to a meeting in which the manuals were being presented. At any rate he taped the meeting, presumably for blackmail purposes."

"How the hell could Mahmoudi put an entire presentation of the Phoenix missile system on a tape-recorder?"

"Technically, it's quite feasible. He bugged the meeting with a simple little ploy. Planted a bug on one of the participants. There are evidently two Sony tapes, each with a sixty-minute recording capacity. That gives you two hours of recording time," Bell explained. "What Mahmoudi did was first to record the entire presentations on sixteen or seventeen miniature tapes and then transfer them all to just two cassettes at very high speed. It's all gibberish if you hear them on a normal tape-recorder. To make any sense out of them you need access to a machine that can slow them down to a crawl."

"Ingenious," said Adel reflectively. "Where is Mahmoudi now?"

"In our care," replied Bell.

Adel started to sweat heavily.

Bell stuck a short thin Davidoff cigar in his mouth and struck a book of matches. "I bring matches from back home wherever I go," he said with exquisite calm. "I hate the damned lethal wax-coated things they sell in Europe; they sputter and go out, or flare up. Lousy things." He inhaled deeply from the cigar and let the smoke leak out of his nostrils in twin wiggly streams.

"Michael, time is short. All this speculation isn't going to get us anywhere. There's a lot to be done and it has to be done quickly. The questions can be –"

Adel shook his head firmly as he interrupted. "Forget it, Bell. And according to you there's nothing to force me."

Bell closed his eyes. "That's not what I said, Adel." He sighed as he stood and paced towards the open window, surveying the view of Port Canto and Les Iles Lérins that faced his quarters. The distant campanile struck eleven.

"I said it's a question of degree." He stood at the bay window, his back to the room. His voice was sharper and more final. "And I'd like your cooperation."

"You're barking up the wrong tree, Colonel. I'm not your man. I'm not trained for this sort of thing and furthermore I don't agree with it."

Bell nodded and paced back from the window, looking upwards at the ceiling as he did so.

Only known effective stimulus available within required time-span is threat to daughter . . .

"You're all we have, and you'll do the job," he said.

"The hell I will."

Bell snapped his head towards Adel. "Call your house," he barked.

Adel squinted, his heart leaping suddenly. Anderson's warning echoed in his mind. *"Natalie! They'll use Natalie!"*

"What did you say?" he whispered incredulously.

"I suggested that you call your house," Bell repeated, his voice flat, his eyes cold and piercing.

Adel's hands squeezed the arms of his chair as every muscle in his body stiffened.

"It's nothing serious," said Bell calmly. "Your wife and daughter should be experiencing minor car problems on the road to Juan-les-Pins. I think a call to your house would confirm my statement."

Adel's head pounded. It was real. It was here. His legs were suddenly very cold. He looked at the telephone. Then back at Bell. Obediently he walked to the telephone and dialled.

"Adel residence," said Usher, after the third ring.

"Let . . . let me speak to Sam, John." He tried to control the unsteadiness in his voice.

"I'm afraid they're not home yet, sir. Madame just called; seems the car broke down on Route Nationale Sept near Juan-les-Pins. I've sent the driver to pick them up; they should be back any minute now."

Adel's mind went blank. He was unable to think or speak. His body was limp and lifeless. And cold.

Usher continued. "Rather unusual, sir. The car only just came back from the garage. I'll get on to them about it immediately."

Adel said nothing. He dropped his hand slowly and replaced the receiver. Then he turned to Bell. His voice came out a whisper.

"Leave them out of this, Bell. You touch them with your filth again and I swear I'll kill you . . ."

But even to himself the threat seemed hollow. The triumphant sparkle in Bell's eyes told him so.

London. Monday, October 22: 10.00 p.m.

Gina Mahmoudi was depressed and a little frightened. It was an unfamiliar mixture of feelings and her character was ill-equipped to handle it. It was a far cry from what she was used to, she thought, as she entered the elevator on the penthouse floor. Nothing resembling a genuine problem had ever really entered her life before. Usually her days were filled with an endless stream of luncheon and dinner dates, shopping and coiffures and beautiful, interesting people. And marvellous places. Paris . . . Rome . . . Beverly Hills . . . Mykonos . . . Sardinia . . . and, more recently, Aspen. She looked in the elevator mirror and admired her exotic features in the soft lighting. Then she moved closer and wiped the rouge on her cheeks a shade lighter.

The elevator came to a gentle stop on the ground floor and she sauntered into the lobby. Think positive. You have things to do, she admonished herself, adding bounce and determination to her movements. After four years Michael Adel had a lesson coming to him and that was the saving grace about this whole mess. If she stopped moping and put some vigour into it, that lesson would start tonight.

"Good evening, Miss Mahmoudi. You look very smart," smiled the head porter, as she passed his desk.

The calculated smile produced its intended result. Gina opened her handbag and found a twenty-pound note. "Thank you, Arturo," she said, adroitly slipping the note to him in her handshake.

She always looked after him, although she didn't have to. After all, her father was the major shareholder in the Swiss holding company that owned this and twenty-seven other hotels across the world. But she did.

She liked Arturo and she needed him too often to rely on company loyalty. She had learned a long time ago that company loyalty went only skin deep. Personal loyalty, reinforced from time to time with financial remuneration, was always far more dependable.

She smiled at Arturo and walked towards the main doors. She loved this hotel, she thought, casting her eyes over the beautiful décor. And some day it would be hers. On her twenty-first birthday her father had promised it to her and it was already duly inscribed in his will.

Of course, he had told her to keep away from the Chelsea Towers and she had been alarmed when he had reiterated it on the telephone last Friday. But now, distanced from it all, it seemed a little unreal. Perhaps he was being over-dramatic; he was getting old and senile and the opium had unhinged him. Leila's death was the final straw. Was it really murder? she wondered as she spotted her dark green Jaguar four yards down the driveway. She doubted it; knowing her sister and her habits, the official version – an overdose – was far more likely.

The uniformed chauffeur opened the left rear door and she stepped in.

"Annabel's, Brian," she instructed, as she sat back on the black leather seat.

As the Jaguar turned left, out of the hotel driveway, a shining black Ford Granada pulled into the traffic behind them, a hundred and fifty yards to the rear. Throughout the journey the distance between the two cars never changed.

In the blurry and spasmodic light of the travelling vehicle, Gina Mahmoudi glanced down at her white low-cut Fendi dress. The slit on the right side stopped high on her smooth bare thigh. She slid her long leg out of the slit and was reassured that the dress was more than appropriate for the occasion.

As usual, Annabel's was crowded, boisterous and dark. Gina Mahmoudi felt at home as she made her way through the packed floor. It had been some time since she had been seen out in London and she savoured her re-appearance on the social scene.

"Don't make a spectacle of yourself," her father had said. But Daddy always exaggerated. That's how he thought he could bend her. Poor Daddy.

She stopped and said hello with all the panache she could muster to the numerous friends who dotted the tables and aisles. But she refused their invitations to stay; tonight she was determined not to be side-tracked.

At the bar she ordered a glass of white wine and scanned the darkness, occasionally blowing a kiss in the direction of another friendly face. If he was there she shouldn't have any difficulty spotting him, she thought. He was at least six inches taller than the average man and almost twice as wide. Suddenly she was nervous again. What if she couldn't find him?

Her father had been adamant on the phone Friday evening. Between waffling about keeping away from her house and the hotel and keeping out of sight, he had told her to contact the Iranian Islamic people in London, immediately. It was all so very bizarre. But then Daddy always knew what he was doing. He was always one step ahead. And what had clinched it was the opportunity to strike at Michael.

"As soon as you can, darling. It must be soon. Tell them about Adel and also that . . . I am sending him to our house in Teheran to steal our hidden land deeds, promissory notes, jewels and things. That's enough for them. Tell them I am sending Adel. Do not put it off, darling. You must tip them off right away. It is of paramount importance. If Adel is caught we have a future. If not . . ." He had not finished, just stuttered nervously and changed course in mid-sentence. ". . . I cannot talk too long. I must go. But do it, my dearest. Do it soon," he had said, hanging up abruptly.

She had needed no urging. At last she had an opportunity to get her daughter back. And what vengeance she would wreak on Michael Adel.

"Archie," she anxiously called the bartender above

the loud Afro-Detroit beat, "have you seen Mr Naderi tonight?" She was careful to seem relaxed, offering him an attractive smile.

"Ahh, let's see," said the bartender, looking up at her while his hands continued to work furiously. He frowned as he tried to recall one face in two hundred.

Her heart skipped a beat as the bartender's expression remained blank.

At last he remembered. "Oh, yes," he said pointing to a dark corner. "I think he's in the back somewhere, Miss Mahmoudi."

"Thanks," she smiled, feeling genuinely relieved.

She squeezed through the crowded floor as nonchalantly as she could and chose an area directly in his view. It had to be natural, she thought. She wanted him to approach her, as he always did, and she would have to be careful to act in character throughout the night. True, they had slept together several times in the past, but if there was anything she had learned about men through the years, it was that they enjoyed the chase. The harder it was, the more they enjoyed it.

Except for that bastard Adel, she recalled with distaste.

She leaned against the support column directly in Keyvan Naderi's view and slipped one leg through the long slit of her dress. Tonight she would give him what she knew he wanted.

God, she thought as her excitement mounted, Keyvan never dreamt of tripping over this sort of information. He had tried so hard, so cleverly, to uncover something about her father: what he was now doing, where he was planning to settle, all ultimately aimed at locating the assets he had spirited out of Iran. But tonight she would present him with someone far more valuable. The information would surely please Keyvan's new paymasters. The old man had pointedly refused to tell her the details, only that Michael was involved and that he had to get caught. Despite her insistence, he had refused to be more specific.

"I cannot talk for long, they have allowed me a few minutes of privacy with your sister before . . . before . . . Just do as I say and perhaps some day I'll explain everything to you. But for now, just do as I say," he had ordered before going on to impress upon her once again the importance of time.

She couldn't understand it. Why was there such a rush to pass on the information anyway? Why was it so imperative for Adel to fail? Why was he to be trapped? Her father had always liked him. She didn't understand it. It was so unlike him. But she shrugged aside the questions. After four years this was her chance to destroy Adel, and nothing else mattered.

Her father had meant her to go to the official representatives of the Islamic Revolutionary government in London. But that would be clumsy and perhaps even dangerous. After all, she was supposed to be in hiding. The old man had forgotten that. Planting a leak through Keyvan would be far more effective. He would channel it straight to where it counted. And, besides, how much more amusing to denounce Michael with another man inside her.

From her vantage point she watched Keyvan dominating the conversation. When he stopped there was a roar of laughter. Another of the slimy bastard's jokes, she thought, as she heard the laughter subside. It was the same old Keyvan, joking and living it up. The only difference in his life was his new paymaster.

A year ago Keyvan Naderi had been a successful wheeler-dealer under the Shah's regime, close to the royal court and SAVAK. Today he was "unofficially" handling commercial transactions in Europe for the new regime. Unencumbered by principles or honour, he was raking in regular kickbacks and commissions. And in the process, to sweeten the pot for the new regime, he had become an informer, a spy who informed on last year's friends and traded information for the right to sell rice, cheese and bullets at inflated prices.

Gina studied his handsome, generous features as he

talked and laughed with his cronies. She could not see the common denominator between him and the new Islamic regime. His unashamedly hedonistic ways were in sharp contrast to the spartan lifestyle of the Islamic movement. Perhaps Keyvan's favourite expression summed him up best: "Man cannot live on bread alone." And Keyvan made sure there was always more than bread on the table; no matter how it was obtained or from whom.

He had noticed her now and was feverishly trying to attract her attention. She turned slightly, away from him, to face the gyrating bodies on the dance floor. Let him work for it, at least, she thought.

A few moments passed before he approached her.

"Gina, dear, you're looking ravishing." His lips lightly caressed her cheek.

"Hello, darling," she said enthusiastically. "How are you?"

"Fed up. This refugee life is beginning to get to me," replied Naderi affecting a serious tone.

"Why? You have no problems."

"Well now, the Home Office is making it difficult for us to stay in England. Funny, isn't it? All our lives we were welcome wherever we went. We used to be rich Persians, running around blowing big money, subsidising tourist industries; now we're boat people, searching for a way to stay alive. Nobody wants to know us."

Gina smiled at his openness but she wasn't fooled by it. Nonchalantly she turned to watch the action on the dance floor.

"Don't worry about it so much, darling, perhaps the pendulum will swing back soon and you can stop being a yacht person." She smiled. "Come on, let's get a drink."

They spent the rest of the evening dancing, dining and gossiping. She spoke of her relationship with Michael Adel, how she continued to love him despite the end of their life together, what a good father he was to Natalie, and how close they still were.

Their talk, when serious, veered back and forth to

Iran, each edging towards the subject for their own specific purpose and gliding away again, lest the other scent the trail too easily.

By two-thirty in the morning the moment had arrived. Curled up in bed, relaxed and exhausted from their lovemaking and intimate as a result of it, Gina rolled over and kissed Keyvan Naderi on the palm of his right hand, holding and caressing it like a drowsy contented child.

"It was good," she purred. "You know you're very good, don't you?" She cuddled closer to him.

All night he had been joking with her and she had tantalised him with harmless bits of gossip about her father and his exile friends. She knew that each snippet was being stored for later use.

Naderi turned in the darkness and felt the bedside table for his cigarettes. He lit one.

"It's good to be with a friend when you're lonely and worried," Gina mumbled.

"Why worried, Gina?"

She paused. "I'm afraid for Michael. He's going to Teheran. Ostensibly to wind up his company. But I heard my father talking to him on the phone last week. Saying something about going to my father's house in Teheran to get some of his valuables out." Might as well spice it up a little, she thought. "I just hope he's not mixed up in all this silly counter-revolutionary talk."

She sounded half-asleep and talking like a silly goose. But she knew Keyvan would sooner or later pick up the lead.

And he did. Was Michael going soon? How brave he was to be going to Iran for whatever reason. Could he, Keyvan, help in any way? Would he be staying long?

In her sleepy voice Gina provided the appropriate monosyllabic responses to guide Keyvan along. Michael at her father's house. A safe. Some kind of rendezvous. Maybe it was just a dealer who wanted to make a quick black-market buck on behalf of some mullahs for the priceless rugs there. But she thought it had sounded much more serious and her father was hardly in the carpet league – however priceless.

"Shouldn't really be saying all this, should I?" she muttered.

The gentle questions and the muffled answers continued until she fell asleep. Keyvan lay on his back staring at the ceiling for a while. Then he looked at his watch and quietly slid out of bed and dressed.

Through her half-closed eyes, Gina watched him tiptoe carefully out of the room. When the door clicked shut, she sat up with a huge grin. She felt mischievous and very pleased with herself. After a minute or so she got up and hung the "Do Not Disturb" sign outside the door. Then she skipped back into bed, wiggled her feet excitedly under the covers and felt warm all over. Tonight, she thought, she would sleep restfully.

London. Tuesday, October 23: 4.00 a.m.

Keyvan Naderi turned right outside the hotel. The night was bitter; cold winds lashed the heavy rains and tore through his overcoat. He bent his head lower to protect his eyes and lengthened his stride to cover the short distance to Sloane Street. He ignored the familiar surroundings; Gina's credibility and the cold were enough to occupy his mind. The problem with Gina's information was that it was incomplete. He had tried to extract more from her but the silly woman didn't know the details. Her father's telephone conversation with Adel had been boring. He shook his head disgustedly. She knew exactly who was screwing whom on three different continents. But a plot to overthrow a government, well, . . . that was too boring for her to listen to.

"Idiot," he muttered. Besides, he thought, the Islamic people had assigned him to entrapping her father. He was not so sure they would be interested in Adel.

Halfway up the block, his thoughts were suddenly interrupted. The shining door of a black car opened a few feet in front of him and Naderi had to side-step quickly to avoid injury. He turned around to see the source of this clumsy move. The emerging figure was a fearsome man of massive proportions. As the body uncurled from the cabin, it stood over six feet, with immense square shoulders on which a head with no neck was seemingly planted. The face was pitted with deep pores and a huge and crooked nose separated two fierce eyes that luckily had not noticed his brief look of anger.

A shiver went through Naderi's body. He bent his head and moved away quickly.

"Later, Wally," Naderi heard the man say flatly, in a southern American drawl. There followed the sound of a closing car door and footsteps that echoed on the wet pavement as they moved away. Another shiver shook Naderi. He had never before seen such an animal. He hoped he never would again.

On the corner of Cadogan Place and Sloane Street, directly across from Coutts & Co., stood two bright red telephone booths. Naderi crossed the road on the zebra crossing and quickly closed the door of one booth behind him, thankful for the relative warmth within. He inserted a tenpence coin in the slot and dialled from memory.

"Come on, come on," he said out loud as he looked through the misting windows at the burly man heading towards the hotel entrance. His right hand, pressed to the metal coin-drop button, trembled in the cold night air as he shuffled with impatience.

Finally, a gruff, heavily accented voice answered sleepily and Naderi pressed the coin into the slot. Eagerly he stuffed his frozen hand into his coat pocket.

" 'Allo," slurred a heavily accented voice.

"Mr Ambassador?" asked Naderi.

"Speaking." The voice was sleepy and distant.

"Naderi here, sir. I'm sorry, but I have to see you right away."

"Now?" growled the Ambassador. "It is nearly three o'clock in the morning."

"I know, sir. But it's important. We cannot discuss it on the telephone. It's too risky."

"Can it not wait until morning?"

"Not if you wish to reach the Imam's ear first, sir."

The Ambassador let out a heavy sigh. "Very well."

The burly man entered the large deserted lobby and headed directly for the hall porter's desk.

"Fifteen-forty-six," he said as he approached.

The elderly night porter squinted through thick spectacles and moved his hands along the numbers.

"Ah, 'ere we are, sir," he said, pulling at the heavy buoy-shaped key-ring and reading the man's name on the little computer-typed slip on the box.

"I need an alarm call at seven in the morning," the man drawled, reaching for the key.

"Not much sleep tonight, eh, Mr Taylor? You Americans 'ave so much –"

"Good night," the burly man said and headed towards the elevators.

On the fifteenth floor he turned towards the emergency staircase that twisted behind the elevator shafts. He walked up two flights of stairs to the seventeenth floor and there followed the signs to Suite 1712-20.

Outside the door he looked up and down the empty corridor and then knelt on the plush dark brown carpet and opened his briefcase. Adroitly he withdrew the Walther PPK and the silencer lying beside it and placed the case upright against the wall. He stood and screwed on the silencer.

He looked at the "Do Not Disturb" sign on the door and smiled as he pressed the buzzer. An appropriate epitaph, he thought.

He pressed the buzzer again, and held it.

"Keyvan?" he heard her ask tentatively, from inside.

He coughed through his handkerchief.

"Keyvan? Is that you, Keyvan?" she asked, her voice more insistent.

His response came through the handkerchief. It was a mixture of a grunt and yes, and it was enough.

The door opened.

The burly man showed no reaction to the look of sheer terror on the naked woman's face. Instinctively he placed one foot inside the doorway and silently savoured the scene. He had always enjoyed this moment. Her eyes were wide and fixed, her complexion grey and cold.

She took only one step backwards, as her hands fell limply to her sides. She made no effort to hide her naked body.

The bullet hit her between the eyes. With barely a sound, it scattered her midbrain and cerebellum on the lime green sofa behind.

The man stuck the gun in his belt, closed the door and picked up his briefcase. He took two steps down the hallway, then walked back and flicked the sign on the door to green: "Please make up this room."

The Voyage. Saturday, October 27.

"I don't know of a single authorised murder by any of our intelligence agencies. Killing is simply idiotic and crude; a proof of failure. And in this business failure is unforgivable. It always comes back to haunt you," Adel recalled Bell assuring him.

"Allen Dulles once observed that assassination and murder are not part of the American character. I agree with him."

"So it was the Russians who killed the Red Indians," Adel had replied, wondering how difficult it would be to convince Castro, Diem, Trujillo, Allende or Lumumba of Bell's words.

Bell's lopsided gaze had turned a trifle cynical. "It's nineteen-seventy-nine, Michael, and the world's a sophisticated place. The state of the art permits us to be far more scientifically efficient than you give us credit for."

Adel shook off his thoughts, reminding himself that he had more immediate problems to worry about. In forty-five minutes he would be in Teheran. One thing at a time, he told himself. One thing at a time.

But his mind still raced. His thoughts had gnawed at him for five hours now, creating a tension that prevented his habitual relief of sleep on long flights. He felt cramped, too, in the 707. There was no upstairs bar and no film to occupy the time. The Nice–Teheran run had lost its glamour; it no longer enjoyed the luxury of a jumbo liner and now even this smaller plane was only half full.

Gradually his mind drifted back to Bell. He heard clearly the smack of the neatly folded parchment document, and the heading his eyes had zoomed in on.

"You just can't get round this, Michael," Bell had said, laying out the parchment neatly to reveal its message:

MANDAT D'ARRÊT
RÉPUBLIQUE FRANÇAIS

Au nom du peuple français . . .
Nous mandons et ordonnons à tous officiers ou agents de la police judiciaire . . .

It was a warrant for Adel's arrest on a charge of kidnapping and blackmail.

"It's waiting to be served."

"It has no date," Adel had responded tepidly, "so it can't be valid."

"Technicality."

"I'll fight it."

"We have affidavits from Gina Mahmoudi, her father, her maid, Barbara, Claudine . . . Shall I go on? Michael, give me credit for having done my homework. We need those tapes. And you're our best bet. We're dealing with a national security issue here. The normal ethical codes that operate between human beings don't apply when problems are of this magnitude. These tapes are bigger than ethics. I will destroy you and your family to get your cooperation. And you have no court of appeal. This operation is sanctioned at the highest possible level. You have no other course available to you, and I think you know that."

Adel did know. He had known for some time.

During the last five days in Cannes, Bell had introduced him to Yuri Allon of the Mossad, who in three short days had tried to teach him the art of clandestine operations and survival.

"He's a fine man, very experienced. He organised the raid on Entebbe, so theoretically this should be a piece of cake for him," Bell had said before Allon's arrival.

The tone had been grudging, thought Adel, as he gazed through the plane's window. Why, he had never been able to detect. Perhaps the use of an Israeli agent had gone against the grain for a man who had spent his life with the CIA and its predecessor, the OSS. Bell had been there at the inception of the agency and had quietly, behind the scenes, contributed as much as anyone to building it into the world's foremost intelligence organisation. He had headed military intelligence in Vietnam and Laos and been a key member of the American intelligence community for over thirty-five years. Now his consulting company, or the Agency, or whoever it was he was representing, was turning to an operative from an upstart little client state for assistance, perhaps because of the recent spate of US intelligence flops. It rankled, and with Bell's discomfort, Adel had suddenly detected a human strain in the man.

"So you want to limit the risks and use proven sources?" Adel had pounced.

Bell had sighed deeply. "If you're referring to the CIA, they have nothing to do with this. As I told you, this is being handled privately, through me."

"Of course it is, Colonel. Of course it is," Adel had answered, closely watching Bell's impassive face. He was determined to play the game out if that was what Bell wanted.

On the first day of his training with the imposing Allon, Bell had shown up for a final briefing. He had drawn him aside to talk privately. "I'll inform one man at the embassy in Teheran to put at your disposal anything you may require. However, we will officially deny any connection should you be unsuccessful. You understand that, don't you?"

"I thought you said this thing was unofficial, Colonel."

Bell ignored him. "Your contact in Teheran will be George Clark, he's in the economic section of the embassy there. His code name will be Khan. Whenever you contact him, use that name at the beginning of the conversation and he'll trigger a scrambler. After that you can talk freely. He's also the man who is arranging the delivery of the equipment you need to your house in Teheran. Probably in the form of a suitcase. It will be delivered two days after your arrival.

"It would probably be better to work out the operational details with Allon and . . . and Gleeson at your own convenience. Oh, that's the man I'll send down to assist you, Gleeson. Jim Gleeson. He's an excellent strategist. I recommend him highly."

Bell had looked at the shine on his shoe and continued, "You're not one to accept suggestions, Michael, but I'd like to offer you a couple. Regarding Clark, I suggest you keep the information to yourself and don't mention it to Gleeson or Allon; there's no point in anyone except you being aware of the various components that make up the whole. It provides you with a secondary escape channel if anything goes wrong. In this line of business, options are what keep you alive."

Adel had been silent for a long time. "Options are what we all strive for, aren't they? I mean, you take a man's options away and you control him, don't you, Colonel?" he had replied.

"The second thing is that Allon must not know what it is you are specifically going in for. He's a good man – probably as good as they come – and he can be helpful to you. But I don't want him knowing about the tapes; in no circumstances must you mention them or what they contain to him."

"Why?"

"Because those are your instructions."

The past gave way to the present as the public address system came alive. "Ladies and gentlemen, we've started our descent towards Teheran's Mehrabad airport. Please fasten your seat-belts and make sure your seat is . . ."

Adel moved his seat to the vertical position, stubbed out his cigarette and turned towards the window. In a few minutes, the lights of the surrounding towns of Ghasvin and Karadj would appear, and minutes later the sprawling city itself.

Teheran. Saturday, October 27.

Teheran's Mehrabad airport had not changed; it retained its prison-like architecture and ambience. A twelve-foot-high barbed-wire fence surrounded the outer perimeters of the huge, city-like compound that acted as the country's main civil and military airport. Guard posts and watchtowers beamed glaring searchlights from differing angles, keeping a constant vigil over every square inch of the massive complex. Armoured cars and tanks dotted the barren landscape, ready to welcome arriving passengers. The airport's outstanding feature, however, was the massive asphalt apron that stretched before the main terminal building. It was large enough to hold ten Xerxes battalions or stage a royal ceremonial for the Shah.

The main terminal building itself was still under construction; it seemed it had always been that way. The roof had caved in under the weight of an unprecedented snowfall in 1974, killing over one hundred people, and still it was under repair. The operative arrival lounge was now a "temporary" expedient off a considerable distance to the right of the main building. And it was too small and ill-equipped to meet even the lightest of off-season loads, let alone revolutionary turmoil.

Adel was the first of five first-class passengers to disembark into the cold night air. He stepped on to the rickety open ramp and turned up the collar of his worn black leather windbreaker to ward off the drizzle. Though his eyes had yet to adapt to the darkness, he could make out the remarkably informal garb of the cluster of guards waiting at the foot of the stairs – a variety of fatigue jackets, bell-bottom jeans of every shade and whatever else was available.

They carried their assortment of weapons casually – Kalashnikovs, M-3s, Uzi submachine-guns, and M-16s waved in the air like the bows of an orchestra's string section. Hand grenades hung on them like strange fruit, while knives and bayonets of varying sizes dangled from their belts. Their pockets bulged and their chests were crossed with bandoliers of bullets. None of the group wore boots, Adel noticed, and clearly they were men unaccustomed to wearing tight-fitting footgear of any variety. Like the people of the bazaar and the rural populace, they were only too happy to adopt the Western way but lack of familiarity undermined their pretensions. So instead they improvised; they wore shoes with the backs crushed downwards and inwards, slipping and dragging as they walked on the asphalt surface.

It took ten minutes before the last of the twenty-four

passengers descended and stood waiting silently in the falling rain, outnumbered and encircled by a motley group of what looked like an Islamic version of Mexican bandits. To Adel they were all too readily recognisable; they were the *pasdaran* militiamen, Ayatollah Khomeini's chosen forces of the Lord.

Adel was closer to them now and he eagerly appraised the forces he was up against. The revolutionary militiamen were a fragmented street-gang. Their average age was no more than twenty-two or three, with many of them mere adolescents. They had no discipline, no efficiency and certainly no coherence, but they swaggered with an arrogance that would have been absurd had it not been so menacing and uncontrolled. They stood, cigarettes dangling, enjoying their new-found power: talking and laughing, rifles swinging carelessly.

"*Autobis nist. Bayad piyadeh berin*," shouted one of the militiamen in Farsi; he appeared to be the mob's leader.

"What did he say? What do we do?" asked an elderly European man timidly.

"There's no bus. We have to walk," replied Adel.

"*Yallah*," ordered another of the militiamen as he swung his Uzi in the direction of the terminal.

"My two children and these bags – can you help me? I can't make it with all this," a young, well-dressed Iranian woman asked distraughtly as she pointed to her unwieldy hand luggage.

"We can't help the passengers," shouted the leader. "It's forbidden. Get one of the others to help you. Besides, you should have thought about it when you bought all that expensive stuff in Europe. Did you steal from the people to pay for it? Or did you get it the usual way?" He pointed between his legs and cackled.

Adel felt his blood pressure rise as the ugly group echoed the man's raucous laughter. Instinctively he stepped towards the woman. But a distant voice pulled him back.

"Blend into the background," the impressive Israeli agent had said. *"Never draw attention to yourself. Never."*

He stopped as the elderly European man moved apprehensively towards the woman.

"I'm not carrying anything. May I help you?" he offered.

"Thank you. You're very kind," she said in English, obviously relieved. She gripped the hand of her eldest child, about five, and pressed the infant closely to her chest. Even in the pale light, her face was pink with embarrassment. The old man picked up her two canvas bags and a large package and together they walked, trailing the other passengers, towards the building.

Inside the terminal the security measures were more menacing than tight. The mob of adolescent guards now outnumbered the passengers by five or more to one. There was a cacophony of conflicting instructions; passengers were ordered first one way, then another, and always at the end of a threatening gun-barrel.

Adel felt both apprehension and reassurance. The air of violence was awesome, but organisation and training were non-existent. He had to blend, disappear into the chaos, he told himself. To hit and run.

At last the line advanced and Adel stood before the unshaven immigration clerk.

"Passport," the official grunted.

Adel held the document out and the man snatched it from his hand.

"Saleh . . . Saleh." The official mumbled the name Adel was travelling under as he thumbed a thick book sitting on the table before him. He stank of onions and sweat. "Saleh . . . Saleh . . . Reza," he repeated.

He closed the huge book with a thump and picked up three crumpled and dirty white sheets of paper. He looked at this second list more carefully. Then he turned his attention to the scuffed burgundy-coloured Iranian passport, one of the old variety now being replaced by a new Islamic version.

Islamic hit list, thought Adel uneasily.

"Hmm," the clerk mumbled. "Height 1.83 metres. Weight 82 kilos," he said, looking up at Adel again. He flipped a few pages. "Businessman. Passport issued in London on February 15, 1976. Valid until February 15, 1980 . . . okay."

He stamped the passport, pushed it back carelessly across the formica counter that separated them, and turned his attention to the next passenger. Adel moved on, relieved to be over the first hurdle.

There was another long wait for the luggage. For the fifth time Adel stood and walked to an ashtray ten feet away, flicked the ash and walked back. He did not do it out of any fastidious habit – the floor was filthy – but it calmed him, and helped curb his impatience. It also gave him an opportunity to look around and size up his surroundings.

As he turned to walk back, he noticed in the far corner an island of composure in the sea of chaos. A group of militiamen surrounded a large rugged man of fair complexion. His powerfully built arms were folded across his chest, one hand occasionally moving to draw on a cigarette. His skin tone, hair and blue eyes branded him Teutonic and he was clearly an object of respect among the darker complexioned militiamen. When he spoke, they listened intently, which in revolutionary times is one yardstick of authority.

Adel looked away and edged back into the crowd; there was nothing to gain from standing and staring. But it was a disconcerting sight; there were very few blue eyed, blond Iranians.

With a shrill screech the luggage-belt jerked into movement and Adel changed direction. He walked towards it, eager to collect his luggage and dispose of the customs formalities.

The young customs girl was wearing the latest Islamic fashion – a *char-ghad* – a cumbersome Islamic scarf modestly hiding the hair, but leaving visible the sight of two thick bushy eyebrows that almost met. She looked at him and smiled. After the most cursory of inspections she stamped his passport and smiled again, this time raising her eyebrow suggestively. Adel smiled back in gratitude.

Khomeini's Islamic honesty and the country's revolutionary principles had made taxi fares a negotiable item: the result was a four-fold increase. Given the time and his eagerness to get off the streets into the safety of his home, Adel was in no mood to participate in the Iranian custom of haggling. It was eleven-thirty at night, he was tired and, he realised, unnerved by the sight of the blond man at the airport. In sharp contrast to the rest of the mob, the man had appeared distinctly professional and highly dangerous.

Adel handed his small suitcase to the first driver to approach, a short, stocky fellow, moustached above and beyond his three-day stubble, and clearly unbathed. His clothes fitted him badly; his trousers seemed too tight everywhere but the seat. There they were two sizes too large.

"Dezashib," he told the driver, indicating a suburb on the north-eastern tip of the capital.

The man lit up at his good fortune; it was the most profitable route in the city.

"You live there?" he asked, throwing the small suitcase on the front seat beside him.

"No. I'm picking up a friend's car," Adel lied.

"Nice friend. A man can't depend on his own family these days, let alone a friend."

The cab moved out. Adel did not want to prolong the conversation; he had a thirty-minute drive ahead of him and he preferred to take in his surroundings, to absorb the feel, the mood of the town. But the driver was in gregarious mood as he swung his battered orange Hillman on to the freeway heading for the former Shahyad Square. Now, Freedom Square.

"You been away long?"

"About a year," replied Adel.

"That's a long time. Why? Do you live abroad?"

"Yes," said Adel. "My wife is a foreigner, and I've lived in her country since we were married." At least half true, he thought.

"Things have changed here in the last year," said the driver cautiously.

"For the better, I'm sure."

"Certainly, certainly." The answer came too quickly. "Agha looks after everything. Everything will be better soon." The cab chugged along noisily, the driver glancing at Adel in the rear-view mirror and muttering inaudibly.

Adel recognised *Agha* as a term of endearment for Ayatollah Khomeini; he was called the Master now. The Shah had been nicknamed *Ra'is*, or the Boss, when he ruled the country.

"Too many spies here," the driver hazarded. "I don't know where they come from. I mean, where were they before? If Agha doesn't start controlling these kids soon, there won't be anything left."

Adel studied the driver's eyes in the rear-view mirror. Was the man asking provocative questions or simply being friendly? Was he probing? Or was he an opponent of the regime, tentatively feeling his way for a fellow traveller?

He could not tell and there was little point in encouraging the conversation. As the driver continued talking, Adel turned his attention to the scenes speeding by outside. The first thing to catch his eye was the inordinate number of mullahs filling the streets. Every second pedestrian seemed to be wearing the turban, gown and sandals of the new élite. The women were all draped in *chadors*, with only a breeze revealing the blue jeans, high heels and human shapes now taboo in Iran. Scattered groups of young men were evident too, all heavily armed. Some huddled around fifty-six-gallon oil drums – makeshift cauldrons – from which orange flames danced. Rubbish littered the street, left by the mobs on their daily protest marches against imperialism, colonialism or whatever. The walls were blackboards of revolutionary slogans, every one of the graffiti preaching murder: *Death to the Shah. Death to Carter. Death to Russia. Death to the Army. Death to Bakhtiar. Death to the US. Death to SAVAK. Death to Sadat. Death to Israel.* At one point, some wit had added in large red letters: *Make sure you don't forget anyone.*

Adel looked around. The occasional minaret broke the contours of the shabby mud-brick, square houses, dwarfed by futuristic high-rise buildings and the shadows of the mountains to the north. The roadside was crammed with hawkers whose dishevelled carts flowed over to the inside lines of the thoroughfare, and a hundred different tempting scents filled the air. Lamb kebabs, hot steamed beetroot, grilled kidneys, marinated walnuts and incense. Afghan and Baluchi tribesmen with long trailing turbans offered medicinal herbs, and others competed to sell a variety of colourful spiced stews from huge copper vats.

The driver's voice broke his thoughts. "I don't understand something. The Shah told us he was guided in his ways by Allah. Mr Khomeini claims Allah leads him in his judgments. Then how come they don't agree? If you ask me, Allah talks a lot but they can't all be listening to what he has to say."

Maybe the man is simply looking for a decent tip, thought Adel.

"Allah is mysterious in his ways," he replied, knowing the cliché would be wasted on the driver as he drifted off into his own thoughts again. The schedule Gleeson had set entailed too much risk. If he followed it without protecting himself, it would provide Bell with what he wanted – a reliable timetable to follow, and there was too much needless risk in that. If Bell was to be a danger, it would be after he had the tapes in his hand, not before. And there was no point in making it easy for him by giving him a hand-picked time and place.

Then again, he thought, perhaps Bell and Gleeson

were being straight. Maybe all they wanted were the tapes and he was letting his suspicion get the better of him. Maybe they knew something he didn't – something that made the schedule essential to follow. They had insisted that the timing was crucial to the plan.

Why then had Yuri Allon been so hesitant? He had never outwardly disagreed with them but that was another disquieting factor. Allon was by nature an undiplomatic man, direct and to the point. He didn't falter or hang back in any other instance. But here, even to the end, Allon had been hesitant and reserved, insisting only that the other ingredients of the operation were more important to its successful outcome than the timing and that they should be given priority.

"*It'll all come together at the airport. That's the critical juncture,*" the Israeli had warned.

"*What about the schedule? What if there's a forced play on that?*"

"*Concentrate on the airport,*" Allon had said. "*The run of the play there on your way out is what's going to buy you retirement. And it's not going to be easy. Build yourself up to that point and remember it may be painful. How painful will depend on how good an actor you are, how well you can improvise. You must make sure they believe two things: your story and your act.*"

"*And the timing?*" Adel had probed, yet again.

The Israeli operative had hesitated before answering, his lined, sunburned face unhappily filled in thought.

"*Planning is the prerogative of generals and you're not even a soldier. These things have a way of changing in the field so concentrate on your own problems. Worry about surviving.*"

Adel cursed under his breath. Right now all he needed was the suitcase containing the equipment and the onus of the arrangements was on them; they were to deliver it to him at the house in the next few days. He would decide later what he was going to do with Bell. One thing, though, was for sure. He was not going to part with those tapes in Iran; nothing would make him hand over the tapes to Bell or his people before he was out safely. London it would be, but on his own schedule. And he would pick the moment. He would not walk into their arms at the bottom of the ramp of a predetermined BA flight. No, he'd have to think of a way to insure himself. But what? How could he cover himself? Whom could he trust?

"Where in Dezashib is your friend's house?" asked the driver, disturbing his thoughts as the taxi pulled up before the battered doors of the small mosque in the centre of Dezashib's seventy-five-yard village strip. The building was daubed with graffiti bearing Islam's message. Quotes from the Koran. Slogans from Khomeini. And the never-ending list of enemies to be exterminated in the Name of God.

On one wall in large red letters a notice read:

America is incapable – Imam Khomeini

Russia is incapable – Imam Khomeini

England is incapable – Imam Khomeini

Israel is incapable – Imam Khomeini

Beneath it someone with a sense of humour – and much courage – had scribbled:

Khomeini is incapable – Mrs Khomeini.

Adel looked past the storefronts to the darkness beyond. "Another two hundred metres or so, up by the old Allam crossroads. I don't know what the new name is."

He was generous with the driver, but not too generous.

"*Blend into the background,*" Allon had said. "*Try to be like a bad commercial. You don't want to be remembered.*"

"Shall I wait for you? Your friend may be out, or the electricity may be off, and he won't hear the bell. We've been having power failures as usual," said the driver, casting his eyes up to Allah.

Adel looked back at the lights on the village strip and answered quickly, "Look back there. The electricity is working tonight and I'm sure he's waiting for me. Thank you anyway."

He ducked into a narrow alley on the crossroads and waited in the shadows as the taxi made a U-turn. There was still another mile to walk to his parents' house, but he waited to gain distance between himself and the departing cab.

"Nothing should be traceable to you. Everything about you must be hazy. If you travel about town, never use one car. Change vehicles often. Never take a direct route. Always keep an eye in the back of your head," Allon had instructed. *"That's where it always comes from – the back."*

Once the tail lights had disappeared, Adel started down the gentle slope that was the start of Farmanieh Avenue, only two miles from the Shah's old palace in Niavaran. A year ago this had been a wealthy and friendly suburb, alive with the hospitality Iranians were once famous for. He glanced at his watch; it was a little after midnight and the place was now a cemetery. The streets were deserted; not a light broke the even blackness. Fear had driven the inhabitants to seek refuge behind the protection of brick walls and darkness. Or flight abroad.

Walking briskly and carrying his small, suitably scuffed suitcase, Adel reached his destination in less than fifteen minutes. Except for a speeding powder blue Mercedes Benz minibus, he saw no other sign of life en route. Across from his parents' old house the once flamboyant Argentinian Embassy stood derelict and lifeless. Inside its compound a few scattered lights gave the occasional window a pale orange glow, while outside two policemen slouched on either side of the black wrought-iron gates. They looked at him casually, uninterested and demoralised.

Adel stood quietly before the door of his parents' house feeling in his pockets for the key. The century-old arched wooden door, with its decorative carvings from the Qajar era, stood high enough and wide enough for a sixteen-wheel semi-truck to pass through; it was also thick enough to stop one. A Judas gate, a smaller door set to the right of the main gate, allowed quicker and more efficient passage for human traffic. It also boasted two traditional heavy circular door-knockers of solid brass. Now obsolete, they had once served an essential function in daily life. The larger one was always mounted higher on the door – out of reach of female callers – and its sound, Adel recalled, was deeper than that of the smaller one. The two knockers were used not only to announce an arrival but to indicate the gender of the visitor and therefore whether a maid or manservant should be despatched to welcome the caller.

Originally, the house had been a summer country estate, sprawling gracefully at the base of the soaring, twenty-thousand-foot Alborz Mountains. Built in 1870, it had been a half-day ride from Teheran, an oasis, comfortably remote from the scorching heat of the city, where his forefathers had spent pleasant summer days in cool comfort and luxury. In those days a private army protected them from bands of nomadic marauders and the massive gate was one of three that connected twelve-foot-high walls surrounding the private park. Now, the house lay neglected and empty, a mocking testament to his family's lost wealth. Most of the other possessions had been nationalised by the Shah; or sold off piecemeal by the playboys of the family in search of lissom young whores in the bars of Paris or the bordellos of Bangkok.

Adel applied his keys to the sturdy ancient lock on the Judas door. It squeaked, but opened easily at his touch.

The sloping grounds spread away in the darkness, and led to a majestic old building positioned on an earthen mound in the centre, overlooking the huge estate. An umbrella of enormous, century-old walnut trees offered sanctuary from the pitiless summer sun, while a jungle of citrus trees, now ragged from lack of pruning, bulked in the darkness, cutting off a clear view of the mansion. A small stream from a fresh mountain spring cut through one corner of the grounds, the soothing sound of flowing water just audible on dark, still nights.

A flood of memories filled his mind. There had been so many wonderful days and nights here. The warmth of his grandparents, his brother Mark, the love of his parents, the glamorous parties during the summer school holidays from England, his first experience of sex. And Gina.

He walked towards the building, remembering exactly where the trapdoor that led to the *qanat* tunnel was: at the end of the garden, to the right of the main gate he had just entered. It had been his childhood hideaway so often while playing hide-and-seek with Mark. Occasionally the boys would pretend they were Ancient Persians digging the narrow tunnel when this subterranean irrigation system was first developed three thousand years ago. In the hot dry summers they loved to splash their faces with the cool fresh water which flowed underground from the mountains to the parched plains. And they would take refuge from the scorching sun in the reservoir that stored the water. Every rural dwelling – and the Adel mansion had been rural when it was first built over a hundred and twenty years ago – was connected to the *qanat* system. The underground network and reservoirs meant that no water, so precious in this hot arid country, was lost through evaporation. The Adel reservoir, like so many others, had been a mine of hidden childhood secrets. Even now in the darkness after so many years it would present no challenge.

Adel lay down on the damp ground beside the steel trapdoor and pulled it open quietly. He extended his arm full stretch into the pit and felt an intricate weave of sticky cobwebs, the cold coarse concrete of the wall, seeking the light-switch. He clicked it, but nothing happened; it had been years since anyone needed to enter this forgotten underground water reservoir.

"Just one more time," he whispered to the darkness below, its dank smell distantly familiar and appealing. "Hide me just one more time," he repeated as he gently closed the heavy door.

Only this time, he thought, it was no childhood game.

Adel stepped back from the trapdoor and headed up the long straight driveway towards the building. A soft yellow light glowed warmly in the kitchen window, setting off the dark loneliness of the rest of the house. As he drew closer, memories of better days came back to him; days when for one brief moment in its long and uncivilised history, the country had flourished. But the gravest error of all had been committed: it had been taken for granted.

In the distance a staccato of gunfire shattered the silent night air and Adel shivered; the deadly sound underlined his thoughts and strengthened his determination. He quickened his stride and made his way through the jasmine bushes of the shrubbery to the side window over the large kitchen sink.

Inside, an old woman, in her seventies now, sat in her usual straight-backed rocking-chair, wrapped in a shawl, a headscarf covering her once-hennaed hair. She was waging war with her knitting, each stitch a victory over failing eyes and trembling hands. For one brief moment, time stood still. She had not changed her habits in over thirty years.

He tapped on the door and called her name.

"Mariam."

She heard but did not seem to remember his voice. Fearlessly, however, she opened the door wide and then, squinting, recognised him. Happy tears welled in her tired eyes as an enchanting smile spread across her wrinkled face. Adel looked at her lovingly. She had always been a small, slender woman but now with age she seemed to have bent under the weight of the years.

"I never thought I'd see you again," she whispered incredulously, the tears meandering down her deeply wrinkled skin as she held out her arms in welcome.

He stepped in and gathered her to him, holding her small fragile frame in a gentle bear-hug. She had been with them for over fifty years now, starting in her early teens as a simple cleaning maid and staying on through the births and deaths of three generations.

He held her closer and closed his eyes, the scent of her body familiar and comforting. She had been the one who had raised them really, him and his brother Mark. Michael suddenly remembered with a pang of regret how close he and Mark had been as youngsters, and indeed still were, although time and work commitments allowed them to see less of each other now. Mark was often abroad and incommunicado, usually for long periods, on business. Hardly surprising that he had never married, thought Michael. Mariam, however, had allowed no one to spoil them when they were young. The fact that both boys had grown up to be well-adjusted was due more to Mariam's strong common sense and discipline than to parental guidance.

Other members of the staff had left in the aftermath of Khomeini's "revolution of the disinherited". Some had sought to blackmail the family through the *komitehs* – the local revolutionary committees which had taken their name from the foreign word – thinking that was the easy way to amass a fortune. The *komitehs* had been set up in each neighbourhood to purge the "sins" of the last regime – and to make a little money on the side; Khomeini's justice gave them the broadest terms of reference; anyone found guilty of "corruption on earth and crimes against God" was punishable. And under the new Islamic law there were only two sentences: confiscation of property and death.

This fragile old lady whom he held in his arms had defended and protected the family property so far.

"You can't get rid of me that easily," he joked, stepping back to look at her.

But immediately she started, "Are you hungry? You must be starved. I have cold cucumber and yoghurt soup and I'll heat up some *dolmehs*; I've got stuffed aubergines, stuffed peppers and stuffed tomatoes. That should be enough, no?"

Knowing the pleasure it gave her and the futility of arguing, he let her make a fuss of him.

"Do you have any whisky, or did they confiscate it?"

"*Goosaleh-ha.* The goats! Of course I've got some. Nobody's taking anything out of this house."

She disappeared into the larder and reappeared, triumphant, with a bottle of Johnnie Walker Black Label.

"Don't worry about alcohol. We've got a basement full," she said, pouring a healthy ration into a glass, and then adding ice from a tray she pulled from the freezer section of the old Westinghouse refrigerator. She put it in front of him with a tumbler of tap water before seeing to the food.

He raised the glass to toast her.

Her chatter continued for two hours. She reminisced happily about the past and then, with a sadness tinged by bitterness, recounted her life in Khomeini's Iran. Her isolation. The hate. The killings. The fear. The inflation. The shortages, especially of heating oil. The hooligans who ran the revolutionary committees. Visits to her few surviving friends. A sharp-minded and sharp-tongued assessment of "the situation in this place today", as she put it.

"There's even a revolutionary office, a *komiteh*, down the road in Mr Mahmoudi's old house."

"Oh," he said nonchalantly, his heart-beat quickening. "What do they do there?"

"Nothing but bother people. In the day it looks like a university; young hooligans flock there and sit around trying to figure out how to steal from people. They're always holding court, arresting people and shooting them without trial. Then, of course, they steal their belongings. Do you remember Mansour, the young barber down the road? Well, they arrested and shot his father and brother two months ago. Just for being soldiers in the Royal Guard. Now they want to confiscate

Mansour's little shop and put him out of business. All this in the name of Islam and God." Her tone was scathing and bitter.

"And at night?" he asked.

"Some guards are left there at night. They sit around smoking opium and drinking the alcohol they steal from people's homes or restaurants. They hang around the front gate and watch cars go by; stopping and searching them purely on whim." She shook her head in disapproval.

"How many of them are there at night?"

Mariam looked at him closely.

"Michael!" she exclaimed. "You're up to something."

He shook his head. "No," he said, "I'm just curious."

She stared at him in disbelief. "Do you think you can fool me?" she asked, a conspiratorial smile on her face. "I know you too well, Michael. What is it? Why do you want to know all this?"

He reached for her fragile hand and looked into her eyes sombrely. "Mariam, this is important. Very important. No one must know I'm here. I don't want you to buy extra food – no bread, milk, eggs, anything. Nothing must be done to suggest an extra person. There's something I have to do, but I can't tell you any more than that. I have to come and go, and I don't want anyone knowing about it. Do you understand?"

She eyed him carefully. "You're not trying to save the world again, are you?"

"No." He shook his head, smiling forlornly. "Just survive in it."

"You're a good boy, Michael," she replied. "You always were."

She removed her hand from his, and spoke in a more serious tone.

"There are about six or seven of them as far as I know. But by about two or three in the morning most of them pass out from drugs and alcohol. They've kept Mr Mahmoudi's old servant, Hossein. He says they're degenerates who drink heavily and smoke opium and some other things he's never heard of. Sometimes they even bring very young girls there. I can find out more tomorrow when I . . ."

"No," snapped Adel. "That's exactly what I mean, Mariam. I don't want you doing anything. There's nothing you can do – except make things worse."

The old woman searched his eyes.

"All right then, I will do nothing."

"This is serious, Mariam. And dangerous." To drive the point home he feigned irritation and cut the evening short. "I need a shower and some sleep. Which room shall I use?"

"Your own, of course," said the old woman, hurt by his abruptness. "The room is all ready; in fact, the whole house is ready. It always is. Perhaps some day we'll all live here together again. Like in the old days. All the family together."

"Perhaps some day," he said, knowing it was unlikely to be in her lifetime.

The old woman sighed and raised herself. "I'll just make up the bed while you take a shower."

They walked up together to the second-floor landing.

Suddenly Mariam exclaimed, "Oh my! I almost forgot. Some man brought a case, a package, for you today. Just this afternoon. I told him you weren't here but he insisted. He told me to give it to you the next time you came. I should have known, shouldn't I? I mean, I should have known then," she mumbled to herself. "Anyway, let me bring it up. You go ahead and get on with your bath."

Adel watched her turn and descend the staircase cautiously, step by step. As he did so he wondered how much of what she had told him was real and how much the product of her outraged disapproval.

He wondered, too, why the suitcase had been delivered ahead of schedule.

Teheran. Sunday, October 28: 4.00 a.m.

The shower had relaxed him, but still sleep would not come. Images of Samira and Natalie intermingled with fear of what lay ahead played havoc with his mind. He looked at his watch for the tenth time; it was four in the morning. He cursed and rolled on to his stomach, but it was useless.

"Damn," he said, finally accepting defeat. He turned on the old bedside lamp and lit a cigarette.

It was impossible not to think of Samira and Natalie and it was a weird, frightening sensation. It was fear, he realised that, but it was more. It was not so much death or danger that terrified him but the aching, gnawing thought that he might never see them again; it produced a combination of deep insecurity and sadness. Yet he was powerless to react in any rational way; there simply was no alternative.

He threw off the blankets in disgust, walked swiftly to the briefcase that lay on the coffee table in front of the fireplace, and spread out its contents on the bed.

There was an Ingram M-10 LISP (Lightweight Individual Special Purpose) machine-pistol with a noise suppressor, night scope and three clips of ammunition; a small magnetic torch which he clicked on to check it functioned; a gas mask with activated carbon canister to offset methane or other gases in the tunnel; a Walther PPK pistol with two boxes of one hundred of the special .45 calibre bullets; fifty feet of thin nylon rope; a miniature rubber suction pump; touch-sensitive black leather gloves; a six-inch knife in a holster to go on his belt; a small stainless steel pry bar; a US army collapsible shovel to dig through any obstruction in the primitive, antiquated *qanat* tunnel, and four small Israeli grenades insulated in plastic blister packs.

The grenades resembled American-Indian, turquoise-coloured stones; exactly the sort and size of ornaments decorating a hippie's belt and similarly designed to fit into his own belt buckle.

The suitcase also contained two passports authenticating Adel as other people. He studied them and admired the quality. At the bottom of the case he found a sealed plastic packet holding five thousand dollars in US currency. It was uncomfortably thick and he wished they'd used larger notes and fewer tens and twenties.

He picked up the Ingram and looked at it. It was clean and ready for use but he stripped it just the same and checked the firing mechanism to be certain. It was an amazing machine, he thought, recalling Allon's words.

"This miniature submachine-gun is a deadly, sophisticated firearm. It is American-made and capable of firing up to twelve hundred rounds per minute at an effective range of two hundred and fifty to three hundred yards. With attachments, it is accurate enough for a sniper. It is the deadliest weapon on the market for your purposes. Some of us had them at Entebbe.

"The Sionics silencer virtually negates any sound, and it reduces the barrel vibration, thereby increasing your accuracy. One other advantage is its sonic boom; because the bullet moves faster than sound, your target will only hear the sound as it leaves him, as it goes away from him. Consequently he will misinterpret the direction from which the bullet was fired. If you miss him, his first reaction will be to move towards you, thinking the shot came from the other direction.

"The Starlight scope, of course, will come in handy. It'll give you night vision of remarkable clarity."

Very carefully Adel put the compact machine-pistol aside and extracted one of the grenades from its protective package, examining the carving in ersatz turquoise. He checked the magnetic clip and fastened it to the belt of his jeans; it held firmly but came away easily when he tugged. He rewrapped the grenade in its protective package and then stowed everything back in the small case, placing it on the top shelf of the cupboard behind some old sweaters, out of harm's way and Mariam's reach.

He gathered up a two-week-old *Ettela'at* newspaper and walked over to the fireplace. He lit the eight-page paper with his lighter, making sure the fire was healthy before tearing the pages from the passport he had travelled with to Teheran, in the name of Reza Saleh, and tossing them into the blaze. He waited and watched as the document twisted and turned into a crisp, black mass of charcoal before using the poker to break up and scatter the ashes.

He glanced at his watch; it was nearly five a.m. He crawled back into bed and snuffed out the bedside lamp. His body ached with fatigue, but still his brain would not stop churning.

He had spent a lot of time during the last week with Natalie and Sam; every available minute away from Allon and Gleeson and the briefings about the mission, the psychology of an operative and the equipment he was to use. It had been precious time, filled with meaning and deep affection and yet, for him, tinged with an apprehension of things to come.

In the darkness he reached for the pack of cigarettes that lay on the bedside table. He lit one and tried to suppress his loneliness and sorrow. But it was useless. Only now lying in bed three thousand miles away from her did he realise how much he loved Samira. Only now when time was running out.

She was such a fragile, delicate being, yet so sensible and strong. It was amazing how powerful a force her love was. How much she had taught him, and how much he needed, and cared for her.

A new thought racked him: if he were to die, would she find another man? What sort of man? Suddenly he remembered another girl he had once known and cared about. Someone whose name kept crossing his mind during the past few days. He thought of Jane Bennett and the agony she had gone through after her first husband had died of cancer. The degradation and pain she had endured in her search to find a substitute, to relieve her grief. The suicide attempts, the hospitals, the humiliations. Would that happen to Sam? Would she be engulfed in the same torment? Or would she be luckier? Would she find the right man quickly? And what sort of man would he be?

He ached inside, overwhelmed by the deep pain of jealousy. But it was also reality. It would happen. Perhaps a year, maybe two, but it would happen. Sam was too beautiful, too alive, to wilt. She would be sought and courted and finally won. It was the rule of life, the law of nature.

He stubbed out his cigarette. Oh, she would ache, even pine for him were he to die. Or perhaps remember him larger than life. But sooner or later . . .

Abruptly he realised that Samira dominated his thoughts. What would happen to Natalie? he asked himself. His precious Natalie, his flesh and blood. But it was only a momentary concern, for he had little to worry about with Natalie. Except for his love, she would miss nothing. Sam would take care of her willingly, completely. Of that he was certain.

But who would care for Sam?

Teheran. Sunday, October 28.

The rattling of Mariam's pots and pans through the open kitchen door grew louder as he descended the staircase. When he entered the kitchen she greeted him with a buoyant smile.

"Did you sleep well?"

"Not a wink," he grumbled.

"That's not new. You never could sleep the first night

back from abroad. Take a nap this afternoon," she suggested. "Now sit down and I'll get you some breakfast."

He did as he was told.

"Did you know he's not an Iranian?"

"Who's not?" he asked, taken aback.

"Khomeini of course. He's Indian."

He relaxed, reaching over and moving the old-fashioned, charcoal-fired brass *samovar* closer, careful to keep the delicate balance of the china teapot that sat atop it.

"East or West?" he asked with a smile as he poured an *estekan* of tea.

"East or West what?"

"East or West Indian?"

She shot him a peeved look. "Don't try to provoke me. He's an Indian and that's all there is to it. And he's illiterate."

"You mean Khomeini can't read or write?" He turned the tap of the *samovar* to dilute the rich, strong tea with boiling water and then dropped three lumps of sugar into the small glass to saturate it with sweetness. "I thought Khomeini was a student of Plato."

"I suppose Mr Plato is one of those Indian gurus," she retorted. "If Khomeini was literate he wouldn't be such a liar about the Koran. All that nasty business he wrote about God. It's shocking. Did you read it?"

"Uhuh," he replied, biting into a piece of hot, unleavened bread and recalling Khomeini's endless rules to guide devout Muslims in proper piety: rules ranging from shaking the last few drops from one's penis to the detailed procedures to be followed and acceptable circumstances in which one could engage in sexual intercourse with one's camel. Or one's favourite ewe. Or one's favourite youth.

Mariam also recalled Khomeini's rules – forcefully and verbally. "So don't tell me the man's literate," she concluded.

Adel said nothing as she shuffled back from the refrigerator and placed butter, goat cheese and honey in front of him. Then she brought a bowl of fruit and a plate covered with sprigs of fresh rosemary, mint and other herbs. The wherewithal of an Iranian breakfast brought a rush of old family memories from his childhood.

"Do you know what they say about him?" she asked, as she seated herself opposite.

"Well, I've heard a few things they call him." He added a generous portion of butter and salty cheese to the freshly baked bread and bit into the open sandwich, quickly adding a couple of seedless Askari grapes for their contrasting flavour.

"They say if you lift his beard, you'll find 'Made in England' printed underneath."

She cackled and he joined in. Then he washed down his mouthful with the sweet jasmine-scented tea that had acquired just a whiff of charcoal from the *samovar*; the contrasting flavours of creamy butter, brittle bread, salty cheese and sweet tea were delicious.

The British were not well loved by Iranians – respected for their cunning but not trusted. For the last hundred years the popular belief was that they were always behind all Iran's woes. In the nineteenth century the tacit alliance between the British Legation in Teheran and the clergy was well documented. Now the British were obviously up to their old tricks again. After all, what other explanation could there be for the BBC's Persian service broadcasts during the revolution? Clearly it was the British who wanted Khomeini to come to power.

Popular belief was irrepressible, mused Adel, especially with sages like Mariam stoking things up from time to time.

The old lady continued, "No religion preaches hate and revenge and murder, especially not Islam; Islam is a beautiful religion, full of forgiving and love. This fool Khomeini slanders it." She slammed the table.

"Do you know how many crimes have been committed in the name of God?" Adel retorted.

"Yes, and that's exactly what he and his sponsors are doing right now – Khomeini, I mean."

"That was delicious, Mariam," Adel said, nodding at the food. "I'd forgotten how good your breakfasts are."

Momentarily she seemed to forget her worries as, suppressing a smile of pleasure, she removed his empty plate.

Teheran. Sunday, October 28.

The rest of the morning passed slowly as he went over and over the plans in his mind. Mercifully, the anxiety and pessimism of the night before had faded, allowing him to take a long afternoon siesta. He awoke refreshed. With little else to occupy his time, he decided to reconnoitre Mahmoudi's house and its surroundings.

If things went well, it might provide answers to the two critical questions Bell and the briefings with Gleeson and Allon had left unanswered: exactly how many guards protected the grounds and where they were posted.

Several times during the afternoon he passed the old mansion which was now the district revolutionary office that attended to the grievances of local constituents; each time on the pretence of purchasing something from the small neighbourhood shops beyond. But it became increasingly clear that without actually entering the premises the answers would elude him. For a moment he thought of joining the long queue of pleaders and petitioners at the gateway to the *komiteh* centre, but it was not moving: those seeking the attention of the new authorities huddled in a sullen line.

By five o'clock in the afternoon he had only managed to confirm the outdoor count – six heavily armed militiamen in paramilitary fatigues, lounging carelessly near the front gateway, occasionally leaving it to wander aimlessly along the wall.

On the three remaining sides of the square estate two militiamen were posted at the mid-point of each wall. These guards did not move from their posts. They did not have to: their view was unobstructed and the traffic on the desolate side-streets was light and easily monitored.

And so the afternoon achieved little; only confirmation of the outside count which was twelve militiamen in all, scattered along the four walls.

But how many more were inside the compound? And where were they posted?

At seven o'clock some civilian workers from inside the grounds went home. But still there was no sign of departing or changing guards. What was worse, as the autumn's early darkness closed in, it drove both pedestrians and cars from the roads, making those that remained more visible and exposed.

All in all it was a wasted day and he headed back to the house disappointed.

"The hell with it," he muttered as he lengthened his stride. He would act immediately. He was damned if he was going to hang around for two more days. Nothing could possibly come of it; nothing would be gained.

The logic of the decision grew more compelling as he thought it over. The actual task would be unaffected by the new timing. After all, it was unlikely that there would be fewer guards on duty on Wednesday than there were today. Besides, he had failed to understand why Bell had insisted on two days of "acclimatisation" in the first place or why the suitcase had been delivered early if it was that essential.

On the other hand, there were several clear advantages to going in ahead of schedule. Not the least of which was the head-start it would give him over Bell. If nothing else, acting ahead of schedule would throw Bell off-balance. It would also give him a couple of extra days to find some sort of protection from Bell, assuming he didn't lose time getting out of Iran.

Yes, he reasoned, opening the small dark green Judas gate. Bell's basic plan was fine; but the original schedule was to his disadvantage. It was as deadly to him as those guards next door. And it was not at all clear who that schedule was designed to accommodate.

When he returned to the house, a worried Mariam was waiting for him.

"You worry too easily," he teased as he sat at the kitchen table and looked up at the kindly old servant. She had always been a devoted woman, he thought. So kind and unselfish. But she was suffering now, her life a desert of loneliness in the wake of the revolution.

"Mariam, when this thing is over, I want you to come and live with us in France," he said impulsively. "There's nothing left for you here and you belong with us. We all miss you."

The old woman thought only for a moment. Then she shook her head wistfully. "No, Michael, this is where I belong. This is my house, my country. This is where I want to die, not among foreigners."

Slowly she shuffled over and kissed him.

"Besides, who's going to look after this place if I go?"

Teheran. Monday, October 29: 1.20 a.m.

Adel heard thunder and cursed. As he walked down the driveway, it was the only sound he heard other than his footfalls on the gravel surface and the howl of a steady wind that was picking up in force and intensity. Overhead, the cumulus clouds hung low; they puffed and billowed, blocking the full moon above and darkening the already stormy night. Ominously they augured even worse.

He was in two minds about the coming storm. The darkness was a godsend. But rain would force the guards to seek shelter inside the house. And that could prove hazardous.

He looked at the storm clouds again. Perhaps he could get in and out of the house before the downpour, he thought, as he glanced at his watch; it was nearly one-thirty in the morning. Getting through the *qanat* tunnel should take about forty-five to sixty minutes, Yuri Allon had estimated. Once he had the tapes, if he got that far, the rain would help. If, that was, the *qanat* was clear. These old irrigation tunnels criss-crossing the country were usually constructed in soft alluvial soil and they were notoriously susceptible to cave-ins. They had been left unused now for over fifteen years, ever since the city water supply had been installed to replace the antiquated system that once carried water from mountain streams to the city.

He took one last drag on his cigarette and crushed the stub beneath his dark blue sneakers. Holding the over-sized briefcase, he dropped quickly and easily into the underground reservoir that led to the *qanat*. The small room smelled stale and musty. His body stiffened as his face brushed against the sticky touch of intricate spider webs.

The heavy silence was punctuated only by the steady pit-a-pat of dripping water. He turned on the flashlight and pressed its magnet to the metal ladder. In the dim light he opened the briefcase and set about unpacking its contents. Carefully he unwrapped and attached the grenades, first rechecking that their primers were secure, then grouping them near his belt buckle, two on either side, in their allotted slots.

He took the Ingram. Marvelling again at its seven pound weight, he attached the Sionics noise suppressor to its nozzle and inserted a clip. Then he fixed the Starlight night scope and slung the almost weightless machine-pistol by a thin strap over his shoulder. The two extra clips went into their pouch on a second belt made of webbing tied more loosely around his hips. He then bound one end of the nylon cord to the belt loop near the front of his black jeans and secured the pry bar, collapsible shovel and small rubber suction-pump in their allotted pockets. He put on the gas mask but it was cumbersome and uncomfortable and it added to the feeling of claustrophobia. He removed it and placed it back in the case.

Dousing the light, he climbed the ladder and placed the briefcase now containing the money, the passports, the gas mask, the Walther PPK and one box of ammunition – at the entrance to the reservoir, behind the clump of roses that hid the trapdoor.

In the dark he descended into the reservoir again. As he entered the narrow tunnel, he was surprised at his own coolness. There was no fear, no consternation, not even foreboding. He had no idea what lay ahead or whether he was capable of handling it. He didn't care if what he was doing was right or wrong, or even if there were an alternative. All he felt was a strong urge to survive. To live to see his family again; to live his own life.

It was cramped; the tunnel was barely more than half a metre high and the fit almost too snug. The ammunition clips attached to his belt scraped the *qanat* walls as he crawled, and he could only pray that the tunnel did not narrow up ahead. The earth beneath was also a problem: it was soft sand and the knees of his jeans were soon wet and soiled, the sharpness of the tiny stones cutting into his flesh.

Gradually the air began to thin and rapidly became foul. The further he progressed the worse the sickening odour and its debilitating effects became. Soon it was unbearable.

He cursed himself for having left the gas mask behind and stopped to construct a makeshift filter round his nose and mouth from a handkerchief. Then he crawled on, faster. He had no choice: it would take too long to go back.

He pushed himself onward, torch in hand, his back occasionally brushing the roof of the tunnel, the nauseous stench making him light-headed and faint. Like a wounded animal he crawled and scraped to escape the pain that seared his lungs; he pulled and pushed his body to flee the gases that had ignited an uncontrollable fit of coughing. He felt himself weakening into semi-consciousness, listlessness. But he forced himself on, refusing to be seduced, pushing himself, remembering the reward would be at the other end. The prize of Sam and Natalie.

Then suddenly the air started to improve. He had arrived at the first reservoir; he was at the neighbour's house, the one that separated his own and Mahmoudi's. He sat on the floor, muffling his coughs and panting, but now breathing fresher, cleaner air. If everything went according to plan, he thought, feeling the fire in his chest subsiding, the next reservoir would be Mahmoudi's house. He was halfway there.

He crawled back into the tunnel and headed on. In the torchlight he noted that the wooden ceiling had completely rotted. The support columns, probably cypress, had rotted through, but miraculously they still held. His luck too was better on this second leg of the journey. The tunnel was not only clear of cave-ins but there were no gases either. Fifteen minutes later he entered the reservoir at Mahmoudi's house.

He stood eagerly and leaned for a moment on the cold damp wall to catch his breath. He rolled his neck, forcing it back as far as he could and then forward to relax his cramped muscles. The flashlight showed a trace of blood on one knee and he could feel the rawness of the other.

He stuck the magnetic flashlight, its light pointing downwards, close to the middle of the metal ladder, and brushed the earth from his clothing. Then he sat on the damp concrete floor of the reservoir and lit a cigarette, inhaling deeply and welcoming the brief rest.

After a few minutes he stood and crushed the cigarette beneath his foot before bending to pick up the butt.

"Leave no trace of your route. No clues whatsoever. If they find your route, they'll find your house – and then you. Remember you have several days before you leave Iran. They'll be looking for you in that period, so protect your route."

He placed the butt in his pocket and climbed the ladder slowly, his heart beating faster, the adrenalin pumping. Slowly, carefully, he pushed the trapdoor. It did not budge. He pushed harder. Perhaps it was locked, he thought, his heart-beat quickening.

He freed the flashlight from the metal rung and climbed back to the door. It wasn't locked; time and lack of use had rusted door and frame together. He refastened the torch and unpacked the pry bar, carefully inserting its sharpened edge between the metal door and the frame. He turned the flashlight off and slowly applied pressure, levering the bar downwards. Still the door would not budge. He pried harder, pulling down violently with his shoulder.

Abruptly it gave.

A thunderous crash split the night's silence as the metal door smashed against the marble surface surrounding the swimming pool. Instinctively, he grabbed the door handle and closed it above his head. Quickly he scrambled down the ladder, missing several of the rungs in his haste and bruising his left shin. At the bottom, he dived into the tunnel, out of sight from above.

His heart beat furiously as he lay there, his ribs pressed against the damp earth. Great, he thought, as he grabbed the Ingram, cocked it and flicked the lever to automatic, the whole neighbourhood had probably heard the crash.

He waited, gun at the ready, frightened and uncertain as to what to expect. Nothing happened. He listened. Not a sound.

Twenty minutes passed before he felt confident enough to leave the relative safety of his hiding place. Thank God for the thunder, he thought, as he slid out of the tunnel into the reservoir, his eyes fixed on the trapdoor above. He climbed the ladder again, and slowly and carefully opened the trapdoor. Through the slit he squinted into the dark pool area that separated him from the building. Then he scanned the rest of the large grounds.

Stoned or drunk, he thought. They have to be. If they didn't hear that, they wouldn't hear anything. Perhaps it was a good omen.

The Olympic-sized swimming pool was some twenty-five to thirty yards from the front of the huge white mansion. Massive colonnades opened on to the building and in the centre stood a large white front door embossed with gold carvings. He opened the trapdoor further for a better look. The ornate door was ajar and light spilled on to the patio. He swallowed and gently opened the trapdoor all the way, resting it on the marble surface. He could see in every direction now as he heard the thunder closing in and smelled rain.

To his right he saw two guards in the gatehouse, a hundred and fifty yards away, down a gentle incline. The men were smoking, talking and laughing, oblivious to danger.

He looked left and saw the mansion.

"*Unless you have to do otherwise, move slowly. Watch and wait. Look for movement. Check the shadows, check the trees, check the building and its windows. It could come from anywhere. Your natural reaction will be to move quickly, to get it over with and get out. Don't. Move slowly. Make certain you've seen everything there is to see before you move from the safety of that tunnel,*" Allon had said.

He checked the gatehouse again. For the moment, the two men presented little threat. They were too far away, too occupied in conversation.

The wind rose, setting up a chatter in the birch trees covering the vast lawns and flower gardens surrounding him on all sides; lightning cut a jagged scar in the black sky. Anxiously he counted the seconds. A sharp thunderclap arrived in under ten – eight or ten miles if I have the right lightning and the right wind speed, he thought. Eight or ten minutes before the storm would pass directly overhead.

He turned his attention to the house. It was ablaze with light. He watched and waited for more than ten minutes, but except for a blur of movement on the second floor, where the rising wind tugged at the curtain of an open window, there was no sign of life.

He glanced at his watch: 03:11:25 – an ungodly hour, he hoped, for Muslims committed to *namaz* – morning prayers – at sunrise.

More lightning was followed by pelting rain; the roar of thunder was now loud and almost overhead.

He jerked himself out of the pit and ran, ignoring the heavy rain and holding the Ingram loosely to his right, ready. Quickly he darted towards the shadows of the nearest rose-bush, throwing himself at its base, twisting and rolling into its foliage. Immediately he positioned himself and lay still.

There was no sign of life, only vapour from his own breath and the loud, heavy pounding in his ribcage. Cautiously he started crawling towards the building, the grass and mud beneath him drenching and caking his clothes.

"*Blend into the darkness as much as you can,*" the Israeli had said. "*In the darkness there is the unknown. In the unknown there is fear.*"

He moved to the steps below the main doors and lay still. There was no sound but the rain, no movement but the wind.

"*Use the setting,*" Allon had said. "*Anything that distracts, even momentarily, is your friend.*"

It seemed like a long time, but when it came, it came suddenly. A streak of light accompanied by a thundering crash momentarily illuminated the entire compound. Fleetingly, it was day. Abruptly it was dark.

Adel moved rapidly. He dashed to the porch and hugged the door, holding the Ingram ready at waist level. Another ear-splitting thunderclap and blaze of light lit up the garden, followed by yet another shattering explosion. He saw no movement in the brief, white glare but knew the storm was now directly overhead.

"Now or never," he told himself.

He grabbed the half-open ornate door latch and pushed lightly. The door gave and he followed it, crouching low as instructed, dashing across the vaguely familiar dark parquet tile floor and kneeling on one knee, his back against the wall. The gun ready.

He waited, but again there was no sign of life.

He knew the house well. The eight glazed mahogany doors in the lobby were in a perfect circle. On the left, a twisting semi-circular glass, gold and chrome-plated stairway led to the second floor. Above this, and extending nearly four floors, a hand-painted sky, complete with cirrus clouds, formed a massive dome.

Was it a replica of some rococo mansion? A bizarre version of the White House? Or simply Mahmoudi's opium-inspired mausoleum; the son of a Kerman pistachio farmer's legacy to his own magnificence.

It was a bordello, thought Adel as he glanced at the serene summer sky painted above. A ten-million-dollar whore-house built by Mahmoudi to accommodate the Shah's extra-marital activities. The Shah's women had been provided by Mahmoudi, usually in the shape of buxom blondes of tender age and expensive tastes. In return, Mahmoudi would arrange the purchase of nuclear reactors, computers, F-14 fighters or any amount of arms, by royal decree. And collect the appropriate commission of course.

Adel stood and walked quickly to the first door on the right, the entrance to Mahmoudi's private study. He opened the door, slipped into the dark room noiselessly and stood there with his back to the door, sweat pouring from his body, but his ears alert, sensitive to any sound. His luck was holding; there was none.

He flashed the torch briefly to memorise the outline and obstacles – chairs, lights, tables. The gaudy room was a jungle of ostentation: everything it held was priceless; but there was just too much. Too many antique tables, chairs, statues and paintings. It looked like the storeroom of a provincial French theatrical company.

In the darkness Adel walked to the inlaid Empire desk; it sat on a small silk Isfahan rug that slid easily and conveniently when pushed. He flashed the torch momentarily on the wooden surface previously covered by the rug and looked for the removable parquet tile above the floor safe. A seam of dirt outlined the two-foot-square panel; quickly he lifted it out with the miniature chrome-rubber suction pump and set it aside.

He paused again to listen, but the heavy rain all but drowned any other sound; there was no possibility of forewarning. He flashed the torch at the three chrome knobs of the safe and spun them to zero. Beneath him as he knelt, a puddle of water formed on the dark parquet surface. His once paper-thin leather gloves were wet and heavy, slippery and insensitive to the touch.

Dial three – turn left once to two.

Dial one – turn right twice to five.

Dial two – turn right once to three.

He pulled the handle and the heavy steel door swung open easily.

The safe was jammed to the brim. He dug in hurriedly, pulling out the contents – jewels, gold krugerrands, documents, opium pellets, small glass phials of cocaine – and laid them carelessly but quietly in a growing pile, ready to be swept back. Near the bottom he found a burgundy-coloured drawstring leather tobacco pouch; inside were two Sony cassette tapes.

He stuck one tape in each kneelength sock and deftly brushed the pouch and pile of discarded valuables back into the safe. He closed the metal door, spun the knobs and replaced the parquet cover.

Abruptly the room was awash with light. For a split second he prayed it was lightning, but a voice behind killed his prayers.

"If you move you're dead." It was a deep, heavy voice.

He did not move. He froze there on hands and knees.

"The passport says Saleh, but I believe Adel is the name," the guttural voice continued.

Adel was gripped by fear as he heard feet move to his rear.

"Very carefully slide the machine-pistol backwards," the voice instructed.

He did as he was told; the Ingram skidded along the floor, scratching the dark wooden surface.

"Good. Now stand up and put your hands and arms around your neck . . . No! Higher!" The voice barked the last two words.

Adel was petrified; a massive weight pressed against his chest making it difficult to breathe. A million icy needles pricked his body.

"Good."

The man spoke English but the accent was indefinable. It was neither British nor Iranian English, Adel observed, as hands moved roughly down his body, removing his equipment. They were thorough in their search and so the tapes did not escape them.

"Now you can turn round, but keep your arms where they are."

Adel turned to face three men. Two stood silently twenty feet away near the glazed mahogany door, confronting him with levelled G-3 rifles and menacing looks. They were obviously militiamen, slovenly and ill at ease. The third man made Adel shudder. Impressively in command, the man raised his rump to sit on the desk. He was relaxed and confident as he shuffled the two plastic cassettes in one massive hand.

It was the man at the airport. The tall blond foreign-looking one in the customs hall. And he looked even more intimidating at close range.

"We've been expecting you, Mr Adel," he said, his guttural accent making the words even more threatening. "Our brothers in London could not tell us precisely when you would arrive. But we knew that you would come to this house." He stopped. "Put your arms down slowly," he instructed.

How the hell could he know I was coming? thought Adel.

"To be honest, we were told to expect you some days earlier. But that is all unimportant now that you are here. What have you come to steal – these tapes, Mr Adel? And what is on these tapes? Please, quickly and honestly, is this what you have come to steal? It would be foolish to lie, Mr Adel. And so much a waste of time."

Adel knew he had only one chance left – the small turquoise-studded Israeli grenades decorating his belt. With his hands down he had a chance. Not much of one, but still something. He hooked his right thumb above the belt buckle, his splayed fingers extending down to the grenades at the front.

"Okay," he said, shrugging his shoulders. It wasn't going to be easy to fool this man and he decided not to try. "I . . . I haven't heard them myself," he stammered, "but they contain information regarding a weapons system." He needed time. He had to freeze the action and hold their attention.

"What weapons system?"

"Ballistic missiles. Something called a Phoenix missile. These tapes carry information about the Hughes guidance system, on-board computers, digital analog micro-processors, over-the-horizon radar. That sort of thing."

He felt no loyalty to Bell or to the US government. Not right now anyway. He had developed a more immediate concern: two G-3 rifles pointing directly at him and an Uzi submachine-gun waving in his vicinity.

The blond man shook his head and grinned.

"That does not seem possible. All that material? And on only two cassette tapes, Mr Adel. Do you take us for fools?"

"No. It's sixteen or seventeen tapes recorded at high speed on to two," said Adel, repeating Bell's words.

But the explanation sounded as hollow as when he himself had first heard it. "That's what I was told," he added.

"You took nothing else from the safe?" asked the blond man, pointing to it with his foot.

"Nothing."

"No jewels?"

"No."

"No documents?"

"No. You saw when you searched me."

Slowly the blond man sauntered back across the room again, his head bent, looking at the tapes in his hand and the priceless carpet beneath his feet. He stopped only inches away from Adel and raised his head. For a long moment he stood silently, his hard, cold blue eyes boring into Adel.

"We are going to have long conversations, you and I," he said turning to walk away. Suddenly he reeled back and the flat of his hand slammed into Adel's face. "And I plan to enjoy our conversation."

Adel rubbed his stinging cheek and watched as the blond man walked purposefully to the door and opened it a slit. "Ahmad, *baatcheha-ra sedakon!*" he bellowed, summoning "the guys".

The accent was guttural, even in Persian, noted Adel. Perhaps he was East European. But no. It was not that sort of accent. It was more . . . Then it hit him. The man was an Arab. And suddenly he remembered Allon's words:

"There is every reason to believe the real power in Iran lies in the hands of Khomeini's PLO advisers. These people are running the show. And they are good. Experienced professionals. If you run into them, be careful. They're merciless."

"Now, Mr Adel, come here and face the wall," the blond mercenary ordered as he took hold of Adel's left arm in a vice-like grip.

He's blond; Arabs aren't usually blond, thought Adel as he felt his limp body being towed towards the wall.

His legs felt weak and ice-water pumped through his veins.

"Put your hands up against the wall . . . high . . . up there." He pointed to a spot above Adel's head. "Very good. Now don't move until you are told to do so. I will ask you one more time. What did you come to steal and what is the number of the safe?"

Adel hesitated as he felt his stomach sink. But of course there were blond Arabs – Crusader seed. The son of a bitch was probably planted in Palestine by some randy German peasant seven hundred years ago.

But now, with his hands high above his head again, he had missed his chance, the grenades were out of reach.

"I told you what I know. They contain highly classified information about the Phoenix missile," he repeated, playing for time, waiting for the chill to leave his bones. "As for the safe combination, it's . . ."

The blond man wrote the numbers down.

"*Any distraction is your friend*," the Israeli agent had said. But what distraction? thought Adel. There was none. Only two guns trained on his head and a man called Ahmad on his way with God knows what else.

"You may put down your arms while we wait for Ahmad, but do not turn. I do not want to make you uncomfortable. Not yet anyway," the blond Arab taunted.

Adel slowly, cautiously moved his hand towards his belt buckle again. It was his last chance. He removed one of the small grenades with his trembling right hand and gripped it tightly in his sweaty fist. Then he removed another.

"Thank you," he said as he did so. He made certain his body protected his movements as he pulled out the two miniature primer pins. It was now or never.

"*Any distraction is your friend*," Allon had said.

"Now, Mr Adel, for the last . . ."

Adel heard the door open and the mercenary stop in mid-sentence; the man called Ahmad had arrived. It was a meagre distraction, but it was all he had.

He flung the grenades behind him and threw himself to the floor.

"Look out," shouted one of the militiamen in Farsi before pandemonium shook the room. A burst of machine-gun fire raked the enclosure and a stream of bullets tore at the wall, inches above Adel's falling, rolling body. An instant later the two grenades exploded simultaneously and a cacophony of additional sounds erupted. Screams and shouts. Breaking glass. A blast of air smashed a chair across his back and the angry sizzle of flying metal tore into his left leg, crushing the limb against the wall.

And then darkness and the smell of smoke.

He was stunned and only half-conscious. He tried to move, but momentarily blacked out from an agonisingly sharp pain in his left calf. In the pitch blackness he could see nothing. He moved his right hand down to feel the wound. The trousers were torn and blood oozed from open flesh. He lay back exhausted and faint, knowing he had to move, knowing he didn't have the time to rest. He forced himself up on to his hands and dragged himself among the tangled bodies of the blond man and the guards, peering into the darkness for his gun. Near the door, smoke rose from a small but growing fire.

He pushed himself forward more quickly, knowing that others were on their way; any second now the door would open and a horde of them would arrive. He heard a groan in the darkness and the sounds of distant shouting from outside. They were coming. He crawled nearer the doorway where the blond man had last stood. He saw nothing but mangled bodies. *The tapes! He had to find the tapes! The gun!*

He was panicking now, brushing the floor in wide circles with his hands. The guards from the gatehouse would be here any second and God knows how many more from inside. He was desperate. *The tapes. The tapes. The gun.*

The fire was spreading quickly, its flames fanning out further and wider. Suddenly, in the flickering light he saw the gun, and the belt that held the ammunition pouch. He pushed himself upright with his hands and lunged eagerly for the automatic. But he landed short – his left leg buckling beneath him. Winded and in agony he buried his face in his hands.

But the shouting was getting closer. He had no time to rest. He forced himself up and crawled the short distance to the gun. There were only seconds left. He had to get out of there . . . into the garden . . . into that tunnel. To hell with the tapes.

He stumbled towards the shattered windows. Two guards were running towards the house about a hundred yards away. He waited for them to draw closer.

Rain was still pouring down, but the lightning and thunder were a distant rumble as he flicked the lever from automatic to single and focused the night scope on the closer of the two figures. Through the visor, night became a green day.

The shot was soundless, exuding only a hiss of air as it caught the first of the runners in the chest. Sixty feet away, the bullet tore a hole the size of a tennis ball through him. The second man stopped when his comrade fell, not knowing why he had stumbled. He never found out. He died standing there looking at his friend's contorted body. Another hiss of air ripped him apart. For the two of them, the revolution was over. They were *shahids*, martyrs.

Adel could see no other movement in the grounds; he crawled back towards the door, praying he could find the tapes by a stroke of luck, hoping they had not been destroyed in the explosion or fire. Frantically he clawed at the wooden surface in semi-circular arcs. Still he couldn't find them.

He was panic-stricken. The fire was now spreading quickly and smoke filled the room. He could hear too, the sounds of running feet from above, inside the building.

Suddenly, he remembered. *The pockets. The blond man had put the tapes in his pocket.*

The body was bent and crushed against the left-hand wall, a confusion of blood and oozing flesh. Both his legs were gone. All that remained were two bloody stumps of differing lengths.

Adel fumbled through the denim jacket pockets on the body. He could feel the sharp edges of the plastic boxes through the heavy material but the pocket openings eluded him. He ripped at the cloth desperately; on the second wrench the material gave. He grabbed the two tapes and crawled towards the door.

At the doorway he steadied himself against the wall and pulled himself up. He was weakening rapidly. His head spun and he had difficulty in focusing his eyes. He staggered through the lobby, using the wall as his crutch. His left leg was agony and his head pounded with pain. He longed to rest, to let oblivion take over.

At the edge of the patio, his leg buckled again and he fell in a heap on the soaking earth. But he forced himself to keep moving, knowing it was his only chance of survival. He grabbed at the grass, digging his fingers deep into the mud and pulled himself towards the sanctuary of the nearest bush.

"Keep moving. Keep moving," he whispered to himself. He crawled on, his leg numb now, the pain receding into half-consciousness. The yearning for oblivion became stronger. More than anything else in the world he wanted to sleep.

He stopped and looked behind at the mansion. It was a blurred mass of flashlights. The power supply had been knocked out and now mobile lights blazed in haphazard circles, sweeping across the garden. He had to move those last few yards to the tunnel. He clawed frantically at the mud.

"*Don't leave any trace of your route*," Allon had urged him.

He opened the tunnel door and slid his body down the ladder. He had to close the door, he told himself . . . he had to . . . otherwise they would know . . . they would trace him. He summoned his last ounce of energy and closed the heavy steel sheet before falling in a heap at the bottom.

Teheran. Monday, October 29: morning.

His eyes would not focus, and the will was not there to force them. Somehow, though, his senses registered a strange familiarity with his surroundings. One by one through the haze of semi-consciousness he identified friendly objects. A familiar painting here, drawn curtains he had known there, furniture he recognised everywhere. Gradually the pieces formed the outlines of a blurred shape and the shape took on a meaning. He was in his own bedroom.

But how long had he been there? And how did he get there? The darkness provided no clues. He raised his head from the pillow to see the clock on the mantelpiece. Its small thin hands merged in and out of focus. He squinted, forcing his eyes to absorb them; it read eleven-fifteen. But was it day or night? Either way, he thought as he slumped back, miraculously they had not come for him. Not yet anyway.

He was weak and his body ached. He wanted to sleep, but his mind raced. How had he got back? He remembered only the struggle to stay conscious in the tunnel.

The tapes. Where were the tapes?

He lifted his head and looked around the room. He could not see them. Through the haze he scanned the room frantically. Still they were nowhere to be seen. His clothes. The gun. There was no sign of any of them. He threw back the bedcovers. Stiff, aching, his leg throbbing, he pushed himself upright.

He started to move from the bed, but pain stabbed his left leg and anchored him to the floor as it spread throughout his body. He was dizzy and sweating profusely.

"Mariam," he cried.

"Get back into bed, I'm coming." Even through the open door, her voice sounded distant and muffled, and it seemed an eternity before she appeared in the doorway.

"Where're the tapes?" he whispered, his throat burning.

"They're safely tucked away. Now get back into bed," she ordered.

A wave of relief swept over him.

Only then did he notice the heavy bandage round his calf. But he asked no questions; he didn't care. He sat on the bed, the urge to rest overwhelming.

"I don't think it's very serious, but the cut is deep and you've lost a lot of blood," said the old lady as she set a tray down beside him. "There may be something in there, too. I can't tell. At my age you can't rely on your eyes."

"How did I get here?" he asked softly, glancing at the traditional Iranian *ash*, thick vegetable and yoghurt soup with meat balls.

"I don't know how you got to the kitchen door. You were in such a mess. Absolutely soaked to the skin and covered in mud. Blood everywhere. Your left leg was caked in it. I had quite a time getting that gun away from you too. You wouldn't let go of it. Anyway, I did and then I got Mansour from down the road – the boy I told you about – to help me get you up the stairs."

He nodded, realising she had had no choice but to get some help to move him.

"Are you sure he's safe?" he asked nervously.

She gave him a reproachful look and instantly he knew it was a foolish question.

"Where's the gun?" His hand shook as he spooned the hot soup.

"I threw it down the well," she said, her lips tight. "I also found a suitcase in the rose-bush by the *qanat*. That's in the cupboard." She pointed to the wardrobe to his left as she sat on the chair next to the bed.

"I couldn't sleep last night," she continued, "there was so much commotion. Shooting and thunder and lightning and I don't know what. When I went to buy the morning bread I found you – well, you fell through the kitchen door, to be more specific." She shook her head in disapproval.

"Where are the tapes?"

"Where you used to hide all your secrets. On the ledge in the chimney."

Adel looked at her and smiled weakly. "Come here," he said, urging her with his eyes.

With the help of her right hand the old woman straightened her back and shuffled to his bed. Adel gently reached out and kissed her.

"Thank you," he whispered.

"That's all very well," she scoffed, shuffling away from his reach. "But what are we going to do about that leg?"

"How bad is it?"

"Bad enough to need a doctor. And if you don't call one, I will," she said firmly.

"Okay. But let me eat something first."

The steaming soup was tempting but he also needed time to think.

"There's an awful clamour out on the street by old Mr Mahmoudi's house," she said, warning him.

Adel stopped eating and looked at her.

"No one knows what happened; someone broke in and killed several guards and then disappeared. They think it was the Forghan group, the anti-Khomeini terrorists. One of the guards is still alive, but he's in a very bad way. He'll probably die, according to Mansour. He's a foreigner, an Arab, I think. He's lost both his legs. White as paper, Mansour said. They took him to hospital."

Adel pushed the tray away. Damn! The son of a bitch was alive. Why hadn't he been more thorough? Why hadn't he made sure?

"Mariam," he said, as he carefully unwound the bandage. "I stink. I need a bath. Then we'll see what we can do about a doctor."

Monday. October 29: 1.00 p.m.

Adel spent a long time soaking in the large old enamel tub, letting the hot water soothe his aches and bruises and thinking about his next move. The wound on his calf was long and deep and Mariam's fear was well founded; there was something in it, a foreign object that looked suspiciously like a piece of metal. He could not risk leaving it there for long. The shrapnel, or whatever it was, together with the slime and dirt from the stagnant *qanat* water, was an invitation to infection; it needed immediate attention. Especially when he thought about the days ahead and all that would be required of him.

As he lay there, left leg resting semi-comfortably on the old tub's metal rim and the cushioned stool beside it, he remembered the blond man. If he recovered the Iranian would point the finger squarely at him. If he hadn't already.

They had been waiting for him in there. They had known he was coming. But how? Somehow there had been a leak.

Adel pulled out the plug and lowered his leg slowly, using his arms to push himself out of the tub. He had to get out of Teheran quickly. Before they came after him.

In the bedroom he used the telephone, dialling from memory the number 8-2-0-0-9-1.

A voice answered after the second ring.

"*Sefarate Amrica*, US Embassy," it said in Farsi and English.

"Extension 2184, please," Adel replied in English.
"Connecting you."
A deep male voice answered after several connecting clicks. "Economic section."
"Khan!" said Adel as he had been instructed.
"I beg your pardon."
"Khan!" he repeated, a flutter of doubt running through him.
This time the voice responded without hesitation. "One moment, please."
The phone clicked. And clicked again.
"Hello." It was the same voice.
"Hello."
"It's okay. We can talk now. This line is sterile," said George Clark, economic counsellor, US Embassy, Teheran. Alias Khan.
"I need a doctor," said Adel.
"Where are you?" snapped Clark. "You were supposed to contact me yesterday." His tone was abrupt.
"You know exactly where I am. I didn't call yesterday because I had nothing to say. Now I do. I need a doctor," Adel repeated, confident that as long as he had the tapes they needed him.
There was a moment's hesitation before Clark responded.
"Very well, but your area is overrun with revolutionary guards and militia. It may take us a little time to set up a watertight reason for being there. We have to take security precautions – for our own sake, as much as yours. Let's say between three and four o'clock this afternoon."
Adel hung up but Khan's words lingered. "Your area is overrun with revolutionary guards and militia."
The US Embassy was monitoring him.

Monday. October 29: 3.55 p.m.

"I think it looks worse than it is," the embassy doctor said, raising his bald head. He was about six feet two inches tall, with a huge egg-shaped body topped by a large shining egg-shaped head. He camouflaged his immense torso with a dreary grey herringbone suit, white shirt and dark blue tie.

George Clark, alias Khan, remained silent, watching from the leather couch to the left of the bed and squinting his grey eyes.

"The only point of immediate concern is that thing in there," the doctor said, squeezing the wound.

"Ahhh! Damn it, take it easy!" Adel winced.

The doctor ignored Adel's pain and pulled the flesh apart for a better look.

"Have that removed as soon as you get to London, assuming, of course, you're leaving right away. Otherwise infection could be a problem; gangrene and so on. All I can do is clean it up, close the wound and give you a shot of antibiotics. You're not allergic to penicillin, are you?"

"Not as far as I know."

"Fine. There may be some bone damage, too. It doesn't look like it, but I can't really tell without X-rays. Just to be on the safe side, I'll put a cast on."

Adel was silent.

"That's about all I can do." The doctor moved away from the bed to sit beside Clark.

Adel thought quickly. The days ahead were uncertain. It was not as if he was flying first class to England and checking into the London Clinic for a month. Just staying alive was going to be a problem.

"That should do it until you get to London," said Clark, breaking the silence.

"There's no guarantee I'll be in London or any other civilised corner of the earth so soon. Why can't we do it right here and now? As you say, it's not that serious." He observed the two men closely.

Clark brushed his blond crew-cut with elegantly long fingers and stood up. He ignored the doctor's uncertain glances as he moved towards the bed.

"You were instructed to follow an itinerary," he said. "And you didn't. Everything's been screwed up already." He was standing above Adel's bed now, looking down. "You need hospital care and attention after an operation of this kind. It's not that easy to arrange."

Adel smiled, mirthlessly.

"As a code name, 'Khan' is perfect for you," he said, looking into Clark's eyes. "It means gentleman in Farsi and no one's ever going to suspect you of being one."

He turned to the doctor. "What can you do with a local anaesthetic?"

The doctor looked at Clark for guidance.

"Put it this way," said Adel, turning back to Clark. "I'm not going anywhere with this leg, and I sure as hell don't intend to turn the tapes over to you until I get out of here. And in one piece." His stare was fixed and cold.

Clark and the doctor exchanged glances before Clark nodded; he did not try to hide the movement.

"I'm only thinking of you," the doctor said uncertainly. "This sort of procedure requires more than we have here. If I'd known, I'd have brought something. God knows what," he added, shrugging his shoulders. He pointed at the leg. "And I can't guarantee this will be painless."

"I'll risk it," replied Adel tartly. "But just make sure it's a simple anaesthetic."

The doctor said nothing. Looking preoccupied he rolled up his shirtsleeves while Clark stared back at Adel, his eyes fixed and curious. They could not understand, but they could not ask either.

"I'll need a few simple things, like boiling water, lots of it and . . ."

Monday, October 29: 8.40 p.m.

Thanks to the morphine, the operation had been painless, but the side effects of the injection had brought uncontrollable lethargy. All evening Adel had been in and out of a stupor.

Something in the back of his mind kept stressing the importance of time and forcing him to consciousness. Only each time the morphine overpowered the movement and drove him back into darkness. All the while he remained as though paralysed, unable to move from his bed.

It was nearly 9.00 p.m. before he could summon enough energy to push his shoulders up to rest against the headboard. It was late, he told himself, and he had so much to do. No more time could be lost.

"Two days," the doctor had said. "You'll be able to move about in two days."

He needed those two days. Bell wouldn't be expecting him before then. Besides, one of those days would be lost getting out of Teheran and that would give him a lead of only twenty-four hours. With one foot in a cast, twenty-four hours was nothing. He had to move.

His mouth tasted like the *qanat* and his stomach was queasy. He moved his hand to the night table and clumsily poured a glass of water from the heavy bedside jug. Slowly he moved the glass to his mouth and sipped the ice-cold water. It cooled his throat and helped to clear his head. He drank another.

He picked up the phone and dropped it on the bed. Wearily, he dialled Mariam's room. There was no answer.

"God damn it," he croaked, his throat sore and dry

again, his tone disappointed rather than angry. She had probably gone out to buy bread or something.

On the night table, beside the jug, he saw an unfamiliar bottle. A bottle of pills – painkillers. The doctor must have left them. He took two of the capsules and lay back.

To the right of the table he saw a pair of old metal crutches and recognised them. His father had once used them after an accident. Mariam must have found them in some dark corner of the cellar.

The pain was bearable now, after the pills. But the grogginess was still there; it came in waves and each time it affected his vision. He knew he had to overcome it. He couldn't afford to wait for it to pass naturally. That would take too long.

He raised himself slowly and rested against the headboard; it wasn't as bad as before, a little strength had returned to his arms. Carefully he put his right leg to the floor. Then the left one in its cast. He used the crutches to get to the bathroom, walking carefully, resting frequently to gather strength and waiting for the dizzy spells to pass. In the bathroom he drew cold water and doused his head repeatedly. Gradually he felt strength returning to his body and the muzziness clearing from his head.

He dressed with difficulty; the left trouser leg was barely wide enough to accommodate the cast. From now on, he told himself, the trousers stay on.

He felt better. He would go downstairs and find something light to eat.

The ground floor was in total darkness as he stepped on to the first-floor landing. He switched on the hall light and started down the stairs slowly, carefully. Then he limped towards the kitchen and reached for the light switch, which hung by a cord in the centre of the room.

The light revealed Mariam; face down on the floor. Dead.

He stared at her uncomprehendingly for several moments; dumbfounded by her stillness, afraid to touch her but overpowered by the contorted position of her body. At last he sat beside her and slowly, tentatively turned her on to her back. Her soft, aged skin felt cold, her eyes were fixed. Tears welled in him but he fought them as he gently straightened her unresisting limbs and smoothed her green and white flower-print dress.

Then he leaned against the table leg and gazed, unwilling to leave her side. But suddenly the numbness disappeared. Something was out of place. Out of character.

The sleeve of her left arm had been rolled up. He grabbed it and looked, pushing up the sleeve even further. Why? Why was the sleeve turned up? She never, ever, did that. It was one of her phobias, her pet hates. Undignified, she would always say.

He turned the arm; two needle marks punctured the inside of her right elbow. Two tiny streams of dried blood meandered down the pale, wrinkled skin of her inner forearm.

Adel felt sick. His stomach churned with anger and disgust. They had killed her. To find the tapes, they had killed her. *The tapes*, he suddenly remembered. Had she talked?

He jerked himself upwards, ignoring the pain, scrambling up the stairs, half-limping, half-dragging himself. Forgetting the pain. Forgetting the crutches. Forgetting the cast. Instead using the staircase and walls for support.

He hurried into the bedroom and to the fireplace, reaching up the chimney and tearing the loose brick from its slot. His heart pounded furiously. If she had talked, if they had found the tapes, he too was dead. Now. Right here. He would never make it out of Iran. Never make it to London, let alone insure himself against any harm Bell might have in store for him.

Then he felt the two plastic boxes and ripped them from their hiding place. Blood and dirt were still caked on their covers.

She hadn't talked. That's why she had died; they had

given her too much. A poor, seventy-year-old woman had died from an overdose of truth serum.

Khan had guessed. He had put it together. If anyone knew where the tapes were it had to be Mariam. And he had killed her. But why? Dear God, why? They had him by the balls – he had to turn the tapes over. Why kill her? Why kill a defenceless old woman?

Tears welled up again but this time he could not fight them. He sat down and sobbed uncontrollably, crying for a woman who had been a mother to him.

Eventually, the anger and sorrow subsided and a new determination took hold. His leg ached again, a dull throbbing pain, and he knew he had damaged it in the rush upstairs. But it was a distant pain; all he could feel was hate.

He limped to the bed, picked up the telephone and dialled: 6-4-3-0-1-3.

It was busy. He tried the second number: 6-4-3-0-1-4.

That, too, was busy. He dialled again and again, frustrated and angry, until he finally got through.

"Hello," a bored male voice responded.

"Mehrabad airport?" he asked.

"Yeah," replied the voice gruffly.

"Revolutionary committee, please," said Adel.

There was a click followed shortly by another.

"It's busy."

"I'll wait."

"Hello." The phone came alive with a rough abrasive voice.

"Hello," he tried to sound hesitant. "Is that the airport *komiteh*?"

"Yeah."

"I'd like to report a crime that's due to be committed at the airport tomorrow," he said, forcing his tone to quiver.

The voice picked up interest. "What crime?"

"Well . . . uh . . . uh . . .," he stammered.

"Go ahead, go ahead. If you know of a crime it's your revolutionary duty to report it."

"There's a passenger booked on the Swiss Air flight leaving at seven in the morning for Damascus and Geneva." He did not offer the flight number. Detail, to Iranians, was always suspicious. They preferred to think in *ousouli* – general – terms.

"He's got a cast on his leg. There's nothing wrong with his leg. It's full of jewellery. Jewellery he wants to smuggle out of the country."

"Who is the man?" asked the voice. "What's his name?"

Adel said nothing.

"Hello. Hello!" The voice grew eager now.

"Hello," said Adel.

"Who is he?"

"A traitor. A bastard who wants to steal our country's wealth."

That should do it, thought Adel. He hung up.

He thought a moment then picked up the phone again and dialled: 8-9-0-6-0-6.

"Hello."

"I'd like a taxi at five in the morning," he said.

"Destination?" asked the man.

"Mehrabad airport."

"Address?"

Adel gave it.

"Okay. We'll have one there."

"I have a plane to catch. Please make sure he's here at five," Adel pleaded. After all, this was Iran, and time, like detail, was only approximate.

"Don't worry, mister, he'll be there."

That night Adel buried Mariam beneath the elegant walnut trees beside the pool. She had always loved that part of the garden because of the protection the trees offered from the merciless summer sun.

Many years ago when they had been children, she had let him and his brother Mark play there – and only there – in the large grass tract, shaded and out of harm's way. And always under her watchful, protective eye. Even in death she had kept her vigil.

The earth was still damp and soft from the rainfall and recollections of Mariam and his childhood were so vivid that the task went by quickly. Tears flowed unchecked down his face and he sat there looking at her for a long time before he found the courage to cover her for the last time. Finally, he kissed her before laying her light body in the shallow grave. He covered her with a white sheet; it was the only protection he could offer her from the ravages of time.

Mehrabad Airport, Teheran.
Tuesday, October 30: 5.30 a.m.

The yellow Shahin taxi, an obsolete Rambler assembled in Iran, inched ahead to a total stop a half a mile from the "temporary" international terminal at Mehrabad airport.

In the gloomy darkness of a cloudy winter morning, hundreds of people pushed and shoved through the tangle of vehicles that had been brought to a standstill. The confusion, partly caused by the inadequate and badly designed facilities, was made even worse by a horde of brutal officials, who worried the anxious passengers with bewildering and contradictory instructions.

A small section of the crowd pushed battered lime-yellow wire carts, stacked with mountains of luggage – suitcases, boxes, cartons, trunks. But most of the travellers were not so lucky; carts, like everything else in the shattered economy, were in short supply. People pulled and pushed their possessions, sweating and cursing profusely. Women, children and the elderly were forced to help their menfolk, sometimes carrying or dragging more than seemed possible for their size.

Adel entered the building and cautiously threaded

his way through the disarray. In the confusion he was careful to protect his damaged leg from further injury but each yard was a physical chore; the hall was packed with nervous, disappointed people.

"What do you mean – the plane won't be coming?" he heard one lady sob as he approached the Pan American counter.

"Why the hell not?" said another. The man's tone was hostile.

"You sold the damned tickets, didn't you?" someone else shouted.

Adel glanced at the young airline official who was trying as best he could to placate the disappointed, desperate passengers. He was as frustrated as they were and unable to provide the answers they sought. Instead, his hands, voice and facial gestures pleaded for understanding.

It was the same at the British Airways counter.

"At least you could have called to let us know," said one man.

"We came all the way from Chemran," moaned a middle-aged woman.

"Can you get us another flight?" asked another, more constructive, traveller.

Adel passed on through the throng towards the Swiss Air counter. One man he passed was busy explaining to his family why he had been turned back.

"It . . . It . . . must be a mistake," he stuttered to an elderly woman, using his hands and shoulders more than his voice. "He . . . he . . . said I was on some . . . some list." The man's face was ashen and moist.

The elderly woman, presumably his wife, burst into a loud wail.

Chaos reigned. Flights had been cancelled, arriving planes were overbooked, passengers were being turned back by three different forces – the *pasdaran* militiamen, the police and immigration officials. No one knew what was going on.

The mêlée at the Swiss Air first class counter seemed

somehow less chaotic than the others and Adel was thankful for it. His optimism, however, quickly turned sour.

What if they don't spot me? What if they miss me and let me through?

Using the cane he had found in his father's wardrobe, he hobbled to the end of the line and dismissed his doubts. It was unlikely; they were expecting him; it could only be a matter of time before they singled him out. Besides, if it went that far, he would have to cause a scene, to draw attention to himself.

Though the queue was short, its progress was slow and tiring. It emphasised the fatigue that had built up. He was tired; to the marrow of his bones he was tired. He felt grubby and dirty, too; he hadn't shaved in days and while he had changed into old clothes, they were ill-fitting and uncomfortable. The slacks barely fitted around the cast. The pain in his leg was dull and bearable; the painkillers were doing their job. But the effects of his brief but violent stay in Iran were beginning to take hold. The stench of cordite and death, the lack of sleep, the aching leg. And Mariam . . . poor innocent Mariam.

And it was not over yet. There was still another day.

Suddenly his thoughts were violently interrupted. There was a frenzy of activity; concentric circles closed in on a given point, causing shock waves of fear and panic among the crowds. Carts of luggage were pushed and upturned in every direction, their value forgotten, with life itself taking precedence. Sounds of panic filled the air. Screams and shouts, tears and cries of horror engulfed him. Instinctively he wanted to move away, to seek cover. Instinctively, he had forgotten.

"Put your hands on your head," a harsh voice rasped.

He was surprised by the size of the arresting party. At least thirty young men surrounded him at a distance of ten to fifteen yards. Kneeling, crouching and standing, they held an assortment of arms, all aimed at him. Adel followed their instructions quickly and to the letter, holding his briefcase in one hand and his cane in the other for effect.

A young man dressed in commando uniform detached himself from the group, rose from a kneeling position and swaggered forward.

He was young, maybe twenty-five, with a crop of unwashed, uncombed wavy black hair; a three-day growth of stubble enhanced the fashionable image of Iran's post-revolutionary guardians. Adel noticed at once that he was carrying a shining Uzi submachine-gun.

The gun did the talking, while his squinted blood-shot eyes indicated his mood. He nodded the direction Adel should follow. As he did so, several uniformed police arrived running, their Colts drawn, ready.

"Do you need help?" asked a tall, thin police captain who sported an Errol Flynn moustache.

The young revolutionary guard sneered at him.

"Late as usual," he said contemptuously pushing Adel towards the centre of the building.

Adel was taken through several cream-coloured, low-ceilinged corridors and seated on a hard wooden chair in the middle of a cramped, fly-infested room. It was situated, Adel had noted, somewhere near the feeder ramp of one of the luggage belts behind the arrivals lounge.

"You are a thief," said the militiaman who had guided him. "What's your name?"

"Me?" asked Adel incredulously.

"I'm talking to you, right?" the militiaman sneered.

"Yes. Yes, you are. I'm sorry. You're the brave guardians of our revolution, but I am not a thief," he said, his voice appropriately servile as his eyes scanned the packed room.

"What is your name?" the man slurred, waving his Uzi threateningly.

"Shariat. Mohammed Shariat."

"Your passport," the man demanded, extending his right hand in expectation.

Adel opened his briefcase and gave it to him.

"What's in that cast?" The militiaman pointed his Uzi at Adel's leg.

"The cast?" said Adel, exaggerating his surprise.

"Yes," the man replied, nodding his head. He passed his machine-gun to one of his cronies. "The cast," he mocked as he turned to the passport and thumbed the pages.

Adel hesitated before replying. "Nothing."

"I am only going to ask you once again."

"Nothing." Again Adel's tone registered surprise. "Why?" he asked.

The commando glowered. "I'll ask the questions."

"Yes, but you're accusing me of something. What? You've no right to treat innocent people this way," replied Adel with rising indignation.

The response was more than he sought. The back-handed blow caught him between his mouth and right eye. Instinctively he grasped his face with his right hand; a trickle of blood flowed from the corner of his mouth.

"I don't know what you're talking about," he moaned. "I've got a badly injured leg. That's all. I am . . . was . . . going to Geneva to see a specialist," he said, surreptitiously glancing at his watch. There was still fifteen minutes to go before the scheduled departure time. He had to be careful. He had to stretch out this scene, to cover the possibility of any delay in take-off.

"Do you know how hard it is to get an appointment with Dr Lucien? I don't know what you're talking about. What could be in the cast?" he whined, dabbing at his cut lip with the back of his hand.

The militiamen pointed to one of his subordinates. "Cut the cast off," he barked.

The subordinate extracted a pair of blunt, stained scissors from the desk drawer and approached Adel.

"Are you mad? What in God's name do you intend to do?" cried Adel as he cowered away.

"Hold him still," ordered the leader, pointing to two militiamen. The two men grabbed Adel's arms and shoulders and anchored him to his chair while the man with the scissors attacked the plaster.

Adel writhed in pain but it had little effect. The man half-cut, half-pulled at the cast with little regard to his agony.

It was painful, but it was not as painful as Adel made it look . . . and sound. Halfway through he asked for a glass of water to use up additional time. Fearing an unconscious prisoner, they provided him with a dirty glass of tepid water. As he drank the water he heard the rumble of a departing plane.

Five minutes later the surgery was over; the cast had been cut.

"There's nothing here," said the astonished scissor operator.

"That's impossible," replied their leader, the man who had hit him. "Let me see." He grabbed the cast.

It was dirty, more so inside than out. The activity of the past night had opened the wound again and dried blood caked its inner wall. Dirt and mud, too, had gathered inside the opening around his toes. But there were no jewels.

"Wrong man," said one of the militiamen as he marched from the room. "What a cock-up," he spat.

"Typical Hossein," said another, following him.

There was a list of additional comments but the tittering laughter made them indistinguishable as one by one the men drifted from the room.

"It could be in the plaster itself," said Hossein Mikhchi to one of the handful that remained.

His suggestion was met with rolling eyes and barely suppressed grins.

"*Khoddah yeh aghli beh to beddeh, yeh pouli beh man* – God give you a brain and me some money," said the man Hossein had addressed as he too turned and left the room.

"Now what?" asked one of his two remaining subordinates.

Hossein Mikhchi was visibly perturbed, his confidence shaken. He seemed as distressed by the physical inconvenience he had caused the cripple as by the loss of face before his peers.

"I'll never make it to Geneva in time," said Adel, writhing in pain. "I've missed the flight and the planes are booked solid out of here. My appointment is for tomorrow afternoon. There's no way I'll make it." He buried his head in his hands.

Hossein was embarrassed; he waved his hands in a signal of silence, and swiftly adopted a subservient air.

"Don't worry, sir, I'll get you there," he said as he strode from the room. At the door he stopped. "Just keep quiet, I'll get you there somehow," he repeated before slamming the door behind him. Two guards remained.

"You people do more damage to this beautiful revolution than all the SAVAK agents around. If only Imam Khomeini knew the pain you cause people. How you alienate his followers and give him a bad name," said Adel, careful to use the words of the Imam himself.

The two men looked at each other.

"I want your names. All of you," said Adel, gradually building his feigned anger. "This isn't right. This is not why we threw out the Shah and make no mistake, I'm going to make sure the Imam hears about this incident. Sadegh Ghotbzadeh is my cousin and I will tell him. I'll go to his house tonight or tomorrow and tell him," he repeated.

The two men looked at each other again, suddenly very worried. The threat of the incident reaching one of Khomeini's right-hand men was enough to put the fear of God into any man, militiaman or not.

"Look . . . ah . . . your Excellency, we will put you on the plane tomorrow, there's no need to make a fuss. What's an extra day? This was a mistake. Really it was. Some pimp called us and said you were smuggling jewellery out in your cast. We really didn't mean to harm Your Honour," said one of the two men, a short, bald fellow with a large, rice-fed pot-belly.

"If we can all keep quiet about this mistake," he

continued, "we'll get you on the plane first thing tomorrow morning."

"Fine. Fine. Just get me to Geneva," said Adel. "You can see I'm in pain and need medical treatment."

The plump militiaman left the room. Moments later he reappeared.

"May I have your ticket, sir?"

"It's in my briefcase," Adel replied weakly.

The man opened the briefcase, took out the blue and white Swiss Air ticket and left the room, the door shaking the thin partition walls as it slammed shut.

Adel smiled inwardly. It was working. It was going as he planned.

Ten or fifteen minutes passed before a murmur of voices rose outside. The door opened a few inches, only to close. Then it opened again, more widely, and closed again.

Adel grew nervous. What the hell were they discussing? The voices were too soft and distant for him to hear. It was unlikely that they saw through his ploy. So what was it? Whatever they were discussing out there concerned him and what to do with him. He had to stop it. He had to decide for them.

He let out a bellow of pain and grabbed his leg with both hands, pulling apart the wound. Immediately blood poured out.

The door banged open. "Keep quiet!" hissed Hossein.

"For God's sake let me out of here. I'm bleeding. Let me get to a doctor." Adel rolled his head in pain as the blood oozed from the cut. "Please let me go. The pain is unbearable."

"Your Excellency, I've got you on the same flight tomorrow morning," said Hossein Mikhchi nervously, distressed at the sight of blood.

"I'm sorry for what happened here today; it was a mistake. But I'm going to make it up to you. Tomorrow morning when you come to the airport, we'll speed everything up for you. We'll get you on the plane first. You won't have to go through all the formalities."

He sniffed and turned to his cohorts. "I'd like to talk to this gentleman alone."

He was obviously the leader, but only just; the others shuffled out grudgingly. Hossein waited until they were alone before he turned to face Adel. Then he walked to the door, making certain it was firmly closed before moving closer. He stroked his stubble nervously before speaking.

"I am willing to assist you on one condition," he said quietly, making sure his words did not carry through the paper-thin walls. "That this episode goes no further than this room. If it does –" he paused, the menace in his tone returning – "we will meet again. The problem we face is that the revolution is young. There are many who are traitors to the cause. Some of these heathens are members of the ex-Shah's secret police, and they look for – sometimes invent – ways to make the *pasdaran* militiamen look bad."

He smirked. "It would be a shame if this reached their ears. A shame for you, that is, because I'll place a kilo of heroin in your suitcase and shoot Your Excellency in the balls for being a pusher. Read me?"

Adel shivered at the thought; he had no reason to doubt the man. Every day innocent people were being framed and shot as drug peddlers; it had become standard procedure.

"We understand each other," said Adel, trying to sound aloof.

Hossein stood and looked down at him, hands on hips. "I am sure it is the word of a gentleman. Otherwise Your Excellency won't enjoy our next meeting."

Teheran. Tuesday, October 30: noon.

"*Pesaram*, my son, it has been over twenty-four hours since we put this man under your care and still he has not recovered consciousness. It is a matter of great urgency for the revolution and even to the Imam himself that we learn what came to pass in this satanic plot. We must learn what is behind this attack on God's government. Can you do nothing to wake him?"

The doctor looked at the mullah, the Islamic priest, listening intently, but fighting a losing battle to suppress the nausea brought about by the man's odour. The short, fat man wore thick round eyeglasses that magnified his protruding eyes and he affected a wide grin that belied his severity. The loose dark brown outer cloak he wore, was soiled and dirty; two dark stains extended beneath his armpits and the front was a polka-dot print of uneven design and colour. The residue of the past month's food intake, thought the doctor. His turban had once been white, but that had been some time ago. Now, various shades dulled it greyish yellow and he wore it as he wore his grin, crooked and offensively. Strands of oily, unwashed hair fell unevenly beneath its grimy border on to his forehead.

The doctor was not taken in by the holy man's amicable smile. On the contrary, he was very much aware of Sadegh Khalkhali's well-earned reputation as "The Hanging Judge". Every day for the past year an average of twenty people had been summarily executed: twenty people whose trials consisted of a one-man judge, jury, defence and prosecution, and that man was now sitting in front of him, smiling.

The doctor, like most of his colleagues, was also aware of the man's medical record. In his vocation, as in most, rumours spread quickly. The word had gone round at the very beginning of the revolution that the judge was a lunatic; a psychotic who had spent seven years in an asylum for an insatiable and uncontrollable desire to strangle cats and dogs. But that had been before the Islamic revolution. He had been a psychopath then. Today he was the Minister of Justice.

"Your Excellency," said the doctor with deference.

"The patient has lost both legs and his left arm. He has lost more than half the blood in his body. We have operated on him twice in the past twenty-four hours. He is weak and close to death; he must be given time to recover."

"Doctor," the mullah said patronisingly, "is there nothing you can do to speed his recovery – even if it is only temporary? He has no reason to live. He is a cripple; a lion cannot survive in the jungle on three legs. Is it not possible with all you have so painstakingly learned in your studies in America to give him something to make him conscious, if only for a moment? There are things we must learn, and only he can provide the answers.

"Many have died in this just cause, my son. What is one more life compared with our high goals of an Islamic Republic? God will smile on you and so will I."

Doctor Bahman Chirazi looked at the religious man incredulously. It was antithetical to everything he had learned about the sanctity of human life.

"Does the Holy Book not compel us, Your Excellency, to minister unto the sick and prolong their life?"

The mullah arched his thick dark oily eyebrows, his eyes blazing.

Chirazi's fears mounted; his heart raced and his stomach churned.

Just as suddenly, the mullah's smile returned.

"The good book has many interpretations, my son. It is the overall message that is important for you to understand and that is the establishment of an Islamic Republic – the establishment of God's government through God's own emissaries – of whom I am one.

"Nothing," he bellowed, "must stand in its way. Nothing," he shouted, "is too high a price to pay."

Chirazi looked at the priest's bulging eyes. What the madman was suggesting was murder. He had to stop it.

Beneath the desk top he rubbed his sweaty palms together and tried a different approach.

"Your Excellency, there are a few drugs we could use,

but at this stage they're just too dangerous. They might cause side effects that could kill the patient by inducing a coma or impeding recovery in any number of ways. Getting this vital information would be impossible if that were to happen. Be patient, Your Excellency. We must be careful not to lose him before we gain the knowledge you need."

The mullah's eyes were distant and glazed, his face distorted by a foolish grin.

"Very well, my son . . .," he said after several moments. With his words the grin faded and his complexion turned bright red. Chirazi recognised the symptoms: the man was on the verge of another fit. Then, abruptly, the colour faded and the mullah rose to his full height of five feet.

"Tonight. I'll be back tonight. At ten o'clock. Have him ready then. And you be here too," he snapped, as he turned and stamped out of Chirazi's office. As the man disappeared round the corner, half a dozen or so heavily armed militiamen formed a protective circle around him and escorted him out.

Chirazi closed his eyes in anticipation of their next meeting.

Teheran. Tuesday, October 30: 5.30 p.m.

Michael Adel watched from the ground-floor library overlooking the long driveway as the two men arrived exactly on schedule at five-thirty in the afternoon. As they drew steadily closer in the fading light he watched and waited. With each step they took towards him, his anger mounted.

"Stay cool," he told himself. "It won't be long now."

But it was hard to do. In his mind was a still picture of an old lady lying contorted and dead, her skirt riding high above her waist uncovering spindly withered legs.

He watched the two men draw closer, watched and hated.

"You'll have to forgive me," he said after greeting them. An uneasy stiffness seemed to hang over both men. "I can only offer you tea, or, if you prefer, drinks. I'm afraid I have no help in the house and a poor excuse for a leg, so you'll have to put up with a dirty kitchen. In all this mess, my maid passed away last night. Heart attack, I think, but I couldn't exactly call a doctor."

The doctor glanced at Khan. George Clark made no response.

Suddenly the doctor noticed his leg.

"Where's your cast?" he asked incredulously.

"Oh, that's a long story," replied Adel. He limped through the pantry into the kitchen, followed by the two men.

"My God, let me look at it," said the doctor with genuine concern.

"Plenty of time for that. Make yourselves at home while I get some ice out."

"Let me see it," the doctor insisted, bending to touch it.

"All in good time," Adel repeated, making light of his discomfort. He took some ice from the refrigerator and glanced through the clear glass of the vegetable compartment. The Walther PPK pistol lay cocked and ready.

"Actually, that's why I asked you here. The leg's a mess, I'm afraid."

"What the hell happened? What did you do?" asked the doctor.

Adel sat down, visibly relieved to take the weight off his aching limb. "I ran into a man who didn't like me."

He poured three straight whiskies and added the ice. "There's no soda in the house but help yourselves to water," he said, pushing across the pitcher on the table.

The doctor fetched his black satchel and busied himself with cleaning the messy wound, mumbling while Adel recounted an abridged version of the airport incident. George Clark said nothing; he sipped his drink and stared blankly at Adel.

"Make the cast a bit large, doctor. There's a lot I've got to get in there this time," said Adel, pointing to his lower thigh, just above the knee.

Clark nibbled at the dead skin around a fingernail. "You're not leaving without our knowing?" he asked coolly.

The time was approaching, thought Adel with pleasure. He looked back at Clark coldly, confident that he was powerless; as long as the tapes were out of his reach he was impotent.

"Where does it say I have to let you know what I'm doing?" he demanded.

Clark shifted in his seat.

"That should do it," said the doctor, patting the new cast.

"How long before it comes off?"

"You must have been a premature baby, Adel. Give the damned thing a chance to heal. There may even be a nick on the bone for all I know. Just remember to get it attended to properly as soon as you reach London."

"If I live that long," countered Adel, his eyes briefly turning back to Clark. He stood up and measured the cast for size.

"That feels a whole lot better. Now, let me top up your drinks."

Neither man objected. Adel opened the refrigerator and felt the ice-cold stab of gunmetal in his palm. He turned swiftly.

"Get up, you bastards."

The look on the two men's faces showed their fear. The doctor was stupefied with fright. His eyes glared, wide and unbelieving, his mouth gaped and his lips quivered. Slowly, as if time was not a rapidly depleting resource, he lifted his hands towards his shoulders and shielded his chest with two shivering open palms.

Clark reacted differently. His eyes reflected his inner horror only momentarily. Then they narrowed and took on the air of deep thought; a man calculating and looking for solutions. His body tensed, ready, while his fingers curled into a ball.

"Out that door," said Adel, pointing.

Neither man replied; they followed his instructions, and moved towards the opening.

There wasn't far to go. Behind the kitchen, some thirty yards in the back courtyard, lay the building's sewer: a deep well that soaked up the refuse, sucking it deep into the earth.

"Your grave is a sewer and it's too goddamned good for you, you mother-fuckers!" he said as he forced the two men at gunpoint towards the large, round wooden door covering the well.

"She was over seventy years old and you killed her. Why? Why, you bastards? The tapes were safe. You knew I had to turn them over to you sooner or later. I had no choice. Why did you kill her?" he asked, his anger rising as images of Mariam's twisted, lifeless body flashed before his eyes.

"I . . . I told him she couldn't stand a second dose. He forced me to . . ." the doctor pleaded, his voice quivering as he stepped forward towards Adel.

The roar of the gun cut him short. The bullet smacked his body three inches above the left rib-cage, tearing his heart out and blasting the corpse backwards to lie in a bloody heap on the damp grass.

"And now you, Khan. The man who would be tough."

Clark's eyes were wide with fright now as he turned back from the doctor's still body. He was deathly white. Slowly he dropped his hands from above his head, knowing it made no difference. The second roar was a carbon copy of the first. It ripped George Clark's heart to shreds.

Adel slowly lowered his right hand and dropped the gun. Then he collapsed on the ground beside it. He was drained. Spent. And suddenly very lonely. He looked at the two contorted figures on the ground and knew it wasn't over.

Slowly, with the last of his energy, he limped towards the two crumpled figures, opened the large, old, wooden door to the deep well and moved back to George Clark. Grasping the corpse by its armpits, he somehow dragged it, half-off, half-on the ground, to pitch it down the dark, bottomless shaft.

The doctor's carcass was heavier and even more unwieldy. Adel had neither the strength nor the will to lift it. He sat on the ground and dragged the bloody hulk inch by inch. The distance was not great, perhaps five yards, but the load was awkward and heavy, and each heave sent a stab of agony through his leg.

He lay back a minute and rested, waiting for the lightness in his head to pass and his stomach to settle. Then with renewed energy he dragged himself up and twisted, turned and pushed the corpse until finally it disappeared down the shaft.

It was over, he told himself as he lay back, staring at the dark, turbulent night sky. It was over. For ever. He could not spend another night in this house.

He dragged himself up from the ground and limped painfully towards the house. Inside, he called for a taxi and while he waited for it to arrive, packed his small suitcase, including the passport and ticket he had used that morning. He stuffed the two tapes, the money and two additional passports – his own and another alias – into the cast, but despite the additional room the doctor had allowed, they pressed painfully against his flesh. He tried to adjust them to a more comfortable position and then limped down the long gravel driveway. At the gate he turned to take a final look at his family home.

Melli Hospital, Teheran. Tuesday, October 30: 10.00 p.m.

Melli Hospital is situated in the heart of Teheran, just south of the main east-west commercial thoroughfare of the old Shah Reza Avenue, now renamed Avenue of the Revolution. Its driveway is narrow and threads between two huge bank buildings, Bank Melli, the government-owned commercial bank, and Bank Markazi, the nation's central bank. Once behind these massive buildings, the road opens on to stunning floral gardens of immense proportions. It also passes within a stone's throw of the small fortress that houses the priceless treasures of the Empire of Iran; the treasures liberated in 1739 by a victorious Nadir Shah who, in one lightning swoop, relieved India of the wealth it had amassed over 348 years.

Shortly after ten o'clock a silver-blue Mercedes Benz 600 – one of a fleet formerly used by members of the Imperial household – screeched right, off Ferdowsi Avenue, escorted by four olive-green Range Rovers carrying a personal squad of militiamen. The fleet of cars sped between the two bank buildings leaving behind a trail of spattered mud and water.

Ayatollah Sadegh Khalkhali did not like being late, especially when he had given his word. A man's word was important if he was to be respected. It should be taken seriously and obeyed. Yes, that was it, he thought. The key to success was to be taken seriously, and now no one joked about him. Oh, there were still rumours about his affinity for blood, how he strangled cats and dogs for enjoyment. But they were taken out of context, voiced by jealousy and spite.

He didn't necessarily enjoy shedding blood, but he was not frightened by it either. The important thing was the use of punishment and discipline to establish an acceptable social order in which right and wrong, good and bad, justice, equality, were based upon the rules of Allah. Not on evil Napoleonic and Anglo-Saxon traditions imported from abroad.

His enemies – and they were all the Shah's agents, his enemies – refused to understand that. They were jealous and frightened. And why were they frightened, he asked himself. Because he spoke the words of the Holy Book and punished as the Holy Book prescribed. They knew he was a man of his word. They knew he would kill every one of them.

He looked out of the window as the floodlit landscape of a beautiful rose-studded park sped by.

"Where are we?" he barked.

The driver cleared his throat. "Just entering the hospital's gardens, Holy One."

"Looks like Hamadan," Khalkhali replied, recalling his home town in west Iran. Well, it was not really his home town. He had been born in Khalkhal in Azerbaijan province in the north of Iran – hence his family name – but his family had moved to Hamadan while he was still an infant and that was where he considered home. He pictured the city's beautiful snowcapped mountains and its rich green pastures. It was so different to this acrid hell-hole of a capital the Shah had built.

And his home. He remembered that too: his grey, wrinkled, doting mother who had been forced by his father to sign the warrant to commit him to the mental asylum.

As always, the thought of his father sickened him. He had been like the others, stupid and ignorant and brainwashed by the Shah's propaganda. The old man had never understood Islam. What good was industry and wealth when women had lost their shame, walking the streets virtually bare-breasted, with legs exposed? When Western materialism was destroying traditional family life and devotion to God?

Khalkhali felt the old feeling returning; it happened

whenever he thought of his father. His head throbbed – that was the most prominent sensation – but he also felt a sudden, almost unbearable heat engulf his body, and an extraordinary tension build up within him. He had first had this feeling when eighteen – or was it nineteen? It had been followed by a full-scale depression, uncontrollable and irrepressible. For a while he began to believe that perhaps his father was right; perhaps he was not normal.

The dejection had gone on for months before finally he had turned for guidance to the house of the Lord.

As luck would have it, it was the best decision he had ever made. The wise man had dismissed his concern with the wave of a hand and a knowing smile. "It is, my son, a normal occurrence in men of unusual intelligence," the Holy Man had said. "The sign of depth of character, of intense commitment." Khalkhali smiled as he recalled the happiness he had felt that night as he left the Holy Man's modest residence. No, he was not insane; he was a man of unusual intelligence.

The limousine swept up to the main entrance of the hospital. Khalkhali stepped from the vehicle and strode towards the building.

Ayatollah (literally, the "Sign of God") Khalkhali did not knock as he entered Dr Chirazi's seventh-floor office.

"Good evening, my son," he greeted as he burst in. "I pray the patient is prepared."

"There . . . there's been little change in his condition," Chirazi stammered, taken aback by the sudden entrance.

"Ah, but we will proceed, will we not, doctor?" The question was rhetorical as Khalkhali rubbed his hands enthusiastically. "Time is short, my son."

"Your Excellency, I'm concerned that the shock of trying to revive him – even temporarily – will kill him," Chirazi ventured.

Khalkhali dismissed his concern with the wave of a hand. "Then that is the will of God. You need not concern yourself with such matters. All that is required of you is to revive him for long enough for me to learn what happened in that house. What happens after that is unimportant."

Chirazi hesitated before speaking. "In my profession, Your Excellency, there are certain technical requirements that have to be fulfilled before I can do such a thing."

Khalkhali glanced at his watch. "Such as?" he snapped.

"I need the approval of one of his family, his next of kin, someone. I cannot take such a responsibility upon myself. It's unethical and illegal."

"I am the law," bellowed Khalkhali, feeling an intense heat spread through his body. "Do not speak to me of law. I decide here what is or is not against the law," he shouted, prodding his chest vigorously with his stubby index finger. "I will sign the paper you need. Give it to me."

Chirazi looked up at the priest. The bulging, maniacal eyes stared fixed and unblinking at him. The face was suffused with blood, the outstretched hand quivering in anger.

Chirazi knew that there was no choice; the man was uncontrollable. He lowered his head and held out the standard "Waiver of Responsibility" form.

Salim Jabeh knew he was in the twilight of his life. He knew because he had seen it so often before. For the past ten years that was all he had seen; pain and death and sorrow and hurt. But now, from up close, there was, curiously, a peculiarly satisfying sensation about it. A feeling of contentment, of calm. There was no more that he could do in his life. He had achieved his aim; he had dealt a blow of immense magnitude to his enemies and he did not mind dying now.

Strangely, his mind seemed separated from his body. It was alive, clear, sharp, while his body lay passive.

Even the smallest detail of his life flashed before his eyes. And yet his limbs refused to obey the simplest instruction. He did not try to fool himself. He knew why. He had seen too much not to know. His right hand was all that remained.

In fact, he had been lucky to last so long. The others in his training unit had long since departed. All of them had been killed or injured or imprisoned in various different missions; mostly against Israel, but some against Israel's benefactor, America, or one of its other surrogates.

The thought of the United States brought contentment. He had dealt them a blow they would not soon forget. A blow, he hoped, that would be the first of many against the imperialists.

In his last moments Salim recalled the minute details of memories which had been too unbearable to contemplate before. His mother and father blown to pieces by an Israeli bomb, the confiscation of his home, indeed the confiscation of his country. The poverty of his two sisters driven from Palestine to a refugee camp in Jordan; their new and permanent home a torn and tattered tent from which there was no hope of escape. The sorrow, the frustration and finally the hate that drove him to revenge. The long and arduous training, the small, meaningless missions for the PLO, and finally to their first major success – Vienna and Carlos. Together they had kidnapped the OPEC ministers. Carlos had received most of the credit and all the publicity, but he had done his part and done it well. So well, in fact, that he had been transferred to the Organisation's most ambitious project: the mission to topple America's pet bulldog – the Shah of Iran.

Now that too had been a success; America's bulwark in the Middle East had been crushed. Only Israel and Anwar Sadat were left. He would miss those, he would miss the dismantling of that impudence, the killing of that traitor. He would miss the establishment of a free, sovereign and secular Palestine.

The Arabs had expected so much from the Americans. But they had turned their backs on the Arabs in their hour of need. They had sold them out to the Jews. They had taken his country lock, stock and barrel, and given it to the Zionists. And now, too late, America, that nation of merchants, had finally realised that sometimes the price of betrayal was high.

The day was not far off when the Arab nations would unite and not a drop of oil would flow to that nation of salesmen. Then let us see what that industrial might is all about, he thought.

There was only one difference between the Russians and the Americans: the Russians knew they were bastards and their regime acted accordingly. Americans . . . ah . . . the Americans, he thought. They called themselves the good guys, people who believed in liberty and freedom and equality and justice and human rights. But that was only an image created to fool. In reality, they lived, breathed, understood and cared about only one thing – money. Profits and bottom lines, cost efficiency and benefit, red and black, acceptable returns on investment and balance of payments. They were a nation of salesmen, a nation who understood quantity – but never quality. They had no values. Not in ethics, not in culture and not in principles. He had been taught all this in the practical education classes of the refugee camps in which he had grown up, and life had borne out his teachers.

His thoughts and dreams and reminiscences were suddenly interrupted. Distantly he heard a voice.

"Salim."

There. He heard it again.

"Salim, my son."

He tried to stir, but his body spurned his instructions. His brain was active and alive yet his eyes refused to focus. He tried more diligently, again the lenses seemed mismatched, they zoomed and retracted in a constant blur. Only a semblance of movement, of life, filtered through.

"Salim . . . Salim. You must answer me. It is very important."

He mustered all his strength and moved his lips, hoping a sound emerged.

Mehrabad airport, Teheran. Tuesday, October 30: midnight

"He's here," said the young militiaman.

"Who?" asked Hossein Mikhchi indifferently as he flicked the pages of the daily circulated list of names entitled "Enemies of God".

"The man with the bad leg."

Hossein Mikhchi looked up from his papers casually, his eyes distant and bored. "He's early, isn't he? It's only just after midnight. His flight doesn't leave for another seven hours."

"Yes, and he looks in poor shape," replied the militiaman.

"Where is he?"

"Sitting in the corner near the Swiss Air counter."

"*Khodah margesh bedeh*!" said Hossein. "That's right next to the police office, isn't it? They'd just love to cause another scandal about us."

He rose and crossed to the window, where he dislodged a piece of jagged glass from the broken pane.

"What time does the plane arrive?" he asked.

"No idea," shrugged the militiaman.

Hossein looked at Samad Nafti. He thought: The man's useless, but at least he's trustworthy. He has no ambition and is therefore unlikely to pull a fast one. He thinks small and all he wants is to move his wife and daughter from that desert village in Khuzestan to Teheran. He had spoken to Hossein about applying for housing in one of the Shah's old army camps. Of course Hossein could do nothing to help but he had promised the man a house. And he knew that he was Samad's only "contact". So Samad would do as he was told.

"Samad, find out exactly what time the plane lands. Then get one of the Swiss Air officials and check this man on right away. The minute the plane lands, get him on board and out of harm's way. In the meantime, keep him out of sight. Check to see which of the offices are empty and hide him there. Whatever happens, I don't want him limping about the place. With his connections he may run into someone and blab his mouth off and that's the last thing we need. Most of all, don't let the police get hold of him. Those bastards can't be trusted; they're all monarchists."

Samad looked at Hossein. He knew that what they were talking about had nothing to do with the revolution or untrustworthy police. It had to do with Hossein's mistake yesterday and the fear of it going higher.

But he didn't care; he had nothing to lose and everything to gain.

"No problem," he said. "With your permission, it might be wiser to keep him out of this building altogether. Maybe in one of the empty private plane hangars would be the best place. They're very safe; no one ever goes into them."

Hossein studied Samad's rough, weatherbeaten face. Perhaps the boy wasn't as stupid as he looked. The hangars were an excellent hiding place and only a stone's throw from where the Swiss Air flight boarded.

"Use the Pars Air Hangar. That's the closest and it's deserted."

Samad Nafti nodded.

"Oh, and Samad," Hossein added. "Keep this to yourself. There's no need to tell anyone about it. Not even the rest of the boys. Just get him out of here; make sure he leaves. If anyone asks any questions refer them to me. Got that?"

"Yes, sir," said Samad.

Mehrabad airport: 3.45 a.m.

For the first time in days Michael Adel relaxed. He was warm and comfortable and, he assured himself, relatively safe. The concrete hangar was well equipped; it had bunk beds, a functioning shower, toilet facilities and a small kitchen. All he needed now, he thought, was a long stiff drink.

Samad Nafti, Adel had discovered after only a few minutes of conversation, was not a devoted revolutionary; in fact, he was hardly a revolutionary at all. Like many others in Iran, he was an opportunist. To him the revolution was merely a propitious event which offered a golden, once-only opportunity for a leg up in life. He could climb from labourer's son to whatever level his cunning – and fortune – would carry him. And Samad was well equipped to handle it. Subservience, or the ability to pretend it, was the essential quality and he had combined this basic ingredient with disarming wit and an agile, if uneducated, mind.

But to Adel, Samad Nafti was a likeable fellow. Twice he had apologised profusely for "any pain or inconvenience my colleagues caused your leg yesterday". He had taken him through the immigration and various other checkpoints speedily. Along the way he had stopped and picked up a backgammon set and commandeered a jeep to spare Adel the long and painful walk to the hangar.

Adel was genuinely grateful; it had been an agonising twelve days. That was all it had been from the moment Anderson had shown up in Cannes. Twelve unimaginable days, of which the last three had been unbearable. But it was nearly over now, he told himself. This was the end of it. Three more hours and he'd be out of this madhouse, tapes and all.

His optimism, however, was short-lived. The thought of the tapes reminded him of Bell.

By now the US Embassy in Iran would be concerned about the disappearance of two of their staff. They would have automatically linked their absence to him. The two men would have logged their visit to his house; departure time, mode of travel, destination and estimated duration of a visit being routine procedure. By now the responsible junior embassy officials would have informed their department heads, who would have communicated with Bell, who in turn would have alerted half of Europe to be on the lookout for him.

And he wasn't ready to see Bell yet. No, he had to insure himself before he did that. He contemplated his options. He had a choice: either he could change flights during the stopover in Damascus, or he could go on to Geneva. The difference being . . .

The door of the pilot's quarters burst open, shattering his thoughts. Adel turned, startled.

Abruptly his heart skipped a beat as his body tensed. A raging, wild-eyed Hossein glared at him from a distance of three yards. He towered above Adel, hands on hips, eyes darting.

Adel considered trying to break the tension but thought better of it. From the little he had learned about Hossein, he was an intimidator; an arrogant, brazen street tough who would bludgeon his target into submission if he sensed weakness.

"Passport," snapped Hossein. Gone was the forced politeness.

Adel felt his nerves pinch as he fidgeted with his briefcase. What the hell could have gone wrong?

Hossein Mikhchi went through the small plastic-coated booklet page by page, scrutinising the various identifying marks. The document Adel was now using was one of the new, post-revolutionary variety, dark brown with gold bordering. Stamped on the cover, in gold, were the words "Government of the Islamic Republic of Iran Passport", in Farsi, French and English.

Adel was not worried about the document's authenticity; he had inspected it carefully. What unnerved him was the possibility of another interrogation, perhaps even a body search. This time the tapes were on him. There would be no escape. He eyed the unarmed Hossein, then glanced over at Sumad's Uzi lying on the counter several feet away.

The blond man. It had to be the blond man, thought Adel, a sickening feeling in his throat. He had recovered and talked.

Hossein Mikhchi clutched the passport as he knotted his hands together, cracking his fingers one by one. After some hesitation he crossed over to Samad and started whispering to him. He tucked Adel's passport firmly into Samad's breast pocket, shot a look at Adel and strutted out of the room, slamming the door behind him.

"It's chaos," said Samad Nafti, raising his hands in helplessness. "Every day there's a crisis."

"What's going on?" asked Adel in as calm a voice as he could muster.

"Seems a man blew up one of the *komitehs* in the north of town and killed half the militiamen in the building before making off with something or other. Today he's the hot item, everybody's looking for him. The only problem is, they don't know who he is, or what he looks like. All they know is his name."

"What is his name?"

"Adel."

Michael Adel cursed himself again for not having followed Allon's instructions more closely: *"If there is any doubt, just remember, it's you or them. Don't leave anything to luck. Kill if necessary but don't leave an iota to chance, not an atom. You'll regret it; it'll come back at you. It always does."*

"So why is your friend Hossein so het up at us?"

"He just wants you out of here. I'm supposed to get you on the plane during the *namaz* – morning prayers – when there are fewer people around. With the increased security because of this character Adel, Hossein's worried you'll be discovered. He doesn't want to have to explain ripping a cast off an invalid."

Teheran – south-side. Wednesday, October 31: 5.00 a.m.

The bright winter sun had only just started to cast its long early morning shadows upon the capital's deserted streets when the two young militiamen arrived at Ayatollah Sadegh Khalkhali's modest residence near the rail tracks. Once this area, with its coppersmiths, spice merchants and rug dealers, had been the hub of the metropolis but that was before the well-to-do had migrated north, towards the cool, scenic skirts of the Alborz Mountains. Now it was a sprawl of tumbling mud brick houses, dilapidated tea-houses and fruit and vegetable stalls.

The trip from the northern tip of the sprawling city to the south-side took the two men over an hour. Figuratively they went back in time, back at least two centuries to a medieval squalor the more fortunate northern dwellers of the city had long since forgotten, or at least chosen to ignore.

They had made the trip separately, from different starting points, but they arrived at the heavily armed building within minutes of each other.

The fraternal familiarity of the Iranian guards did not exempt either of the two men from a thorough search; the Ayatollah's Palestinian "advisers" – who even after years of close coopération did not leave certain details to their Iranian brothers – insisted upon the formalities.

After the close scrutiny, the two men were shown into a drab room. Its main feature was a cheap, worn Gashghai tribal rug of orange, brown and red design. A small dilapidated wooden table was the only furniture the room possessed. On it stood a chipped, smoked glass ashtray adorned with the inscription, "Royal Teheran Hilton".

The two men were informed that they had been excused morning prayers by the Holy Man himself and were left in the musty room to await his pleasure. After only the briefest exchange, they sat quietly on the floor, thankful for a few moments' rest; they had not slept now for close to thirty-six hours and the prospect was not promising. At times like this when the Holy Man showed abnormal energy, he expected the same from his disciples. Perhaps more.

Shortly after five-thirty a.m. their brief respite came to an end. The Ayatollah's new adjutant, an erstwhile comrade in arms who for the past six weeks had been withdrawn from the troubled streets to the more pleasant and less dangerous duties of his uncle's offices, opened the door and aroused them.

"*Baradarha*, brothers, he is ready for you," he smiled, making the event a matter of some significance. Without further word the Ayatollah's nephew showed them through the dark grey corridor and into the Holy Man's office.

The large room was, like the rest of the house, sparsely decorated. A huge, recently "liberated", antique Kashan silk carpet covered the entire floor. At the far end of the room, in the centre, the Holy Man sat cross-legged on the floor; opposite him rested three tall fair-haired men, obviously Westerners. Their legs, unaccustomed to lengthy periods in a semi-lotus position, seemed tangled and uncomfortable. It was a far cry from the plush facilities of their European news bureau headquarters.

". . . therefore is not necessary to try criminals. Once a criminal's identity has been established he should be taken out and executed." Khalkhali said in heavily accented English.

The two militiamen stood hesitantly near the door while the Holy Man spoke.

One of the three journalists, a fair-haired, bespectacled man asked, "But what if there's a mistake? What if an innocent man is executed? A case of, say, mistaken identity? It's more likely, you must admit, Your Worship, without proper safeguards to establish guilt."

"No matter," responded the Holy Man earnestly. "That is of no consequence. In such case victim is blessed. He will go straight to heaven."

Khalkhali looked at the two militiamen. He waved permission for them to enter, indicating a corner of the room for them to occupy.

"This won't take long," he said to them in Farsi before turning his attention back to the three foreign correspondents who were carefully taking notes between expressive glances at each other.

"My friends call me 'Wrath of God', my enemies 'Cat Killer', but both groups respect me, gentlemen. I do not care what they call me. I have duty to fulfil. To put it in – how you say? nutshell? – I have a most difficult yet gratifying job. I am Iran's Islamic Revolutionary Court. It is heavy burden to carry, but vengeance is religious duty and I am determined to rid Iran, and indeed world, of those guilty of 'corruption on earth'. Those so far executed can be likened to Nazi war criminals. They had done evil and incurred wrath of God. Like Nazis, they have been justly punished. Your nations authorised Nuremberg trials, gentlemen, so you understand evil, do you not?"

He did not wait for a reply.

"All of this is simply first phase; we have only just started to cleanse. We will export this purification and spread word of God to entire world, even to your countries, gentlemen," he said waving his hand in an arc to include all three men.

"But for time being," he went on, slapping his knee to indicate the end of the audience, "you will appreciate that there is much to be done right here; much that I must attend to. Regretfully, we must terminate this meeting. Hopefully we meet again in very near future to continue these thoughts. Perhaps even, we will meet in your countries," he said, bursting into a loud cackle. "But if that is to be case you must accustom yourself to working these early hours of day, gentlemen. You all look exhausted." He bellowed with laughter.

The three journalists stood up eagerly. Under the circumstances, there seemed to be no appropriate final question to ask.

Once the door had closed Khalkhali turned quickly to the two men and motioned them closer. His expression turned businesslike and sombre as he switched to Farsi.

"Mehdi, what did you find at the airport?" he asked anxiously, motioning the man to sit before him on the carpet.

He needed a crisis to show Imam Khomeini his worth once again. His enemies had greatly influenced Khomeini against him recently, telling the Imam lies about his unpopularity, his insanity, his exaggerations. He prayed for a positive response.

"Nothing suspicious. Nothing worth mentioning."

"Well, mention it anyway," barked Khalkhali.

"Ah . . . well . . . the man out there – a Hossein Mikhchi – is most uncooperative. I don't think he wishes to be connected to our brotherhood. He's arrogant and difficult and I think he might well be communist."

Khalkhali smiled. "His time will come. Very soon now, it will come," he said turning to the second man. "You . . . Farhad. Did you get the file?"

"Yes, sir," the young man replied, placing a thin plastic folder on the coffee table in front of the Ayatollah.

Khalkhali took the file and opened it. Holding the papers close to his eyes, he squinted through the thick, curved glass of his spectacles.

Farhad Samandar stuttered, unsure of himself. "After . . . after I collected the file I . . . I went over to the Farmanieh *komiteh* headquarters to take a look for myself. I enquired around and found something interesting, sir."

"Well?" said Khalkhali his eyes scanning the file.

"This man . . . Adel . . . his house is only one away from the *komiteh* headquarters, sir."

Khalkhali looked up abruptly.

"And?"

"Well, I went to his house, Holy One; there was blood everywhere, especially near the *qanat* entrance. I also found a gun near a well and from the smell of it, I think it's been fired recently."

"Good. Good," said Khalkhali, his voice distant but his eyes alert. "That's very good."

Samandar took a photograph from his pocket.

"This may prove useful too, sir. It's a picture of Adel. It's signed here," Samandar said pointing to the inscription: To my beloved parents. Michael.

Khalkhali peered intently at the photograph.

"One other thing, sir," Samandar interrupted.

"What, my son?" Khalkhali asked kindly, looking up at the man.

"There's an American Embassy car parked near the house, in an alley. At least I think it's one of theirs; it looks exactly like the ones they use. The black four-door sedan type with no hub-caps or white walls. Only the Americans use those."

"Does it have diplomatic plates?" asked Khalkhali.

"Yes but I haven't been able to gain access to the vehicle registration office. They don't open till eight."

Khalkhali nodded and smiled contentedly. He had found the crisis he needed. Spies sent into Iran, secret tapes stolen from a *komiteh* headquarters, killings. And now an American Embassy car in the neighbourhood. Yes, he thought. With a little embellishment, this would do very well. As a conspiracy it would do very well indeed.

He held his smile as he pushed the photograph towards Mehdi.

"Have this circulated right away," he said. "I want

this picture in every air terminal, train station and border crossing in the next twelve hours. I want it stuck on every wall, in every shop, in every government building of every town and village in the country. I want this man caught and brought to me immediately. You can leave right away and drop everything else you're doing. This is of utmost importance."

Mehdi stood and left the room quickly. As he did so Khalkhali turned to Samandar.

"What do you think the next step is?" he asked.

"I'd like to search his house. I think we might find some interesting things in there."

"Yes . . . yes," Khalkhali answered distantly, preoccupied with planning how, what and when to tell the Imam to make it most effective.

"I would also suggest we learn more about that car parked in the alley. We should contact the American Embassy to learn more . . ."

Khalkhali snapped out of his thoughts.

"Samandar, I'm putting you in charge of this. Search the house. Find out whatever you can. Here" – he threw the SAVAMA secret police file in front of his deputy – "read this and find him. Get those tapes. I must inform the Imam himself of an American plot against our revolution.

"In the meantime I don't want anyone to know about this. Not the Prime Minister nor Bani-Sadr nor Yazdi nor Ghotbzadeh. Especially not Defence Minister Chamran or General Fardoust. Keep it to yourselves; discuss it only with me. Some of these men are foreign agents," he said as he rose and walked towards the door.

Mehrabad airport, Teheran.
Wednesday, October 31: 7.30 a.m.

The whirr of the DC8's four engines blasted through the open hatch as the pilot revved once again. Over and over he had gunned the motors in a bid to arrest the needless last-minute inspection the *pasdaran* militiamen were conducting. It was seven-thirty: already the flight was half an hour late, and it went against the methodical grain of the Swiss pilot. There was no obvious reason for the harassment either; the passengers had already undergone countless thorough searches prior to boarding, yet still the scraggy militiamen walked up and down the aisle brandishing their firearms. The engines calmed to idle again; waste, too, was anathema to the Swiss.

Michael Adel sat in the left-hand window seat of the front row of the first-class cabin. He sat quietly, hiding his anxiety and watching the constant flow of traffic on the tarmac below; each arriving vehicle brought fresh tension, each parting one a measure of relief. He moved his unwieldy cast to a more comfortable position and glanced at the elderly man sitting beside him. Mercifully the man did not appear to be the talkative type and Adel turned away to the oval window as the high-pitched whine of the engines picked up again. Relax, he told himself. Just a few more minutes and it will all be over. But still he could not quite overcome his nerves.

To occupy his mind and drown the pain in his leg, Adel stared beyond the airport into the distance, where the sun bounced off the snowcapped Alborz Mountains, giving the long rugged range a shimmering coat of stately majesty.

"Mr Adel," a voice beside him said.

Adel snapped his head towards the old man. But he

was gone. In his seat sat Samad Nafti, a 9mm Browning, partially concealed beneath his olive denim jacket, showed its ugly nozzle in his hand.

"Mr Adel. That's your *real* name, isn't it?"

Adel did not, could not, answer. His heart thumped furiously at his ribcage.

"A few minutes ago a jeep brought this to the plane." Samad thrust a folded piece of paper into Adel's lap. "That's you, isn't it?"

Adel's hands shook as he unfolded the paper to its full eight and a half by eleven inch size; he recognised it immediately. It was an old picture taken in Huntington Beach, California in 1963; it had sat on his father's desk at the house, a gift from Adel to his parents on his twentieth birthday. It was an old picture, but its significance was up to date. They knew everything; who he was, how he had broken into Mahmoudi's house, the tapes, everything.

Samad's voice interrupted his thoughts. "The poster you have in your hand is one of the first batch to be distributed. In a few hours there'll be more pictures of you plastered to the walls than Imam Khomeini's, if that's possible. There'll be no way out for you."

Adel bit his lip and nodded. There was little else he could do. He tried to think but his mind refused to function. He barely heard the young man's words as wildly impractical ideas raced through his head. He was literally cornered on the plane and there was nothing he could do about it.

Abruptly the man's words broke through the nightmare.

"But I'm willing to make a deal with you, Mr Adel."

What the hell was he talking about? In his terror and panic, Samad's words made no sense. He nodded again but avoided Samad's eyes, and shrugged his shoulders helplessly. It was easier than talking, and it bought time.

Samad looked around in search of prying ears before continuing. "These people are never going to last," he whispered. "Sooner or later their time will come. If we're lucky the Americans or English will do it. If not, the Russians will."

Samad stopped as a militiaman went by. He looked up at his comrade and smiled casually. "I'll be right with you," he said.

He waited for the man to gain distance. "It cannot last much longer like this," he said, turning back to Adel. "It's a mess."

He stopped, waiting for a reaction. His rugged features revealed a sharpness previously hidden by the leathery skin.

Adel nodded, a brief nervous smile forming at his lips.

"It's a simple deal, Mr Adel," said Samad flatly. "You look after me when the country returns to civilised government, when people like you return. You look after me then. Tell them I worked with this mob but that I never killed or hurt anyone. You look after me then and you're free to go now."

Adel looked away from Samad. He couldn't believe it . . . the boy was letting him go. Offering him his life back on a half-baked promise of future help.

"That and ten thousand dollars cash."

Adel stared at Samad. It made more sense now. Even though he didn't have the ten thousand, he felt an ease come over him; he was on familiar ground; he knew the figure was negotiable.

"I don't have that much money," he said, eager to capitalise on his luck and conclude the negotiations.

Samad Nafti looked at him, his expression cold and hard. "How much do you have?"

"Five thousand. I can give you four thousand," said Adel, leaving some leeway for Samad to haggle in true Iranian fashion.

Samad held his hard expression for a moment. Then he grinned, "I suppose you need a little pocket money. Make it four thousand five hundred and you can owe me the rest."

Adel hid his relief. "What about the others?" he

whispered, glancing down the aisle at the other militiamen.

"Leave that to me," said Samad confidently.

Adel hesitated a moment. "I have to use the lavatory to get to it."

"Okay, but hurry," said Samad nervously.

Adel moved to stand but Samad's powerful arm held him back.

"If you have any ideas, take a good look around you," he whispered. "You don't stand a chance."

Adel had no ideas; he returned quickly and as he sat he passed the bulky envelope that had been in his cast to Samad.

"I hope it's all there." Samad measured the weight of the manilla envelope. He looked at Adel and started to open it, but his action was cut short by the approach of two militiamen.

"Your passport," said one of them as he drew closer.

Adel felt for the breast pocket of his leather windbreaker but again Samad's arm stopped him.

"This gentleman is all right," said Samad as he stood to face the men on equal footing.

"We have instructions to inspect everyone's passport and hand luggage. Your passport, please," insisted the militiaman.

"Why?" asked Samad Nafti. "They've been searched ten times."

The man shrugged coldly. "Orders."

"Come here." Samad motioned the two men closer.

They huddled closer and Samad whispered. As he did so the men's brusqueness seemed to wilt. Their eyes darted, and they seemed flustered. But the inaudible conversation continued.

Adel felt a feverish sweat break out on his body as the debate went on.

"I'm sure His Excellency understands," said Samad more loudly, at last. He turned towards Adel and his face suggested relief as his eyes urged Adel to put their minds at rest.

"No problem brothers," croaked Adel. He cleared his throat and smiled as casually as he could. "It's good to see men of your calibre, your dedication."

The two men smiled back and nodded the traditional Iranian bow of servility before moving away nervously.

Samad waited for them to disappear before sitting. He looked at Adel, a wide grin on his face.

"I told them you were one of Khomeini's relatives on a delicate mission to Europe," he said, obviously pleased with himself.

Adel did not reply and Samad continued in the same serious tone he had used before. "I don't know what you've done and I don't want to know. Maybe you deserve to die, maybe you don't. But it doesn't make any difference here. They kill you first and then ask questions."

Adel looked at the luggage rack above his head. Then he turned towards Samad, a relief he had never felt before surging through him.

"What about you? What will they do to you when they find out?" he asked.

"I have my orders. They're to get you out of here without any more problems. And that's what I'm doing."

He turned and looked up and down the aisle, then back at Adel. For the briefest of moments the two men's eyes met before a small, almost imperceptible smile appeared at the corners of Samad's hard mouth. Then, suddenly, he was gone.

Five minutes later the plane was airborne.

London. Wednesday, October 31: 11.30 a.m.

If there is an airport in the world built for inconvenience it is London's Heathrow, thought Adel as he hobbled down its drab, seemingly endless corridors to the terminal building. He anticipated with dread the long delays still to come at immigration and customs control, and glumly predicted that with the Iranian passport he was using there would be additional unnecessary aggravations. But he forced himself on, thinking of Sam and Natalie and how close he was to them. He told himself, too, that good luck was not everlasting, that it came and went in cycles. And his had lasted a long time now.

It had lasted through Damascus, where he had changed planes, opting to continue his trip with a new identity and on a different flight. To offset the computers that relayed their information around the world to every major intelligence agency, he had ignored his booking through to Geneva. He had simply stood up and left the aircraft with the other departing passengers.

The Swiss Air flight had arrived in Damascus a few minutes after eight in the morning local time, nine-thirty Teheran time, six London time. In the terminal, concealed in a battered cubicle in the men's room on the ground floor, his privacy guaranteed by a stench so foul that it discouraged the idly inquisitive, he had discarded the Iranian passport in the name of Mohammed Shariat, first smudging the name and number from the document with soap and water for the ink and a razor blade for the identification numbers on each page.

He had stuck the indistinguishable document behind a row of books in what resembled a bookshop next to the lavatories. It was not important if the document was found, so long as it was not in the next few days. Given the rather unappetising selection of English and French books and an airport clientele predominantly made up of Soviet advisers and Islamic priests, book sales were hardly flourishing. The document was unlikely to be detected for some time.

He had checked out of the small airport on to the parched desert wasteland of Syria using his own American passport, then returned to catch the British Airways flight 232 leaving for London at nine-thirty a.m. local time, seven-thirty London time. This time he used the second passport he had secreted in his cast; another Iranian one. Hopefully the Syrian officials were, if forced, alert enough to notice that one Michael Adel was still in the country.

Even more important, his luck had held with the telephone call he had made. The only person who had come to mind, the one unmarked person who might provide assistance – albeit of an erratic and undependable sort – was luckily in London. And expecting him.

Now, standing in the immigration line marked "Others", indicating his failure to meet the stringent qualifications of the faster moving lines marked "British Subjects" and "EEC", he longed for relief from the overpowering pain. A strong painkiller, a shower, a shave and a long, long bath. He desperately needed all of that, and sleep.

London. Wednesday, October 31: 2.05 p.m.

On Wilton Place, sandwiched between the pedestrian bustle of Knightsbridge and the heavy traffic of Hyde Park Corner, stands the Berkeley Hotel. Discreet and elegant, it goes unnoticed by the casual observer, for, to its credit, it does not rely on ostentation. Rather, its reputation is secure among a relatively small but highly satisfied clientele.

As Adel stood in the hotel's only second-floor suite overlooking the park, he watched the silent tangle of traffic outside through double-glazed windows and tucked a white cotton shirt into black slacks. The painkiller and new clothes purchased by the hall porter had aroused a new sense of optimism and energy. But still momentarily he yearned to stop his running and spend a week doing nothing, being cosseted by the hotel. That, though, was impossible. Once before he had ignored Allon's words of caution and it had nearly cost him his life. He was determined not to make the same mistake again.

"*Insure yourself,*" the Israeli had said. "*As far as possible always insure yourself. Nothing is too small.*"

He grabbed his old black leather windbreaker from the hanger in the hallway and considered calling his brother Mark. Then he thought better of it. This time round he would listen to Allon, right down to the last detail. There was nothing pressing about contacting Mark. Not yet. But should he place his other call . . . no, that should wait too. First he would insure himself, he thought. First he would visit Harrods and insure himself.

Adel walked past the roaring fire in the hotel lobby and picked up a newspaper from the stack that lay on the counter marked "Enquiries".

"Have the evening papers arrived yet?" he asked the young man behind the desk.

"I think so, sir." The youth dipped below the counter as Adel glanced at the paper in his hand: a huge picture of Israeli Prime Minister Menachem Begin and Egyptian President Anwar Sadat laughing and shaking hands.

Adel looked no further. He remembered how it had all started and the words of Don Anderson.

"*That's not possible; we can't use our own people; there's some sort of problem with it. I don't know what it is. Only thing I can think of is that the President doesn't want anything to tarnish the Camp David Agreement. He's pleased as a kitten with it; it's still too fresh and vulnerable.*"

The memory reinforced his predicament and the importance of time.

"Here we are, sir," said the young man, holding out the evening paper.

"What time is it?"

"Five past two, sir."

"Thank you." Adel adjusted his watch two hours back from the Damascus time it still showed, took the paper and walked away, the picture and its ramifications still filling his mind. He glanced at the evening paper absentmindedly. But it provided no relief.

SHAH SELLS SURREY MANSION

The Shah of Iran's mansion in Hascombe, Surrey, was being stripped today of all its priceless antiques for shipment to America where the former ruler is at present undergoing emergency medical treatment at Sloane Kettering Hospital in New York.

Strutt and Parker, the London estate agents, believed to be handling the sale of Stilemans estate near Godalming . . .,

Adel folded the two papers and stuffed them in his windbreaker. Time was a luxury he could not afford. At any moment now Bell and his organisation would trace him. At most it would take them a day. More likely they would be here in the next few hours. That was all he had. A few hours to insure his future.

And no estate in Surrey to sell.

Outside the Berkeley, he turned his jacket collar up against the light drizzle and hobbled right, across the street, towards Knightsbridge and Harrods.

In front of the small post-office on the corner he noticed a bespectacled, robust blonde in her late thirties step from a black de Tomaso Mini Innocenti. Her raincoat rode upwards with her skirt as she struggled to unknot herself from the small cabin; beneath were revealed legs of extraordinary length and beauty. Adel looked at them longingly. It had been a long time, he thought.

He limped across Sloane Street thinking of Samira and welcoming the gentle refreshing touch of the rain on his face. On the Brompton Road he remembered the last time he had been here with her; it had been Christmas, only ten months ago. He pressed the bell on the door marked Kutchinsky and waited for the buzz of the security lock to open from within. It was one of her favourite jewellers and suddenly he felt a strong urge to remind her of his love. Besides, Harrods was next door and it would only take a minute.

He chose the evening watch she had admired; a thick gold identification bracelet with a timepiece on it and studded discreetly with diamonds.

"Are you sure this is the one she liked?"

"Yes sir. Mrs Adel has been in to see it several times," the formally attired middle-aged salesman assured him.

"Okay, I'll take it," said Adel. "But I'd like something inscribed on –"

The words caught in his throat. The blonde woman with the fine legs passed the window a second time. He had seen her the first time but put it down to coincidence. But a second time? Actually, it was a third time, he thought. She could have been waiting for him outside the hotel.

"What would you like engraved on it, Mr Adel?" the bald salesman prompted politely.

Adel stared at the window. "Ah . . . ah . . . just put 'I love you', my initials and the date."

"Yes, sir."

"Oh. And . . . ah . . . can you send it to her? You have the address."

"Certainly, sir. Do we bill you, Mr Adel?"

"Yes . . . yes . . . that'll be fine," he replied distractedly as he headed for the door.

On the Brompton Road he turned left towards Harrods, but immediately started across the road, weaving through the stalled traffic to the opposite side. He was careful to act like a man with a purpose, a man with a destination to reach.

He entered Richoux, the small continental teashop across from Harrods, and took the narrow staircase down to the café's lower floor. Exactly five minutes later, at twenty-six minutes past two, he placed a one pound note on the table to cover the tea he had ordered but not touched and came back up.

He snapped the café door open and looked quickly both ways, up and down the pavement. Several doors down, to his right, blonde hair disappeared into the Rosenthal Studio House.

"Shit."

They had found him.

He crossed the street again, his heart pounding, his mind racing. He needed time. Another few hours. He wasn't ready. Not yet. He had to lose them, he had to shake free.

He was in front of Harrods now, directly in line with the doorway hiding the blonde. Her back was to him as she carefully studied the china in the shop window; and, no doubt, his reflection in the glass. He hailed a taxi.

"Where to, guv?"

"Hammersmith across to Barnes," he replied, stepping into the cab, his eyes trained on its rear window and beyond.

The fair-haired woman ran across the road, barely missing an oncoming car as she did so. She ran to the front of the taxi-rank outside Harrods and said a few words to the alighting passenger. Then she boarded the cab and set out after them.

Adel turned to the driver. "How would you like to make fifty pounds?"

"That depends," the driver responded cautiously.

"Someone's following me and I'd like to lose them."

"Like taking candy from a baby," the driver bragged as the vehicle surged forward.

"Drive over to Barnes, then," Adel instructed.

The driver made a slight detour and headed up Exhibition Road towards Hyde Park. The traffic steadily decreased as they passed Kensington and left the West End; after Olympia the flow became uninhibited. The pursuing taxi adjusted its speed and kept pace at a distance that varied between one and two hundred yards. Adel's heart pounded as he watched out of the rear window. He had to lose her.

Then suddenly, as they passed the old St Paul's School buildings the pursuing vehicle turned into a side street.

Adel was surprised; it made no sense. She had been following him – he was certain of that. From the Berkeley to Richoux and then the taxi; it had to be more than coincidence.

Then it hit him. This was not Khomeini's rabble he was dealing with. These were professionals, real professionals. "Sidewalk artists", as they called themselves.

Adel turned to look through the rear window again. "Which one of you is it?" he muttered as he watched the vehicles behind.

It was impossible to tell.

The taxi made its way past a large church and over Hammersmith Bridge into Barnes; within a suspicious distance, a motorcyclist, two taxis, followed by numerous cars and a red double-decker bus came with them.

"Take a right," ordered Adel after they had passed the second set of traffic lights. He had to separate them, identify the hunter.

Only one taxi followed.

"Take a left," snapped Adel his head moving like a windscreen-wiper between the driver and the rear window.

Again the same vehicle gave chase. A taxi, he thought. If that was all, he had a chance. He watched to see if any other car followed but none did.

"Pull up ahead," he instructed.

The taxi swerved over to the kerb and stopped. Adel stepped out.

"Listen carefully," he told the driver as he leaned into the window. "I want you to pick me up in two minutes at that . . ."

"I thought you said fifty quid, mate," the driver interjected, full of indignation.

Adel gave the driver a cold, hard look. He did not want to pay the man, not even what was on the meter; he had to be sure that the cabbie would return.

"Look in your mirror," he said. "See that taxi back there?"

"Yeah."

"Well, we haven't lost him yet, have we?"

The cabbie's attention alternated between Adel and the rearview mirror.

"But we will," smiled Adel, giving him confidence. "Drive around the block and pick me up on that corner in two minutes," he said, surreptitiously pointing to the intersection ahead.

"Two minutes?" the driver asked suspiciously.

"Exactly two minutes," said Adel, leaning back from the window. "And not a second later."

"Two minutes it is," the cabbie replied, realising he had no choice.

Adel's eyes followed the parting cab until they rested on the predator behind. He wore a dark hat and a cream-coloured raincoat; nothing else about him stood out. He was of medium height and build, and he was paying the taxi.

Adel started limping down the quiet Victorian street at a leisurely pace. Except for the two of them, there was not a soul in sight.

The distance to the crossroads was too short to justify two minutes at a normal pace and the casual saunter he chose masked the anxiety he felt. It was meant to consume time and unnerve the man in pursuit. He stopped twice along the route, once to admire a brass hound's-head doorknob and once to touch the soft petals of a late-blooming rose, but still he arrived at the corner some twenty seconds early. As he stood waiting he fought the urge to turn and observe the predator's movements. Instead, he stood there, holding his ground, confident that the hunter was baffled by his behaviour, confident too that the professional had committed what Allon called the cardinal sin: he had underestimated the opposition.

The clack-clack of the diesel engine was a welcome sound; he heard it before it came into view from a side street to his right. It pulled closer and stopped in front of him. Adel at last gave in to his urge. He looked back at the perplexed face of his predator before he stepped in.

As the taxi pulled away, however, the hunter showed no sign of panic; he quickly pulled a small square object from his pocket, raised an antenna from it and bent his head to its surface. Then he looked up and down the street in search of a vehicle.

Adel turned to the driver. "What's the nearest underground station?" The walkie-talkie beaming its message across London left him no choice.

"Ahh . . . Hammersmith station, I'd say."

"Drop me there."

Two minutes later the taxi pulled up at Hammersmith underground station and Adel hopped on to the wet pavement. He stuffed the sixty pounds he held ready into the driver's hand.

"Thanks," he said as he headed away.

He had lost them. But it would not be for long.

Harrods, London. Wednesday, October 31: 3.20 p.m.

It was three-twenty when Michael Adel entered the radio and television department on the second floor of Harrods department store, confident that he had not been followed. En route, he had gone to great pains to make sure he was alone. Twice he had changed trains; twice more he had lured any would-be pedestrian followers into the open.

Now he hobbled past turntables, amplifiers, tape-recorders and televisions and quickly scanned the department's salesmen.

It was important to choose correctly; quickly and without fuss. It took a few minutes before he spotted a young assistant, nattily dressed in a suit that was obviously beyond his means. Adel watched him for several minutes in search of a telling sign. But there was none; the young man behaved normally in every way. Yet something about the boy smelled of moonlighting, of subsidising his tastes. He watched the assistant closely for several more minutes but still there was no concrete reason to back up his suspicion.

He had to move quickly; he had to decide. Out there, Bell had an army looking for him. Time was running out.

As he hovered beneath a sign that read "Audio Accessories" Adel decided to trust his instincts. He waited for the red-headed young man to finish with his customer, and then moved closer.

"Can I help you, sir?" asked the young man.

"Perhaps," replied Adel cautiously.

"What is it you're looking for?"

Adel reached in his pocket. "Something a little unusual."

"Well, we have *almost* everything at Harrods," smiled the young man, "and if we don't carry it, we can always order it for you, sir."

"Yes. I'm sure you can. But I'm not looking for anything in particular, just someone who's willing to make himself a hundred pounds legally and quickly."

The young man's eyes flickered but he was neither insulted nor shaken. He merely scanned the floor for a supervisor.

"I . . . I . . . don't know, sir," he stammered. "A hundred pounds? What is it you want?"

Adel removed the two tapes from his jacket. "Duplicates of these."

"Well, sir," replied the salesman, obviously mollified – it was, after all, a relatively simple task –

"that's not exactly permitted, but let me see what I can do."

"I know. That's what the hundred's for," Adel replied, holding five twenty-pound notes in his hand.

The red-headed salesman scanned the floor again. "Leave them with me," he said nervously, grabbing for the tapes and the money.

Adel pulled back. "That's the snag," he said, stretching the words. "I want to hear them while you do it."

Harrods, London. Wednesday, October 31: 3.39 p.m.

The two Gale speakers erupted in a deafening, high-pitched hiss as the makeshift recording cubicle burst into life. Perched on a high stool, the red-headed salesman stretched quickly and depressed a lever marked "volume", reducing the outburst to a more tolerable level.

Adel frowned and glanced at his watch in nervous anticipation. Then he picked up the small cassette jacket the salesman had placed on the deck and read once again the simple, handwritten red letters: "The Trust 1975. Tape 1."

Still the words meant nothing.

The sounds emitted were a steady drone of mumbling, intermittently shattered by a flare of laughter or a raised voice that momentarily stood out, clear and distinguishable, only to fade again beneath a medley of clashing interference.

Adel suddenly felt uneasy and confused. "Is this working at normal speed?"

"Sure." The salesman looked at him curiously. "Why?"

"It's a lousy recording," muttered Adel distantly, his mind drifting back to Bell.

"It's all gibberish if you hear them on a normal tape-recorder. To make any sense out of them you need access to a machine that can slow them down to a crawl."

Why? thought Adel. Why the hell had Bell lied? The tape was recorded at normal speed and it was patently decipherable at that.

"Listen," he said to the boy, "give me a pair of earphones; that way I can turn it up and the sound won't bother anyone." The real reason was different; Bell's lie had unnerved him; he didn't want anyone listening.

"That's marvellous," replied the salesman. "Because I've got to be seen on the floor so I'll be coming and going." He handed Adel a pair and left.

Adel felt a surge of adrenalin as a clear, single voice burst through the jungle of murmurs.

"Gentlemen. I've requested this extraordinary formal session because of the grave and impending nature of the crisis we face."

Adel sat up with a start.

"I think you'll consider the inconvenience of flying in to New York at such short notice justified as the ramifications of the problem become apparent."

Adel cocked his head as he registered a hint of recognition. That voice, he thought. That inflection. He knew them. He had heard them. And what did a crisis in New York have to do with the Phoenix missile anyway? His stomach rumbled with nervous anticipation.

"I'll be as brief as I can on the background so we can reach the crux of the matter quickly. As you are all no doubt aware, the Shah of Iran is presently on the last day of a ten-day state visit to Rumania. During the course of this period, intelligence reports started coming in indicating that top secret negotiations were taking place between the two countries that, if successful, could shake the very foundations of our organisation."

What organisation? What the hell was he talking about?

"Unfortunately, these negotiations have now been successfully concluded. Mahmoudi, who went along as the Shah's Finance Minister, has just flown in from Bucharest. He's here on a round of previously scheduled talks with the people in Washington and he's brought with him a copy of the final accord."

"Incidentally," added the same tantalisingly recognisable voice, *"Mahmoudi is standing by next door should any of us have any questions."*

"What," asked a second voice, palpably uninterested in Mahmoudi's whereabouts, *"are the terms of this arrangement?"*

The first speaker responded without hesitation. *"The accord itself is inconsequential, Sol. It's a barter agreement. The Iranians are to supply one hundred and fifty million dollars' worth of oil per year and receive in return an equivalent dollar value in agricultural equipment and foodstuffs. But the ramifications, as I am sure you are all aware, are devastating."*

There was a momentary silence, and Adel shifted uneasily on his stool. Again he thought, what the hell had this to do with the Phoenix missile?

The voice in the earphones continued. *"On its own the deal is peanuts. But it's the first entry into the market-place by an OPEC nation. That,"* said the voice gravely, *"is what's wrong."*

It was a calm, refined baritone. Deep and resonant and tinged with a mid-Atlantic timbre. Adel frowned and leaned forward, trying to force his memory.

"Fundamentally, what the Shah signed in Bucharest last Friday – the document is dated February 28, 1975" – the voice paused, obviously for effect, *"is an assault on our monopoly."* Again it paused. *"The overt challenge, gentlemen, by an oil producer to bypass our marketing apparatus and acquire independent markets."*

God damn it! thought Adel. Of course he knew that voice! He knew it well. It was the voice he had heard only days ago. The voice of his friend. The man he had trusted. The man he had turned to for advice and guidance.

It was the voice of John Alexander Case, chairman of the board and chief executive officer, Enerco Corporation – the largest energy company in the world.

Suddenly his worst doubts and fears were a reality. "Phoenix Missile, my ass!" he spat bitterly, turning to deliver an angry look at the outsize speaker.

The voice that responded to his glare was a new one. It was fragile and barely audible. Like the two which had preceded it, its inflection was American. But there the similarity ended. This voice was more elderly, its tone even more confident and assured.

"*How deeply does it cut into the marketing network, Jacey?*" it asked flatly.

Jacey, thought Adel bitterly. Those were his initials – J.A.C. – John Alexander Case. Jacey to his cronies!

"*The answer to that, David, is it doesn't,*" replied Case. "*Not significantly, anyway. But it's the precedent we've been watching for. Like everything else about OPEC, it'll lead to leap-frogging. Once the Iranians get away with this deal – and knowing the Shah he'll find some absurdly glittering manner to proclaim his achievement – every OPEC nation will seek its own market. Kuwait will want to enter Australia, Bahrain, Japan, Nigeria, Brazil, and so on. They'll bypass us.*"

"*Well,*" remarked David, with a heavy sigh, "*as I understand it, this isn't altogether unexpected. Clear-cut contingency plans designed to handle just such an event have been in existence for some time. The drawback has always been our reluctance to activate them.*" The confidence of the voice was emphasised by the consummate calm of its delivery. There was not, Adel noticed, a trace of the emotion the other two voices exuded. "*The time has obviously come to put that reluctance aside.*"

"*Er . . . Gentlemen, David Thorncroft has a cogent point . . .*"

Shit! thought Adel. But there was no time to think

further. The voice was a new one and it was unmistakably British.

"*. . . but the reluctance is not whimsical, it's based on very valid concerns. The region is not a stable one, and the intricacies – indeed the variables – of these so-called contingency plans are numerous and the outcome uncertain. Very high-risk stuff, all this, in what is strategically the most important area in the world. That's why this contingency thinking was always seen as a last resort. I'm not sure a minuscule barter agreement constitutes quite that.*"

The course of the discussion had only one natural direction, thought Adel. And it sure as hell didn't include the Phoenix missile.

So far, he observed, four voices had spoken. Besides Case, only one other had been clearly identified. It was the voice of one of the richest men in the world; a man who owned a controlling interest, both overtly and covertly, in several of the largest oil companies in the world. It was the voice of David Thorncroft.

Even worse, it was not difficult to guess the names of the others present. Not with the Christian name of one and the British accent of the other. Not when he had, in various degrees of proximity, known and worked with each and every one of them: Solomon Horowitz, Arthur Sinclair and Baron Gerome Steendijk van Lochem. The rulers of the world's oil industry.

The Mall, London: 3.58 p.m.

At precisely that moment, less than two miles from Harrods on the fifth floor of a Regency mansion on The Mall, Colonel Grover Cleveland Bell stood contentedly at the window, reflecting on the awesome history that the sprawling majesty of Buckingham Palace epitomised. After a moment's consideration he turned to the unimposing heap of Victorian buildings standing directly in front of him, across St James's Park. It was there, however – in Whitehall – that history had been made, and not in the impotent splendour of the palace to his right. His reflections on the ironies of power were cut short by the buzz of his telephone. He turned from the window and pressed a button.

"Yes, Ann."

"It's Mr Gleeson, sir."

Bell pressed another button and reclined in the chair behind the desk.

"Hey, Jim. How's it going?" he asked with all the assurance of an untroubled mind.

"We've lost him."

"What!" Bell elongated the word in astonishment as he snapped the chair upright.

"We lost him," repeated Gleeson.

Bell stood ramrod straight. "How the hell did you do that?"

"He engineered it. He slipped his tail around Barnes."

"Who," snapped Bell, "is Barnes?"

"It's a neighbourhood, Grove. Just across the Hammersmith Bridge."

"Terrific." Bell paused. "You got twenty-seven men and eleven vehicles to follow a fucking cripple and you can't manage it," he hollered. "A fucking amateur!"

"He knows what he's doing, Grove. He executed the slip perfectly."

"When did it happen?"

"About an hour ago. Around two forty-five."

Bell hesitated before he spoke. When he did, his words were delivered with military precision. "Call in the rest of your unit and deploy them over six areas: Soho, Mayfair, Belgravia, Chelsea, Knightsbridge and Kensington. I'll get domestic assistance to cover the rest. Circulate an exact description of what he's wearing and key on recording studios, stereo stores, tape and record shops – anywhere he could duplicate the tapes."

Bell walked to the far end of the large office and back, barking orders as he did so.

"If I know the bastard he's going to double back to the areas he knows best, and that, Gleeson, is the six you're covering, so for fuck's sake pull your finger out of your ass!"

"What about known associates?" Gleeson asked.

Bell stopped pacing. "If he's good enough to slip you, Gleeson, he isn't going to drop in on his aunt for tea, is he?" He paused and covered himself. "Let domestic stake the knowns. We'll liaise with domestic here. I'm going down to the Sit. Room now so I'll be plugged into all the communications traffic. I want to know every step you're taking, Gleeson. Have all the vehicles do a Howard Cosell. I want ball-by-ball coverage."

"Yes, sir."

"Find him, Gleeson. I don't care what it takes, find him. I don't want that mother fucker getting close to a tape-recorder."

"Yes, sir."

"Oh, and Gleeson . . ."

"Yes, Grove?"

"Don't forget the larger department stores: Selfridges, Fortnum & Mason, Harvey Nichols, Harrods – all of them."

Harrods: 3.58 p.m.

It was David Thorncroft's voice that broke the silence of the tape. "*This is a watershed problem, and I think it might help if we reflect a moment before we go any further.*" His elderly assured tone betrayed not a hint of the tension of his colleagues. He seemed to be trying to appease the two distinctly different factions that Adel had heard emerging over the past twenty minutes of discussions. It was not clear to Adel what the differences were. Only that the interests of the Americans who wanted to act and the Europeans who advocated caution clashed.

"The essence of this Trust has been its ability to retain its unity in times of stress. It might be useful to keep that in mind as we go over the intricacies of this crisis. I urge you to recall the preamble to our constitution: 'Only through cooperation comes power.' And remember how well those five words have served us in the past. I suspect they may be the reason behind any future prosperity we enjoy."

"Your point is well taken," replied the clipped British voice of Arthur Sinclair testily. *"No one is questioning 1928. I'm committed to it. Gerome here is committed to it, and so, clearly, are the three of you. Yes, indeed, 1928 forms the basis of any decision we take. But in addition to cooperation, 1928 also suggests that responsibility and risk be equally –"* – he paused and repeated the word – *"equally distributed among the economic units. The area in question is only of peripheral interest to three of those present. To Gerome and myself it endangers all four of our sources of supply: Iran, Iraq, Kuwait and the Arab Emirates. Your prime concern – the Saudi production – would be unaffected. The pipelines you've built down to the Red Sea ensure that. You're not affected by the Strait of Hormuz and its closure."*

"That's true, Arthur," responded Case firmly . . .

Adel shook his head in amazement. 1928 was the year the major oil companies had secretly met at Achnacarry Castle in Scotland and signed the so-called "Status-quo Agreement", an accord eliminating all competition in the energy industry and dividing the world into separate but equal sectors to be shared among the major international oil companies who were signatories to the agreement. The 1928 "Status-quo Agreement" was never published. In fact its existence was always vehemently denied by the oil industry. But here were today's potentates of oil, not only testifying to its existence, but privately discussing its details.

He moved his hand up to massage his forehead and felt the sweat of fear.

. . .*"The contingency plans present far more of a danger to your two European units than they do to us, but that's why the reserves and production facilities we intend to develop before the plans go into effect are slated to be in your spheres of influence and under your direction."*

"But it's the old story of a bird in the hand, isn't it?" snapped Sinclair. *"It's a very high-risk game we're playing. Perhaps we could still explore other less drastic options. Perhaps a more political, less violent solution."*

What violence? What high-risk game were they playing? What the hell was going on?

Again, David Thorncroft brought his authoritative voice to bear. *"Over the years, Arthur, the power base of this Trust of ours, the essence if you will, has been its ability to recognise when the time has come to make difficult decisions. And never attempt to skirt them. We must be careful not to lose that ability."*

"Look, Art," said Solomon Horowitz, *"the circumstances in 1928 weren't too different to what we've got today. The world's economies were growing too fast; we've got that today. The oil industry was facing excessive demand; we've got that today. Supply sources had not kept up with demand; we've got that today. Competition between marketing units was getting out of hand; for all intents and purposes after the Shah's Bucharest agreement, you can say we've got that today. For Christ's sake, what we're talking about here is excessive market competition. Destructive market competition. If the OPEC people are allowed to establish a foothold in the marketing end of operations, we're finished. They have the oil; all they need are the markets."*

"These decisions," declared David Thorncroft quickly, the moment Horowitz had fallen silent, *"do not lend themselves to emotions or questions of right and wrong."* He spoke with what seemed a purposely calming cadence, the words a buffer to Solomon Horowitz's aggres-

sive tones. "*They concern the survival of our world and way of life – the Western world and free democracies – and, incidentally, the health of this Trust. If we are going to retain our position, I submit that we must be up to the challenges of today, even if that means employing the sternest of measures and taking a modicum of risk.*"

While softly spoken, the words sounded conclusive. The elderly voice seemed to arouse a measure of authority that cut through the atmosphere. It even cut through time and forced itself on to Adel. What he was up against was daunting.

At length another voice broke the silence. "*Does there exist any evidence of Russian connivance in this barter agreement the Shah has concluded?*"

Adel felt vindicated. It was the distinct voice of Baron Gerome Steendijk van Lochem, head of a Benelux energy conglomerate. He recalled clearly the last time he had seen the baron. It had been a luncheon in The Hague. Adel remembered the baron's clumsy mixture of cold, enormously precise Prussian bearing and his affected, outmoded English mannerisms, his slicked-down hair, the Savile Row suit and the horsy features of his face.

"*The short answer is, yes,*" responded Case. "*Mahmoudi claims that the Shah was flown off in the middle of the night by helicopter and that the man who negotiated on Rumania's behalf was Alexei Kosygin himself. Now you'll recall Kosygin kept a high profile when we were negotiating with the Soviets. He, with Khrushchev, Suslov and Mikoyan signed the agreement we concluded in 1962, after their ploy with Mattei ended with his fatal accident and they became willing to play ball. This Rumanian thing with the Shah is a clear breach of those understandings. It may well be a new pincer movement by the Soviets and they wouldn't do it unless they thought the timing was right. A response, gentlemen, and an unmistakable one, is imperative on more than one front.*"

Mattei too, thought Adel with a shiver. But he had

little time for reflection. Only enough to recall that Enrico Mattei the head of ENI, Italy's oil giant, had tried to buck the system and a bomb had torn his private plane to shreds outside Milan's Linate airport.

"*Speaking on my own behalf,*" said the baron, "*I am not opposed, and neither have I been in any one of our previous discussions on this subject, to the concept of the dismantlement of OPEC. I see the eventual need for it. The disquieting element, as Arthur suggests, is the radical nature of the proposed operation and the somewhat uncertain outcome.*" He spoke in an exaggeratedly measured English tone that hadn't quite crossed the Channel. The "o"s came out as "ue"s and the voice sounded half-throttled, but the words and their meaning were more than clear. These ghouls were calmly planning the destruction of OPEC.

"*Look,*" broke in Horowitz impatiently. "*We could have accomplished every one of the things we accomplished with OPEC in other ways and without losing supply side-control.*"

What did this mean?

"*Now the Shah of Iran – this creature of OPEC – is going for our balls and here we are sitting debating whether his assault on the marketing end of operations is or is not acceptable.*"

He paused. "*Well, I'll tell you something. If he's allowed to succeed you can all rest assured of one thing: every OPEC member will seek its own market and with the discounts they can offer to acquire those markets, it'll be a bush fire. They'll nibble away until all that's left is a couple of gas stations in Climax, Nevada, for us to play with.*"

Adel closed his eyes and leaned forward as the barrage of revelations continued. A picture of Horowitz, the major shareholder in the largest independent oil company in the world, formed in Adel's mind. He was slight and sloppy in appearance. His balding head sat on constantly hunched, narrow shoulders and its most noteworthy feature, besides the ever-present grimace, was sharp, dark eyes hidden behind brown photochromic lenses. He was variously described in the media as controversial, outspoken, brash and arrogant. The entrepreneurial skills that had taken him from a penniless Russian Jewish immigrant to the pinnacle of American corporate power were awesome. His immense fortune, used to spread patronage and philanthropic largesse, was legendary. The Horowitz private art collection was envied and coveted by the world's major museums.

The curt British tones of Arthur Sinclair snapped Adel's attention back to reality. "*Really, Sol, you're being rather uncharitable on the OPEC decision. Establishing OPEC has unquestionably been the single most complex undertaking we've ever attempted and its success must be close to perfect.*"

Adel reeled. This was the biggest bombshell yet.

"*Every one of us has benefited enormously from it. There's no question of anyone being harmed,*" he concluded.

"*Yes,*" Case broke in quickly, before Horowitz could take issue, "*your reticence regarding the OPEC option is on record, Sol, and I think I can say we've all appreciated your spirit of cooperation in going along with us. I know you've had misgivings all along. But I think I have to agree with Arthur here.*"

Case, Adel noted, was coming to Sinclair's aid. The art of diplomacy. Case was already certain of Horowitz's support; he was going after Sinclair's.

"*There was no choice. We had to diversify to alternative sources of energy, and the OPEC option we triggered fifteen years ago has just about put us in reach of our goals. Without the price increases they forced through, how could we have financed the development of alternative energy sources? No, Sol, it was the right decision. And it's right on course. By 1984 or 5 it will have served its purpose.*"

If he were not hearing all this with his own ears, Adel felt, he could never have believed it possible. Loud and clear it was coming through: OPEC with all its swagger had all along been a ploy of the oil companies.

"*Yes, quite so.*" It was now Sinclair hammering the points home. "*The only politically acceptable way of getting prices up to the required levels was to get the producers to do it. And the only way that could have happened was to organise them. The perfect foreign organ which seemed to be giving us a beating. Very neat, really. I can't say any of us has cause to complain.*"

"*Fine. It's served its purpose,*" conceded Horowitz grudgingly. "*But it's grown too independent now.*"

The Mall: 4.17 p.m.

The Otis elevator that Grover Bell entered serves only two points of the sprawling mansion on the Mall: the security clearance room on the ground floor with its visual identification procedures, and the basement which has two electronic checkpoints, one at the elevator door and another at the end of a long tunnel. These measures are additional to the two clearances necessary to enter the building itself, and the closed-circuit video camera that records all who enter and leave the room at the end of the tunnel.

No one is allowed to circumvent the security measures that lead to that door marked "2001SX". To ensure against the unlikely event of someone trying, guards from the US Marine Corps stand by with weapons powerful and advanced enough to penetrate any bullet-proof equipment known to Western scientists.

As he entered into the cave of electronic wizardry, Colonel Grover Cleveland Bell felt foolish. The sophistication of the room was, he admitted, a classic case of overkill for his purposes. The capabilities it held were mind boggling. All the technological marvels of the twentieth century were condensed into that one room.

It was in fact one of four such facilities in the Western world: the Strategic Air Command Headquarters outside Omaha, Nebraska, the Joint Chief of Staff Command Centre in the Pentagon, US Military Command, East, in Guam, and this – Strategic Command Europe – the least publicised of all.

Every military and intelligence capability that the Western world possesses is available in that one tennis-court-sized room. The vast electronic surveillance gadgetry (ELECTINT) of the CIA, NSA and DIA, the sensitive human grid (HUMINT) of the SIS, Mossad and SDECE, the American military satellite and land-based intelligence network, not to mention the conventional security forces of law and order.

In that room, coverage of world events is available at the touch of a button. It can zoom in with high-resolution satellite cameras on the havoc Afghan rebels are wreaking on Soviet troops in the Pamir Mountains, and establish with remarkable accuracy the quantities of arms, boots and ammunition they have captured. It can listen in on Ayatollah Khomeini's daily domestic conversation in North Teheran; provide the exact numbers of central American rebels about to attack a government post, or assess the calibre of companion any particular targeted politician might have chosen for that particular night's activity. It can monitor – and provide simultaneous translations in every language – all ground-to-ground, ground-to-air conversations throughout the globe, or assess the load of a tanker in any sea, not by its obvious size but by the exact level of its water-mark.

All of which was of little use to Bell, for he had neither the time nor the inclination to re-route satellites to search for Adel.

What he did need was the vast domestic communication capability this room contained: the ability to contact anyone at the touch of a button – the keeper in the lighthouse off Land's End, the Chief Constable at his desk on the Shetland Islands, the Prime Minister, the Head of MI5, each and every government department and every transportation outlet, store or service provided publicly or privately in the country.

Harrods: 4.20 p.m.

The voice of David Thorncroft cut in. "*We have to be careful here to differentiate between the desirability of dismantling OPEC and the actual mode of destabilisation. The mode of execution is not something we are in a position to assess. That's for Operations to decide, isn't it?*"

Adel braced himself and looked at the progress of the tape in the cassette.

"*Yes, it is,*" responded Case solidly. "*And they're fully prepared. What we need to decide is whether or not the timing is right.*"

"*I'm not sure the time is ever quite right for these things,*" said the baron wistfully. "*It's more a question of whether OPEC is controllable or not. Rumania seems to suggest it isn't. Or at least it seems to suggest it soon won't be.*"

"*Yes,*" agreed Sinclair. "*If Rumania is allowed to succeed it would seem a fair bet that the Russians would at the very least seek to expand the barter concept to their other satellites – Poland, Hungary, and so on. It would have a snowballing effect: unstoppable after a certain point.*" He spoke distantly, as if deep in thought, his initial trepidation forgotten.

The speakers were silent momentarily. But the silence was worse. It drove home to Adel the claustrophobia of the small room.

"*How does Operations see a project of this magnitude, Jacey?*" asked Arthur Sinclair.

"Well," Case sighed, *"we've really got two problems rolled up in one. The first is the issue of the Shah's future; and the second – the issue of OPEC. From what I understand, Operations' plans revolve around the fact that for the most part OPEC nations need our money more than we need their oil. At least, in the short term that's true. The development dreams of the producing nations are enormous and their dependence on oil revenue is absolute. That, gentlemen, is their Achilles heel.*

"Operations suggest that if a glut situation could be manufactured for, say, a period of one or two years, the internal fiscal pressure on every OPEC member except Saudi Arabia would be such that it would lead to pressing financial shortages and consequently a price war within OPEC. In effect, OPEC would self-destruct."

"And how do we bring about such a glut scenario?" asked Horowitz.

"Operations will be making a presentation shortly," replied Case. *"It's based on the destabilisation of one or both of the moderate elements of OPEC – Saudi Arabia and Iran – who between them produce half of OPEC's oil – that is, one quarter of world production. That way the moderate element would lose its plurality to control; this would lead to gradual price increases; a panic in the West as we stockpile more oil; further price increases, much larger this time; conservation and probable economic recession in the West, with OPEC left holding a high-priced baby that no one wants. In other words, a glut."*

Adel found it impossible to take in the full implications of the taped voice. The chairman of the board of the most powerful energy company in the world was admitting to the largest conspiracy of all time – a conspiracy to subjugate hundreds of millions of people throughout the world, whole nations, so a handful could profit and prosper.

What was worse, Adel realised, was that his own problems had only just begun. Everything – the killings, the pain, the fatigue – had only just started. What he had suffered had been merely the prologue.

"If the choice for destabilisation is between the Shah and King Khaled, it's simple, isn't it?" said Sinclair. *"One's a megalomaniac, the other a reasonable man content with his hawks and his hunting."*

"There are technical elements involved, too." It was Horowitz's crusty voice. *"Iran has reserves of fifty billion barrels; Saudi Arabia one hundred and fifty million. Iran has a daily export capability of eight million barrels, Saudi Arabia fourteen. Iran is on the Soviet border, Saudi Arabia is a thousand miles away, separated by a gulf."*

"My main concern," continued Case patiently, *"is the preliminary years. We'll have to generate a major programme to increase Western reserves and supplies in order to ensure adequate energy levels throughout the transitionary period. Six million barrels of Iranian oil – that's a hell of a loss of supply."*

"It's not a problem technically, Jacey," said Horowitz. *"We can do it by carrying out some in-fill drilling in existing major fields. And start major exploration efforts in areas of the continental United States, Alaska and Mexico. There's so much we've located but left fallow. Once prices rise, we can open completely new areas such as the North Sea quite economically. And the Saudis will always go along with production increases. Tell 'em the incremental growth will be applied to strategic military stockpiling only. They always buy that."*

"I seem to have missed something somewhere." It was the baron. *"Why do we need to lose the Iranian production? Is the outcome that uncertain?"* He stretched the "that".

"No, Gerome, you didn't miss a thing. The thinking on this is that we can set the price programme ahead by a few years. If a revolution occurs and six million of the Iranian production goes off the market it would seem a natural time for a shortage to occur. That being the case, the projected prices in effect at that time which are . . . ah . . . ah . . ."

"*Twelve dollars and change,*" said Horowitz over the rustle of paper.

"*Yes,*" said Case. "*The twelve dollars or so projected to be in effect then can be engineered upward to the thirty dollar range. That's when the alternative sources we are now so heavily committed to can be brought on-stream economically. An unfriendly new regime in Iran's going to lead to a scramble for oil. The whole world's going to be terrified of the Strait of Hormuz being blocked, so everybody's going to rush to stockpile. And we, of course, can help that scare programme along.*"

Adel shook his head in disbelief. That was exactly what had happened. On January 16, 1979 – the day the Shah left Iran – the price of oil had been twelve dollars a barrel. Today it had reached thirty. Six months. That's all it took them. A one hundred and fifty per cent increase in six months. He nodded as he thought of his own fate.

Case went on confidently: "*After a decent interval, the energy glut we just talked about can be manufactured. The glut that hopefully will force OPEC nations to internal competition, discounts and, eventually, disintegration.*"

Suddenly the door of the studio opened. The salesman entered and said something.

Adel did not reply. He was mesmerised.

"*Gentlemen,*" said Case firmly, "*we must arrive at a complete and final solution . . .*"

Abruptly there was silence.

The Mall: 4.39 p.m.

"The cab dropped him off at Hammersmith underground station, sir."

Bell jerked his head up from the small computer screen to the right of the conference table. Sitting, he looked up at the wiry young man and the clipboard he held.

He pointed. "What else have you got there?"

Christopher Cappelli shook his head. "That's about it, sir. We traced the taxi through the number John had, and that's all the driver knew. Hammersmith underground station."

"What time was that?'

"An hour and a half ago. Two forty-five. Three o'clock. Somewhere in that time frame."

Bell glanced away, his eyes slowly scanning the eight silent film screens on the three walls in front of him. He bit his lower lip and swivelled on his chair.

"He's doubled back. I can feel it," he muttered. His eyes narrowed, deepening the lines around his eyes and crinkling the thin sliver of a scar on his right cheek. "To the crowds, to where he knows best." He stopped swivelling and slowly withdrew a pack of cigarettes from his pocket.

"Patrolmen wired in this town?"

"The bobbies? Yes, sir. They carry walkie-talkie systems. Not too sophisticated, but they can be reached."

Bell stood and nodded his head. "It'll do. Circulate a description to every cop on the street and stress the fact that his limp is barely noticeable. Then, Cappelli, I want to know what happens to this town on Wednesdays. What time the stores close, if there are any late closing areas, and anything else that's special about Wednesdays."

Harrods: 4.45 p.m.

Michael Adel watched in a daze as the salesman ejected the first cassette and replaced it. His life had been uprooted during the past two weeks, but this latest twist was shattering.

"Any good?" blurted the salesman.

Adel looked at the boy. Have you any idea of the enormity of what you're witnessing? he thought. No, but you wouldn't have, would you? That's what it's all about; that's what makes it work for them. Our ignorance, our preoccupation with ourselves, our fecklessness. The Shah of Iran had to go, the man had said in 1975. Four years later, he was gone. Now it was OPEC's turn.

"Yes," Adel said, replacing the earphones and pointing to the salesman to start the second tape. "It's good, all right."

"*Without any more ado I'm going to turn the floor over to Operations,*" the tape boomed. "*Gentlemen, James Farrar.*"

It was the same voice as on the first tape. John Alexander Case, resonant and eloquent.

James Farrar's voice was different; it was scholarly and soft and it held the remains of a southern lilt.

"*The strategy for this exercise is,*" he said, clearly jittery, "*in a general way, always prepared. This is as true of all potential targets as it is with Iran. Each has its own particular idiosyncrasies; each depends on timing and the course of events – past, present and projected – and at the point of execution, the strategy may or may not require refinement to accommodate the desired outcome.*"

He cleared his throat self-consciously before continuing. "*The system we use for destabilisation models is Operations Research and Analytical Logic, or ORAL, as it has come to be known. Most of you are familiar with the use of this programme to solve problems of planning for your companies. But these same programmes can be adapted to accommodate various other applications.*"

Again Adel heard that nervous clearing of the throat. "*The programming software is essentially the same. In the case of this particular ORAL programme, the computer is programmed to pretend that it is Iran – in terms of the economy, the military, the intelligence, the gov-*

ernmental and religious systems, the demographic movement of the population, the communications and transportation systems, the agriculture . . . and so on.

"To apply ORAL to Iran, one in effect selects a variety of potential strategies that could result in destabilisation. The computer then reports the relative success or failure of each strategy and/or a combination thereof."

As Farrar talked, Adel found a picture of him forming in his mind. It resembled the sort of man he'd seen countless times in airports or on flights, in trains and restaurants. He imagined him to be fortyish and of slight build with fine, thinning blond hair. He wore wire-frame glasses and had eager eyes that darted swiftly beneath a large forehead. His idea of a good dinner was a barbecued steak during the half-time interval of ABC's Monday Night football games. But with wine, not beer.

". . . These strategies should hold probabilities in the neighbourhood of eighty-five to ninety per cent if they are to be looked at as potentially successful programmes. They must, as well, be practical, both in operational and economic terms.

"We know from experience that destabilisation – by definition a euphemism for an engineered revolution – is far less costly, in both human and material terms, and with a higher success rate, than traditional military methods. The cost/benefit experience with systems such as ORAL . . ."

The voice of John Alexander Case interrupted. *"I think most of us are reasonably aware of the marvels of the computer age,"* he said brusquely. *"Perhaps we could proceed to the actual programme."*

There was a moment's silence before Farrar continued, the nervous jerkiness of his voice even more apparent now. *"Based on our studies to date, any destabilisation programme for Iran must take into account the following critical factors: One: The 1973 oil price increase by OPEC led to Iranian oil revenues soaring from five billion dollars in fiscal 1973 to some nineteen billion dollars last year, fiscal 1974. Even with major new investments for military equipment, the economy is unable to absorb this income."*

Adel leaned forward and allowed his mind to refine its Identikit impression of Farrar. White Brooks Brothers' button-down shirt. Gold Cross pen stuck in its breast pocket. Regulation striped tie – synthetic. Grey dacron and wool pinstriped suit. Trousers at half-mast. Heavy, brown, wingtip shoes. His one peccadillo: long side-burns, a throwback to Rice University campus fashion during the 'sixties.

"Two: Lacking the necessary infrastructure, the country's economic programme has been a fiasco. It has ignited wave after wave of socio-cultural shock. The bottom line is rampant inflation and a severe overloading of all support systems – transportation, communication, housing, etcetera.

"Three: Dramatic public aspirations, aroused by the Shah himself when he launched his so-called 'Great Civilisation Programme', have now been severely disappointed. The result is complete political disaffection.

"Four: The Shah himself is demoralised by the lack of progress. The Shah's realisation that his 'Great Civilisation' is a fantasy has induced bouts of severe depression in the man."

As the salesman stood to leave the room again, Adel noticed that the trepidation in Farrar's voice had given way to a newfound confidence. His voice did not falter as he ran through the causes for the effects which were being engineered.

"Five: The historical tension between the mullahs . . . that is the clergy . . . and the Shah's government has always been a basis for open conflict. The Shah's undermining of clerical power through land reform, the secularisation of education, marriage and divorce procedures and so on have all posed an increasing threat to the mullah caste. Subsidies from the Shah and the CIA to keep them in line have only added to the resentment of radical elements among the priests.

"Six: Corruption is rife throughout the society. A general decadence, a growing sense of cynicism and a feeling of helplessness to influence the destiny of Iran permeates the professional and technocrat levels who form the core of a small but ambitious middle class.

"Seven: The offshoot of this disaffection is a level of communist infiltration that is higher than has generally been admitted. Needless to say, the communists are tactically available to participate in the destabilisation of the country, albeit for their own ends.

"In short, gentlemen, Iran is fertile for destabilisation."

Adel was aware now of a tenseness, a tautness, throughout his body. Every muscle was hard, every vein bulged. He recognised the feeling. It was fear – a very different fear from the one he had experienced over the past few days. That was the fear of danger, of pain, of personal loss, but there had always been a chance. The enemy was a rabble. A zealous, cruel, vindictive rabble, but thankfully unworldly, uneducated and untrained.

But these people were different. They were psychopaths with machines and psychiatrists at their disposal; they had analysts and strategists; they owned organisations and companies throughout the world; they used trained, professional killers. And they were patient. They had all the time in the world.

Hell, he thought. This tape had been made four years ago, in 1975. It was a precise analysis of every weakness in the Shah's regime, the pinpointing of every pressure point. They had probably gone through the same process with him and there was only one conclusion they could have reached.

He knew too much.

The Mall: 4.46 p.m.

"Domestic are getting uptight, sir. They say we're cutting into their basic everyday security needs."

"Cappelli!" hollered Bell as he stomped across the room. "I don't give a shit what domestic thinks. So it'll be a good day for pickpockets, so fucking what? We have clearance."

Cappelli and the older man with him followed in Bell's wake through the frenetic activity of the now buzzing room. A cacophony of electronic sounds seemed synchronised to the variously coloured wall and panel lights that lit and dimmed with the incessant sound of ringing phones and clacking teleprinters. The eight screens on the walls, too, were now alive. Maps in varying scales lit the immaculately white walls as London became within the reach of a button and the glance of an eye.

Orange lights followed the path of every vehicle involved in the dragnet. The cold, wet route of every policeman on beat was being flashed in yellow, while green indicated the scattered locations of eight helicopters ready to descend upon a given point. Red signalled every potential sighting that was reported, and white indicated every stationary informer at the disposal of British security: underground ticket offices, planted train and bus station employees, airport officials, pavement flower, vegetable and newspaper hawkers, pushers, hookers, ice-cream vans, beggars, petrol pump attendants and hotel staff.

What the lights and screens did not indicate was the bank of telephone and teleprinter monitoring systems being employed on the floor above. Every CB channel was being eavesdropped upon, every regular radio taxi, minicab and international call to the South of France was being followed.

And the operation was still in its infancy. Within the

hour the net would expand further, to every bus-driver, conductor, taxi-driver, combing the streets of London. To callgirls, cinemas, theatres and pubs as they opened. To superintendents of buildings and parks and rent-a-car outlets.

Bell reached the large square wooden conference table that dominated the room and dropped the navy blue dossier he held on it as he turned.

"If domestic have a gripe," he said, staring at the man accompanying Cappelli, "they should call their superiors."

He held his glare for a moment before turning back to Cappelli: "What do you have for me?"

"McNulty the man from Scotland Yard has it," replied Cappelli. He pointed to the man beside him without taking his eyes off Bell.

Bell looked at the man sternly again. "Well?"

"We have three late-closing nights in London each week," said the middle-aged McNulty in a Scottish accent. "Each night pertains to a different . . ."

"Skip the commercial, McNulty," Bell cut in icily. "Wednesday. Night. That's all I'm interested in."

McNulty flushed, flustered by Bell's American bluntness.

"All areas close at five-thirty except Knightsbridge and the King's Road. They close at seven," he responded.

Bell bit his lower lip. "Every other area in London closes at five-thirty? In thirty-seven minutes?"

McNulty nodded.

Abruptly, Bell reclined on the swivel chair and locked his fingers behind his head. His eyes gradually glazed with thought and, as was his habit in such circumstances, he bit his lower lip again.

"He hasn't had time," he murmured at length, and to no one in particular, swivelling towards the bank of twinkling electronic maps on the right wall. "Those tapes are over two hours long. No matter how you figure it . . ."

He stopped and turned back to the two men.

"How long does it take for the streets to empty after closing time, McNulty?" he asked.

"It's an attrition process. About half an hour, I suppose."

Bell nodded and stabbed the air with his right index finger. "Let's close the net at five on the two late-closing areas," he commanded. "Cappelli, I want everyone in Gleeson's group combing those two districts from five onwards. The domestics can cover the rest. And you," he said, turning to McNulty, "after five-thirty, re-assign as many men as you can from the other areas to these two parts. Just keep skeleton groups operating in the areas you think appropriate. Assign five – no, make that ten – of your people to start calling at every shop with the facilities for recording tapes in those two neighbourhoods. If he hasn't been in, tell them to call you if he does. Circulate his description: last seen wearing black pants, black leather windbreaker, white shirt, five-ten, 175 pounds, black curly hair, everything. And make it formal. Use official language . . . call him a nut, dangerous, Jack the Ripper, whatever it is that turns you people on."

Harrods: 5.21 p.m.

In the claustrophobic cubicle at Harrods, the voice of James Farrar droned on.

"Based on ORAL's findings, the following preliminary programme sets out the optimum strategy for controlled destabilisation, re-grouping and establishment of a new, friendly and compliant government.

"One: The annual CIA subsidy to the mullahs – an estimated four hundred and forty million dollars a year initiated at our behest in 1953 to calm the growing unrest of the country at that time – must be halted forthwith.

These CIA subsidies are obviously counter-productive to the new goals."

There had been widespread rumours of this in Iran. But Adel had always dismissed them as foolish, hysterical and paranoid.

"Two: The strategy depends on an extensive roster of reliable Iranian nationals to carry through key tasks at all stages. It is a list of competent individuals with a prior record of assistance."

"Have these people been approached?" asked the voice of John Alexander Case.

"No, sir. The timing is still vague. The operation hasn't received final authorisation yet. Only the preliminary phases have been activated."

"Very well. Please go ahead," said Case.

"Two opposing views presently make up Iranian – indeed world – public opinion. One is the sympathetic view that the Shah's errors are natural and could be expected since he had so little with which to begin. Coupled with this is the belief that external pressures on him prevented wide success.

"The opposing view is that in the heady intoxication of power, the Shah has blown a unique opportunity for development and modernisation by attempting too much, too soon, and too corruptly.

"The propaganda process in the West will be adjusted to encourage the latter view.

"To undermine the support being given to the Shah in the west, SAVAK's record of ruthlessness, torture and total disregard of human rights must be given full exposure. In due course we hope to create an atmosphere in Western public opinion that will strongly discourage continued support for the Shah's regime. This is the core of the entire programme; the Shah's confidence must be shattered, turning a basically indecisive man to impotence."

The dull voice then proceeded to outline the steps that would be taken in Iran itself. Iranian "Friends" already in important positions in the Shah's administration would encourage the Shah towards immensely ambitious development programmes, which the country's infrastructure clearly did not have the capacity to handle. The resulting chaos, corruption and discontent would be phenomenal. Care would have to be taken to involve all – he stressed "all" – the Imperial family in the corruption and pay-offs. Public discontent would over a period of two or three years be brought to fever pitch, stoked by an economic expansion apparently out of control.

Eventually, in order to extricate himself and buy back the people's loyalty, the Shah would be encouraged to embark on a political liberalisation programme. The press would be gradually unmuzzled, politicians allowed to express their views and some political prisoners released.

"*If matters proceed as we project, that's when the dam bursts and the regime begins to disintegrate.*"

And how right the bastard's "projections" had been, thought Adel.

"*What's the catalyst to bring things to a head, Jim?*" asked Case. "*We already got the Shah to castrate just about anyone with balls. What's left?*"

"*We recommend a force used often in the old days, but one that has been dormant in more modern times. The use of religion. It is easily the most effective force to mobilise and cement a revolution in Iran. The vehicle of religion lends itself well to other parts of the Middle East if and when it becomes necessary – Iran, Egypt, Saudi Arabia, Libya or wherever else Islam is a force. It really makes no difference. Once Islamic fundamentalism is born, nothing can stop it. Armed might is ineffectual when faced with aspiring martyrs.*"

"*How about leadership?*" asked the raspy voice of David Thorncroft.

"*In that context we sought the advice of our British counterparts who, because of their historical role in the fanatical Muslim Brotherhood and their widespread contacts with the clergy in Iran, are more finely tuned to*

Islam than we are. They have agreed with our conclusion. The movement must be led by a fundamentalist theologian with the appropriate personality, eloquence and charisma."

"*Do we have one?*" Again Thorncroft.

"*Yes, sir. The man we've selected is Ayatollah Ruhollah Khomeini.*"

The Mall: 5.40 p.m.

"Gleeson's unit is forty minutes into their sweep, sir," said Cappelli, pointing at the wall to Bell's left. "Those two screens isolate the late-closing sectors. The right is Knightsbridge, the left King's Road."

Bell slowly closed the dark blue leather dossier he had been studying and looked up from the desk, first at Cappelli and then at the wall.

The scale of the maps, he noticed immediately, had tightened. Not only were the major arteries, streets and alleys pinpointed but now buildings, shops – even street stalls – were discernible. The flashing lights were closer and more numerous – so close in some cases that they seemed like ever-changing, multi-coloured clusters of space invaders on some twenty-five-cent electronic arcade machine. The pace of the lights had quickened too, but that, he knew, was an optical illusion; the areas the men and vehicles were covering were smaller, their concentric sweeps shorter, their beats more concise.

The clock above the screens read five-forty-two p.m. There was still a little more time, he thought, but not very much. He studied the dark areas of the maps, those that fell out of the range of the lights or between them. He studied the huge mass of the Harrods building and further down the road, Harvey Nichols and considered the heavy flow of human traffic that circulated around them in Brompton Road, Sloane Street, Sloane Square, Hans Crescent, Hans Road and up towards Beauchamp Place and the museums.

By now Adel knew, thought Bell. Whether he had duplicated the tapes was another matter and beside the point. Knowing was enough. He held his gaze as he barked:

"Get some more domestics in! There's too much black up there." He pointed to the wall.

Cappelli didn't move. "If you want results, sir, you'll have to tell McNulty yourself," he said. "He isn't exactly listening to us."

But he was unfortunate. His words were lost on Bell. The unilluminated mass within the perimeters of Harrods had absorbed the Colonel's attention.

Harrods: 5.40 p.m.

"*You may recall the man,*" said Farrar. "*In 1963 he violently opposed the Shah's land reforms and enfranchisement of women. He orchestrated widespread protest riots which were mercilessly crushed by the Iranian army.*"

He paused, seeming to shuffle papers.

"*Mean-looking bastard,*" said Case. Farrar had obviously passed round some pictures.

"*This guy's got class,*" piped the high-pitched voice of Solomon.

"*I say, very Old Testament,*" muttered Sinclair.

"*Gott verdamme,*" intoned the baron.

"*Tell me, Sol, could this be the Messiah you people have been waiting for?*" asked David Thorncroft.

They all chuckled and after a respectable interval, Farrar continued: "*He is a religious mystic, sir, whose only motivation outside sharia or Islamic law is limited to his personal antipathy to change in any form. He is a kind of idealist, with a bizarre conviction in his holy mission as an ascetic spiritual leader. Like the Shah, he believes he is the instrument of God and therefore above error. He is also blessed by Allah with that most impressive of talents: arousing the masses to the rage of jihad, or holy war."*

Adel shook his head and rubbed his damp forehead in despair. Mariam was right. The sceptics, the cynics, had been right: Khomeini was a company man, and his support came from outside, from the same men who once helped the Shah.

He felt cold as he recalled the old woman's words: "If you lift his beard you'll find 'Made in England' printed underneath."

But by now nothing surprised him any more. The last hour had numbed him.

"Khomeini's simplicity and lack of any twentieth-century experience makes him enormously malleable. In essence, the last person the Ayatollah talks to is the person who forms the Ayatollah's attitudes.

"It is essential, therefore, that from today onwards we keep him on a very, very tight leash. We have taken the necessary steps in this direction already; several of our people, both Iranian and otherwise, with a history of opposition to the Shah, have moved to his home in Iraq. Their instructions are to provide him with organisation. They are busy setting up what we have called the Khomeini International. It will be a terrorist network in association with the Libyans, Syrians, PLO, the fanatical Muslim Brotherhood and other groups, and will operate active cells within Iran."

So that's who they were, these Ghotbzadehs, Yasdis, Bani-Sadrs who suddenly blossomed from nowhere.

"Khomeini himself, however, is only an instrument. And then on a short-term basis. Options for the long-term government of Iran have been purposely kept open. It is . . ."

Suddenly, Adel knew he wasn't alone in the room. Slowly, very slowly at first, the sounds of the tape faded, and his body hardened into a weapon of defence.

He jerked sharply around on the stool to face the door. There, in the doorway, stood a tall, well-dressed, powerful-looking man. His eyes exuded the welcome of a smiling cobra.

Rutland Gate: 6.01 p.m.

Directly across the street from Harrods, less than two hundred yards away, Jane Bennett dropped her pink bathrobe to the floor and stepped down into the sunken Jacuzzi in her Rutland Gate apartment. As was her habit, she tested the temperature of the water on the first step before plunging in.

She sat on the mosaic seat at one end of the bath for a moment, and lit the cigarettes she held. Then slowly she lowered her slim body into the turbulent water until it was submerged completely – all, that is, but her head and her right arm. That, like a periscope, stuck straight up in the air, protected from the occasional spray of the competing currents below.

She took a deep drag and held her breath for a full ten seconds before exhaling. Then she repeated the action twice more in quick succession, only now she submerged her head, held her breath and released her breath below the water. It was another habit she had acquired. Whether at the end of an arduous day of shooting or the start of a long evening ahead, the marijuana combined with the sensuous, gentle massage of the Jacuzzi relaxed, refreshed and aroused her as the occasion demanded.

She lay back and took another drag, opening her legs to allow the bubbles to caress her all over.

It was, she admitted as she gazed at the smoke-mirrored ceiling, the very essence of self-indulgence. She dragged once again and let her eyes roam round the luxurious bathroom. What a shame that her mother had not lived to see these days. She had witnessed only her daughter's rough, raw initiation to success, never the happy content of its achievement.

She recognised the beginnings of a morbid trip and switched off. She took one last drag before tossing the roach into the ashtray on the side and submerging herself, twisting on to her belly as she did so. Even below the water she heard the trill of the telephone.

Harrods: 6.01 p.m.

The icy stare of the man seemed to last an eternity. He stood quite still in the doorway, his eyes challenging, ready to pounce. Then slowly and silently, he unbuttoned his white trenchcoat, his eyes never leaving Adel's.

He was trapped. The thought pounded in his head. Bell had found him and he wasn't ready. Not yet. He hadn't had time; he had to insure himself. He had to escape.

"Who are you?" asked the man.

Adel played for time. He smiled at the man and slipped off the earphones.

He had to get out. And to do that he had only one choice. He picked up the long, heavy microphone and casually started unscrewing it from its base.

"I asked you a question, young man," said the intruder as he moved closer. "Who are you?" He placed his hands on his hips and glared down.

Adel curled his fingers around the disengaged microphone unit and gripped it tightly. He looked up at the man and prayed he would take one step closer.

"What are you doing here?"

Adel did not hear the rest. His eyes, his attention, his

very being were on that one small rectangular green badge adorning the man's lapel.

The Mall: 6.01 p.m.

"McNulty," said Bell as the tall, bespectacled, middle-aged man approached his desk, followed by Cappelli. "See that up there?" He shouted, ostensibly to beat the noise of the whirring machines. But the unhurried pace of the man also grated.

"Yes, sir," responded McNulty after taking his time in studying the two blinking, bleeping electronic maps on the wall.

"It seems to me that there's still a hunk of black up there. Does it look covered to you?"

McNulty studied the wall at length before responding. "Nothing is ever quite airtight, sir," he said with measured calm. "The Yorkshire Ripper slipped through the net despite fifty different interrogations."

Bell nodded gently and tried to suppress the anger he felt inside. "Terrific." He glanced at Cappelli, then down at the desk. "He is not the Yorkshire Ripper, McNulty," he said in a slow, deliberate monotone. "We are not the CID and we have only one shot at it." He looked up, straight at McNulty, and gave him a vicious, piercing glare. "And we have less than an hour to do it in."

The Scotsman said nothing.

"There's hunks of black up there, McNulty," said Bell, his face a paralysed mask, his eyes unblinking. "And I want them lit up. Like a Christmas tree I want them lit up, especially the two large department stores, Harrods and Harvey Nichols."

Harrods: 6.02 p.m.

Adel sighed deeply. He waited, waited for the build-up of tension and violence to ease from his body. Still gripping the microphone, he turned to look up at the imposing figure. And his green Harrods badge.

"What does it look like I'm doing?" he asked, trying to sound like a cocky British worker. "Mending the equipment, that's what I'm doing."

The man scrutinised him for a moment. Then he slowly looked around the small disorganised room full of boxes and components and a haphazard mix of other electronic equipment. His gaze stopped at the unscrewed microphone in Adel's hand.

"Oh," he replied, less assured. "Never seen you around here before. Where's Kevin?" He was flustered slightly but not enough to admit it to a lower being.

"Sick," snapped Adel confidently, busying himself with re-assembling the microphone. He wanted desperately to sigh. A long deep sigh of relief.

"Oh," repeated the man. "Poor chap. Nothing serious, I trust?"

"Nah."

"Good. Well, must run," he said airily, hanging up his raincoat next to Adel's black leather jacket. "Cheerio."

Adel slumped on the stool, staring at the closed door. After a long moment he turned wearily and slipped on the earphones. Immediately the voice of Farrar emerged. But obviously he was now on to something else.

"*. . . which leads to the topic of the Shah himself,*" said Farrar over the distinct sound of pages being turned quickly.

"*Is this the psychograph?*" asked the baron.

"*Yes, sir, it's the non-specific summary. A full*

psychographic study is a lengthy, intimately detailed analysis of a specific target's personality and behavioural traits. Each sector of a target's make-up is examined to determine its influence on his or her life. Areas such as childhood, traumas, fixations, sexual behaviour, religious upbringing, influences, response to stress, defence mechanisms, friends, etcetera.

"*What I'm reading is a very general summary. If any further information is required . . .*"

"*No,*" said the baron. "*That won't be necessary.*"

There was a murmur of agreement.

Farrar started again. He seemed to be reading. "*Mohammed Reza Pahlavi was a shy, sensitive boy, lacking self-confidence . . .*"

Adel listened to a precise, perceptive discourse on the Shah's history and personality, his shrewdness and intelligence, his indecision, weakness and sense of insecurity; his domination by an unbending father and a ruthless twin sister; his love-hate relationship with the West – the awe he had of it and the deep, paranoid anxiety it instilled in him.

"*Domestically, the same traits are apparent. His regime has a veneer of democracy but it is superficial. Severe personal insecurity leads to fear of opposition from any quarter. This in turn pre-empts adoption of any Western institutions. Checks, balances and the diversification of power are concepts alien to him. He tends only to promote and feel comfortable with individuals whom he can dominate. He therefore surrounds himself with sycophants and opportunists of little value in matters of state. They manipulate his weak psychological make-up, doting on him while simultaneously plundering the country.*"

There followed an analysis of the Shah's three marriages, with special emphasis on the artistic and cultural pretensions of his present wife, the Empress Farah.

"*The Shah's extra-marital life is extensive. These activities are primarily relationships with 'filles de plaisir', to use the French term. They are inevitably young, blonde, buxom and of the wholesome Californian variety. Insecurity, shyness and lack of confidence drive Mohammed Reza to spend these hours in pleasant conversation and chit-chat over tea. The consensus of opinion among his female companions is that he is pleasant, well mannered, considerate, intelligent and very, very lonely. He is not sexually prolific.*

"That, gentlemen, is Mohammed Reza Pahlavi, the Shah of Iran," concluded Farrar.

"Did you say 'tea'?" pounced David's fragile voice.

"Yes," replied Farrar. *"Tea."*

"That in itself suggests an inefficient use of resources. The job's wasted on him," said David Thorncroft.

There was a roar of laughter.

6.15 p.m.

Bell closed his eyes and lifted his feet from the table. The man standing before him was not being difficult, he decided. Not intentionally, anyway. He was just ponderous and British. Every proposed action was arduous, every idea impossible, every speed slow. He had just wasted another ten precious minutes on this idiot from Scotland Yard.

"McNulty," he said with controlled patience. "We are not talking about our field assets; no one wants to increase the number of operatives involved. We are talking about bringing a major portion of these assets together, in one place, at one time. We are talking about cordoning off one section of one area, and a very small and inconsequential area at that."

"Inconsequential!" cried McNulty, suddenly coming to life. "That inconsequential area you are talking about, Colonel, is Harrods department store, which has a four-and-a-half-acre ground plan consisting of fourteen acres of selling space, eight and a half acres of stockrooms and back-up services, eighty display windows, fifty lifts, twelve escalators, and over thirty-five doors of one sort or another. It also has twenty-five thousand automatic sprinkler heads, one hundred and ninety-seven hydrants, eight hundred and forty-one fire extinguishers, nine hundred and ninety automatic fire-resistant doors, two thousand two hundred and twenty-six heat sensors and one hundred and fourteen hose reels."

He paused, withdrew a pack of Senior Service cigarettes and lit one, holding on to the burning match. "Even an amateur could manage to create pandemonium with what Harrods has to offer. All it needs is a bit of intelligence," he said, moving the match an inch forward. "Can you imagine, Colonel Bell, what chaos, panic, death and injury he could cause by merely using his initiative? One wrong move in that store and there'd be a string of questions to be answered."

He took a slow drag of his unfiltered cigarette, shook the match and dropped it in the ashtray on Bell's desk. "You know Harrods is no ordinary store Colonel," he said grandly. "Why, the Queen of England shops there."

6.19 p.m.

"*Domestically – in the United States, that is*" – Adel heard Farrar clarify quickly – "*the tide of opinion is turning against the Shah. Many of the nation's top corporations, once anxious to play ball with Iran, have become disenchanted by the Shah's grandiloquence. The military and intelligence communities are concerned about an excessive reliance on one man . . .*"

Case's resonant voice interrupted. "*Yes, and the Shah's fortunately managing to alienate a wide variety of other powerful interest groups too. The human rights advocates, the nuclear proliferation lobby, the oil price control lobby, the arms control lobby, the anti-Israel lobby, the pro-Arab lobby, the Left, the Democratic Party and the liberals, particularly the Kennedys – they'd all be quite happy to see the Shah go.*"

6.19 p.m.

He had a point, thought Bell, glancing at his watch.

"Besides, Colonel Bell," suggested McNulty. "In the circumstances, it seems unnecessary to cordon off the entire store; perhaps a handful of people would put your mind at rest. After all, the manager of the radio and television department has been contacted and he clearly insisted that Harrods does not provide such a service. Certainly not at the speed we are talking about."

6.22 p.m.

"*The pro-Shah element in the West – particularly the United States – must be held in check. Many of the grandees of the Republican Party, like the Rockefellers, the Annenbergs, the Scrantons, have established close personal relations with the Shah. The axis of mutual flattery between Teheran and mid-town Manhattan is a powerful one. Dr Kissinger, of course, lends it much respectability,*" said Farrar.

"*Timing is critical. The influence of these people must be kept in check at least until the operation has reached the point of no return and its momentum has become unstoppable. They must be . . .*"

David Thorncroft intervened. "*I don't think it's necessary to dwell on how to handle what you call the pro-Shah element.*"

"I'm sorry, sir – I only meant to . . ."
"Yes, yes. Please proceed."

The flimsy door of the studio crashed open and the young salesman appeared, gesturing nervously.

Adel withdrew the earphones and stopped the tape.

"Look, sir, you'd better get out of here. The manager is asking about you."

Adel said nothing; his mind raced. Of course. Bell would know. And out there on the streets Bell would have an army looking for him.

He glanced at the progress of the tape. It was almost finished. Five minutes, maybe ten, were left. And he needed the copies to be complete.

He rubbed his shirt to soak up the sweat and looked up at the flustered salesman.

"Five minutes," he said. "I'll be out in five minutes." He pressed the start button. As he placed the earphones back on he heard the panicking voice of the retreating salesman.

"That . . . that's fine with me but . . . but . . . I'm leaving and I'll deny any involvement."

"The man we've chosen to coordinate this entire programme – for many reasons – is Colonel Grover Cleveland Bell."

Adel suddenly felt queasy as he recalled his conversation with Case; his stomach churned. He lit a cigarette quickly and inhaled to fight the unsettled feeling the salesman's warning and the mention of Bell's name had created.

Knightsbridge: 6.30 p.m.

Jim Gleeson scanned the crowd as the unmarked police car crawled past Sloane Street on to the Brompton Road. To his right he saw the Scotch House, and to his left, one fashionable boutique after another: Lucy's, Fiorucci, Yves Saint-Laurent, Charles Jourdan. Each was packed with a cosmopolitan assortment of customers.

The rain was a godsend, he reflected, as his eyes registered the slowly quickening pace of the red, blue and silver fox coats, the occasional Blackglama mink and the Burberry raincoats and umbrellas that flashed by. The faster pace of pedestrians seeking to escape the approaching downpour served to isolate the smallest unhurried movement. The brittle bones of the arthritic, the slow movements of the elderly, the casual amble of lovers or the slightest limp had all become easily discernible.

"Gleeson." Bell's voice barked over the unmarked police car radio cutting straight through the endless communications between vehicles, walkie-talkies, police stations and Cappelli and McNulty in the Sit. Room.

Gleeson grabbed the microphone and pressed its button.

"Yes, Grove."

"Where are you?"

Gleeson looked out of the rain-speckled side window of the car. "On the Brompton Road. Just outside Mappin & Webb."

"How far is that from Harrods?"

The CID officer driving the car pointed to the huge, glittering department store looming up ahead.

"Fifty yards."

"Great. Go to door number five. That's in Hans Crescent. There's four of you in the car and another four are waiting at the door. Check it out, Jim. The manager responds negative. But let's check it out ourselves."

"Sure, Grove." He turned to the driver and waved a hand casually. "You heard the man." But Gleeson did not mention that never in twenty years of working for him had he heard Grover Cleveland Bell sound so urgent. Or so worried.

Harrods: 6.30 p.m.

"*The overriding issue that influenced our selection of Colonel Grover Cleveland Bell,*" said Farrar, "*is our inability to count, as in the past, on formal government support.*

"*Colonel Bell's background in this area goes back twenty-five years – to the birth of the CIA and before. He's occupied pivotal positions within the intelligence community; OSS agent, planner, plotter, spy-maker, military intelligence, Vietnam, etcetera, and of course, finally, the coordination of the entire covert activity of the nation. Recently Bell's had more than his fair share of problems with a mistrusting President and the growing public disenchantment with the operational side of intelligence activities. Unfortunately for him, but fortunately for our purposes, he has become one of the victims of Watergate.*"

Adel looked at his watch.

"*. . . intricately aware of the workings of government in London, Paris, Teheran . . .*"

A minute had passed since the salesman had left the cubicle. And out there in the streets the net would be closing.

"*. . . and many of those in positions of power and influence owe much to Grover Cleveland Bell . . .*"

Should he leave? Now? Adel glanced at the revolving tape. There was very little left. A minute. Maybe two.

Knightsbridge: 6.31 p.m.

The Rover 2600 pulled up sharply at door number five of Harrods department store. The driver disregarded the turning heads his screeching, sliding stop had attracted. He made no effort to park carefully. He stopped at an angle, the car's tail jutting into the driving lane, its nose angling into a space barely wide enough to accommodate its width. A few yards ahead, another empty, unmarked, white Rover waited, half-on and half-off the pavement. From its exhaust the fumes of an idling engine rose into the damp, cold night air.

Beneath the door's wrought-iron and glass awning, four burly men in beige trenchcoats stood waiting, blocking the hurried movements of the heavy pedestrian traffic. As the car stopped they turned to the four alighting passengers and with barely a nod of recognition the eight men moved through the swinging doors into the massive, bustling complex. Not one of the group noticed the disapproving expression of the green-clad doorman. His warning on parking tickets went unheeded.

Instead they moved quickly and silently through the crowds to the base of the escalators.

"Let's spread out," said Gleeson. He turned to his domestic counterpart, the man who had shared his car for the past five hours. "How do we cover this place, Henry?"

Henry Pearce did not hesitate. "The radio and television department is on the second floor," he said. "And the subject has a gammy leg, so presumably his natural inclination will be to use either the escalators or the lifts. If we scatter and join upstairs we can cover eight of the possibilities at his disposal. That's the best we can do, I'm afraid," he concluded with the snap logic of experience.

"How long do we have?"

Pearce looked at his watch. "The store closes in twenty-seven minutes."

"Fine," snapped Gleeson. "I'll take these escalators. You guys separate and fan out."

Harrods: 6.31 p.m.

The last two minutes of the tape seemed to go on for an eternity, grinding out compliments to Bell's organisational skills, knowledge of the Iranian political scene and back to his influence base in Washington and the hold he had on the capital's power-brokers. It put him in the same league as James Angleton, Richard Helms, William Colby.

"*He can, shall we say, persuade the reticent,*" was how Case put it when referring to Bell's famous files on congressmen, senators, senior bureaucrats and lobbyists.

"*And thirdly . . .*" Case paused.

Adel again looked at his watch. But he was yanked back by the words that followed:

"*. . . he's frankly the toughest son-of-a-bitch any of us is ever likely to come across. He has a healthy element of the brute in him which could be useful in the more delicate moments of this operation. Now, Mr Farrar, please continue.*"

"*Ahh . . . yes, sir. To break down the Iranian security and armed forces, we have elicited the assistance of the top man the army has assigned to Iran – the deputy chief of European . . .*"

Abruptly, the steely, ice-cold voice vanished. The tape had ended.

Michael Adel hit the stop buttons and leaned forward on his stool. He closed his eyes and massaged his tense, throbbing forehead.

He was exhausted. Exhausted, lonely and frightened. There seemed no point to it all. No point in running. Sooner or later they'd catch up with him. He opened his eyes and despondently pressed the eject button on the four machines. Out there they were looking for him. An army of them. Trained men, equipped, and well rested. And what did he have going for him? he asked as he wearily gathered the tapes.

He looked at the two dirt-stained original Sony tapes, then at the six brand-new plastic boxes that constituted three complete copies. They were his only hope. Somehow he had to find a way to insure himself. He had to find someone Bell hadn't covered.

Before he could do that, though, he had to get out of here. He had to slip through the cordon that was drawn around the brightly lit, late-closing streets of Knightsbridge.

He stood and walked towards the coat-rack and reached for his jacket. Abruptly, he pulled back. That's what they were looking for. A man with a limp. A man with a black leather jacket, black slacks, white shirt. It wasn't much in the way of deception or camouflage, he thought, as he grabbed the outsized white trenchcoat the man had hung next to his jacket, but it was better than nothing. He stuffed the tapes into its deep pocket before putting it on. It was too long and baggy – perfect. He looked heavier and, he hoped, shorter. He lifted the material above the belt he tied loosely to give an even more bulky shape to his torso.

There was just a chance. The streets were crowded. He had to get out of there before they emptied. He glanced at his watch; it read six-thirty-three. Twenty-seven minutes before the shops closed.

Quickly he scanned the room for a pair of scissors, a razor-blade, anything sharp.

His luck was holding. He found a tape-editing device and quickly extracted the blade it held. Crudely, quickly he attacked the cast, surprised at the sharpness of the blade, pulling and tearing at the cast as he cut. With three strokes of the instrument he tore a slit through the plaster above the knee, then he ripped it even further apart with his hands. Now there would be no limp; the knee could bend. It was stiff. It was painful. But it could bend.

He opened the door and looked up and down the corridor.

Adrenalin pumped through his body as he walked down the corridor and stepped into the huge crowded radio and television showroom. His eyes scrutinised the room briefly before he started to walk across the floor, absorbing the excruciating pain but camouflaging it and hiding the stiff knee. He walked quickly, determinedly towards the far end of the room to the elevators next to the pet shop.

He hesitated at the elevator doors, then moved on quickly to the stairs directly behind. They were safer. The odds were against a man with a cast using stairs.

Though Michael Adel had no way of knowing it, those same elevator doors opened just twenty seconds later. Henry Pearce stepped through them just in time to greet Jim Gleeson as he walked into the lobby between the pet shop and the radio and television department. Neither man glanced at the stocky figure stiffly descending the stairs to their right.

Qum. Wednesday, October 31: 10.13 p.m.

Ayatollah Sadegh Khalkhali watched as the grim old man of eighty shuffled down from the rooftop balcony in his flat white slippers, a coterie of disciples clutching his arms to assist him.

Outside, the feverish crowds attending one of the Imam's rare prayer ceremonies numbered close to a hundred thousand and their impassioned roar shook the thin glass panes of the windows.

"*Allah Akbar, Marg bar Cart-er, Marg bar Shah, Marg bar Amrica* (Death to Carter, Death to the Shah, Death to America)," they chanted over and over. Each time the fervent bellow grew louder and more resonant.

It had been eight months now since the victorious Imam had returned to Iran but still the crowds in Qum grew in intensity and number. Still they came to worship the Twelfth Saint in this holy city.

He was walking majestically down the hall now; immediately to his right was his son, Ahmad and, to his left, the bespectacled Foreign Minister, Ibrahim Yazdi. Just behind followed the renowned Sadegh Ghotbzadeh, a tall, stout man with thinning hair and a bulbous nose.

Khalkhali was honoured to be among such world leaders. As he watched the entourage move down the modest hallway of the school building towards him, he was genuinely glad and spiritually uplifted to see them. It had been nearly two weeks since he had had the pleasure, and a fortnight was a long time where men of such calibre were concerned. Yes, he thought, he missed sitting and deliberating with them in this simple school building that had become the nerve-centre of the world.

And then, of course, there was the Imam himself. It had been such a long wait, but now, Allah be praised, it was over. The Twelfth Imam, the saviour, sent by God to stop corruption on earth and crimes committed against Him, had arrived. And it had all been worth it.

He took a deep breath and bent his head low in respect; Imam Khomeini was passing directly in front of him.

London. Wednesday, October 31: 6.43 p.m.

It was precisely seventeen minutes to seven when Michael Adel stepped out of Harrods into the heavy rain. Instinctively he slid into the centre of the fast-moving crowds on the pavement and let them bump and carry him towards Hans Crescent.

Hyde Park, he thought, careful to conceal himself in the middle of the pack of shoppers; he had to get to Hyde Park. It was the most ludicrous place in the world in this storm, but where else was there? His brain ticked furiously, trying to come up with a more hospitable retreat. But the thought of the tapes and the power he was up against foreclosed on each option.

He waited at the pedestrian crossing, his eyes darting everywhere yet uncertain what it was they sought. A crawling car, a lingering gaze, behind, in front. It could come from anywhere. A private army.

He shuddered as he saw two policemen turn and wait at the opposite side of the crossing. Had Bell co-opted the police too?

The lights changed and Adel held back to let a wall of pedestrians precede him. Then he started across the Brompton Road, his hooded eyes trained on the two dark blue uniformed men on the other side.

He had to get to the safety of darkness. To a wilderness where no one existed. He had to think.

The two policemen started crossing the street towards him and instinctively he added a bounce to his walk. It was excruciating but necessary. They went by without a glance.

He turned left on the other side of the road, then hard right into the relatively dark solitude of Lancelot Place. Dropping the jauntiness from his stride to reduce the painful jabs from the sharp, torn edges of the cast, he embarked on the last two hundred yards before the safety of the park.

The tapes had been cloned, he thought, and in the process he had learned why Bell had lied in that hotel room in Cannes. They had nothing to do with the Phoenix missile, or Soviet threats. They had to do with revolution and death. Planned, premeditated mass murder. And their message was not gibberish. It was crystal clear.

Ignoring the pouring rain, he dodged the traffic on Kensington Gore and entered Hyde Park.

What chance did he have? What chance did anyone have? And what did it matter anyway? Life and death and poverty and wealth. It was all a game. A chess game played by remote control; only the pieces were live. Kings and Queens, knights and bishops and rooks were all expendable pawns. Sacrificial offerings to the Merchant Gods. In Iran thousands had died in the streets. Thousands more had been made homeless. A revolution had been promoted from afar, for profit and gain.

Millions had been whipped up to religious fervour by slick propaganda programmes. Disinformation, they called it. The innocent, ignorant masses had been disinformed in the name of God.

But the reality was different. Full control over the world's energy and ever-increasing energy prices, that's what it was really about. Lower prices could not be tolerated. Not until they had cornered and consolidated a monopoly of the alternative sources of energy. That ruse was for public consumption only.

In any case it was the Shah who had forced their hand; that ungrateful army sergeant's son had overstepped the boundary. Khomeini too was merely another pawn. Like the Shah, he was expendable. Another would soon follow. And another. Until the wells dried. Until the wind and sea and sun had been harnessed. For the time being, however, he would do; a new Shah, only this time masquerading in religious garb. Devoid of the trappings of grandeur and anxious to please. Grateful for his elevation and eager to stay. Puppet-grateful.

Same shit, different colour, thought Adel as he snapped back to reality. He looked at his watch; he had been walking aimlessly for over two hours in the pouring rain oblivious of the dull ache in his leg. Through the darkening twilight and the mist and blur of rain he recognised the Serpentine a hundred yards off to his right, surrounded by a forest of trees.

He looked around again at the deserted park, the stillness, the beauty. And felt an overpowering isolation.

He needed warmth. Human warmth and loving. And a little care. He craved Sam. To talk to her and hear her innocent chatter. To feel her arms around him, protecting him from this hell of loneliness and fear. But that was a dream. It could not be.

He started walking again, limping southwards towards Knightsbridge. Through the mist, a small children's playground loomed ahead and Adel hobbled towards it. He sat, gently rocking on a swing, as the rain subsided to a gentle drizzle. He sat thinking, analysing, weighing his options. None seemed attractive. The more he considered his position, the more restricted it looked. His only hope was an unstable one – erratic and unpredictable.

"*Insure yourself. Always insure yourself,*" Yuri Allon had said over and over, repeating himself almost every hour for three days. Had the Israeli agent tried to warn him? Or was it just his mind playing tricks on him? Somehow he had to convince Bell that he was more valuable alive than dead. But how? Who else, other than Jane, was there close enough to trust; close enough to risk involvement and yet too distant in the past to be linked to him, too fleeting in his life to be recalled? Someone more dependable than dear, loyal, temperamental Jane.

Sure, he would act in character; he would go to the people Bell expected him to go to; his brother Mark and his banker in Switzerland, Claude Boissy. But he would have to do more. To survive his insurance would have to be foolproof.

But who? Who else was there that he could depend upon? Who else was there who was unknown, even to his family and closest friends?

He shook his head as his mind selected and rejected, one by one, his friends and even his casual acquaintances. The ugly truth was that Bell would have gone through the very same process. Only he would have done so with machines. In his computer file they would all be branded, like every detail of his life. As for his acquaintances, there was no reason in the world why they should be loyal to him – except for money, and money generated greed which led to blackmail. No, that would not do.

No, it would have to be Jane. Their relationship had been too distant, too fleeting, too anonymous to be remembered. He forced himself to concentrate. To remember the details of their relationship and if anything of substance had occurred to be important enough to be an asterisk in his life. To be accessible to Bell.

He had known Jane Bennett a long time, twelve years at the least. She had been a high-flying Paris model on the brink of fame when they had met by chance at a private party thrown by a mutual friend at Régine's, and for two mad, fun-filled secret weeks thereafter they had spent sleepless nights, laughing and screwing; crazy days combing the *marché aux puces*; and weekends at a rented cottage near Deauville. They had had a ball, and the relationship had been spiced by the fact that Jane was married.

After an emotional parting marked by unkept promises, Adel had gone on to his work in Iran and she to the first of her divorces and to a liaison with a famous English actor who fell insanely in love with her. Pouring money into film after film, he had pushed and shoved her to stardom.

But scandal after scandal erupted into headlines as the actor's jealous rages led to public temper tantrums; he had beaten her and imprisoned her. Their careers demanded long separations for location filming and naturally the press had fanned the flames. After about a year of marriage Jane's third husband suffered a heart attack that nearly killed him.

Finally, depressed and defeated, she had divorced. Adel saw her once more after that, recovering in a Paris hospital after a suicide attempt.

Physically she had been unaffected; she was still as beautiful as ever; but inside she was crushed. Shattered. "If this is what success brings," she had whispered sadly, "imagine what failure offers."

For the last few years, Jane Bennett had dropped out of his life. At the hospital she had sensed the importance of his love for Samira and accepted it gracefully.

Yes, she would do. She was safer than Mark or Claude Boissy. They were known quantities, marked men; traceable and controllable. Sooner or later Bell would get to them. But with Jane it was different, he thought as he stood up from the swing. During their brief time together, she had insisted on the most extreme secrecy to protect herself from her husband. There were no records of their affair. No tell-tale letters. No phone numbers. No pictures.

There was a chance.

As he hobbled towards the black wrought-iron mass of Rutland Gate a terrifying thought struck him. What if he was wrong? What if Bell had her on his files too? And under scrutiny?

Qum. Wednesday, October 31: 11.00 a.m.

"Have there been any new developments, Ayatollah?" asked Imam Khomeini after Khalkhali had settled beside him on the floor of the spartan reception room he used for his audiences. The Imam's face was expressionless; his beard formed a halo of white around baleful eyes that stared at the floor directly in front of his crossed legs. Despite the late hour, the Imam looked majestic. An immaculate black cape covered his daunting figure and his black turban was carefully angled to hide a receding forehead.

Khalkhali answered, his head bent respectfully.

"Yes, Hazrat Imam. Lamentably, it is worse than we imagined. Far worse. An old woman was buried in a shallow grave in the grounds of the house, her mutilated body barely cold. Two other corpses were found dumped in a well. They too had been viciously murdered."

"Who were they?" asked Khomeini, his voice, as always, passionless and barely audible.

"American Embassy officials, Holy One. The identification they had on them showed they were Americans and this was later confirmed by their embassy. But it is a matter of some mystery. Everything points to an alliance between this animal, Adel, and the Americans, yet there are two dead Americans in the house. There is no doubt a simple explanation, but time has been short and we wish to be very careful in our investigation."

Khomeini sat motionless, his face devoid of expression, but Khalkhali was not unduly concerned. The Imam was always calm. Even when his infant daughter had died, thirty-odd years ago, he had shown no weakness. Khalkhali had looked into the Imam's eyes that day, knowing how he adored the child, but neither sorrow nor hurt nor longing were evident in the Saint's bearing. His strength on that occasion had been almost unnatural. "He who gave the child has now recalled her," he had said as he knelt to pray. Those were the first and last words he uttered on the death of his beloved youngest daughter.

"But we found no tapes, Holy One," Khalkhali continued. "We searched the house from top to bottom and there is no sign of them."

Khomeini's frail hands shook slightly as he reached for the plate of goat cheese and mint leaves. "Was anything else revealed in your labours?" he asked, his voice low and gravelly.

This was the moment Khalkhali had been waiting for, the moment to capture the Imam's attention and arouse his interest.

"Yes, sir," he responded, looking into the Imam's eyes with an air of sincerity. "The car we found in a nearby alley has been positively identified as an American Embassy vehicle. No one came to claim it so we approached their embassy. The officials there professed ignorance as to why the car was in Farmanieh."

Khomeini nodded and Khalkhali continued: "The equipment Adel used was scattered in various hiding places in the grounds. We also have definite proof now that he was the man who entered the *komiteh* building through the underground *qanat* between the two buildings."

Still there was no reaction from the Imam.

"Everything we've found suggests that he has been generously assisted by the Americans. Many, many things suggest that, Holy One," Khalkhali lied.

To obtain full authority to handle this affair his way, without interference from that fool Prime Minister, Bazargan, it was imperative to arouse the Imam and the only way to do that was to link Adel directly to the Americans. Khalkhali was confident, too, as he wove fact and fiction, for no one could dispute him. He alone had interviewed Salim on his deathbed.

"The Palestinian, Salim, was a dying man, weak and mumbling, but he was very clear on this point. He said Adel told him that the tapes were to be delivered to the American Embassy. Surely it is safe to assume Adel made that delivery after his escape. And if so, the tapes are still there – in the embassy's compound. We moved very quickly, Holy One. The Americans did not have time to despatch them out of the country. No diplomatic pouches have left Teheran since this incident."

Khomeini raised his bushy black eyebrows. It was the first sign of emotion he had shown. He leaned forward to talk, and Khalkhali bent closer.

"Why would Adel want to kill the two Americans?" whispered the Imam.

Khalkhali answered cautiously, for the old man was shrewd. He instinctively spotted weak links in the arguments of his associates. And he was a highly suspicious man, too.

"That is a more difficult question to answer and we must first interrogate Adel, Your Eminence. The scientists believe that the evidence points directly to this man. They say the bullets that killed the two Americans are of the same type as those used in the assault on the *komiteh* building."

"Is that unusual?"

"The experts claim it is, Holy One. They say the bullets are special ones, used only by assassins. They travel faster than the normal variety, and what is more worrying, such bullets do not exist in Iran."

Khomeini lifted his eyes from the silk Kashan carpet and nodded. "But that does not explain why Adel would want to kill his American employers."

"Perhaps there was some sort of falling out among them, Your Eminence."

"Perhaps," said Khomeini doubtfully.

"We will not know the answer for sure until we interrogate Adel, Holy One. And that, *insh'Allah*, is only a question of time. We've clamped down hard on every exit from the city; the roads, the trains, the airports. Every vehicle, pedestrian, even mule is being thoroughly searched. I've also ordered the opening of the diplomatic pouches of every embassy in case the Americans should want to use one of their surrogates to export the tapes. The only country not to comply with my instructions are the Russians, and they withdrew their pouch; they did not . . ."

Khomeini's whisper interrupted him. "Adel is unimportant."

Khalkhali was surprised; he shifted uneasily on the hard floor.

"But the tapes. That is another matter. They are very important indeed."

Khalkhali made no attempt to mask his puzzled expression.

London. Wednesday, October 31: 9.00 p.m.

The front door of the flat opened in answer to his ring and her eyes glistened with delight at the sight of him. Adel slumped against the wall with relief.

"Michael," Jane Bennett cried, as she grabbed and hugged him.

"Hello, Jane." He placed an arm tentatively around her, instinctively peering into the flat beyond.

She pressed him close. "It's so lovely to see you," she said softly in his ear.

Adel stepped backwards, away from her embrace. "I did call to give you warning."

"And what a terrible line. Where were you ringing from?"

"A long way away."

"Come in. Come in," she said, pulling his arm.

Adel was eager to respond. He needed warmth and friendship. And she looked stunning.

"My God, Michael!" she exclaimed as he limped in. "You look terrible. What's wrong with you?"

Adel negotiated the three steps up to the sitting-room.

"That's exactly how I feel." He pointed at the damp patch on her dress and made a stab at light-heartedness. "You should watch who you hug these days."

"What happened to you? What's wrong with your leg?" she asked, glancing down at the stains on her blood-red silk dress.

"If you don't give me a towel, the whole place will be like that."

She glanced at the water dripping from his raincoat

on to the thick white carpet and pushed him into a corner of the room.

"God, you're a mess. Just stand still."

She began removing his clothes carefully but quickly.

"You need a bath. That's the first thing. Then some food. A good hot bowl of soup is the best thing for you."

He gratefully slipped into the luxurious soft towel robe she had provided. "Regular mother," he kidded, as she left the room again; already the tension was subsiding.

Within minutes she was back. "The soup's on the stove," she said, smiling.

"Great."

She bent down and kissed him lightly on the lips.

This was the difficult part, thought Adel. Her feeling for him had never completely died; it was he who had always discouraged and resisted it. But tonight it was going to be difficult – no, impossible – to do so.

"I need a joint," he said, knowing that unless things had changed radically, she would be able to supply one.

She smiled, walked to the cabinet and withdrew a small cherrywood humidor. "What's wrong, Michael? Why are you in such a state?" she asked, offering it to him.

He took two joints and looked up at her. "First the bath."

He inhaled on a joint of high quality Acapulco Gold as he soaked in the bathtub. It felt good; a warm, relaxing sensation suffused his body. His mind was alternately sharp and befuddled as he gazed at the water in the tub. Was the water hot or cold? He splashed his face and the scent of the jasmine bath salts from Floris filled his nostrils. Flashes of reality intruded on his reverie. He saw Mariam's wrinkled face as he buried her, interposed with Khomeini's diabolic eyes. "Made in England" printed under his beard Mariam had said. How she had chuckled. The water was too hot and he turned it to cold. It felt better and he rested his torn cast on the stool more easily. He could feel his body unwind and his mind turn away, if only for a moment, from the horrors of reality. Slowly he sank into oblivion.

He awoke suddenly. The gentle touch of Jane's caressing hands had startled him. A tray now sat across the tub.

"Thanks," he slurred, dazed but hungry.

She pulled up a stool and sat close to him. "I won't insist you tell me what happened – despite the wreckage: that beaten look, the broken leg, walking about like a madman in the rain. Of course, if you want to tell me, I'll listen."

He spoke between spoonfuls of pea and ham soup and croutons, "You're an absolute wonder. You're worth a hundred shrinks."

"Well?"

"Well what?"

"Well, are you going to tell me what happened or not?"

He closed his eyes and dropped the spoon carelessly into the bowl. He was tired and it was far more than an explanation that he would have to give. It was a trap he had to lay. A noose tied tightly around her neck . . .

"Not tonight, Jane. I'm tired and . . . Maybe tomorrow," he said as he grabbed clumsily for the edge of the tub.

She smiled in understanding and gently clasped his penis.

"We'll see," she said tugging it gently.

Both of them laughed as she helped dry him and then led him into the bedroom. She stripped the gold-patterned chintz bedcover to reveal black satin sheets.

Adel fondled the shiny material. "What the hell is this?"

She looked at him in surprise. "What's wrong with it?"

"Nothing. I've just never been seduced in a coffin before."

Tomorrow he might regret this brief interlude of

warmth and loving. But what the hell, he thought. How many tomorrows were there?

They made love without inhibition, for time had neither dulled nor reduced the burning sexual attraction they had once enjoyed.

She went down on him, slowly at first – flicking, nibbling, teasing – and gradually she loosened him up, transforming his pent-up remorse and anger to energy. Her tongue darted non-stop, building his desire, increasing his need and at the same time arousing her own body. He lay back savouring the flickering wet massage on the nerve endings and let her build to a frenzy.

But his needs were more than animal. He needed loving and warmth and proximity. He grabbed her head and brought her up to him and kissed her. It was a long, passionate embrace of the lips and they held it as they rolled over and over in the huge king-sized bed, the soft, slinky satin sheets sensuously caressing their skins.

Abruptly he entered her. At first she relished the moment, clinging to it and making it last. Then, slowly, she let it slip. She slid down on him gently, her face an open book of delight. Just as suddenly, her mood and needs changed. Like a savage mare, she started bucking wildly as she closed her eyes and bit her lower lip, digging her nails into his shoulders. As she gradually increased her ferocity, Adel forced himself to hold back – to wait – until finally she gasped and cried out again and again.

Qum. Thursday, November 1: 1 a.m.

"Ah, but the occidental mind is simple," sighed Ayatollah Khomeini gently, a faint contemplative smile on his face. He reached for the prayer beads that lay on the small wooden side-table, beside the black old-fashioned telephone, and his fragile fingers took to toying with the one hundred green *jovain* beads, moving them one at a time, first in one direction, then back again. The movement was slow and deliberate, like the words he spoke.

"They have a marvellous ability to judge everything by their own false standards. They have never had the flexibility of thought to adapt to the subtle nuances of Islam. Some have done better than others . . . the English, the French. But the Americans, they do not comprehend the beauty and joy of Islam."

The old man seemed suddenly tired. Tired and saddened by the unwillingness of some to heed his warnings.

"Islam is not a religion; it is an all-encompassing way of life. It is not an empty slogan like Christianity. It is a rigid, serious way of life and since it is the government of God, it must adhere to the principles He has clearly outlined in the Good Book. We do not need manmade laws and punishments, we have no use for Western playthings."

Khomeini sighed deeply. "But they cannot comprehend us. And I am the representative of that which they cannot understand. It suits them better to think of me as some sort of Prime Minister, or President, or Pope – as someone they can easily categorise. They refuse to believe the divine destiny with which I have been charged. They cannot comprehend that my government is Allah's government and that it is the first lawful government on earth in twelve hundred years."

Khomeini's right hand brushed and stroked his bushy white beard. "They compare me to the Shah," he said, with a short, scornful chuckle. "But they are wrong, Aghayeh Khalkhali, and do you know why?"

Khalkhali knew the Imam was not seeking an answer; he remained silent.

"The human soul, my son, is complex. It cannot be easily satisfied. It needs profound nourishment. The Western culture creates an atmosphere of dark despair in which avarice is its colour and greed its shape. Their people are mentally and emotionally deprived. They spend their lives subsidising this aesthetic void by amassing great fortunes: large houses, expensive cars, coloured stones, airplanes and boats. They do this to give their empty soulless lives meaning because that is what they have been brainwashed to believe. Success, they are taught, is material wealth and hedonistic pleasure.

"The germ of greed once planted, my son, is difficult to remove." The old man raised his eyebrows, his gaze fixed on Khalkhali now. "But they can never achieve happiness, because the path they embark upon, encouraged and indoctrinated century after century by their corrupt governments in partnership with their misguided churches, is wayward and devoid of meaning.

"They are not blessed with the way of Allah. Instead of meditating and looking inward, like stubborn rams they butt their heads against the wall of material wealth in search of a security and happiness that cannot be found on this earth."

Khalkhali was puzzled by the Imam's speech. What had this to do with Adel and the tapes? He listened intently to catch every syllable.

"And so, of course, they are awed by death. They are in terror of the state where aches and pains disappear, where troubles evaporate, where the warmth of constant security and relief from labour mesh with unlimited meditation and rest to form true happiness. The state of communion with God."

He shook his head and smiled. "*Halah man-ra tahdid mikonan*, now they threaten me with death, my friend; they seek to frighten an eighty-year-old priest with martyrdom." The smile turned to laughter and his chest and belly bounced with joy. "I who value death above all else.

"They are children, are they not?" he asked rhetorically, as the laughter subsided and he reclined on the large, silk back-rest pillow.

Khalkhali sat waiting. The Imam had not finished.

The old man's whisper returned. "My son, we worked together recently, the Western world and I. It was a marriage of convenience; we needed each other to remove the cancerous regime of the Shah."

Khalkhali listened intently as the old man outlined how he had allowed the Americans to, as they thought, manipulate him. How he had permitted Ayatollah Beheshti to play along with them in the negotiations – conceding point after point on the post-revolution power structure of Iran, its government, intelligence organisations and armed forces.

"Now they want to blackmail me with exposure of this past relationship, believing my people will be disappointed to learn of my association with the West in defeating the Shah. Of course, Allah forewarned me; I knew such a day would come. It is something I, with the help of Allah, have prepared for."

"Allah Akbar," said Khalkhali.

"Six months ago in France that creature of corruption, Ali Mahmoudi, passed word to me that he had information on tapes secreted somewhere in Iran which recorded the relationship between the Americans and us. He had stolen it from the Americans. That despicable wart on God's earth desired to sell us these tapes, but naturally we ignored him. Undoubtedly he has now sold them back to the Americans or they have at least found out about them somehow, and now wish to retrieve them for their own purposes."

Khalkhali nodded but said nothing. He did not know what to say in the face of the Imam's revelations.

Khomeini frowned and the monotone continued. "Actually it is unimportant where these tapes are for I am sure the Americans have copies. And I doubt you will find them, no matter how efficient and dedicated your efforts."

"Then how must we stop them?" ventured Khalkhali cautiously.

Khomeini turned slowly towards his disciple. "My son, never fear the mighty," he said with exquisite calm. "For the mighty are not motivated by victory. They are preoccupied by defeat."

A smile spread slowly across Khalkhali's face. "As with the Shah, Holy One."

"Precisely, my son. The Americans, this nation of infants, have provided us with the very stick with which to beat them and all they have stood for in this country."

"Holy One, by what means?" Khalkhali prompted.

"I will inform you. I will inform you at the appropriate time."

London. Thursday, November 1: 10.00 a.m.

"American Embassy, good morning," said the polite female operator.

"My name is Michael Adel and you have fifteen seconds to connect me to Colonel Grover Cleveland Bell."

Immediately the line clicked and Adel knew that his guess had been right.

"Congratulations, Michael, you did very well. I must admit your speed and efficiency surprised even me. I suppose you called to finalise this whole thing?" The phone exaggerated the chirpiness in Bell's voice.

Adel watched the moving second hand on the Imhof clock beside the telephone. "Sure," he responded curtly.

"There's a small house in Shepherd's Market, near Curzon Street. It's off the beaten track and quite safe. Are you familiar with the area?"

"Birds of a feather flock together," mumbled Adel.

There was a moment's hush before Bell responded. "What was that?" he asked.

Adel thought the moment's silence exaggerated. "I know the area. It's where two-bit hustlers walk the streets."

There was another, even longer pause.

"Things turned out well, Michael. It's all over now. We don't need to fight about it. The location of the house is safe, nothing else."

Adel's eyes were riveted to the clock. "Safe for whom, Bell? If you're worried about me, I'd prefer to meet somewhere more public, a place swarming with people. Besides, there's a couple of things that might interest you, things that might persuade you that my well-being is in your best interest."

"Back to that again," sighed Bell.

They were one minute ten seconds into the conversation, Adel noted as he replied. "Let's say the lobby of the Berkeley Hotel."

"Half an hour suit you?" asked Bell.

"Only if you're willing to wait several hours. No. Let's say six o'clock this evening, Colonel. And alone. No bodyguards, advisers, *consiglieri* in drag as waiters or doormen."

"That suits me fine," agreed Bell. "Tell me, Michael, was it easy getting out?"

The elapsed time of their conversation stood at a few seconds over two minutes and Bell was obviously trying to stretch it out. Adel pictured the wires and computers buzzing and clicking and humming in a desperate search to make the right connection.

"Six o'clock, Bell," he replied and hung up. He checked the clock and then looked at the telephone. "Bastard."

"Is that your way of saying good morning?" came the sleepy voice of Jane Bennett.

He turned in the bed and kissed her. In the dim light, two flawless dimples receded attractively on the small of her back. He swung the cast over the smooth heart-shaped curves of her hips and she arched her back in assistance.

London. Thursday, November 1: 3.00 p.m.

By three o'clock, Adel had finished his letters. One was addressed to his brother, Mark, the second to his banker friend Claude Boissy in Switzerland. Both were attached to heavily taped envelopes that, as the covering letter instructed, were to be kept sealed until his death. Inside, each manilla envelope contained two tapes, clones of Mahmoudi's originals. There was also a short note identifying the voices and companies he had been able to recognise.

The covering letters requested that in the event of his death the tapes be transcribed and duplicated, then sent to selected journalists, newspapers, writers and scholars taking in the whole political spectrum. He stressed that neither the tapes nor the transcripts should be released unless and until he died and he urged both men to conceal the tapes as cleverly and securely as possible and to withhold any information or knowledge of the tapes from even the closest of confidants.

At any rate, he told himself, he was going through the motions, acting in character. He had no choice; the existence of both men was known to Bell; they were the obvious choices; Bell would intercept the tapes.

He sat for a long time wondering if he was actually exposing the two men to any danger. He decided he wasn't. Besides, it was a risk he had to take. And what did it matter anyway if Boissy faced a little danger. Even Swiss bankers had to face some responsibility from time to time. Boissy had made enough money off him over the years. Now he could start to earn it.

His brother Mark was another matter. There he could take no chances. Mark was more than a brother to him. Since childhood each had been the other's only true friend. He couldn't bear the thought of endangering Mark. Any insurance policy he took out with Bell would have to cover Mark too.

From Jane's living-room he dialled Mark's number at his house less than a mile away in Chelsea. It rang a long time before there was a response.

"Hello." It was Mark's longtime housekeeper.

"Hello, Theresa. Let me talk to Mark," he said brusquely, cutting through the formalities. He would be expected to call him. So even if Mark's phone was tapped, he would have to go through the motions. But quickly, before they could trace the call.

"I'm afraid he's not here, Mr Michael. He's not in London at the moment."

"Where is he?"

The hesitation was momentary but unsettling. "I. . . I don't know, sir. Probably the States."

Adel frowned; Mark was never out of touch with his house. As an independent consultant, specialising in commercial risk analysis, he usually worked from home and in the absence of a wife, Theresa acted as the conduit. She always knew where to contact him.

It didn't make sense, thought Adel. It was highly unusual – especially in view of their close relationship, of which Theresa was well aware.

"Well, I need to talk to him urgently. When do you expect him back?"

"He didn't say. Not for a few days, sir."

Adel thought for a moment before speaking. "Listen, Theresa. There's a letter I've got to get to him. I'll send it round in a little while. The important thing is for him to contact me as soon as he sees it. I have to go over a few of the details with him. I'll send it over by taxi shortly."

If the phone's tapped, that should do it, he thought.

"Very well, sir. I'll be in all day anyway."

Adel was puzzled. Why was Theresa reluctant to tell him where Mark was? Or was he being unduly suspicious and paranoid? Maybe Theresa really didn't know. Or perhaps she was making a mountain out of a molehill – God knows she did that often enough. To her, secrecy was a door to romance. Mark was probably off to some conference or other, and she was being self-important again . . .

"Now, what do you want to talk to me about?" said Jane, interrupting his thoughts. She walked through the bedroom door and into the sitting-room dressed in skintight black leather that set off her blonde hair.

"You look great," he said.

"It's all for you, sir." She pirouetted slowly on the ball of one foot.

He patted the couch beside him. "Come here."

Once she was installed he talked in a purposefully sombre tone. "I need your help," he said, looking at her intently. "But you have to listen carefully and memorise everything. You can't write anything down. You think you can do that?"

"I'm an actress, remember? Memorising is the nuts and bolts of the business."

"Good. Now listen, Jane, this isn't a joke. It's probably the most important thing that's ever going to happen to either of us. So be serious," he said, letting his concern reflect on his face. "I'm going to give you two cassette tapes and two different addresses. I want you to hide them. Do you have a safe-deposit box at a bank?"

"Ah . . . sure. Yes," she stammered, surprised by his gravity.

"Good, bury them there. Put them in the vault and forget about them until the right moment."

"But why? What are they?"

He pointed to the envelopes on the coffee table. "I'll get to that in a minute. The first thing you have to do is to forget about me. I mean completely. You mustn't mention my name again. Pretend, act, do anything you want, but make damn sure no one finds out we ever knew each other. Just like before. Repeat: no one must ever know we've seen each other or know each other."

She looked at him questioningly. Her eyes searched

for reassurance and guidance, but found none.

"Are you serious? What's wrong? What kind of trouble are you in?"

He nodded. "Yes, I'm serious, but you don't want to know. Not about this, Jane. Just trust me and do as I say. Don't mention my name; for your own sake as much as mine."

Adel stood and limped towards the fireplace to gain distance from the hurt he was about to cause.

"Why?" she frowned. "Are you and Samira having problems?"

"Hell, no," he grimaced. "It's nothing like that. It's a long story and, as I said, you don't want to know. It'll only make things more dangerous for you."

"Dangerous! Are you being serious, Michael?"

"Very."

Jane frowned and moved forward to the edge of the couch, her body tensing. "What danger? What's all this about?"

Adel ran his fingers through his hair. "There's a lot to it, Jane. And I need your help."

He glanced at her but she said nothing.

"If anything happens to me I want you to take the tapes from your safe, duplicate them, and send a copy to two people."

He pointed at the papers on the table in front of her. "You'll find two names and addresses in the letter I've written for you; one is to an old friend of mine right here in London. He's a writer and a good one, but I don't want him touching this material unless something happens to me. The other is to an address in the States. He's a friend too, but he's a little more devious. If anything happens to me, maybe they can make life hell for those responsible."

Again he pointed to the table. "I didn't have time to duplicate enough tapes. So you'll have to make a copy for the American address, if and when the time comes. Don't make any extra copies for yourself. In no circumstances must you do that. Just do exactly as the note says. No more, no less. And don't do it before the right time, don't touch it before . . ."

"What's all this about, Michael?" she snapped. "Who are 'those responsible'?"

He looked at her for a long moment before answering. "Jane, I'm trying to make this easy. I'm trying to keep you as far out of it as I can. Don't ask questions. You don't want to know."

She stood up slowly but her eyes did not leave his. They were worried, uncomprehending eyes. "First you tell me I'm in danger, then you tell me I'm better off not knowing why. Does that make sense to you?"

It was getting more difficult. "No, it doesn't. But that's the way it has to be."

She stared at him suspiciously and squinted as outside the sun broke through London's habitual cloud cover and filtered through the window, catching her in its golden path.

"Does that leg have anything to do with this, Michael?"

"In a fashion."

She glanced at his leg. The physical evidence of danger underlined the gravity of her own plight. "How?" she asked, the colour draining from her face.

"Drop it, Jane. The less you know, the better off you are."

"I don't believe this," she said, looking away as if there was a third person present and she was arguing her case. "You make all these dark statements about secrecy and tapes and danger and you don't want me asking any questions?"

"Exactly."

She was surprised by his abruptness. "Why?" she asked, a little less assertively.

"Because that's the only way I know for both of us to survive."

She was silent. Lost. Confused. She crossed the room for a cigarette and fumbled with the lighter as she lit it. "He is serious," she whispered to herself.

Adel said nothing. He felt enormous guilt and sorrow as he watched the slow disintegrating process at work. He had to remind himself that there was no other way, that it was a scene that had to be played.

"Why? What's going to happen, Michael?" she asked in a whisper.

"Nothing, I hope. It's just a precaution, Jane. Sort of an insurance policy. Just trust me and do exactly as I say and it'll be all right."

She walked away from his approach and then swivelled around to face him from a distance. "I don't like it, Michael. You're frightened yourself and you're getting me involved. Why? Why do you need me?"

Adel said nothing; there was nothing to say, and there was nothing he could do either.

"What's wrong, Michael?' her voice pleaded. "Please tell me. Please explain."

"You're right. I am scared," he said softly. "But I can't tell you any more than I already have. Not without making it worse."

He looked at her. Her uncertainty and distress had given way to anger. It would soon revert to helplessness.

"How can I convince you?"

"You can't," she said, her face taut and angry. "I'd just like you to leave."

Adel stretched his neck back as far as it would go and sighed. It was cruel, heartless and mean. But there was no other way.

"It's too late for that, Jane. I can't go and I can't tell you about it either," he said. "Not if you want to live."

She gasped and her tear-filled eyes widened as instinctively the trembling hands of a little girl moved up to form a protective cup around her quivering lips.

It was against everything in his nature, everything he believed in. He wanted to cross the room and hold her, tell her, console her, but some alien urge was stronger. It stopped him. It told him that it would do no good. That it would only make things worse. It would expose her to more than she could handle. And it told him he had no choice.

Even worse, it told him that this was the precise juncture at which he would succeed or fail. It was now that he had to drive the point home; now that he had to make certain she fully understood the importance of silence.

"The only way you'll stay alive is if you do exactly as I tell you. Otherwise they'll kill you. And not a person in this world will ever know why," he said coldly, with no compassion. His words were past threats. They were past warnings. "So just stick to exactly what the letter says."

She crossed her legs and squeezed the padded armrests until her knuckles were white. "Why, Michael?" she whispered as tears flowed down her cheeks. "Why did you have to get me involved? Don't you think I have enough problems of my own?"

It was a fair question.

Knightsbridge: 6.00 p.m.

Michael Adel stepped into the lobby of the Berkeley Hotel quickly but cautiously. His heart thumped as his eyes scanned the small space, searching for a Bell surrogate, expecting danger.

The small foyer was elegantly decorated, with light orange painted walls and grey and white marble flooring. A blazing fireplace extended like a beer belly into the foyer, discreetly forcing visitors to pass the alert, discriminating eyes of the enquiries desk to the left, and the hall porter to the right. Three steps up from the hall porter's dark wood counter was a small cocktail lounge, ceremonially solemn and regal, in keeping with the hotel's image. It was discreetly but expensively furnished with high-backed leather armchairs and polished wooden tables, thoughtfully positioned to ensure maximum comfort and pockets of privacy for the clientele. But Adel was relieved by the normality of the scene. It was quiet and reserved, nothing appeared untoward, no one seemed out of place. He glanced at his watch; it read 5.37 p.m. It was pointless searching the place, he thought. He was powerless to change anything, even if it was out of line. Besides, it would probably be impossible to detect any of Bell's men; they were professionals. Even if Bell had heeded the warning not to bring anyone to the hotel, he was sure to have covered himself. At the very least, the entrances of the building would be watched and guarded. And word would have already gone round that he had arrived.

Convincing Bell, he thought as he headed up the steps to the lounge, that would be the hard part. He chose a comfortable leather chair at the entrance of the room, overlooking the foyer, and slumped into it.

"Mr Adel?"

Adel froze.

"I'm afraid ties are required," the waiter whispered politely.

"Yes . . . yes, of course they are." Adel sighed with relief, trying to camouflage his disquiet.

"I can serve you in the breakfast-room across the hall, if you wish, sir," the waiter offered in the same soft tone.

"Thank you." Adel followed the waiter's glance across the foyer to the single room reserved by the hotel for its more "informal" American guests.

"Glenlivet and water, please. No ice," he said, getting up from his chair.

The breakfast-room was just as good a vantage point; he couldn't miss Bell from there either.

And he didn't. At precisely six o'clock, the Colonel passed through the revolving door. For a moment he stood unobtrusively to one side of the lobby, his well-attired frame stiff and upright, his pale blue eyes slowly taking in the space as his hands adjusted the black knitted tie at his throat. Then he spotted Adel.

"It's difficult to get a taxi at this time of day," he declared as he extended a firm, dry hand. "Especially when it's raining." He sat in the chair opposite and straightened the trouser crease of his crossed right leg.

"Drink?" asked Adel, pointing to his own.

"Yes, let's see . . . ah . . . something warming. Vodka, I think, a vodka martini."

Adel signalled the waiter across the lobby and ordered the martini and another whisky for himself as Bell first smoothed his hair, then rubbed his hands together vigorously.

"Damned weather. Don't know what it is about London. Temperatures seldom drop below freezing but the chill goes straight through you. Probably age," he added, chuckling affably.

"What's wrong with your leg?" he asked with what seemed like genuine concern.

Adel felt a twinge of anger. Bell knew exactly what had happened. He knew an hour or two after the event. Or however long it took George Clark to contact him from Teheran.

"Let's get this over with," he snapped.

"Very well, very well," said Bell, ignoring the hostility.

Adel looked resolutely at him. "I don't know much about your profession, Colonel, but I know more than I did two weeks ago. And you were right. I seem to have some natural inbuilt ability. I've learned quickly. Had some good field experience too. I've killed seven people, give or take a few, and I've betrayed and endangered the lives of at least three more."

Bell reached for his drink.

"And I don't think I'd stop there." Adel's stare was hard and angry. "You were right about that, too. To survive, you seem to stoop to any level."

"That's true of most people, Michael. It's instinct. If you think about it, though, every profession has its unpleasant side. Doctors only save lives if they're paid.

Lawyers will defend the most terrifying homicidal maniac if the rewards are right. Accountants are used to rip off the government. There's always a nasty side. One has to do a certain amount to protect the things one believes in. The end does justify the means."

Adel looked at the distinguished public servant sitting in front of him. Elegantly dressed. Cool. Establishment. But that was the veneer. Inside was a madman who compared assassins to doctors and accountants.

He forced himself to relax, to concentrate. He had to somehow convince this psychopath of his claim to a longer life.

"Perhaps," he said. "But you're conditioned to that attitude. I'm not. It's totally alien to me, a way of life I can't take." He wanted to say hate, despise, abhor, but he checked himself. All that was beside the point. He had to convince the man to let him live. He put his hand in his jacket, brought out the two original tapes, and placed them on the table in front of Bell. The Colonel's face showed no reaction.

"In my world, it's rather different, Colonel," he continued. "I don't believe in deception as a way of life. Not for me, anyway. It's important you understand that and believe me because if you don't – we're probably both dead."

As he pointed at the table separating them and the two small rectangular boxes that lay there, Adel noted that his threat had not brought any noticeable reaction from the Colonel.

"Those are the tapes from Mahmoudi's safe. They're yours. And that's my side of the bargain. Your side is to leave me and my family alone to our lives. And I expect you to keep to it."

Adel paused. He wanted his words digested and etched in Bell's mind. Then he went on, slowly, deliberately: "There's a red-headed young man who works in the radio and television department in Harrods. I don't know his name, but he'll vouch for the existence of three copies of the tapes you have in front of you."

Bell's steely blue eyes opened just a fraction, otherwise there was no reaction.

"I've distributed them in such a way as to ensure the widest possible exposure should you choose to renege on our bargain."

Bell smiled faintly as he shook his head. "That wasn't very wise of you."

"Let me tell you why first, Colonel. You've only been told half the story about Teheran, I'll tell you the rest." Adel felt angry again; he wanted to forget about survival, to tell the son-of-a-bitch why he couldn't trust him, why he was a cheap two-bit thug.

"Your man Khan and a doctor friend of his overdosed an innocent seventy-year-old woman to get those damn tapes out of me. Not just any old lady, Colonel. One I loved. And I killed them for it."

Bell looked at him placidly. "Yes, I thought as much; I thought it was probably the result of some sort of falling out among you," he said calmly. Then his face took on a more serious, concerned air. "But why would they kill this lady? Aren't you letting your imagination run away with you again?"

Adel ignored the barb. "You were certain of getting the tapes. Who gave them the authority to go around me, Colonel? To go for a short cut?" asked Adel, not waiting for an answer. "Well, whoever gave them the authority, killed them."

Bell's hand stretched for the martini again. "Why would I have an old lady killed to get information from you? Why wouldn't I just have them get to you?"

"Ahh . . . Colonel. What was it you said in Cannes? Options. You had to keep your options open, didn't you? The risk element was too high. If you'd tried it on me with the same result you'd be in a whole lot of shit now, wouldn't you? You'd have lost the tapes again, perhaps for good. But with the old woman, there was just a chance that she knew. And if she had talked . . ." The image of Mariam's corpse came vividly to mind. "Well, poor soul, she'd be dead anyway." He lifted his head and stared coldly at Bell. "But so would I. They'd have taken me right then and there – in my sleep – wouldn't they, Colonel?"

"That's rubbish, Adel," snapped Bell. "Why would we kill you when we control the strings? That's poppycock. The product of a warped mind."

"I don't know. Maybe the exit part of my trip bothered you. Maybe you wanted to get your hands on the tapes through the safe anonymity of the diplomatic pouch. Maybe you knew I wouldn't just take your word for it, that I would listen to the tapes. I don't know. You tell me."

"Look, Adel, no one gave any such order and I don't know a damn thing about any of this. I gave my word and I'll keep it."

"Yeah . . . well . . . just in case you change your mind, I've insured myself."

Bell looked at Adel intently, concentrating on his eyes. "Have you listened to them?"

Adel smiled. "Yes, Colonel, and it's all gibberish. You can't make out a word of it," he said, his tone dripping with sarcasm.

"Michael, these things are dynamite. They contain the most sensitive, dangerous material imaginable. If there's an error in your judgment and they're made public there would be a scandal of unprecedented proportions and worse. They'll set off a chain reaction that would jeopardise the entire structure of the Western world. It could lead to the destruction of the whole system: governments toppling, economies crumbling, intelligence networks dissolving, our entire system of alliances undermined. The chaos could lead to the power vacuum the Soviets have long been waiting for. Is that what you want?"

"No, Colonel. The Western world is strong enough to excrete its crap without damaging itself to that extent. Perhaps it'll even grow stronger."

"Listen, Michael . . ."

Adel pounced, sensing the moment. "No, you listen

for once, Colonel. I want to live and you're not exactly a man who elicits trust. Leave me . . . us . . . all of us, including my brother Mark . . . alone and there'll be nothing to worry about. No one will ever see the tapes, much less hear them. They'll stay buried and the scenario you foresee will be avoided."

"It's an unnecessary risk, Adel," said Bell. "You're not protecting yourself this way. You're making it worse."

"Don't threaten, Colonel Bell. Listen. Let me explain so there's no misunderstanding."

Bell said nothing. He pressed his hands together in front of his mouth, his piercing eyes fixed on Adel.

"If anything happens to me or my family," Adel continued, "it'll set off a chain reaction in which your oil company friends will become the sole targets. Even if you track down one or two of the tapes, you won't find them all. Not in time. That's the way it's set up. And if they do come out . . . if the shit does hit the fan . . . not even your powerful government cronies will be able to help or protect you or your oil company friends. If the exposure is right, they'll be forced to turn on you. And I assure you, Colonel Bell, it's right. The exposure I've set up is total. Once the dam breaks, the flow of dirt – fifty years of dirt – will be impossible to stop. It'll create a scandal so staggering, so immense in proportion, that your usual tactics of lying, stonewalling, getting rid of evidence, killing, won't do you any good. It will be too late for all that.

"Quite simply, your government friends will turn against you. They'll come in and split your Trust apart seam from seam because they'll have no choice. They'll make you and your Trust the scapegoats so they themselves can survive."

Adel looked away contemptuously, his throat dry and hoarse.

Bell sighed and closed his eyes before reaching for his drink. He gulped it and thought: How did this man slip the net? It had all been arranged: they had picked him up at Heathrow airport and then lost him. For twenty-four hours they blew it, giving him the opportunity to wreak all this havoc. It had all been projected, of course, but no one had any idea that a man with no previous experience could slip through a net of professionals. Professionals, he mocked silently. They were clowns.

He said: "Presumably you think you're protecting yourself this way."

Adel gave a hollow laugh. "Can you think of something better?"

Bell's eyes narrowed to slits. "Use your head, boy," he spat, slapping the table harder and more loudly than he intended. He turned and continued in a quieter but no less abrasive voice.

"All you're doing is lengthening the chain, increasing the possibility of a weak link and the chances of a leak. A simple operation is getting totally out of control because of your paranoid suspicion and mistrust." He shifted uneasily in his chair and brushed the sleeves of his jacket. "Look, if you did make copies, you'd better go round them up and get them back to me before it's too late. Before it blows up in your handsome face," he threatened, leaning forward and resting his elbows on his knees, his face red with anger.

"I wouldn't trust you as far as I could spit, Colonel."

Bell looked at him and smiled menacingly. "You refuse to take my word; everything has to be a conspiracy with you, doesn't it, Adel? Well, if you believe the world can survive without order, you're a dreamer. A fool."

Adel was taken aback by Bell's sudden passion.

"The Great Conspiracy – as you would think of it – is merely an attempt to give the world and its affairs rationality and stability." Bell felt in his pockets for a cigarette. "Thus we can go some way to control chaos and avoid waste. It means that you can forget about World War III. It means, Adel, that without order the world would destroy itself, and I would have no reason to lie to you," he said, his voice gaining in volume and impatience as he spoke.

"You wouldn't even stop at genocide, would you?" Adel said softly.

"Tut, tut, tut. I'm surprised at you, Michael, and at your naivety." Bell stuck a cigarette in the slit of his mouth and lit it. "There's no such thing as genocide because there are no 'genotypes' left. At least, no such thing as an American or an Englishman, or a Frenchman, or even an Iranian – they're all mosaics, genetic mosaics. What you in your self-righteous smugness fail to see is the overall scenario. It's the march of time and the imperatives, the priorities of every second of that march. Order is the only imperative, and it doesn't come from God. He left in despair a long time ago, Adel. It's up to us now. And if control is not exerted every second, every hour, every day, the world would slide towards anarchy and chaos . . ."

"And for the moment the imperatives are that the industrialised world is running out of resources and America doesn't have a resource pot to piss in. Is that it?"

Bell inhaled and let the smoke curl out from his thin nostrils. "Look, Adel, we can't engage in an undergraduate discussion on ethics now. There isn't time. Be reasonable. You can't fight this. No one can. Tell me where the tapes are. Tell me where you copied them and if anyone else heard them."

Adel smiled nervously and lit a cigarette. Bell was mad. But within his crazy scheme it was all logical, everything had a place. Order, as he called it. And now he, Michael Adel, was disturbing that order. The sense of panic returned. His only hope lay with the tapes. Without them he was dead.

"I told you. They were duplicated at Harrods. Three copies to be exact and there was a red-headed salesman in the room off and on, but he wasn't listening. I mailed the copies to various corners of the world yesterday, with letters outlining clearly what should be done if anything happens to me."

"Mailed yesterday?" muttered Bell distantly. "Well,

it's still possible to retrieve them. I need to know where you mailed them from. And where you sent them." He fell silent before mumbling again. "The redhead's no problem."

"What?"

Bell smiled his same menacing lopsided smile. "It means you killed him, Mr Adel. That makes a total of eight notches on your gun. Unless you wish to take the credit for the death of His Excellency Ali Mahmoudi and his daughter Gina, too. And there'll be more . . ."

Oh my God. He's killed Gina. Images of Natalie's mother flashed before his eyes. The young Gina, the girl he had once loved so desperately, with whom he had shared his youth and his daughter. The woman who had caused him so much happiness in life. And pain. He remembered their first kiss at the house in Teheran. And their last at the hotel in Paris.

This madman had killed her. And Mahmoudi, too. He'll go on killing. On and on and on. He'll kill them all. He'll kill Mark . . . and he'll kill . . . Jesus Christ Almighty, stop him . . . he's a lunatic . . . I'll give him the bloody tapes . . . he can have them . . . just tell him to leave . . . to get out of my life . . . to leave me alone . . .

But no. He'll never do that. Even with the tapes he won't stop. If he gets his hands on them, he won't let anyone live.

"Those tapes are all I have to protect me and my family from you. Or from worse; if there is any worse. There are three duplicates out there," Adel said, gesturing to the world outside. "You can't stop it," his voice pleaded. "Leave it alone, Colonel."

Bell finished his drink and set the glass down gently on the table. He looked directly into Adel's eyes. He had no reason to be civil now.

"Tell me, Adel, what makes you bigger or better than the Shah? Let me answer that for you. Nothing. We had him by the balls, so you're no problem at all. If I can topple a man of his stature, just imagine what I'm going to do to you." He picked up the two original tapes from the table and slid one into each breast pocket. Even as he stood, his eyes never left his target.

Adel looked up at Bell and felt sick with loathing.

"You're a reptile, Bell. A slimy snake that slithers and grovels in filth."

Bell looked down at him and smiled.

"The only difference is, I have feet, Adel. And no matter where you go, I'll be there."

London. Friday, November 2: early morning.

At the Berkeley Hotel, Adel had tossed and turned all night; images of pain and fear were joined by new emotions – guilt and sorrow. Guilt about Jane and the hurt and damage he had caused her. Genuine sorrow at the demise of Gina who was after all Natalie's mother, and a woman he had once loved.

At five-fifteen he threw off the bedcovers. There was nothing he could do about it, he thought, as he hobbled from the bed towards the shower. He could not change the past and there was no guarantee for the future. In a few hours he would be home, to Samira, to Natalie, to the warmth and security of his home. Perhaps there, in time, the images of the past would fade.

London. Friday, November 2: evening.

The five men had arrived at the detached, two-storey, neo-Georgian redbrick house on the north side of Hyde Park separately and by various routes. They had arrived at predetermined times between seven-thirty and eight-thirty in the evening, to coincide with the arrival of other carefully selected dinner guests.

To the casual and not-so-casual passer-by, it was clear that this middle-class residence in the Paddington district of London was, like several of its neighbours, celebrating the weekend. Its ground-level double reception room glowed with bright lights that filtered through fine white lace curtains on to the street outside. From there, too, one could just make out through the partially opened windows the inconsequential rise and fall of the voices and laughter of the guests inside.

Unlike the other neighbourhood parties, however, the celebrations at 18 Sussex Gardens were camouflage. The windows that fronted the lace curtains were half an inch thick, and bulletproof, and the building itself was structured deception – a safe house, as it is called in the trade.

Inside, the five men, who had mixed with the guests for a suitable period of time, were now gathered in a basement that did not show on the house plans publicly available at the city and borough planning departments. Nor did it show on the designs on file at the real estate agents in Kensington who had originally been charged with selling the building in 1966, when it was constructed. In fact, none of the high-security additions to the building were visible or on file anywhere. They had all been added in decorative form by a branch of US naval intelligence in 1972 when the house had been purchased by the Central Intelligence Agency. The lead-lined basement walls, to offset electronic eavesdropping, the bulletproof glass, the heavy steel-sheeted doors, the narrow tunnel that burrowed under the road to the small private park across the street, were all well kept secrets. The outdoor high-resolution cameras and microphones too were camouflaged, but the dozen television screens inside provided a 360° view, with zoom ability to pinpoint anything within view and an electronic net added audio surveillance with extensive mix and isolate capability for the immediate surroundings.

"What do we have on Adel?" asked Bell, looking at the wiry blond young man sitting opposite him at the round table.

"On him personally, sir? Or the whole background report?" asked the man, nervously thumbing through the pages of a folder in front of him.

Bell glanced at the swarthy, suntanned figure sitting next to him, then back at the young man.

"All of it," he said curtly.

The younger man shuffled the papers back again.

"Well, Adel left for the South of France this morning. BA Flight 342 to Nice/Côte d'Azur airport at eleven o'clock to be precise."

Bell nodded, scrutinising the dark scholarly looking man to his left.

"We've recovered both tapes, sir," said the younger man, giving the good news first. "The first set of documents was recovered, as you suggested, from the Cheyne Walk address in Chelsea; the residence of a certain Mark Adel," he said.

Bell observed the swarthy man's nervous twitch as he raised his glasses on to his forehead.

The young man continued. "The package contained two Narela cassette tapes. Numbers seven-four-five-three-seven dash E stroke R dash forty-six dash seventy-eight and seven-four-five-three-eight dash E stroke R dash forty-six dash seventy-eight. It also contained a five-page handwritten letter, a summary of which I'll get to in just a minute, if that's all right with you." He looked round the table for approval.

No one objected, so he continued. "The second package was located with the assistance of our British counterparts. We could have waited for its receipt by Mr Claude Boissy in Switzerland before retrieval, but at your suggestion, Colonel" – the young man nodded deferentially at Bell – "it was decided to put an early stop on it here in London. This was done for two reasons. First, because while Boissy was classified simultaneously cooperative and safe, it was thought that an appreciable reduction in the risk factor could be obtained through the prevention of his exposure to the contents of the package, if, that is, it could be achieved. The second parameter was a sizeable reduction in the time factor. It was determined that early access to both packages would increase our cross-check capabilities and thereby increase the accuracy factor of our comparative analysis. This we believed would substantially improve our chances of understanding fully the planned offensive in the shortest time frame."

The younger man looked up at his audience; they were attentive. "Through our British counterparts we placed an immediate stop/search on all parcels to Switzerland above the size of a letter. X-ray scanning on four thousand, one hundred and eighty-three packages, destination Switzerland, point of origin British Isles, in the last twenty-nine hours isolated and recovered the target package at the foreign sorting facilities at Mount Pleasant.

"The second parcel was almost identical to the first. It contained two Narela cassette tapes numbered seven-four-five-four-zero dash E stroke R dash forty-six dash seventy-eight and seven-four-five-four-one dash E stroke R dash forty-six dash seventy-eight . . ."

"Cappelli," Bell interrupted. "Just give us the gist of your report. We can go through the details with you individually if need be," he said, overriding his earlier instruction.

He had been through all this before and the meeting was bound to be a long one.

Christopher Cappelli cleared his throat nervously and continued. "The package also contained a letter. The two letters were remarkably similar; if there was a difference, it was in the wording. Boissy's version was more formal and more detailed. In the circumstances, this has been adjudged normal," said Cappelli, looking up to check Bell's expression. "The letters instruct the recipients that, in the case of unusual circumstances regarding the subject's well being and safety, the tapes are to be made available both in audio and transcript form to a mixed assortment of outlets: governments, institutions, a broad spectrum of the media, lawyers, writers, radicals and a variety of companies, both friendly and otherwise. The word 'unusual' is defined by the subject in the broadest terms."

Cappelli looked at those seated around the table.

"Some of those listed are not in our sphere of influence," he said, his voice youthful but appropriately grave. "On the contrary, if one or two of those outlets found access to this information it would be impossible to contain." He paused, waiting for the implications of what he had just said to take hold.

"As for the Narela tapes, their point of origin is the CKY manufacturing plant just outside Tokyo, Japan. The first series of numbers on their identification tags which I partially read," he said, looking at Bell meekly, "indicate the number of the production run. The E stroke R indicates that they were manufactured specifically for the European market. The forty-six indicates that they were made in the forty-sixth week of 1978, which is identified by the last digits.

"CKY manufactures high quality tapes under a variety of brand names; it has no distribution arm of its own. These tapes and other CKY products are shipped to London by container, warehoused and distributed throughout Europe by various distribution companies under a variety of brand names. Narela Corporation is a British distributor and is considered top of the line."

Cappelli placed the papers in his hands on the table and looked up. "In a nutshell, that's the gist of the task force findings. The originals – tapes, letters and our assessments – have been forwarded by courier to Washington for review and in-depth analysis. We should get their results and recommendations back in thirty-six hours."

Bell nodded and slowly leaned forward, his elbows resting on the polished table. There was a moment's silence in the room as the group digested the information.

Bell turned to Cappelli. "See if you can get Washington to speed things up," he said. "What's a realistic minimum?"

Cappelli thought for a moment. "Another twelve hours. Say some time tomorrow morning. Afternoon at the latest."

Bell looked around. "Are there any questions for Cappelli?"

The elderly, emaciated man to Bell's right shifted in his seat. He was the more senior of the two scientists at the table – men trained in the general area of covert operations but specialising in one exacting aspect.

"Yes, John," said Bell, anticipating a comment.

Dr Johan Brandt withdrew his glasses from his narrow, bony face and placed them on the red folder in front of him.

"I wonder, Mr Cappelli," he said, smiling meekly at the younger man, "where was the letter to . . . ah . . . ah . . ." his left hand shook as he replaced his glasses and referred to his papers for help ". . . Mr Boissy mailed from?"

"Sloane Street," replied Cappelli.

"Yes. Good . . . good . . . good," Dr Brandt repeated. "I wonder, did you put a stop on the other mail from that box, Mr Cappelli? Presumably if the subject mailed anything else, which is doubtful, it would not be unreasonable to assume that he mailed it at the same time as Mr Boissy's package, would it?" he asked, smiling. He blinked frequently behind thick curved glasses that distorted the shape and size of his eyes.

Cappelli smiled back but it was an uncomfortable smile. The doctor's gentleness was unsettling, especially since Cappelli had only recently read his personal file. Like all the men present, the doctor was an intelligence expert, but there the similarity ended. He and his colleague sitting opposite him were a different breed of specialist. Their expertise lay in a rapidly emerging new science – human behavioural engineering. Part doctor, part psychologist, part interrogator, the two men were manipulation strategists who correlated the likelihoods, odds and percentages of a human being's future behaviour based on past patterns. They looked at his loves, hates, desires, fears, but most of all his weaknesses and vulnerability. And then they would calculate what stimulus would produce what result.

Cappelli answered cautiously. He knew the two men were analysing his every word, and the thought unnerved him.

"Sure. Sure it occurred to us." He nodded at the doctor. "But let me explain the logistical problems involved. We had a clean handle on Boissy's letter. His name was one of two hundred and thirteen we had isolated and targeted. We knew the approximate time it had to have been mailed. And we knew its destination. If those two parameters are available it is always, relatively speaking, a simple task to isolate a specific piece of mail. We intercepted the package because we had a potential destination and enough time to locate it. When we did so, then, and only then, did we identify Sloane Street as the mail drop, but of course by that time something like six to eight hours had elapsed, during which the mail from that box had been sorted and mixed with the ah . . . ah . . ." he flicked the page of his folder . . . "one million, two hundred thousand other pieces of mail that on average leave this country daily.

"As soon as we were aware of the Sloane Street drop we put an immediate stop search on all mail originating there. But practically speaking, it was too late, the pouches had already been sorted and mixed by destination. We're trying to isolate the Sloane Street mail back again but it's a horrendous task. The British are more optimistic about the outcome than we are, but then again they're very efficient at this sort of thing. They have dozens of people working on it and we should have an answer by the morning."

Johan Brandt nodded his head as he doodled. "If we

had another parametric characteristic . . . a destination . . . a name . . . something, I'd feel far more confident myself. But you thought about it, did you?" he asked, nodding and smiling approvingly.

"Yes, Doctor."

"Have you considered stopping all the outgoing mail?"

Cappelli smiled nervously in anticipation of a long grilling ahead. "In essence that's what the British are doing. Although perhaps 'delaying' is a more apt description."

"I have no other questions, Colonel."

Bell looked around the room from left to right. There was silence.

"Any questions?" Bell asked the man to his right.

The dark, scholarly looking man puffed at his pipe and shook his head.

"Thank you, Cappelli. Wait with the others," Bell ordered.

There was silence as Cappelli closed his folder and left the smoke-filled room.

Bell waited for the door to close. "Well, John," he said to Brandt, "what do you think?"

Brandt pursed his lips.

"It's an interesting one. This man is behaving awkwardly. In fact, he is acting downright unpredictably," he said, his accent thicker now, his eyes fixed on a corner of the ceiling. "Perhaps there has been a change. Maybe we missed something." He shook his head and then continued: "It is unsettling. Up to a given point, in every single instance he acted as projected. We have to presume that it was because the created stresses resulted in a controlled and predictable environment. He had no choice; he had no alternative but to cooperate with us. First and foremost, he had no means with which to fight back, and second, he had quite a considerable amount to lose. So naturally he reacted in the expected manner. The question is, why did he veer from that pattern of behaviour? Why does he feel so confident now under the very same conditions that have, theoretically, existed all along? I don't know.

"The possibility does exist that he has found this so-called third outlet and no longer feels the pressure so overwhelming. Perhaps this third source has reduced his insecurity. Either that or he has finally succumbed to the rather lengthy period of high stress to which he has been subjected. If that is the case, it is impossible to predict what he will do next, or indeed, what he is capable of doing. He is now unbalanced and totally unpredictable." He paused.

"It's worth thinking about, isn't it?" he asked, his voice worried but his eyes alive with professional interest. "He's certainly a challenge."

Edward Rogers, Brandt's colleague sitting opposite him, joined in the conversation. He looked at the doctor and said, "I don't know, John. I see it a little differently. The key part for me is that in retrospect it's pretty clear that, from the start, the programme has been just a little off target and all the misjudgment has been in what I'd call the 'obeisance factor'. Adel simply hasn't been as compliant as projected. No, that's not strictly true. He did act predictably at the very outset, when his daughter was threatened. Since then he hasn't, though; he's been fighting every step of the way. He didn't accept our field operatives," he said, ticking the points off one by one on the fingers of his left hand. "He didn't keep to the schedule. He killed two of our operatives. And while we clearly projected the likelihood of his duplicating and then retaining copies of the tapes if he had the opportunity, we had no idea he would go so far as to mass distribute them. Now, as Grove tells it," concluded Rogers, pointing to Bell, "even his daughter has taken on a secondary importance."

Brandt turned to Bell, aware of the practical problem at hand. "Basically, Colonel, we need something we don't have – time. We need to go back and take another detailed look at all this in the lab. See if a possible third source exists in London or if it's simply a product of his imagination. It could be that he is a more complex animal than we perceived him to be."

"Let's call a spade a spade," said Rogers. "Someone in Operations blew it. No matter what the behavioural deviations have been, we projected clearly that he would duplicate if he could. From the start we insisted that a high coverage grid be placed around him from the moment of his departure from Iran; in fact, we even suggested that his surveillance should start from the moment he laid his hands on the tapes. That's" – he paused – "where the fatal error was committed. This problem should never have come up."

He looked at Bell for a reaction. While the Colonel's face was a little more haggard than usual, it betrayed no emotion.

"True, he's not acting specifically as we projected, Grove," Rogers continued. "But all the deviation relates to one specific factor; we've been accurate in every other dimension. The fact remains that a rank amateur was selected to execute a highly technical and dangerous task based only on capabilities and personality traits displayed in quite different areas of endeavour. And it's been a highly successful operation. Let's not forget that side of it. The question is, as you point out, John, *is there a third outlet*?"

Bell toyed with his lower lip as he studied the speaker's light blue eyes. They were calm, analytical eyes which had for two decades weighed and evaluated statistical data on human behaviour.

"What do you think, Ed?" he asked. "Deep down do you think that the projections are wrong? Do you think there's someone . . ." he let the words trail off.

"That's the sixty-four-thousand-dollar question." Edward Rogers smiled but the smile faded quickly. He tugged at his blond curls and, after a moment's thought, continued sombrely: "No, Grove. I don't believe that we're that far off. There is nothing – nothing," he repeated as he fanned the pages of the thick red binder in front of him, "to suggest a third outlet. Not in London, anyway. Remember, you're not talking about a simple favour from an acquaintance. You're not playing with the kids in the alley. You're talking about deep personal involvement and awesome risks." He smacked the binder heavily with the back of his hand. "Hell, there's nothing to suggest the existence of such a person here. If I had to bet on it I'd say he's bluffing. But it's a dangerous poker game we're playing."

"In a sense, he's right," said Brandt nibbling at the arm of his glasses. "The chances are he's lying but I would suggest we wait for Washington to respond. That is a more cautious approach. Let them study the knowns at length in the laboratory where they have access to the computer files. Meanwhile we can all sleep on it. Give it time to . . ."

Bell interrupted, his tone reflecting his sombre mood. "We have severe time restraints. He's already left for France. Every hour we do nothing extends the circle of exposure and correspondingly the risk factor. We can't afford that. Either we do something quickly or we might as well forget it. It'll be too late, and then we can only sit back and wait for it to blow up in our faces."

"Yes, Grove," broke in Rogers. "But on the other hand, if you eliminate the man and find he's got the royal flush . . ." He didn't need to finish the sentence.

Bell gently dropped the yellow pencil he was twirling over and over in his right hand on to the table. It bounced on the eraser at one end and fell to the floor.

The swarthy man's eyes followed the pencil's path as he spoke for the first time. "The risk is too great. There are too many ifs involved," he said, looking up from the floor at Bell. "For a start, there is a good chance he didn't mail anything; he could have hand delivered the third set. After all, that's what he did with one of the recovered packages." He made no indication that he, Mark Adel, was the recipient, even though he was aware that everyone in the room knew.

"Then there's also the possibility of him asking someone – whoever – to mail the package in a week or two, or ten. That would hardly be too much to ask anyone, would it? It wouldn't require a good friend or even a close acquaintance. In those circumstances he could approach just about anyone. A hall porter, a secretary, virtually anyone."

"Yes, that's true," said Brandt, rubbing his forehead. "The fact is, something is wrong. It was never thought the subject would behave so erratically. The question of multiple sources was never approached. That was an error on our part. In fact . . ."

"Look," broke in the swarthy man impatiently, "we're all sitting here talking as if the manipulation of a human being is an exact science with proven laws upon which one can depend. It is not. It is a crude art in an embryonic stage. Let's stop getting carried away with its accuracy and reliability. The fact is that the success of Operation Peacock in Iran – the changing of a regime – had nothing to do with this so-called science of human manipulation. That, gentlemen, was a planned military and intelligence operation. Only in part – a very small part at that – did it rely on the manipulation of one man – the Shah. It would be fatal to continue to ascribe proven propaganda and destabilisation tactics and their successful execution to this . . . this science of human manipulation or whatever it is you call it. You can't sit here and project exactly what anyone is going to do – ever. Let alone a complicated, sensitive, tough human being who is fighting for his life," he said, his tone conspicuously angry.

Dr John Brandt looked at the swarthy man. "Yes. Well, if we are restricted by time I suggest we use what little we have constructively. I don't see this man Adel's behaviour as being that divergent from the original projections. Divergent, yes, but not so radically as to suggest a total departure from the programme. It is impossible to project an animal's behaviour exactly in the existing state of this science," he said, glancing contemptuously at his colleague. "Perhaps some day we will reach that level of accuracy. And we all knew that from the start," he said, again resting his eyes on the swarthy man. "It has been ninety per cent accurate up to now and I for one can live with that sort of success level."

He slumped back in his chair. "Given the complexities you have, Colonel, I would recommend that we wait for Washington to respond. Let them run the data again, see if there is a correlation between the recipient list the target has provided in his two letters and the known acquaintances we have on file. In addition, the lab could scour the names again and see if there is a distant girlfriend, a former business acquaintance, tennis partner or karate teacher, someone we might have missed."

Bell held his gaze on the doctor for several seconds even though his mind was elsewhere. He thought: Mark Adel is no longer a valid contributor. His personal involvement is blinding him to the realities and dangers of the situation. As one of the foremost military strategists and an outside consultant to the Agency on the Middle East and Iran, he was one of the key planners in Operation Peacock. But he was a left-over from that project. It was wrong to have brought him into this operation, however unfeeling and professional he actually was. Even now he's showing no emotion or personal interest. That's what's incongruous about his behaviour. He's trying to argue professionally, strategically, and it doesn't make sense.

He stored the information and turned to Rogers. "What about you, Ed?"

Rogers followed the doctor's lead and tilted his chair back on to its hind legs. He was slow to answer.

"I think we should all try to remember," he said at length, "without getting emotionally involved, that this man is no longer a stable human being. The strains of the last few days must, at the very least, have caused considerable shock. After all, it was an alien and frightening experience for him. The result is, we may well have a lunatic out there armed with enough information to destroy our entire system of democratic government. I submit that, even if we do not call his bluff, even if we leave the matter totally alone, let him go his own way, never see or touch or talk or contact him again, there is a facet – a proven facet – of this man's character that we must not forget. I'm speaking, of course, about his need for revenge and his sheer determination. Look at the elaborate lengths he went to for the recovery of his daugher, Natalie.

"This is not a man who will sit back and take defeat graciously. I submit to you that in the days and months and years ahead, the resentment he presumably feels will become uncontrollable. It will obsess him and force him against us. At some point in time he will be unable to stem that drive; it is an integral part of his make-up. At that point – and it is impossible to predetermine it – he will come after us."

"Terrific," said Bell as he watched Mark Adel shift in his seat.

"I further submit to you that this vengeance might take a different form. He could simply publicise the information contained on those tapes, even if he is lying and there is no third set of tapes. With time, he will recall or piece together much of the information even if he doesn't have an actual copy. Perhaps the proof will be missing but the facts will be there, available and ready.

"He must not be given that opportunity; we must not give him time to draw up a strategy that would be difficult to neutralise; let's face it, he is a competent man."

There was a hush round the table; no one could argue with the wisdom or logic of the words, not even Mark Adel.

The meeting lasted until midnight, but nothing more of consequence emerged. Bell, Brandt and Rogers talked around the various options but Mark Adel stayed silent, contributing no more than his previous warning.

At one in the morning Colonel Grover Cleveland Bell saw the three men to the door of the office. He was tired and it was obvious nothing positive would come from continuing.

At the door Mark Adel nodded his head, mumbled brusque farewells and left quickly. He was followed shortly by Dr Brandt, who was in better spirits. Ed Rogers took the Colonel's hand and shook it.

"There's one more thing, Grove," he said. "I didn't want to bring it up in front of ah . . . everyone. If you go through with this, be careful. There's no room for error. He's the same in enmity as he is in friendship; he gives it everything he's got."

Bell looked into his colleague's eyes and nodded, then the two men turned in opposite directions.

The Colonel walked back into the wood-panelled room and towards the desk at the far end. He needed facts, figures, odds, percentages, ratios. Judgment calls were dangerous – anathema in this business, he thought as he reached for the telephone.

He knew that Adel was lying; he could feel it in his bones. Brandt and Rogers agreed with him. They had to, the likelihoods dictated it; but, like him, they were worried about the risk. And they had no actual proof, no hard evidence. If anything went wrong, all hell would break loose. And this time there were very few candidates for scapegoats, he thought wryly. He picked up the black phone and pressed a button.

"Tell Gleeson to come in," he barked into the mouthpiece. He leaned back on the swivel chair, closed his eyes and reclined, placing his feet on the table and locking his fingers behind his head. "Judgment calls," he spat in disgust.

There was a loud knock on the door.

"Come in," growled Bell without opening his eyes.

The door opened and the lean, wiry frame of Jim Gleeson entered.

"What happened with the sales clerk?" asked Bell for the umpteenth time, hoping that with repetition something new, perhaps previously forgotten, would emerge.

Jim Gleeson sat in the chair across from the desk and answered again.

"He was in the room, Grove, taping the duplicate copies while Adel listened to the tapes. "Claimed he hadn't heard them himself. He said Adel had listened to the whole thing on earphones. But he gave a hell of a description of Adel. Right down to dimples-when-he-smiles detail."

"Terrific." Bell's eyes were still closed.

"He knew enough to be dangerous," Gleeson reiterated. "After our visit and the attention it must have aroused, it would have been dangerous to let him go."

Bell snapped his eyes open.

"He won't be a problem, Grove," explained Gleeson quickly.

Bell was unmoved. He looked away. "If the kid had been that smart he would have remembered how many copies of the tapes he'd made. Now the only one who knows is Adel."

"We tried everything, Grove. He just didn't remember whether it was two or three copies. The problem was, since he was working a fiddle, there was no receipt from the store to show the sale of four or six tapes. He claimed he was out of the studio most of the time and Adel could have popped extra tapes into the apparatus without his knowing."

Bell closed his eyes in thought again and the room was silent. After several moments, he abruptly swung his feet to the floor, sat up straight and looked into the eyes of his colleague.

"This is a rough one, Jim," he confided. "A mother! We have to wait a couple of days to see what Washington comes up with. The problem is, we can't afford the time."

He sighed and bit his lower lip. There was a moment's silence before he spoke again. "Have you set up the surveillance grid in the South of France?"

"Yes, it's all in place."

"Okay, you better get down there and activate it. Keep your eye on the bastard," ordered Bell.

"Sure, Grove."

"Yes," said Bell as much to himself as anybody. "Get down there as soon as possible and keep a tight leash on him; we don't need another fuck-up like London. Remember, Jim, this thing is critical; it's as big as anything we've ever handled, probably bigger. Keep everybody on their toes. The man's no fool and we don't need him spotting it. I want him to relax, to unwind and feel like it's all over. I want him to drop his guard and perhaps that way we can learn something. If he spots it like the last time . . ." Bell hesitated and turned away from Gleeson.

"We know what to expect this time, Grove."

"Well, it's encouraging to know that after twenty years in this business, you're still learning. I suppose, all we can hope for is that Adel isn't a faster learner," he snapped.

Gleeson looked away from Bell's piercing glare.

"Okay, you better get going."

Gleeson stood and walked towards the door.

"Oh . . . ahh . . . Jim," Bell called.

Gleeson turned to face him.

"Wait for Davis. He'll be coming with you."

Gleeson nodded and left the room.

Bell was alone again now. He rested his left elbow on the table and rubbed his eyes; they were tired and bloodshot with fatigue.

Was there a third set of tapes? Was there a third outlet? He could not stop the thought repeating itself over and over in his brain.

The salesman had no reason to lie. He had said that there were three sets of tapes. Three, four or forty, what was the difference to him? Davis and Gleeson had gone too far, especially Davis, he thought, making a mental note to reprimand him. Between the two of them they had mixed the fool up, repeatedly asking him if he had included the original tapes in his figures or not? Had he made three copies or was it three in all? Four with the originals or three? On and on until the poor fool's brain jammed. The kid had no reason to lie. His original answer had come forcefully and without hesitation or reflection.

And Michael Adel? he thought as he walked to the conference table. Who on earth could he have found in London that was not on the records? No one. That's who. There was no way. There were only three sets of tapes and all three were already safe. The bastard was bluffing. Adel was lying.

He picked up a pack of cigarettes from the polished, mahogany table and lit one. Beside the cigarettes the spread-eagle emblem on the blue leather folder caught his eye. He fanned its pages absentmindedly, not stopping to see what was written. He didn't need to. He had read them so often he had memorised them. Abruptly he turned his back and started pacing the floor.

There was nothing to be gained from the papers. Nothing, not even a hint of a third person, especially in London. Even outside, there was no one. Only his wife. But that he would never do. He would never involve her.

"He's lying," he said forcefully as he picked up the phone and dialled.

"Theresa, let me talk to Mark," he ordered.

There was no third person, he thought again as he waited. Michael Adel had very few friends; that was one of the reasons he had been chosen in the first place. No, he thought, the facts were indisputable. He crushed his cigarette in the ashtray.

"Hello," came the deep English accent.

"Mark, I'm relieved you went straight home," said Bell.

"Good." The tone was abrupt.

"Mark, the more we delve, the more it looks like your brother is lying. There's simply nothing to substantiate the existence of a third person in London." He added quickly, "Without our knowing."

"We went through this at length before the meeting, Colonel. Whether he's lying or not, the risk you're taking isn't justified. You've become too involved in all this. It's become a personal vendetta. My advice, and that's what I'm here to give, remember, is to let it cool down. Wait for Washington to get back to us. There's nothing to be gained by acting rashly. And a great deal to lose," said Mark Adel coldly. "You're exaggerating the time restraints."

"The timing is critical," snapped Bell. "Every hour his exposure increases. Besides, as for personal involvement . . ."

"Don't be stupid, Colonel," Mark Adel growled. "It's the logic that's wrong. It has nothing to do with personal involvement." The whole perception of these people was off, he thought angrily. It was offensive. An insult to his professionalism. They saw a weakness in him that wasn't there. And he was powerless to convince them. No matter how persuasive the logic of his arguments, they saw it as an attempt to save his brother. An emotional issue. And they were wrong.

Bell's clipped tone broke the silence.

"I want your professional judgment, Mark."

"Okay. You want a formal response," said Mark Adel, his voice cold and angry. "Here's my professional opinion. Carve it in your brain because it'll come back to haunt you. I don't know who the third person is, but I don't think Michael's lying. Nothing you have proves otherwise. Until you have such proof, the risk is not worth taking. That, Colonel Bell, is my formal response. I'll have it to you in writing in the morning."

Bell felt a shudder. What if Mark was right and he was wrong? What if there was a third outlet?

"Look, Mark, this has been a horrendous task. It's got to all of us. I really do understand your position. They should never have involved you on this. It was too much to expect," he said, trying to sound conciliating.

Mark Adel's voice bristled. "When I was assigned to this project, I made up my mind to be impartial. To help you, Colonel. And that is exactly what I'm trying to do. I have tried endlessly to explain to you that there are things above and beyond facts and figures and computer analyses. There's a thing called feel and it comes with years of close proximity. You can't acquire it by feeding a machine and playing with variables. Especially with this human being, you can't."

He fell silent, then picked up again more calmly. "You're all right, Colonel, when you talk about my brother's fascination for the concept of revenge; we've discussed that endlessly. But you refuse to listen to the man who knows him best and you're only partly right: you've overlooked something crucial. It's not revenge that drives him. It's something totally different. It's winning. And to win you have to be cautious, calculating."

He waited to let Bell absorb the meaning fully and then continued: "None of that shows up on your computers, does it, Colonel? That's the part you missed – the critical part – and you refuse to listen to me. He's not bluffing; there is a third outlet. He's too careful to gamble without it." He said softly, "Michael won't lie down and die. Not without being reasonably certain that one way or another he'll eventually win."

He's a cold fish, this one, thought Bell. In all his years in this business, he had never known anyone quite like Mark. The man really wasn't pleading for his brother. He was merely pressing a professional viewpoint. What was bothering him was not the danger his brother was in. He was angry because the voting was going against him.

Let's test him, thought Bell. "Mark, all that's well and good but it has nothing to do with a third outlet. You're worried about your brother and that's understandable. But we have time restraints and we know he's lying."

Mark Adel sighed audibly. "You're wrong, Colonel – on both counts. I keep trying to tell you, there's no emotion involved. In this profession, emotion is a bad habit. And there is a third outlet."

There was something eerie about Mark. Something Bell couldn't quite put his finger on. He was cold and humourless, always scowling behind his scholarly features. From the very beginning Bell had felt uncomfortable with him. Nothing he could isolate or classify, just a sixth sense of unease.

He ignored the feelings. "He's lying, Mark. I'd bet my life on it."

There was no hesitation in the response. "You probably are, Colonel."

Bell looked at the dead receiver, surprised. He replaced it slowly and leaned back in his chair. The guy has a point there, he thought.

He picked up the phone again.

"Ask Gleeson to come in," he ordered. "And Davis, too."

Holding the receiver, he clicked the phone dead and looked at the antique Victorian clock; it read two-thirty in the morning. It was a good hour for what he had in mind and even better when you added the extra hour to get French time. He dialled the thirteen numbers for the South of France and listened as the staccato of clicks made the connection. His palm was sweaty and he switched the receiver from one hand to the other, surprised at his own nervous excitement.

He would tell Michael Adel that his offer was acceptable. No. Better yet, he thought, he would tell Adel that his superiors had overruled him, that they had ordered him to accept Adel's offer. That it was all over, because the risk of exposure was too great.

"Adel residence," a sleepy voice finally answered.

"I'd like to speak to Mr Michael Adel."

"Who may I say is calling?" the polite male voice enquired.

"Bell. Grover Cleveland Bell."

The response came immediately. "Mr and Mrs Adel are out for the evening, sir."

Bell looked quickly at his watch again. "It's three-thirty in the morning," he said incredulously. "What do you mean, he's out?"

"There is no curfew in the South of France, sir," replied Usher, his voice calm and measured.

"Yes," muttered Bell feebly. "Well, tell him I called to

let him know we've accepted his offer. Tell him that we've agreed to his proposal. And ask him to call me."

Bell hung up and reached for another cigarette. It didn't make sense. It wasn't normal for a man under this kind of pressure to be out dining with his wife until three-thirty in the morning.

"Come in," he bellowed, more from anger than necessity, in answer to the knock. Adel's behaviour made no sense, he thought, as the two men approached his desk. He lit his cigarette and waited for them to settle in chairs.

"We've got to move, Jim," said Bell, looking at Gleeson. "It's too risky to let it just hang."

He bit his lower lip and looked at his watch. "Set it up for tomorrow, Jim. We'll have the report in from Washington by then, so if need be we can always abort. If not, we'll go ahead."

"Oh . . ." he added. "I want to be there myself. I want to be certain that there's not a trace left of him."

Menton, France. Friday, November 2: 3.30 a.m.

Et la vie sépare
Ceux qui s'aiment,
Tout doucement,
Sans faire de bruit.

Et la mer efface
Sur le sable
Le pas des amants
Désunis.

Adel hugged Samira closer on the crowded dance floor. They were not dancing; they merely swayed to the strains of the Spanish guitarist vocalising in French. To

Adel it was bliss. The suffering and violence of the recent past was easing from his body, displaced by love. He held her even tighter, feeling her firm breasts through the thin black chiffon of her couture dress and feeling too his excitement as their hips pressed together.

"Where did you hear that before?" he whispered into her ear.

She caressed the locks of black curly hair at his neck. "Boulevard St Germain, the day we met."

He smiled in satisfaction and kissed her forehead. "Who said you were just a pretty face?"

"God, I love you." She pulled his head down and kissed his lips gently. "I've missed you."

"Let's see how you feel next week."

The trio broke into a fast samba rhythm. He gestured to their table and she agreed. Adel cautiously guarded his damaged leg as they made their way through the swaying Monaco winter crowd that packed the small dance floor.

"*Salute*," offered Samira, raising the glass of Dom Perignon even before she had sat down.

"*Cento anne*," he responded without thinking. A shiver moved up his spine as he remembered Bell. He would settle for less if he was pushed, he thought.

"There," said Samira. "That's the look I was talking about. It crosses your face every now and then. You seem so troubled."

"Nonsense," he said, a little sharply. Quickly he tried to cover himself. "I need a joint. I'm a little uptight, that's all."

"So have one." She shrugged offhandedly, before continuing in a more serious tone. "Why are you so tense?"

Her large brown eyes stared straight into his. They were worried eyes but they sparkled just the same.

He picked out a joint from among the cigarettes in the Marlboro box and lit it.

"I don't know. I guess I'm tired."

"It scares me, Michael. It really does. I've never seen it on you before."

"It shouldn't. I'll be all right in a couple of days." He looked at her provocatively. "Besides, it could be something else."

She smiled, a flush appearing.

Suddenly a bright orange flare illuminated the restaurant's private beach front. Instinctively Michael Adel snapped his head towards it as his body shied away. He ducked, waiting for the explosion to follow the orange flash of burning phosphorous.

It did not come.

Just as quickly he turned back, trying to camouflage the violent movement. But it was a useless effort. Samira stared at him, her eyes filled with suspicion and worry.

Mercifully the strains of a waltz sounded in a loud fanfare, cutting off conversation.

> Oh, how we danced
> On the night we were wed.
> We vowed our true love,
> Though a word was not said.

The singer and his accompaniment serenaded a middle-aged couple sitting next to the windows overlooking the now brightly lit beach front. Outside, the restaurant's traditional anniversary ceremonies were unfolding. As the stormy waves crashed against huge jagged white rocks, two swimmers emerged from the freezing Mediterranean Sea with large bright flares held aloft. They ran across the narrow beach front and up the gently inclined steps into the restaurant. Inside, the amplifier was turned up a notch or two and the waiters hopped from table to table pouring large glasses of champagne for the customers. "Compliments of the gentleman," they would say, pointing to the couple and quickly topping up the glasses. "It's his twenty-fifth wedding anniversary."

The song ended in a cacophony of sounds. Clapping and shouting and laughter were accompanied by music of the sort played at Italian weddings and suddenly the room was filled with the friendly chatter and joyous laughter of a private party. Le Pirate Restaurant was at its best; the lush, loud, decadent spirit was difficult to resist. Even more so as the marijuana took hold, clouding and distancing reality.

Samira stretched across the table and took his hand. "It worries me, that look," she said, refusing to be sidetracked. "And your lying makes it worse."

Adel looked out of the window alongside the table and lit a cigarette. It was the same old story. Nothing could be gained by telling her. She would only worry herself sick about it and be dragged into the quagmire like the rest of them. He looked at her and pressed her hand.

"You're making a mountain out of a molehill. I'm tired and jumpy and the leg hurts a little, that's all," he said, patting her hand. "But don't go on about it."

"Are you sure that's all?" she asked, offering him another chance.

He closed his eyes impatiently. "That's all I know."

She held her look for a few seconds and then relaxed. "Okay. Enough said." Her full lips stretched into a delicious, irresistible smile.

It was nearly sunrise when they arrived home; and quite some time later before they slept.

Qum. Saturday, November 3: 7.00 a.m.

On the floor of that austere reception room that was soon to mesmerise the entire world, Ayatollah Khomeini frowned and his sullen features took on a sinister expression as his hand reached for the traditional Iranian *ghand palou* tea. Carefully he selected a medium-sized slow-dissolving sugar cube and dunked it in the piping hot liquid before placing the lump in his mouth and using the strong rich blended brew as a chaser to wash the sweetness down. His frown lingered throughout.

"So the *pasdaran* militiamen have been infiltrated too?"

"It would seem so, Holy One," Ayatollah Khalkhali responded deferentially.

"The fact that this Adel has been escorted out of Iran confirms that the Americans are still everywhere in this country. Their net reaches even the Prime Minister."

Khalkhali nodded in agreement. "You will be satisfied to learn that at midnight last night we tried and executed Hossein Mikhchi and Samad Nafti, the two American spies who worked at the airport."

Khomeini brushed aside the reassurance. "If Adel took these tapes out of the country, it can only mean one thing: that the Americans are in a hurry. There could be no other reason to risk rushing them through the airport. They could simply and safely have smuggled them through our vast unguardable borders like we used to do."

Khalkhali remained silent, trying to anticipate the Imam's thoughts.

"No, my brother, they wish to use these tapes against us," continued Khomeini.

He thought for a brief moment before speaking again in the same unemotional whisper.

"They wish to blackmail us with them. They wish to discredit us with our own people, trying to show that we collaborated with them. No doubt they will again attempt to place their puppets – lackeys like Bazargan, Yazdi, Ghotbzadeh – into power."

Khalkhali was amazed at Khomeini's lack of emotion.

"But did I not say they are like children? They have done for us what we have sought to do since the success of this revolution. They have given us the opportunity to eradicate their stooges for ever. And more. Much, much more."

Slowly the Imam lifted his gaze from the floor. He looked at the plain whitewashed wall at the far end of the room. "This peanut-grower has handed us the perfect tool with which to carve anti-Americanism into the very souls of our people."

Khalkhali looked at the Imam with awe. "How, Your Holiness?"

Khomeini turned slowly and spoke with a barely concealed rage. "We shall take their embassy. We shall take their spies hostage. And we shall hold them. And hold them. We shall hold them until those tapes are useless to Carter and his cronies. Never again will either East or West dominate our land."

Cannes. Saturday, November 3.

It was ten-thirty in the morning by the time the sleek white Leopard yacht drifted gracefully out of the gateway to Port Canto. Serenely the luxurious vessel turned outwards towards the Estorel, Les Iles Lérins to her port, Le Vieux Port de Cannes to starboard. Despite the bright sun, a light haze clouded the shimmering glass surface of the water, hampering visibility.

Once clear of the tranquil harbour, Michael Adel gradually pushed forward the two gunmetal black levers beside the wheel and instantly the twin diesel Caterpillar D/334 engines picked up momentum, raising the vessel's majestic bow and belching a stream of turbulent froth from its stern. Adel handed the wheel to the captain and headed aft, down the three steps, past the kitchen and into the lounge. The cast on his leg felt looser and more comfortable from use, making the chore of adjusting to the boat's movement a relatively simple task; still he took the added precaution of steadying himself on the railing.

He slid open the cabin door and stepped in.

"Damn!" he barked, feeling a surge of pain move up his leg. He grimaced and glared at the door sill as he hopped into the cabin and slumped on the beige suède sofa. He looked at the door sill angrily as he hoisted the cast atop the white lacquer coffee table and stretched to massage the bruised toes below it.

"Are you all right?" asked Samira.

"I guess so."

"You really have to be more careful. Stop moving around so much."

The whiff of freshly brewed coffee caught his nose. "John," he said a little louder so Usher in the open kitchen to his right could hear. "Can I have some coffee, please?"

Samira was relieved by the quick recovery. She picked up a cushion from the couch and made light of the incident. "I wonder how much damage you're going to cause the furniture before you're better," she said, as she placed the pillow between the cast and the table's delicate finish.

Natalie giggled at him; it was a game father and daughter played when either was scolded.

"Think that's funny?" he asked, looking at her in mock seriousness.

"Uh-uh." She nodded excitedly, her face smiling, her eyes alight with mischief.

"Thank you, John." Adel lifted a cup of steaming black coffee from the wicker tray Usher held and placed it on a side-table. Then he turned back to Natalie and looked at her for a moment. Some day he would have to tell her about her mother. Somehow he would have to explain it all to her. And the only thing he could do to soften the blow was to ensure that his little daughter had warm loving memories of Gina. In his mind he promised her that. It was the least he could do.

But not now, he thought. Not today. He wasn't up to

it. And she was far too young still to understand the tragedy.

Instead he wagged his finger at her. "Come here."

Natalie dived on to the sofa next to him and gently he caressed the side of her face.

"How would you like me to start Sam on all the homework you should be doing right now?" he whispered in her ear, just loud enough for Samira to hear.

"Oh, that's not fair," she pouted. For an instant her face reflected deep thought. Then she whispered even louder than he had, "I'll be on your side if we can eat at Tahiti Beach."

Samira and Adel both smiled. It was Natalie's favourite restaurant, for it served a delicious, charcoal-broiled corn-on-the-cob dipped in butter sauce.

"Come on, that's enough whispering," said Sam. "Natalie, fetch the backgammon set and I'll play you."

Natalie ran happily from the room even before Sam had finished, disappearing down the narrow staircase to the cabins below.

Sam turned at once to Adel. "Michael . . ." she said softly, and hesitated.

Adel set down the cup and looked at her. She sat cross-legged on the floor in a white jump suit studded with golden buttons. Her large doe-eyes, youthful and innocent without make-up, were worried.

"You really have to snap out of it. It's starting to affect Natalie. She's asking a lot of questions."

"Like what?"

Samira studied him, an appraising coolness in her eyes, as she brushed back her billowing jet-black hair. She waited for him to say something, to open up, to explain. It did not come.

"Why you didn't call when you were away? Why you're so quiet now? Why you're sad? It's all fairly obvious, you know. I have to live with your explanation. I'm not very happy about it and I figure you'll tell me when you're ready. But children are different, they don't think that way. They respond on simple, emotional levels and Natalie senses something. I told her it's some trouble with your work."

Samira dropped her eyes, her fingers nervously picking at strands of the dark green carpet as she continued. "But it wasn't good enough for her. She thought about it – you know the way she does – and said, 'Well, Dad should get a different job, then.' I didn't want to bring it up again, Michael; it's obvious you don't want to talk about it. But if you don't change, it'll affect her."

Adel felt irritated; it grated to be told the obvious. He was tired of acting; sick of performing and camouflaging his despair. Over and over he had had to do it. Mariam, Jane, and now Samira and Natalie. There was no end to it. And, besides, he wasn't exactly doing a masterful job. He closed his eyes in frustration and disciplined himself once more.

"Sometimes it has to be that way," he said. "Sometimes you're better off not knowing."

Samira said nothing but her eyes were unsatisfied.

"I hope you believe me because that's all there is to it," he explained brusquely.

She did not reply for a moment; when she did, her voice was severe. "I don't think you have the right to make that kind of judgment. What's better or worse for me, or for us, is something you have no right to decide alone. We share things, good and bad. Besides, we aren't talking about me."

"Assuming you're right," he snapped, "assuming there is some goddamn thing wrong. You're not doing anyone a favour by going on about it. Leave it alone."

She lowered her gaze and played with the strands of carpet for a moment longer, then she stood and moved to him, nestling her head in the curve of his shoulder and embracing him.

"Please, Michael," she whispered. "I hate this feeling. I can't stand it. I don't know what it is, but it scares me. You're frightened, I see it in your eyes all the time. And, then, sometimes, it's even worse. It makes you unreachable. And you won't even tell me what it is." She kissed him gently on the neck. "At least tell me it's all over."

He wanted to tell her. To scream that he did not know – that he would never know; not until it was too late. A split second before a silent bullet smashed his forehead. A flash before his car blew up. Or poison tore his guts apart. To tell her he would never have the luxury of living without the fear of death hovering over him.

Instead he caressed her face and kissed her. "I think so . . ."

Mercifully Natalie cut him short in mid-sentence. She rushed into the cabin clutching a backgammon set and chattering happily.

"Let's play in turns. You know, whoever wins plays the next guy."

"Okay," he said, relieved and eager to be alone. "You play Sam first. I have to go on deck for a second. I'll play the winner."

A fleeting frown crossed Samira's face. "Come on, Natalie. We'll play," she said good-humouredly.

Adel kissed Samira's forehead and offered her a reassuring wink but she did not respond.

The sea air was fresh and clean. With the help of the wooden railing, he made his way up to the bow of the boat, ignoring the chilly discomfort of the cold, strong headwinds that tore through his windbreaker and the occasional light spray of sea water. He sat on the teak surface at the tip of the bow, his back to the sea. A mile or so off to starboard he could just make out Porte la Galère with its shining white stucco buildings and red-tiled roofs, tranquil and stately in the quiet winter season.

He thought about Sam and knew that he could never tell her. It was enough that his own life was cursed. To make gentle, fragile Sam a party to his fear and guilt would be more than he could bear. She was right about one thing, though: it couldn't go on like this. He was nervous and uptight, like a coiled spring ready to unwind, snapping and snarling at random. Nothing was enjoyable. Nothing and no one.

He had been through it a thousand times, but the conclusion never changed. The fact was, there were no guarantees. There was nothing to depend on. No security; no peace of mind. His whole case was built on the shifting sands of credibility. That and the fear of exposure of the tapes. Credibility and fear, two qualities Colonel Grover Cleveland Bell knew little about. And there was little else to cling to.

He shrugged and lifted the wall phone.

The captain answered.

"*Gérard, est-ce que Usher est là?*" he asked.

"*Oui, monsieur.*"

There was a moment's silence before Usher answered. "Yes, sir."

"John, have you been able to contact my brother, yet?"

"No, sir. And not for lack of trying."

"Thanks." Adel hung up.

And that was another thing. Where the hell was Mark?

Nice – Côte D'Azur airport. November 3: 11.00 a.m.

"What time is it set for?" asked Bell as the three men stepped out of the door marked "Domestic" in large yellow letters over a dark blue background.

"High noon," replied Bill Davis, glancing at his watch. "We picked up Adel's conversation with the captain on the wire-tap. He called for a ten o'clock departure. Even if there's a delay, it's built in to the safety factor."

"An hour," said Bell, more a statement than a question.

"Yes, sir," replied Davis.

The three men crossed the narrow access road and made their way down the white sandstone stairs to the large apron in front of Nice-Côte d'Azur airport. To the spectators on the observation deck above, it was obvious that two of these men were American. One could not mistake the loud check trousers cut shorter than continental fashion allowed. It was more difficult to identify the third man from his clothing; he wore a conservative grey Savile Row suit.

"Not even transportation to and from the planes in this damned place," Bell grunted.

"Only when it's raining, Colonel. Conservation of energy; something we're learning back home rather quickly," said the grey-clad Jim Gleeson. He pointed to the clear, turquoise-coloured water. "Besides, with the Mediterranean surrounding you on three sides, it sure is pretty enough for a short walk."

Davis nodded in agreement as Bell flashed a quick look at the sea and then at Jim Gleeson before lengthening his stride to cover the three hundred yards to the west of the ramp more quickly.

"Have we got the vessel sighted?" Bell shouted above the clatter and whine of the AB-206B helicopter's jet engine.

"We've got a radar track on it, sir. It left just over thirty minutes ago," Davis bellowed, stepping aside to let the two men precede him up the crude, narrow ramp.

The pilot casually saluted the three men and made certain they fastened their seat-belts before engaging the main motor and watching the tachometer crawl steadily upward. After the briefest of communications with the control tower, the sky-blue helicopter lifted forward and upwards towards the Estorel.

"Who's winning?" asked Adel as he stepped carefully over the sill and closed the cabin door.

"I am," blurted Natalie. "And I'm playing really well."

Adel slid on to the couch next to Samira and smiled at her atrociously placed pieces.

"I'd throw in the towel if I were you."

She looked at him coldly. "There's a lot of things you'd do if you were me."

Adel turned his regard to Natalie and was silent for an instant.

"You're right, Sam," he said softly to hide the tension. "But you'll have to bear with me. Just give me a little time."

Samira threw the dice. "It's not me you have to worry about." She glanced at Natalie, then turned away.

"Now you, Dad. Now you," cried Natalie excitedly.

Adel forced a smile and busied himself positioning the pieces in their appropriate spots. "I'm going to have to do something about it."

"I hope so," said Samira in a more gentle tone. "For all our sakes."

He placed his hand on hers and pressed it gently. "It'll be all right. Don't worry."

She smiled wanly. "I hope so," she repeated.

The sun entered the helicopter from the left and slightly to the rear as it gained altitude to 2,500 feet and flew due south-west at 170 knots.

Colonel Bell felt nervous and uneasy as he looked through the window at the hazy sea below beating against the tip of Cap d'Antibes. Visibility was slightly impaired, he noted, but it was still good enough for a visual sighting. And that was why he was here, he reminded himself. He did not want to rely on the instruments on board, no matter how reliable, no matter how efficient. He was here to see it for himself, not to rely on dots and colours and weird sounds and echoes.

But the uncertainty refused to budge. It had haunted him for several days now, seeming to feed on itself, growing and spreading its dark pessimism until it produced an even more distasteful emotion: the need for reassurance.

He turned his head towards Jim Gleeson and again tried to check his anxiety. He looked at his colleague for some time before pushing the intercom transmitter button. What the hell, he thought. What's the harm?

"What do you think, Jim?"

Gleeson turned slowly to face Bell. He was more surprised by the worried tone of Bell's voice than the question; he had no idea how to react to such a tone; he had never heard it before.

"I don't know, Grove," he said carefully. "I just don't know. It might be premature."

"Even after Washington?"

Gleeson faced Bell again. "Washington was vague, Grove. They didn't really take a position, did they? It seems to me they just threw the ball back in your court. It's the 'establish veracity' part that gets me," he said, unable to hide his own trepidation, yet unwilling to take a position.

" 'Without risk of exposure' – they said that too," responded Bell testily. "And this asshole's touring the world."

"Yeah, Grove," Gleeson agreed with a sigh. "That's true too. It's a bitch."

Bell turned abruptly towards the window. What if he was wrong . . .? He didn't want to think about it. He couldn't be wrong. There was no third set; there was no third outlet. There couldn't be. They'd been back to ORAL again and even Operations Research couldn't find a new lead. Friends, old classmates, ex-girlfriends, business associates, a couple of whores, even another relative – but nothing. Zero. Every one of them had an alibi. Besides none of them was close enough to Adel for this sort of dependence and trust. And risk. No, if there was a third set it was down there, close to him, within easy reach. Either that, or it was at the house in Cannes. That was human nature and the odds lay stacked in its favour.

"There's your boat. Up ahead, there," shouted the

pilot over the engine clatter. He pointed ahead and a few degrees to port.

Below, the sleek white yacht glimmered in the hazy sun, its turbulence cutting a silent path through the calm sea.

"Keep well away," ordered Bell.

Instantly the pilot veered starboard towards the land mass on the horizon.

But what if he was wrong? What if there was another outlet? The thought returned and a million ice-cold needles punctured Bell's body. Again, he called up his armoury of will and discipline to suppress the weakness and doubts. He wasn't wrong; he couldn't be. The facts were there.

The intercom came alive; it was Gleeson's voice.

"What gets me, Grove," he said "is that Mark. But I guess it's natural for him to see things differently."

The mention of Mark Adel's name destroyed Bell's hard-won composure. Even now he remembered his emotionless scholarly tones over the telephone as clearly as Gleeson's voice over the intercom.

"It's not revenge that drives him. It's winning. And to win you have to be cautious, calculating . . . He's not bluffing . . . There is a third outlet . . . He's too careful to gamble without it."

Bell shuddered as he recalled the words and the man. He was ice, thought Bell. Cold and heartless. And he always moved in the background, too; in anonymity – silently, efficiently and without feeling.

He bit his lower lip and turned to the window.

"I'll come with you," cried Natalie.

Michael Adel pointed at her authoritatively. "Get your coat on, then."

"Meanwhile I'll get presentable for St Tropez," said Samira.

Adel let Natalie up the short ladder to the upper deck before following her. The cold headwind was too strong to allow loitering anywhere except behind the protection of the large perspex windshield in front of the upper controls. As they sat on the small pilot's bench, the steady drone of a helicopter filtered through. Adel was curious; he looked around but the glaring wintry haze obstructed the view.

"Can I drive, Dad? Please, please," pleaded Natalie as she clapped her hands in excitement.

"Sure," he smiled, gently caressing her windswept hair.

He picked up the intercom. "We'll take it up here for a little while, Gérard," he said into the mouthpiece.

The earphones of all four men in the helicopter suddenly erupted above the roar of the engine.

"Gibraltar Ground Control to Dragon One. Gibraltar Ground Control to Dragon One. This is urgent. Repeat urgent. Do you read me? Over."

The pilot pushed a button. "Dragon One to Ground Control. Dragon One to Ground Control. I read you. Over."

"Gibraltar Ground Control to Dragon One. I have an urgent call for Barracuda. I have an urgent call for Barracuda. I'll proceed to patch it through. I have instructions to inform you to switch to scrambler. Do you read me? Over."

"I read you. Barracuda standing by. Repeat Barracuda standing by. Scrambler activated. Over." The pilot pointed to Bell to take over.

"Colonel Bell?" a voice demanded.

"Yes," said Bell. He did not recognise the voice.

"Hold on please, sir."

The next voice that all four men heard even through the cackle and metallic tone of the scrambler was easily distinguishable. It was refined, its tone mid-Atlantic and confident, but the calmness that was usually an integral part of it was missing.

"Colonel Bell, can you hear me?" the voice asked.

Bell pressed a button and responded. "I read you. Over."

"Good. I hope I caught you in time. There's a tape missing. At this point in time we have in hand two original tapes and four copies. I am talking to you about the copies. We have Narela seven-four-five-three-seven and eight. We also have Narela seven-four-five-four-zero- and one. Please note that Narela seven-four-five-three-nine is missing from the sequence. We believe that there is a third set and that this missing tape has a mate most likely sequential in nature. We have reason to believe that seven-four-five-four-two is its mate.

"This information has only just been observed. No sales slip exists. But unfortunately the store confirmed less than an hour ago that these six tapes are missing from both the stock and the sales records and that they were indeed part of a batch received by them. Since only one number is missing from the sequence the possible existence of a third set is high. Too high. Consequently all plans must, repeat must, be postponed until this point is clarified. I repeat, abort all plans immediately and indefinitely. Do you understand me? The man must be left alone until clarification is made. Until we are certain. Do you understand?"

Bell's complexion turned an ashen grey. He sat staring at the control panel uncomprehendingly, unable to move.

"Do you understand? Do you hear me?" the voice blurted.

Bell seemed paralysed. He sat staring, his once-poised figure now slumped.

"Goddamn it, Bell! Can you hear me?" John Alexander Case, chairman of the Trust, shouted.

Bell's right hand slowly grasped the microphone attached to his headset. Needlessly he felt it and adjusted its already perfect position. "It . . . it may be too late," he whispered gulping involuntarily.

There was a moment's silence before the voice spoke coldly. "I don't think you can afford that, Colonel. There has already been one serious and unnecessary blunder."

Bell looked at his watch. It was 11.55.

"Over," he said curtly, grabbing the pilot's brown leather jacket. "How long would it take to get on to that boat's frequency?" he said, pointing at the yacht below.

"A couple of minutes," said the pilot.

"We don't have that kind of time. Drop down and I'll use the bullhorn," Bell instructed. The pilot went into a steep dive even before he had finished speaking.

"That's called a depthfinder, darling. It tells you how deep the water is."

Adel found himself talking steadily louder, competing with the ever-increasing roar of what seemed like a jet helicopter. He realised suddenly that the noise was far too close. Quickly he turned, his slitted eyes, scanning the bright, hazy sky.

Then he saw it and his heart missed a beat. Instinctively the face of Colonel Grover Cleveland Bell flashed before his mind.

A light blue chopper swayed carelessly from side to side two hundred yards behind the boat and only a few feet above the sea. But it was closing in quickly. Adel grabbed Natalie and pushed her beneath the bench wedged between two fixed wooden lockers on either side. It was not much cover but it was all that was available. His heart was speeding now, pumping violently as his mind raced with fear. He grabbed the phone.

"Take over the boat and tell Samira to stay down there," he shouted at Usher. There was no way down. Not with Natalie anyway. He crouched beside her, gaping at the recess dead centre beneath the closing helicopter. It was a machine-gun and it was trained directly on the bench.

"*Adel. Michael Adel. Listen to me.*" The monotone was easily recognisable. Even through the uproar it was recognisable.

"*Get off the boat. There's a bomb aboard,*" the monstrous voice boomed as the chopper swayed only a few feet from the stern.

"*It's set for twelve o'clock.*"

Adel looked at his wrist. 11.58 it read.

"*Get off. We'll pick you up.*" Bell's voice bellowed even louder.

What bomb? Who put it there for Bell to drop from the sky to be his saviour?

Adel thought of Sam and Natalie. What if it was a ploy? A set-up. A lie. What if Bell didn't pick them up? What the hell would he do with his two girls, in the middle of a winter sea, two miles from shore?

He couldn't think. The questions were coming too fast. It didn't make sense.

"Dad, Dad, what's going on?" asked a petrified, bewildered Natalie.

He looked at her sprawled beneath the bench. Confusion and fear filled her innocent face. Her eyes were bright with tears.

"Nothing, darling. Just stay there," he shouted over the clatter.

He looked back up at the helicopter; it was following now fifty yards away. Suddenly Sam's face appeared through the hatch. She was dripping wet, a pink bath-towel her only protection from the chilly winds as she took the steps quickly, lost and horrified. He stood up and pulled her down beside them. When he looked back up the helicopter had dropped back a little and gained altitude.

"*Listen, Adel, you have less than a minute. Jump. For God's sake JUMP!*"

Adel could hear the alarm in Bell's voice, but was it feigned? Dear God was it feigned?

"What is it Michael?" screamed a panic-stricken Samira. What's going on? What is that man saying?"

"I don't know. I . . ."

"*Michael,*" boomed Bell's voice, "*it's a mistake. There's a bomb in the engine-room put there to kill you. But it's a mistake. It was put there by mistake . . .*"

The helicopter was dropping back and gaining altitude.

"I know what you're thinking," said Bell. *"And you're right. We were wrong. Just get off with your wife and daughter. I'll explain everything. Please. Just trust me."*

There was urgency in that voice. And panic. At the same time it shouted and pleaded. And the helicopter was dropping back too. It was close to two hundred yards behind now and there had to be a reason for its increasing distance.

"Dear God Almighty," Adel shouted as he grabbed Natalie and dragged her to her feet.

"Jump, darling. J-U-M-P," he screamed at Samira, pushing her forcibly towards the side with his free arm.

At the railing he picked up his petrified daughter and handed her to Samira. "Hold her, Sam, and don't let go. No matter what happens, don't let go. I'll throw you a raft."

"What about . . ."

He pushed them – hard to clear the vessel's wake – and immediately turned towards the nearest wooden locker. Opening its door he grabbed for the orange life raft and pulled the black knob at its top. Instantly it began to inflate. As he threw it overboard he felt relief. Twenty yards behind he could see their heads bobbing above the water.

There was one more thing to do, thought Adel as he turned back swiftly to the control panel. Then he would join them. He picked up the intercom.

"Gérard," he barked. "There's a bomb on board. Tell Usher and get off the boat now. Jump. And do it quickly."

He dropped the receiver and ran towards the railing.

Bell, Davis and Gleeson craned their necks as they watched the three frantic figures dashing towards the yacht's upper railing. But from above, the movement seemed in slow motion. They watched aghast as the man below hurled his wife and daughter into the sea and turned back towards the boat. Their necks craned even further when the figure dropped the raft overboard and turned inwards yet again.

"Fuck them, man, jump," said Davis as he watched Adel pick up the intercom.

"Come on. Come on. Get out of there," pleaded Gleeson through gritted teeth. "Jump," he shouted.

"Way to go. Yeah. Way to go," Davis encouraged the scrambling figure dashing once more towards the railing.

It worked, thought Bell, feeling the cool breeze of relief on his body as Michael Adel climbed the yacht's railing. Bell slumped back on his chair and closed his eyes. That was too close for comfort, he thought, thankful to the gods of luck. He touched the corner of his right eye to control the slight twitching movement it had acquired and drew in a deep lungful of air.

But his relief was premature. Only by seconds, but still premature. The explosion smashed into the helicopter, driving it backwards, the engine unable to rise above the torrent of air that blasted it. The roar followed later, deafening the four men in the pandemonium of chaos that followed as the helicopter was battered by flying debris. Only their seat-belts saved them from worse as the pilot rode the turbulent punch and climbed with it, upwards and to the rear.

When he straightened out at 900 feet, the debris was still rising, but now it resembled black confetti drifting aimlessly in a soft whirlwind. All that remained of the proud vessel was a small fire where the engine-room once stood. The remainder of the structure was obliterated.

The three men were speechless. They slumped in their assault chairs. Their expressions reflected awareness that they would be held answerable.

After a lengthy shocked silence, Bill Davis could control himself no longer. He turned his eyes away from the two figures in the choppy waters desperately struggling to board the orange liferaft and looked at Colonel Bell.

"Shall we have them picked up?"

Bell was silent a moment, his drooping head forcing the tired, defeated skin of his neck into a sudden double chin. Then slowly he gazed upwards, through the perspex of the cabin into the distance as a tape of Mark Adel's voice played over and over in his mind. "*You can't rely solely on machines . . . you can't rely solely on machines . . . it's not revenge that drives him. It's winning . . . it's winning . . . it's winning . . . it's . . .*"

"No," he whispered, his eyes locked on the black confetti shimmering in the distance. "Leave them alone."

"What'll happen to Egypt and Saudi Arabia?" mumbled Jim Gleeson. "What will happen to those projects?"

But his question fell on deaf ears.

Cannes. Sunday, November 4: 6.00 a.m.

One of the three men accompanying the sleepy bathrobed figures of Gleeson and Davis slipped his brass master key into the Fichet lock, eased the white wooden door open and reached for the light switch. The two Americans entered the sumptuous hotel suite and froze.

It was the dull look on the dead man's face that shook them the most. The fixed, glazed, dilated eyes locked on the ceiling. A stream of blood had trickled from the pebble-sized contusion at the man's temple, down past the thin scar on the right side of his face, forming a pool on the light-green carpet. A Smith & Wesson .38 calibre Service revolver lay on the floor beside the corpse.

"Call the police," said the short, slim manager of the Carlton Hotel to one of his security men.

Davis and Gleeson rushed forward, but the two hefty French security men blocked them.

"You will touch nothing," said the manager. "You will leave the room."

The two Americans looked up from the prostrate body of Colonel Grover Cleveland Bell. Then a pale, angry Gleeson swivelled round to face the manager. "Listen, asshole, this is over your head. You'd better contact the DST security people in Paris before you go any further."

The manager reached into his breast pocket. He withdrew a small, worn, leather wallet and snapped it open. Beneath the bright red stripe and his picture were the words: *Direction de la Surveillance du Territoire*.

"My instructions are to escort you to Nice airport. You will board a flight to New York which has been arranged for you. Any further explanation will have to wait till the other end."

Gleeson and Davis looked at each other in astonishment. Before they could utter a word, the manager of the hotel held out a folded copy of *Nice Matin*. "Perhaps this will explain something," he said.

Gleeson stared at the Frenchman. Then slowly he dropped his eyes and scanned the glaring headline.

EXPLOSION MYSTERIEUSE D'UNE YACHT.
CINQ PERSONNES SAUVÉES. PAS DE MORTS.

MYSTERY EXPLOSION ABOARD YACHT
FIVE SAVED. NO FATALITIES.

EPILOGUE

At 3.03 a.m. Washington time on Sunday, November 4, 1979 the United States Embassy in Teheran was occupied by Iranian students, "Followers of the Imam's Line", they called themselves. Sixty-five United States Embassy officials were taken hostage. Two weeks later, thirteen of these hostages – five women and eight black men – were released. The other fifty-two remained in captivity for four hundred and forty-four days.

International Herald Tribune – January 19, 1980

SHAH SAYS OIL FIRMS HELPED TO OUST HIM
By Norman Kempster
WASHINGTON, Jan. 18 (LAT) – Mohammed Reza Pahlavi, the deposed Shah, charged in an interview broadcast yesterday that international oil companies had sacrificed his regime to reduce Iran's oil production and thus drive up prices.

. . . The Shah said that two years before he was overthrown he had "heard from two different sources connected with oil companies that the regime in Iran would change. We believe that there was a plan to ensure less oil was offered to the world markets in order to bring about a price rise." He added: "One country was to be chosen for the sacrifice . . . It seems that the country chosen to drop its oil production was mine."

International Herald Tribune – March 4, 1980

CARTER IGNORED CIA IN CUTTING IRAN ISLAM PAYOFF, JOURNAL SAYS
WASHINGTON, March 3 (UPI) – President Carter

abruptly halted CIA payments supporting Iran's Islamic religious affairs in 1977 despite warnings that the cut-off would undermine the Shah, according to *Politics Today* magazine.

Daniel Drooz said in an article that details of the events were provided by six agents, former agents and intelligence analysts with connections in Teheran, the US State Department and the White House.

Mr Drooz said that the CIA payments began in 1953 following the overthrow of the Shah by Premier Mohammed Mossadegh. The CIA assisted in restoring the Shah to the throne and began payments to the country's ayatollahs and mullahs – in essence buying support for the Shah.

"For the next decade the Shah and Iran's religious leaders coexisted more or less peacefully, while the CIA quietly sent regular payments to help support the mullahs," Mr Drooz said.

Mr Drooz said that at least one source contended that the amount paid had reached $400 million a year, while other sources said that figure was too high.

The payments came to an abrupt halt shortly after Mr Carter became president in 1977 when the *Washington Post* revealed payments of $10 million a year to King Hussein of Jordan, Mr Drooz said.

At 12.33 p.m. Washington time on Tuesday, January 20, 1981 – the day Ronald Reagan was inaugurated as the fortieth President of the United States – the fifty-two hostages from the US Embassy in Teheran were released. Among the various other conditions of their release, the United States government publicly pledged never again to interfere in Iran's internal affairs.